OF FIRE AND STARS

AUDREY COULTHURST

OF FIRE
AND
STARS

BALZER + BRAY

An Imprint of HarperCollins*Publishers*

Balzer + Bray is an imprint of HarperCollins Publishers.

Of Fire and Stars
Copyright © 2016 by Audrey Coulthurst
Map copyright © 2016 by Saia Jordan
All rights reserved. Printed in the United States of America.
www.epicreads.com

ISBN 978-0-06-243325-1

Typography by Torborg Davern
16 17 18 19 20   PC/RRDH   10 9 8 7 6 5 4 3 2

❖

First Edition

For the members of the Austin Java Writing Company—
Thank you for lighting the fire under my ass
that made this book possible. You will always be
among the brightest stars in my universe.

Dennaleia

WHEN I WAS SEVEN WINTERS OF AGE, MY MOTHER caught me in the hearth stacking red-hot coals with my bare hands.

That evening had found Spire City chilled to the core with the kind of cold that only Havemont knows, when early sunsets leave the afternoon dark as midnight and the sky swirls with relentless snow. My sister, Alisendi, and I knelt in the High Adytum, the most sacred temple in the four Northern Kingdoms, the two of us small beneath the cavernous apse depicting the aspects of the fire god. Flames dancing in the hearth brought the walls to life, from the forge and cookfires painted at the bottom clear up to the ceiling, where sunbeams gave way to a dusky sky streaked with falling stars. We were supposed to be spending a few minutes at prayer after our studies until our mother, the queen, came to fetch us.

Instead, we flicked wooden offering chips as far as we could over the warm stones, giggling as the temple cat pounced on the skittering pieces. But then the fire settled, and one of the burning logs toppled out of the hearth in a shower of sparks. Alisendi screamed and leaped back. Yet something held me in place as a tingle raced through my fingertips. When I grasped the log and shoved it back into the fire, the flames felt like no more than a whisper against my skin even as the ends of my woolen sleeves smoldered.

"Look, Ali," I said, picking up one of the cinders that had tumbled out. In my still-tingling palm it lit again, glowing bright as the heart of the fire. A thrill hummed through me as I watched it burn. I had no idea it was possible to hold fire in one's hand, but it answered a question in me to which I had never been able to put words.

"You shouldn't do that," Alisendi said, tracing the symbol of the fire god in the air before her.

"But it's like the tales about the great mages," I said. "What if people still have those powers? And what if the other stories are real, too? The dragons and the fae? And the people who take on the shapes of animals?" It made me giddy to imagine that the world could truly be filled with such incredible things—and exhilarated to think that I might be one of them.

"Those tales are made up to put us to sleep," Alisendi said. "We're nearly too old for that nonsense."

I scowled and held out the ember in my palm. "So this isn't real?"

"I don't know," she said, and stepped back. Her uncertainty was strange to see. One day she would be queen of Havemont, and she already carried herself as though she knew everything. I had always wanted to be like my perfect older sister but always seemed to fall short—too shy, too bookish, too impulsive to be a true leader. But finally I could do something that she could not.

"It's real," I insisted, and stuck both hands into the fire, showing her that the flames did not harm me. I pushed a log aside, built a tower of coals, and drew the crest of our kingdom beside it in the ashes.

That was when our mother arrived.

She shrieked and pulled me out of the flames, her panic turning to fear when she brushed away the cinders and found unblemished skin beneath the soot.

"Princesses don't play with fire," she scolded me.

Frightened by the tears in her eyes, I promised never to do it again—a promise that would prove impossible to keep.

Later that night, my mother told me that the fire god must have bestowed a gift upon me because our kingdom held the fire god closest to our hearts. She said perhaps my prayers in the High Adytum had been answered with magic because the temple was so high on the mountain that the Six Gods barely had to bow their heads to hear us pray. By then it was too late to rescind my betrothal to the prince of Mynaria, even though the people of his kingdom believed the use of magic was heresy. Mother insisted that ignored and untrained, my Affinity for fire would fade away as many people's small gifts did. She forbade Alisendi and me to tell another soul.

In the years that followed, I tried to ignore the lure of flame. But the desire to indulge the tingles that danced through my hands or cheeks was more insistent than a nagging itch. Between my lessons in history, etiquette, and politics, I brought out the magic when alone and played with it like a parlor trick. By age ten I could make a fire burn more brightly or a few sparks dance across the floor. My magic was small and quiet, like the rest of me, and easy to keep hidden.

My daily life remained a rehearsal for the moment I met my betrothed, and my secret seemed like a trivial thing. I believed that as long as I followed my training, nothing could go wrong.

But some things are stronger than years of lessons.

The draw of fire.

A longing for freedom.

Or a girl on a red horse.

ONE

🪶 *Dennaleia*

SUMMER HUNG HEAVY OVER MYNARIA THE DAY I arrived to meet my future husband. As my carriage clattered over the cobbled streets toward the castle west of the city, I couldn't say whether nervousness or the constricting bodice of my dress made it more difficult to breathe. Citizens lined the roads, cheering and waving squares of colored cloth, and the clamor rang in my ears long after my maid and entourage split off at the gates of the castle and my lone carriage drew to a halt in the innermost courtyard.

"May the Six give me strength," I whispered to steady myself as the footman opened the velvet-lined door.

I stepped out onto pale flagstones, greeted by a line of horses in full barding. Their armor glinted in the sun and embroidered silk fluttered from their reins. Colorful banners hung from the battlements above them, alternating the plum of my homeland with the deep blue of Mynaria. Behind the gatehouse the castle loomed, a massive structure with square towers jutting into the sky. It looked naked without the twisting spires that had crowned the palace where I grew up, and the strangeness of it made my throat tighten with homesickness.

Before I could step forward, a bay mare tossed her head and bumped her hindquarters into the horse next to her, sending a ripple of pinned ears and fidgeting hooves through the line. The prince sat astride her, wearing a welcoming smile. My stomach fluttered with nerves.

"Quit," muttered the person on the chestnut horse beside him.

I fought the urge to shrink back from the horses and instead plastered on a confident smile, drawing myself up to make the most of my diminutive stature. My first impression needed to be one of poise and dignity, not anxiety and resignation. If Alisendi had been in my place, she would have already swept into the castle and won over half the court. I felt like a meager offering in comparison.

"Her Royal Highness, Princess Dennaleia of Havemont!" a herald announced. The riders dismounted in unison and bowed. I answered with a curtsy. The prince handed his reins to the person beside him and stepped forward. The portraits I'd seen back home hadn't done him justice. Every seam of his doublet was perfectly tailored to his body. His blond hair gleamed in the sunlight, just long enough to curl behind his ears, and his bright-blue eyes matched the cloudless sky.

I waited to feel something, for some spark to light in my chest at the sight of his broad shoulders and strong jawline. Even after the years of inevitability surrounding my marriage, part of me hoped we might fall in love.

Nothing happened, and my confidence wavered.

"Welcome to Lyrra, the cresthaven of Mynaria, Your Highness," the prince said, and bowed. "I am Prince Thandilimon, at the service of the crown and the Six."

I curtsied formally in response. Another man stepped up to flank him, wearing the robes of a steward. They shared the same straight nose and fair coloring, though the steward's hair was more silver than blond. He had to be the king's brother.

"Lord Casmiel, steward to the crown," he said with a wide smile, and then took my hand and kissed it in the old-fashioned way, much like my father sometimes did. The familiar gesture comforted me. But before I could complete my curtsy, the prince's mare snapped her teeth at the sleeve of the girl holding her.

"Quit!" the girl said, bumping the horse's nose away with an elbow. The mare flattened her ears, swung her hind end over again, and landed a solid kick on the chestnut horse.

Chaos erupted as the big chestnut reared and lurched away from the others, heading directly toward me. Sparks flew beneath the horse's iron-shod hooves as he scrambled over the stone. Panic rose in me, and my magic surged with it as my control faltered in a way it never had before. I tried to step out of the way of the oncoming horse, but his shoulder slammed into mine. All the air rushed out of my lungs as I hit the ground flat on my back.

"Catch him!" a voice shouted.

Boots scuffled around me and bridles jangled as people steadied their horses and tried to regain control of the situation while I gasped for breath.

Someone dropped down beside me and placed a gentle hand

beneath my ribs. I looked up into a pair of long-lashed gray eyes, surprised to see the face of the girl who had been holding the horse that ran me over. She had a scattering of delicate freckles across her nose and auburn hair that stood out in sharp contrast to her dark-blue livery.

"It's all right," she said. "Try to relax. Use these muscles to let the air in."

The melody of her voice soothed me, and the muscles in my stomach unwound. I took a few shuddering breaths, each one easier than the last. She pulled me carefully to my feet, steadied me, and left my hand filled with the pins and needles of barely suppressed magic when she dropped it and walked away. In the past my gift had sometimes seemed closer to the surface when I was upset or afraid—but never like this. Then again, I'd never had an important occasion like today turn into a catastrophe so quickly. But I had to stay calm.

The girl took the chestnut horse's reins from a footman holding the animal warily at arm's length. The horse yawned as if entirely bored.

The prince strode past me and stopped in front of the girl.

"Get that filthy cull out of here now," he said. Behind him, the liegemen eyed one another uneasily. Casmiel hurried toward them, ushering everyone back into line.

"If you bothered to correct your horse when she kicks, it probably wouldn't have happened," the girl replied. Her blithe tone and lack of deference surprised me.

"I don't care whose horse did what. You were to keep the horses in order for Princess Dennaleia's arrival. I swear to the Six Gods, I ask you to do one thing for me and—"

"Yes, yes, because this is all about you." She snorted, a sound that probably would have been better suited to her mount.

The prince's face reddened. "You can't expect to have that animal of yours run over an honored guest—a soon-to-be member of the royal family—without any repercussions."

I pressed my hand to the place where the girl had touched me. She had come so swiftly to my rescue. Mother had always said that servants needed more kind words than harsh ones. As the prince opened his mouth to unleash another round of castigation on her, I stepped between them.

"Let's not make too much of it," I said. "It was merely an accident." Though my voice stayed steady, my magic seethed within me, and I couldn't fathom why. I swallowed hard and stared down at the hem of my dress, trying to regain control.

"Are you all right, my lady?" Prince Thandilimon asked.

Before I could respond, a flame sprang from the bottom of my skirt, power pouring from me in an uncontrolled rush.

"Your Highness!" the footman shouted. He dove toward my feet, scrambling on the ground to snuff out the fire with his gloved hands.

I watched in horror, afraid to move or speak.

"I believe it's out, Your Highness." The footman stood up, panting, his white gloves covered in dirt and singe marks.

"I don't know what happened," I lied. My surging emotions since my arrival must have been to blame. Regardless, I had to make sure no one guessed the truth.

"It's been a dry summer," Thandilimon said. "The sparks from the horse's shoes must have kindled it." He stepped closer, regarding my charred skirt with concern.

"Well, this has certainly been an eventful reception," I said. "Perhaps I could have my maid change me into a new dress?"

"Of course," he said, as though suddenly remembering his manners. He waved a dismissal to the servant girl.

Her face remained unusually calm given the circumstances. She caught my eye over the prince's shoulder and smiled the tiniest bit before turning on her heel and sauntering out of the courtyard, her horse following placidly.

"Days like this make me wish I could ship her and that ugly horse somewhere far enough south that the seasons come in reverse," the prince muttered as they disappeared from the courtyard. He offered his arm and I took it. Four delicate bracelets peeked out from the bottom of the prince's jacket sleeve—cachets. Like all Mynarians, he wore braided bracelets made from the tail hairs of each horse he had started under saddle.

Having restored order to the welcome party, Casmiel reappeared at the prince's side. "My lady, I apologize for such an inauspicious welcome to our kingdom. Please allow us to escort you into your new home."

"There was no harm done," I said as we entered the castle. The hall arched above us, made of the same sandy stone as the exterior. Sconces in the shape of horse heads lined the walkway, unlit, sunbeams warming the polished brass.

"Pardon me for asking, my lords, but the girl whose horse got away—why do you keep her employed if she's so incompetent?" I asked. My father would have dismissed her on the spot.

The prince sighed, and I could have sworn Casmiel smirked.

"No choice," the prince said. "Mare is unsuited for anything else at this point, so Father lets her train horses. She's good at it, and it's about the only useful thing she's willing to do."

"Is she a liegeman?" I asked.

"I apologize. We should have made a proper introduction," Casmiel said, eyeing Thandilimon meaningfully.

The prince sighed. "Mare is my elder sister—Amaranthine, Princess of Mynaria. I assure you she is not an accurate reflection of our people or the royal family."

My mind raced. Princess Amaranthine had been mentioned so little in my schooling that I had assumed she was already married off. At age eighteen—two years older than me—she should have been. Most of what I knew about the Mynarian royal family beyond King Aturnicus and Prince Thandilimon was about how they interacted with the Directorate, the group of representatives who helped govern the kingdom. But even if Amaranthine wasn't involved in politics, or married, playing horse trainer seemed like the last thing a princess should have been doing. I was puzzled—and curious.

"Shouldn't she have taken on the duties of lady of the house when Queen Mirianna passed away?" I asked.

"Mare can be difficult to persuade—" Casmiel began.

"Stubborn as a mule, more like," Thandilimon interrupted. Casmiel shot him a warning look, but the prince continued in spite of it. "She has no idea what it means to serve the crown. If she had any sense, she'd pick someone to marry and get it over with before my father makes the decision for her. At least right now she has a choice."

"It is nice to have choices," I said softly. His words stung. There had never been a choice for us. If he resented me as a result, I didn't know how we would survive. Hopefully we could find something besides duty over which to bond, like books, or a particular style of music, or even something as simple as the sour fruit candies that came up from Sonnenborne in winter.

"Indeed," he said, his expression resolute. "At least the alliance will force Mare to do something with herself. I have no intention of continuing to let her run wild once it's up to me."

After we ascended a flight of stairs, two liegemen stepped aside for us to enter the chambers that had been prepared for me. A receiving room with a fireplace and a spacious seating area opened into the bedroom through another set of doors. Large windows overlooked the grounds and the fields beyond. In the far distance, I imagined that I could see the mountains of my homeland shrouded in faraway clouds, even though I knew they were half a moon's journey to the northeast.

Beside one of the plush chairs in the receiving room, my maid, Auna, curtsied in greeting. Her familiar face made the room feel a little more like home.

A page rapped on the door and delivered a whispered message to the prince.

"I'm sorry, but I have some business to attend to," Thandilimon said after the page dashed away. "Casmiel will show you around the castle grounds, and I'll see you later tonight at the welcoming feast. Tomorrow we'll have a breakfast at which you can meet some of my father's most important advisers in a more private setting."

"I look forward to it, Your Highness." I curtsied.

"As do I, my lady." He bowed and left the room, the liegemen closing it quietly behind him.

After an entire life of preparation, our first meeting had been too brief and too filled with calamity, leaving me unsure what I should feel. Mostly, I wanted to go home.

I excused myself to have Auna help me into a fresh, unsinged dress, all too conscious of Casmiel waiting on the other side of the door. The surprise of Amaranthine's presence had me worried about what other gaps might exist in my knowledge of Mynaria, but her unconventional role intrigued me. Decorum suggested that it would be polite to seek her out and properly thank her for coming to my aid, and it sounded like there was only one place she'd be. I stared out my windows to where the royal stables lay on the hillside. I knew the first place I'd ask Casmiel to take me.

TWO   ✦ *Mare*

I HUMMED A BAWDY TAVERN SONG WHILE DIGGING PACKED
dirt out of Flicker's front hoof, grateful to be back at a familiar task
after the disaster of Princess Dennaleia's arrival. Though my brother's
rotten mare had been responsible, taking the blame didn't bother me.
It meant my father and Thandi wouldn't want me to help with anything else for a while. That spelled freedom—my favorite thing. But
no sooner had I scraped the last of the dirt from alongside Flicker's
shoe than a shriek tore through the stables, shrill enough to make
my heart race. Flicker shied and jerked his hoof away, barely missing my toes as he stomped down.

"Easy, boy," I said, putting my hand on his shoulder. If this was
another instance of a stable hand showing a kitchen maid the true
discomfort of a "roll in the hay," both of them would need my boots
dislodged from their rear ends. Scowling, I wiped my hands on the
rough fabric of my breeches and marched out of the stall.

Princess Dennaleia stood across the aisle, clutching one hand with the other, her face ashen. Lovely. As family scapegoat, whatever had happened would undoubtedly be my fault, despite my uncle Cas standing next to her.

"What's going on?" I asked.

"It bit me," she said, her voice shaky.

Dennaleia was half a head shorter than me, the kind of delicate girl who made me feel like a dirty, lumbering oaf. Her yellow silk dress from earlier in the day had been replaced with a ruffled lavender affair, and she looked like she should be on top of a cake instead of in the middle of my barn.

"Bring her to the tack room," I said to Cas. We each took an arm, directing the princess out of the aisle to seat her on a trunk. She whimpered a little as I examined the bite. It was only a surface scrape, probably with bruising to follow. I'd seen far worse injuries. Experienced them myself, in fact. She'd heal in less than a week.

"Mare will get you fixed up and everything will be all right," Cas said, passing her a handkerchief to dab at her eyes.

I sighed and pulled some cleanser and a poultice from a wound kit. The blood on her hand washed away to reveal soft, white skin marred only by the horse bite and a shadowy ink stain on her middle finger. A scholar, then. No wonder she seemed as out of place in the stables as lace on combat tack. After gently applying the herb poultice, I bound her injury with a strip of clean cotton.

"All done," I said, eager for both her and Cas to leave.

She stared at the floor, her head crowned with brown hair so dark it swallowed the light.

"I'm so sorry, Your Highness," the princess said, eyes still downcast. "Perhaps I shouldn't have come. But I've read so much about Mynaria's warhorses and their significance to the foundation of the kingdom, and the stables themselves are one of the few remaining examples of early-era stone architecture—"

My mind drifted almost immediately after she opened her mouth. The girl was word-vomiting a history book I had no interest in reading.

"It's fine," I interrupted her. "You don't have to apologize. But for the love of the Six, don't 'Your Highness' me. I go by Mare."

"Princess Dennaleia of Havemont, at the service of the crown and the Six." She used her good hand to execute a remarkably graceful seated curtsy.

I rolled my eyes. Protocol made my head ache, and it wasn't as though I didn't already know her name.

"The bite wasn't her fault," Cas said.

"So how exactly did she end up with her hand in Shadow's mouth?" I glared at him.

"I was giving Princess Dennaleia a tour, and she asked to come by the stables. I didn't think Shadow would be a problem."

I sighed. Shadow was well-mannered under saddle, but everyone knew she had a tendency to be mouthy, a habit encouraged by the grooms, who hand-fed her treats. Cas spent enough time around the horses that he should have known better.

"I assumed Shadow would be her mount for the Gathering and the wedding ceremony," he continued. "I was trying to introduce them. But Dennaleia has no experience with horses, and—"

"How in the Six Hells is that even possible?" I interrupted. The idea of a noble who didn't know how to ride was as ridiculous as a stable hand not knowing how to push a wheelbarrow.

Cas rubbed his temple. "I visited Havemont about ten years ago. The roads up to Spire City are barely fit for goats, much less horses. They would've had to ship her halfway to Mynaria for lessons. Even the carriage that brought her here had to meet her entourage at a town in the foothills. It probably made more sense to wait, but she'll have to be trained in time for the wedding."

The girl finally looked up, her eyes an unexpected shade of pale green.

"I should get some basic instruction as soon as possible," she said with surprising resolve, given that she seemed to be cursed where horses were concerned.

"That's a splendid idea." Cas smiled at her and then gave me a pointed look.

I shook my head and set my jaw. The last thing I wanted was to teach a rank beginner who would constantly be under the watch of my brother and father.

"Give her to Theeds. He can put her with the liegemen trainees," I said.

"That's not an option. She has only a few moons before the wedding, and you know damn well that putting her in with a mixed class above her level isn't going to teach her anything. Besides, there's no better instructor than you."

I ignored Cas's flattery. The earnest tone he used with the more recalcitrant members of the Directorate wasn't going to work on me. "Not a chance."

"Riding with the liegemen is probably fine," Dennaleia said. She looked about as enthusiastic about the lessons as I felt about being saddled with her. "Surely you know what's best—"

I ignored her attempt at diplomacy and spoke directly to Cas. "You can figure it out."

I stalked out of the tack room, but Cas caught me by my sleeve outside the door.

"Mare, I'm sorry, but you're going to have to do this," he said in a low voice.

I jerked my arm away.

"Think how pleased your father will be that you're doing something to help the princess."

"I don't have time to fix up every delicate flower who wanders through the barn with an idiot for a guide," I said.

Cas let my insult roll off him like rain hitting waxed leather and fixed me with a grave look. "You need a different way to occupy your afternoons until the alliance is settled."

A jolt went through me. He was breaking our agreement. On afternoons when I wasn't occupied with the horses, I often sneaked out of the castle. Cas overlooked my excursions and didn't tell my father in exchange for the useful information I sometimes brought him.

"People will be coming from all over the Northern Kingdoms to witness your brother's wedding. Not all of them will be happy about it," Cas said. "The city will not be as safe as it once was."

He must have known I didn't always stick to the best parts of town or sources he approved of. Damn him and his spies.

"Teaching Dennaleia to ride is important," he continued. "She needs to seem like one of us as soon as possible. Her people may believe in our gods, but that does not undo all the years they've turned a blind eye to the Zumordans using Havemont to gain access to our kingdom."

"That's not my problem," I said.

"It is now. Don't give me reason to tell your father what you've been up to."

"Fine," I said, furious. He left me no other option. "Just keep her out of here until I teach her which end of a horse will bite her." Fuming, I stalked back to Flicker's stall.

"Mare—" Cas called out, but there was nothing else for him to say. I should have felt guiltier for being so rude—he sympathized with my point of view more than my father or brother, and even advocated for my interests from time to time. Still, he would never understand what it felt like when what little freedom I had was taken from me. Now that my brother had a princess to wear on his wrist like another cachet, there should have been even less pressure on me to be lady of the castle. I had counted on it.

I made my way to Flicker's last hoof in need of cleaning. After digging out a pebble wedged alongside his frog, I brushed the hoof clean and set it down gently. He craned his neck around to look at me between bites of hay.

"Sorry, boy. You're all done now." I stroked his neck, his summer coat bright as copper even in the dim light of the barn. Usually I would have lingered, but the sun already rested above the hills, dusting the sky with hints of pink. Tonight I'd be forced into attire I hadn't worn in years for Princess Dennaleia's welcoming feast, and my maids had serious work ahead of them with the snarled state of my hair.

I exited the stables and walked the least traveled path from the barn to the castle, feeling like the walls of the palace gardens were closing in on me. The thought of being trapped for the rest of the summer thanks to Dennaleia's stupid lessons made me ache for escape—blending into any crowd, teasing out the most valuable information from informants, or haggling with vendors at the market in Cataphract Square. To the street buskers and bar musicians I was a patron like any other, a hand from which to earn a coin for an apple or a heel of bread. Anonymity gave me choices that my title never would. It allowed me to pretend, if only for a moment, that someday I could be a simple horse trainer in a small town somewhere, doing the one thing that mattered to me.

At least at the feast there would be one place I could put my troubles—at the bottom of a flagon of wine.

Several sunlengths later I scowled at the silver horses staring back at me from the ends of my dirty flatware as conversations flew over my head. Across the table lay the remains of the summer feast: toppled piles of fresh berries in melted pools of whipped cream, bones from the tender honey-glazed venison, kernelless corncobs, and crumbs of oat bread scattered amidst it all. My stomach lurched at the thought of more food, especially the rich, dark chocolate cream pie covered in imposing spikes of toasted meringue that the chef had come up with to honor Princess Dennaleia's mountain home. I twisted my cachets, counting the minutes until I could be somewhere—anywhere—else.

My father lifted his glass and tapped his fork against it in six ringing tones.

"I would like to give thanks to the Six Gods for the safe arrival of our guest, Princess Dennaleia of Havemont, and for the bounty of the feast we have enjoyed in her honor. We welcome her to our kingdom and look forward to riding with her by our side. May the Six bless the crown and those who serve."

As the hall rang with blessings, I raised my glass and took a small sip of wine, studying the princess. Her glass aloft and head held high, she showed no sign of her earlier trauma. The flickering light of a wall sconce warmed her pale skin. Long, loose curls draped over her back, almost black against the burgundy evening dress that swept below her shoulder blades. I briefly entertained the idea of making her clean stalls, relishing the thought of what manure would do to the hemline of a gown like that.

Her ignorance about horses might have been amusing if she weren't now my problem. I downed the rest of my cup and poured myself a refill.

"How do you like the wine tonight?" the man beside me said. His white doublet was of an unusual cut and he wore a thin gold band on the fifth finger of his left hand. He had to be the ambassador from Sonnenborne—the closest thing that kingdom had to a ruler since he'd managed to unite several of its nomadic tribes under his banner. Though he had arrived a moon or two ago, I had not spoken to him before.

"It's fine," I replied, taking another hearty swig. What he didn't know was that I'd been taught to drink at the common alehouses in town. I was in little danger of being swayed by any charm he possessed, even with the help of alcohol.

"The new princess is lovely, is she not?"

"Of course." I smirked. "More a princess than I'll ever be."

"You know that's not true, Princess Amaranthine." He spoke with kindness, not knowing how irritating I found his choice of words.

"I hate that name," I muttered.

"Pardon?"

"I said I'll have more of the same." I held up my half-empty glass.

"Baron Endalan Kriantz of Sonnenborne, pleased to be of service," he said, and refilled my cup. "I hear you're the person to speak to about horses."

"Oh?" I sat up straighter. At least someone wanted to talk about something interesting, for a change.

"One of the men I was introduced to down at the stables mentioned you. He said few others possess such a detailed knowledge of warhorse bloodlines." He tipped his wineglass lazily in his hand, watching the liquid swirl within. "Can you tell me your opinion of the Flann bloodline? I'm trying to determine whether they might cross well with my desert horses." He smiled, the edges of his grin lost in a closely cropped black beard.

"Flann horses have good endurance that would closely complement a desert horse, but they throw height. Since your horses are much shorter than ours, you wouldn't be able to guarantee much consistency of stature or build. I'd pick a bloodline with a little less endurance but more reliability as far as height. Azura, perhaps?"

"I'm impressed," he said, and took a sip from his glass.

Warmth rushed through me at the praise. "What exactly do you need the horses for?"

"As my people become less nomadic, we need to prioritize

defense," he said. "Our desert-breds are swift, with great endurance, but less sturdy than your warhorses. Good when one needs to outrun an enemy, but a poor choice for standing one's ground."

"If you're dealing with skirmishes, definitely keep your horses small," I said. "You can add muscle without sacrificing speed over short distances."

"That's exactly my hope, Your Highness," he said.

"I can't stand that 'Your Highness' nonsense. Save it for the people who care about it." I jerked my head toward the end of the table, where Dennaleia was smiling insipidly at my fool of a brother.

"So I should call you . . . ?"

"Mare." I held my head high, daring him to mock me.

"As it pleases you, Mare." He smiled, no trace of mockery in his tone or expression.

"Thank you," I said, impressed with him despite myself. Either Sonnenbornes had remarkable manners for a bunch of mostly lawless tribesmen, or he hadn't discovered the depths of my reputation yet.

"Would you like to dance?" he offered.

"Why not?" I surprised myself by agreeing. Usually there wasn't enough wine in the kingdom to pull me onto the dance floor. I had all the grace of a crippled antelope thanks to dodging most of my lessons.

Lord Kriantz stood up, unfolding smoothly out of his chair to offer me his arm. I rose and wobbled on my heeled shoes, grabbing the back of my chair until my balance felt steady. I cursed under my breath and vowed to demand flat shoes next time. It baffled me that women could walk in such pointy demon hooves all the time, much less dance. Ridiculous.

Jewel-toned skirts swirled in hypnotizing patterns across the wooden floor, accompanied by a small chamber orchestra in the corner of the hall. We joined them and twirled through the crowd, with me clumsily following the baron's lead. Almost immediately, I bumped into a pair of men dancing. They gave us a dirty look, but I didn't care. In spite of myself, I enjoyed the feeling of lightness as Lord Kriantz spun me. Besides, if the timing worked out, I'd be near the door when the song ended and could make my escape.

We completed the last steps of the dance smiling and breathless, right near the exit.

"Thank you," I said in a tone that made it clear there would not be another turn around the floor.

"I hope we will meet another time, perhaps for a ride," Lord Kriantz said. He bowed politely and disappeared into the crowd.

I had almost made it to the door when the orchestra slowed and began to play a version of one of my favorite pieces. A hush rolled through the room as Princess Dennaleia stepped out for her first dance of the evening with Cas alongside her. She bowed her head in my direction and looked up through her lashes, her eyes catching mine as her gaze followed a flourish of her arm. The intensity of her focus sent a little jolt through me. If her hand still hurt from the horse bite, there was no sign of it in the way she moved. My pulse hammered in my ears until she twirled away, the flames of the sconces seeming to flicker and leap as she passed. If she'd been anything other than a problem to me, I might have found her rather alluring.

Once the music wound to its close, the princess curtsied to Cas amidst thunderous applause. It was a showcase, no doubt—he was among the best dancers at court. He then offered his arm to his wife, Ryka, the captain of the guard. I had no idea what he saw in her grave demeanor and severe uniform, but he was the only one who could make her laugh. A pang of fondness for my uncle hit me in spite of my earlier frustration with him.

The musicians picked up a bright peasant tune, clearing my head of the dancing princess. If one pretty piece of music could addle me into thinking she was attractive, it was definitely time to leave. I slipped out the door, chucked my offensive shoes behind a nearby shrub, and stalked off to my quarters. I'd had more than enough of being a princess for one day.

THREE

🪶 *Dennaleia*

I ENTERED BREAKFAST ON MY SECOND DAY IN MYNARIA with one mission: to redeem myself after the disasters of my first. Sheer white curtains along the east side of a high balcony blocked the morning sun, shimmering softly like drifting clouds. Beyond the arcade, the city of Lyrra spread out below us in a burst of colorful rooftops trailing down the hillside and onto the plains. Prince Thandilimon walked over to greet me as soon as I arrived.

"Good morning, my lady," he said. "I trust you slept well?"

I hadn't, thanks to lying awake haunted by everything that had gone wrong the day before. The unabating heat hadn't helped, either. Fortunately, he didn't wait for my answer before continuing.

"A few of my father's most trusted advisers have joined us today," he said, gesturing to a group of dignitaries caught up in a conversation about archery.

King Aturnicus stood near the head of the table, having a more serious discussion with a dark-skinned woman who fixed me with a glare that could have melted glass. I recognized her immediately as Hilara, the director of foreign relations. My mother had warned me about her. Hilara's vote for a Zumordan alliance had been overturned in favor of the one with Havemont, and apparently her ire had never faded. A deep-blue dress almost as sheer as the curtains clung to her willowy frame, and while she looked rather young, judging by her long history on the Directorate, she had to be at least my mother's age.

I returned her glare with a gentle smile, even as my heart quickened with fear and magic prickled at my fingertips. Ever since leaving Havemont, I had felt my gift closer to the surface, rising at the slightest emotional provocation.

"Let's go speak to my father," the prince said.

Fortunately, the king stepped away from Hilara to meet us. He shared Thandilimon and Casmiel's fair hair, but his eyes were more gray than blue, like Amaranthine's, which reminded me that I hadn't seen her yet. Where was she?

"It's such a pleasure to have you here, Princess," the king said.

"Thank you, Your Majesty." I curtsied.

"No need to be too formal among family," he said cheerfully. "I'll be relying on you to keep this son of mine in line. It has been too long since we've had a woman's touch about the place."

I stared at him, trying to decide how to react. I wasn't sure what he meant, given that many of the directors were women. I looked to Thandilimon for guidance, but he only shrugged sheepishly.

"Let us take our seats," the king said, ushering us toward the table.

Before anyone could sit, the curtains rippled as Amaranthine swept onto the balcony, her face flushed.

"Late as always," the prince muttered as he escorted me to the end of the table between Hilara and the king.

No one else paid Amaranthine any attention, but I couldn't stop sneaking glances, shocked that nobody made her apologize. Her green dress made her hair glow like fire, and she wore the gown as well as she had her livery the day before.

I finally tore my eyes away as Thandilimon sat down across from me. He smiled warmly, which I hoped was a sign that he had put the previous day behind us.

The servants dashed around, delivering an extra piece of flatware—a spoon the size of my smallest finger—for the first course. I marveled at it, wondering if we were to eat poached fleas or some other absurd delicacy. But instead I was presented with a shallow bowl filled with ice chips, upon which rested something that looked like a wobbly gray hunk of old liver inside a jagged shell. It looked like something the palace cats might throw up. I tried not to panic.

"Your Highness, Casmiel has told me that you'll be taking riding lessons with Mare?" Hilara said.

She would have to ask me about the only thing I dreaded more than eating the horror on my plate.

"Yes, Director," I said, forcing my face into a benevolent smile. "I look forward to learning more about the warhorses."

The dark expression on Amaranthine's face almost convinced me that she, not I, was the one at the table most likely to set something on fire.

Everyone else busied themselves with the food on their plates, some applying a bit of what smelled like vinegar and shallots. They swallowed the things whole right from the shells, slime and all.

"Tastes like a perfect day on the ocean," Hilara commented with a venomous smile. A challenge.

I tipped the shell to my lips and let the whole thing slide down my throat as the others had. Brine filled my mouth, salty, cold—and shockingly delicious. I smiled and set the empty shell back on my plate.

"Quite lovely," I said. "Where does one get these?"

"They're Royal Cove oysters from Trindor province," Thandilimon said. "We usually only have them in winter, but a Trindori noblewoman is visiting court this season, and her family sent them as a gift to the crown. These are the only ones they harvest in summer, extra deep in the ocean where the water is cooler, and they have this diving equipment—"

"Now, now, Thandi, I doubt Princess Dennaleia shares your enthusiasm for sea exploration or marine life," the king said.

"Sorry," the prince said, embarrassed. "I've always wanted to see the ocean."

"I understand," I said. Like me, he had no doubt spent enough time at his studies to find out how big the world truly was—and to realize how little time he would have to explore it thanks to his future duties as king. "I've never seen the ocean either, but at least I grew up in one kingdom and now have the opportunity to live in another. I can't wait to see more of Mynaria."

"Oh, but we'll have to do something about the Recusants before we can have you out in the city." Hilara sat back, looking smug.

"Recusants?" I asked. I had never heard the word before, nor had I heard about any problems that would impact my presentation to the people of Mynaria.

"Nothing to be too concerned about," Casmiel said. "The Recusants are a rather elusive group of heretics unhappy about the alliance, since it will block magic users from accessing the High Adytum in Havemont."

I frowned. That had not been part of the terms of the alliance. Most magic users were from the eastern kingdom of Zumorda. They had no temples of their own, as they did not believe in the Six Gods—only the power of magic—but they considered the High Adytum a place of pilgrimage for their middle-of-summer rituals. In Havemont, the Zumordans and other magic users had always come and gone in peace.

"Defacing buildings with their symbol or burning them down outright is plenty of cause for concern, if you ask me," Hilara said.

"It's to be expected from a bunch of magic-loving traitors," the king growled, mopping bits of caviar from his mustache. "We'll purge them from both kingdoms in time."

The metal of my fork grew so hot in my hand that I dropped it on the table. I was shocked. No one had ever told me that my marriage meant magic users were unwelcome not only in Mynaria, but in my homeland as well. If an official ban came to pass, strife would undoubtedly follow.

"Protecting our citizens comes first, of course," Casmiel said. "But we must proceed carefully in accordance with the law to keep people happy with the leadership. We wouldn't want to compromise the fondness your people have for you, Your Majesty."

"Of course not," the king said, mollified by Casmiel's reasoning.

"But if the Recusants are responsible for violence in the city, we should round them up and punish them now before they become a bigger problem," Thandilimon said. "We can't have them threatening the safety of the kingdom."

"The antimagic fundamentalists are responsible for most of the outright violence," said Captain Ryka. Her tone suggested she was the sort of person with little patience for anything but facts.

"This all would have been avoided if we had set up an alliance with Zumorda by now," Hilara said, clearly enjoying the quarrel she'd stirred up.

"We can't ally with a kingdom run by heretics." The king waved his knife to emphasize his words.

"Clearly the best response to something you don't understand is to attack it," Amaranthine said, her sarcasm sharp enough to cut.

I clutched my hands tightly around my cool glass, desperate to hold in my magic and not to reveal any anger or fear. The king and the Directorate clearly not only hated magic users, but also planned to persecute them based on the consummation of the alliance. I had to try to smooth things over until I could find out more.

"Perhaps there is another way to placate these Recusants and prevent further violence?" I offered. "Few of them would make it to the High Adytum in their lifetimes. Perhaps it's a matter of finding them a new place of worship locally."

Casmiel nodded thoughtfully.

"But they're apostates," Thandilimon said. "The crown can't risk looking like we support a group of heretic magic users."

"Of course not," I agreed. "It's crucial to find a solution that satisfies both sides and lessens the backlash from the fundamentalists. Perhaps it would help to learn more about what each group wants?"

"True," Thandilimon said. "It couldn't hurt to gather more information."

Hilara frowned, no doubt irritated that she couldn't find fault with my suggestion.

"Princess Dennaleia has a good point," Casmiel said. "It hasn't been easy to track down the Recusants, though. No one is eager to trade information pertaining to magic."

Amaranthine looked at Casmiel keenly then. "Maybe if my afternoons were free, I'd be able to help—"

"You have lessons to teach," the king cut her off. "This is the last I want to hear of you trying to get out of it."

I winced as she slumped back in her chair. We barely knew each other and she already hated me. I had to change that. If I couldn't win over another princess, it would be preposterous to consider myself worthy of a queen's crown. After so many years of etiquette lessons, I should have been able to charm snow out of a clear blue sky.

"Eadric, what do you advise on the matter?" the prince asked. "Surely our director of religion should weigh in, since this is so closely tied to the proper worship of the Six."

Everyone turned to the far end of the table, where Director Eadric was slowly consuming a noodle of interminable length in a way that precluded speech. He had nearly white hair and the distinguished look of a seasoned courtier, but his gaze seemed rather vacant.

"Showing the Recusants a path to the light is the only way," he finally said. He sketched the symbol of the wind god languidly over the table with his fork, a noodle still dangling.

Everyone stared at him except the king, who had moved on to gnawing on a leg of smoked chicken, sucking the meat directly off the bone. The news of unrest in the city and policy changes to the alliance made me wonder what other watered-down information Havemont had been receiving, leaving me uninformed.

The conversation eventually picked up again and turned to more general topics, but I could not stop worrying about what else I didn't know. Each course was more picturesque and delectable than the last, and yet I scarcely tasted the food. We rose from our seats to mingle for the final course, a jewellike dessert with a flavor like violets, served with fresh berries and a milk caramel that had been lightened with whipped cream. Amaranthine took the opportunity to vanish, giving everyone something to complain about for the remainder of the breakfast in between talking about some of the formal events they hoped I would help plan. By the time it was over, my feet could not carry me to my chambers quickly enough. I wanted to do something useful—not be responsible for the social calendar of every noble in Lyrra.

"Your Highness." Casmiel caught up to me in the hallway before I called a page. "May I walk you to your rooms?"

"Of course, my lord," I said, and took his arm.

"I apologize for Amaranthine's attitude about the lessons," Casmiel said.

"It's understandable," I said. "She's so busy, and I hate to take her away from her other duties. Perhaps there is someone else who could teach me?" It couldn't hurt to make one last attempt to escape the lessons, particularly if it might put me on better terms with Amaranthine.

"There's no better instructor," Casmiel said. "She's a bit rough around the edges, but she has a good heart. Truly. Give her a chance."

"Of course. I am sure she's quite skilled." I forced a small smile. Her teaching skills weren't the problem. Of the two of us, she was the one not interested in giving *me* a chance. She seemed eager to spend her time doing almost anything else.

"She's the most skilled rider in or out of these walls. And she has a way of sometimes turning up with useful information, even if it's gathered from sources that are, shall we say . . . unconventional."

"Oh?" I said, curious what he meant.

We stopped at the end of my hallway, out of earshot of the liegemen patrolling near my door.

"But I'd like to talk about you for a moment," he said. "You've only just arrived, but I see in you all the things I hoped to. You listen and observe. You pay attention to people and relationships. You understand how to help people with divergent opinions find common ground, as you did during the discussion about the Recusants this morning. You also stepped in to keep Mare and Thandi from each other's throats yesterday, and that's no small feat."

His compliments bloomed in me like morning glories unfurling toward the sun. Everything since my arrival had felt like a series of accidents, and it heartened me that he had seen more to me than those mishaps.

"Thandilimon has much of his father in him," he said. "They are strong, charismatic people in need of temperance from time to time. It is important for them to have trusted advisers who can keep them steady. That is who I am for King Aturnicus. That is who I hope you will be for Thandi."

I nodded, feeling stripped bare by the depth of his gaze. He had Amaranthine's intensity without any of her harshness. "It is my deepest wish to be of service to the kingdom however I can," I said.

"I'm pleased to hear that," he said. "If you're interested, I'd like to take the time to meet with you each day after your riding lessons to discuss matters pertaining to the Directorate and the governance of the kingdom. It's a lot to add to your already busy schedule, but I see that it matters to you. I hope you will consider me a friend and a mentor during your ascension."

Hope surged in me. I didn't care that meeting with him would take up the only remaining free time in my days, which would soon be booked with mornings full of social breakfasts with courtiers, afternoons riding with Amaranthine, and evening dinners or entertainment with the royal family. Casmiel could help me lay the groundwork to become the ruler I aspired to be.

"Nothing would please me more," I said.

"Excellent. We can begin tomorrow," he said, his crow's-feet crinkling as he smiled and bowed a farewell.

I entered my rooms giddy with the promise of Casmiel's mentorship, too excited to bother closing the door. Tingles of magic danced through my arms and fingers. Auna, my maid, looked up from the embroidery she sat working on near the windows and beamed to see me so happy.

I imagined a cleansing breeze rushing through my rooms, blowing away all my fears and doubts. Behind me, the door to my rooms slammed shut, and I stopped in my tracks. The sensation in my arms had completely vanished, and my head spun a little.

"My lady . . . is the door to your chambers weighted?" Auna asked, her voice tentative.

"I don't know," I said. Fear eased in where the magic had been seconds before.

"It must have been a breeze that closed it." She sketched the symbol of the wind god in the air.

"Yes, a breeze," I murmured in agreement.

But as it had been everywhere in the castle that morning, the air was absolutely still.

FOUR

✦ *Mare*

AFTER NEARLY A WEEK OF ONEROUS COURT EVENTS following Princess Dennaleia's arrival, I had no intention of spending my last morning of freedom inside the castle walls. Just after dawn I let myself into the liegemen's barracks and yanked the covers off my best friend, Nils.

"Time to go out on the town!" I said cheerfully.

He groaned. "By the Six, why do you do this to me?"

I gave him a few good knocks until he swung his legs over the side of the bed to sit up.

"It's too early to have one of your girls in the barracks," a nearby bunkmate complained, flipping over and mashing a pillow over his ears.

Nils stood and rummaged through his trunk for a shirt. We were the same age, but somehow in the past few years he'd outgrown me and turned into a broad-shouldered liegeman with the kind of biceps that made his vocation obvious and most of the women—and some of the men—in the castle take note.

"I'll meet you at breakfast in a quarter sunlength," I said. "Don't be late."

In spite of the curses he grumbled at my back, I knew he wouldn't be far behind.

We ate a quick breakfast and took off on horseback—Nils on his gray gelding, Holler, and me on a nondescript mare borrowed without permission from the pen of green four-year-olds. The clop of our horses' hooves and the metallic squeak of my mare champing on her snaffle quickly got lost amidst the noise of other traffic as we rode into Lyrra. The enormous stone houses of wealthy nobles towered on either side of us, surrounded by gated gardens and footpaths that were already swept clean for the new day.

"So what in the Sixth Hell was important enough that you had to drag me out of bed barely after the birds started up?" Nils asked.

"Showing Cas that he's making a mistake wasting my summer with those stupid riding lessons," I said. If I could find some new information on the Recusants, he'd have to reevaluate.

"Riding lessons? You don't need those." He gave me a puzzled look.

"Not me, numbskull. I've been ordered to give lessons to Princess Dennaleia, starting this afternoon. Right now when it comes to horses, the girl's as much use as tits on a saddle."

"That's not all bad. I've found there are many benefits to befriending the noblewomen at court," he said with a sly grin.

"Maybe for you." I snorted. "If I befriend Dennaleia, it'll play right into my father's and Cas's plans. They're probably hoping she'll turn me into a perfect princess who will be happily married off before winter. I'd rather eat hoof trimmings. Besides, no noble with half their wits about them would befriend me."

"I befriended you," he said.

"You were different," I countered. He wasn't noble, so he didn't have a court reputation to destroy. We'd constantly been in trouble together in our horsemanship classes. Friendship was inevitable, as was what had come after—even if it hadn't lasted.

"Or I possess no sense of self-preservation," he teased. "So where are we going?"

I drew my mare to a halt at the end of the next street. Above our heads the painted outline of a circle in bright white adorned the side of a merchant's shop, and across the road a building had been burned nearly to the ground. My stomach dropped a little.

"Recusants," Nils said grimly.

"Let's start at the Deaf Dog," I said. A favorite of off-duty liegemen, it was one of the cleanest pubs in town—and a good place to trade money for information. I'd intended to drag Nils to the Pelham, but the burned building made me think twice about heading straight for the seediest alehouse in Lyrra.

We hitched our horses to the rail outside the Deaf Dog and took seats inside near the window. People in the passing traffic laughed or jeered, hurried or took their time, unconstrained by formality and protocol. Tension melted out of me. Outside the castle I didn't have to deal with people bowing as I passed, or the smirks I pretended not to see.

"Coffee for ye, m'lads?" a rumbling baritone asked.

I looked up and smiled at Graum, the proprietor.

"Make it a double," Nils said.

"Aye! Nice to see ye. It's been a while." Graum clapped me on the back with a meaty hand, nearly knocking me into the table. "Black tea, no sugar?"

"Exactly right. Thank you," I replied with a smile.

"Always such nice manners on ye, lad." He grinned. "Your mother raised you right."

My smile faltered at the mention of my mother, but he didn't seem to notice as he lumbered off.

When Graum returned, he barely glanced at the coin I'd left crown side down on the table. Nevertheless, it vanished into his hand somewhere between setting down my tea and asking me if I'd like anything else.

I placed two fingers on the edge of the table, the code for politics.

He moved my tea mug to the left side of my plate. New information.

I picked up my fork to indicate that I would stay.

He placed four fingers on the edge of the table, and I exchanged a look with Nils. What I wanted to know wasn't going to come cheaply.

I hesitated for a moment, not wanting to give away the ease with which I could pay his price.

"The food is good," I said at last, agreeing to his terms.

He nodded and walked off, the grin back.

A few minutes later a man slid into the bench across from us. His unmemorable face was crowned with jet-black hair, neatly trimmed. The cut of his clothing was almost too simple, and definitely too clean for the working-class style he wore—the subtle hallmarks of a spy.

"Two mugs?" he asked.

"Yes," I answered, passing a handful of coins to him under the table. His palm was rough and warm against my fingers.

"Many think the crown has gone soft thanks to the false security provided by the alliance with Havemont," he said, his voice pitched to be barely audible above the buzz of the pub. "A group of heretics known as the Recusants opposes the alliance. The extremists among them want to see the High Adytum reclaimed only for magic users rather than worshipers of the Six. Conversely, those who feel most strongly that magic is heresy believe that the Directorate and the king are not doing enough to quiet these pockets of unrest and to keep Mynaria safe and pure."

I gnawed anxiously at my lip. It wasn't anything I didn't know. But while I agreed that the Directorate was full of stuffy old windbags who rarely got anything done, the alliance had been in the works for so long that it seemed inevitable, and our kingdoms had been at peace since the signing of the decrees years ago. The High Adytum couldn't be the only problem.

"What else?" I asked.

"The Recusants have always counted on being able to use Havemont as a roundabout gateway to Zumorda. Some say that Zumorda has counted on it as well, for the trade of illegal goods. Havemont's borders are far less regulated than the one between Mynaria and Zumorda, as the people of Havemont are less stringently opposed to magic."

"What does that mean for the crown?" Nils asked.

"It's been suggested that the Zumordans may rise to side with the Recusants," the spy said.

"What?" I squeaked. If an entire kingdom was willing to step up and fight for the interests of a small rebel group, the problems were far larger than Cas had told us. No one knew exactly how powerful Zumorda might be, but given that it was the only kingdom to offer refuge for magic users, making an enemy of it would be unwise at best.

The man's gaze held steady, but a muscle twitched in his right cheek.

"Magic users from the east—" The spy cut off as an eruption of shouting began in the street.

Nils set down his mug and craned his head out the window. "Six Hells!"

"What's going on?" I asked.

Other patrons had already surged to their feet and flooded out the front door.

I turned back to the spy, only to see that he'd slipped away, unwilling to get caught in a situation that seemed to be going east. One coin remained on the table—the price of not getting me all the information I'd been promised. I swore under my breath.

Nils and I ran outside straight into a brawl. Fists flew in a surging crowd of people that seemed to be continually increasing in size. Our horses skittered at the hitching rail, the whites of their eyes showing.

"We need to get out of here," Nils said, already untying Holler.

But then I saw what had started the fight. At the end of a nearby alley, half a white circle on the side of a building still dripped with fresh paint. My heart jumped into my throat.

"This started with the Recusants," I said, sidestepping a man who nearly staggered into me as he reeled from a punch.

"An even better reason to leave," Nils replied.

We swung into our saddles and urged our horses away from the riot. As we broke free of the crowd, so did a man, with three others right on his heels. I did a double take. White paint was spattered on his arms. He had to be the Recusant who'd started it. The four men dashed down a narrow alley between two tall buildings, and I took a hard right to follow them.

"Dammit!" Nils yelled behind me. I hoped to the Six he'd follow.

The three men pounced on their victim halfway down the alley, flinging him against the stone wall of a building. He slid down into a trickle of water that reeked of garbage.

"How does that feel, you dirty scum?" one of them said as he landed a kick.

"Hey!" I shouted.

The three men looked up, faces twisted in identical expressions of hate.

"Are you a magic lover too?" the tallest man sneered. One of his front teeth was broken in half, and it looked like a fist had adjusted the position of his nose more than once.

"Oh, for the love of the Six," Nils muttered as he rode up alongside me.

"What did he ever do to you?" I asked, hoping I sounded cockier than I felt.

One of them spat on the fallen man. "Sold my youngest son to the Zumordans, they did."

And then the men were upon me, one of them trying to tug

me out of the saddle by the leg, and another reaching for my mare's reins.

Holler leaped forward. Nils swiped a broken broom handle from a trash pile, brandishing it like a jousting lance. One of them tried to grab it from him, but he thrust it into the man's chest and knocked him flat. Then he cued Holler to lash out with his back hooves, narrowly missing the second. I held out a hand and took the broom handle from Nils, hoping the skittish little mare would hold steady for me. I squeezed her forward and swung the weapon into the tall man's head, tossing it back over my shoulder to Nils afterward. When the men saw Holler bearing down on them again, they ran like a pack of stray dogs.

I slipped out of the saddle and crouched next to the man on the ground, helping him into a sitting position. He was better dressed than the others, but not much, with the wiry look of a courier. Dark, shaggy hair streaked with gray hung into his eyes, and blood dripped from a split lip.

"If you answer my questions, we might let you go," I said. "First, what's your name?"

He eyed us mistrustfully, wincing as he probed his ribs. Nils shifted his grip on the broom handle, and the man put up his hands. "Alen!" he said. "My name is Alen."

"Is it true you sold that man's child to Zumorda?" I needed to know if he actually deserved our help, or if we'd be better off trying to haul him in.

"We don't sell children. We save them," Alen said, swiping at the blood drying on his chin.

"Save them from what?" I said sharply.

"Parents who think purification rituals will cleanse Affinities," Alen said bitterly. "We send gifted children to Zumorda, where they can be trained and won't hurt anyone by accident. We only want to keep everyone safe."

If Cas knew anything about that, he hadn't mentioned it. In theory, Alen and his cohort were providing a useful service to the kingdom, even if the methods were questionable.

"Who is 'we'?" I asked.

"The Syncretic Circle," he said.

Apparently the Recusants went by more than one name. I rocked back on my heels and looked up at Nils. He frowned, no doubt wondering how deep the manure was that we'd stepped in now.

Feet pounded over the cobblestones as three men and a woman appeared at the far end of the alley. Alen waved weakly in their direction.

"Let's go. Now," Nils said, giving me a look that forestalled any argument.

I reluctantly mounted my horse. I wanted to interrogate Alen further, but we couldn't take on four others, especially if any of them had magic on their side.

"We'll find out more at the Pelham," I said as soon as we were out of earshot.

"Oh no, I don't think so," Nils said. "We can't risk another fight. You're already covered in blood, and don't you have a lesson to teach this afternoon?"

"I'd prefer the Pelham," I said.

"Mare." Nils gave me a pleading look.

"Fine," I grumbled.

Several minutes passed before he spoke again.

"You know I'd do anything for you," he said softly, his brow furrowed. "But as a liegeman, I can't run around playing vigilante. I got lucky that those brutes were cowards. Sure, I'm trained to take down three men—with a sword or spear. Not with a broken broom handle."

"I'm sorry," I said, and reached for his hand. "If anything ever happened to you . . ." I couldn't even finish the sentence.

The expression on his face didn't change, but he took my hand. We walked our horses side by side that way for a while, until the tension of the fight left his grip.

"You wouldn't deliberately endanger me. I know that," he said.

"I wouldn't," I said firmly. I shouldn't have been so careless. Even though we were no longer lovers, he was so much more to me than a bodyguard, and always would be. I hoped he knew.

As for me, I was already planning to sneak out alone after Dennaleia's lesson to broker a second meeting with that spy.

FIVE

❧ *Dennaleia*

MY HANDS SHOOK WITH NERVES AS I HEADED TO MY first riding lesson. Thandilimon accompanied me, seemingly oblivious to how ridiculous I looked in riding breeches. The hot afternoon sun beat down on us, amplifying my dread as we made our way through the castle gardens toward the stables. Thandilimon kept a brisk pace, telling me a story about a time he and Amaranthine had gotten in trouble with Captain Ryka for trying out the mounted archery course before they'd had any instruction.

"We could barely keep our ponies going in straight lines, much less shoot anything. Arrows were sticking out of every place except the targets. If we had been anyone else's children, Ryka might have shot us. It was Mare's idea, of course." He laughed.

"It sounds as though Amaranthine makes her own rules," I said. His story was almost a good distraction, but I couldn't get over feeling strangely exposed in my outfit and anxious about dealing with Amaranthine.

"Mare's rule book is a mystery to us all. Will your sister have similar stories about you when she arrives for her visit?" he teased.

"You'll never know. Ali keeps my secrets." I tried for what I hoped was a flirtatious smile.

"Do you have something in your eye?" he asked.

"Only the sun," I said, embarrassed. Flirtation had evidently not been adequately covered in my etiquette classes. I quickly changed the subject. "Has the Directorate made any progress getting more information on the Recusants?"

"Not much," Thandilimon said. "Many of the leads Casmiel's spies followed turned out to be dead ends. The fundamentalists are throwing around a lot of baseless accusations hoping to criminalize the Recusants however they can. We receive more and more petitions to the crown every day."

"That's unfortunate," I said. A whisper of fear crept through me. More paranoia meant that the eyes of the people would be sharply attuned to anything that smelled of magic.

As we entered the stables, I whispered a small prayer to the Six to help me survive my lesson without looking like a clumsy fool. I needed to impress Amaranthine with my competence if I wanted to win her over.

"Well, I'm off to ride Zin," Thandilimon said. "Good luck at your lesson."

He departed with a bow and a smile, leaving me stranded in the middle of the barn. Horses stood in various sets of cross ties being saddled, unsaddled, bathed, and a number of other things I couldn't put a name to. Straw flew as stable hands cleaned stalls, hurrying past me with wheelbarrows or brooms. I had no idea whether to search for Amaranthine somewhere in the building or outside in one of the many practice arenas.

"Excuse me. Are you looking for your lesson, Your Highness?" A tall man with sun-aged skin stepped into my path.

"Yes, thank you," I replied, straightening my shoulders.

"Jamin Theeds." He introduced himself with a bow. "I'm the stable master and head trainer here."

"Lovely to meet you," I said.

"Come this way." He led me through the barn and out the far end at a brisk pace. Outside, a sturdy-looking horse the color of mead stood in the middle of a small, round arena. His ears flopped to either side like a mule's as Amaranthine scratched behind them. My mouth went dry and I clutched reflexively for skirts I wasn't wearing. Theeds escorted me into the pen, dust curling up from beneath the soles of his boots.

Amaranthine faced us with one hip cocked, wearing her plain shirt and breeches as though they were the vestments of a queen. Like her brother, she towered over me. Cachets of every color adorned her right forearm, the thin bracelets stacked almost halfway to her elbow. Despite my tailored riding clothes, I felt as homely and small as a sparrow beside her. A few loose pieces of hair swept the edge of her jawline, which was set in a challenging expression.

I crumpled beneath her stare.

"Thanks, Theeds." She nodded a dismissal to him, already busy pulling down the stirrups.

My stomach knotted, and a familiar tingle raced down my arm. I jabbed my fingernails into my palm until the magic faded into the pain.

Amaranthine finished with the saddle and finally faced me. Despite my memory of her eyes, they still took me by surprise—a mutable gray that reminded me of earth and sky all at once.

"Princess Amaranthine." I finally found words. "I appreciate you doing this for me."

She growled. "For the love of the Six, don't call me that. Just Mare. Yes, like a horse. Stupid, I know, but I can't stand Amaranthine. What a ridiculously overlong and pretentious collection of syllables."

I couldn't quite bring myself to say it. In Havemont it would be offensive for anyone outside of immediate family to shorten the name of a royal.

"Anyway, we're wasting time. Let's get you on this horse. Stand facing the saddle and bend your left leg at the knee."

I stepped up to the left side of the horse, self-conscious in my breeches, wondering if wearing pants would stop feeling odd after enough lessons.

"This is Louie, by the way," she said, gesturing to the horse. "Whoa is his favorite speed." He flicked his tail as if answering to his name.

Before I had time to ask what came next, her hands cupped beneath my bent knee, flinging me into the saddle as though I weighed no more than a sack of flour. I fumbled at the leather, trying to find my balance.

"Thanks for the warning," I muttered.

Amaranthine didn't answer. A corner of her mouth quirked up, but I couldn't tell whether it was due to amusement or disdain.

I jammed my feet into the stirrups and sat up, grateful that Louie seemed so uninspired to move.

"Keep the stirrup on the ball of your foot if you can. Here." She wiggled the stirrup out from under the arch of my foot.

"Like dancing." I thought back to the welcoming feast, when Amaranthine's eyes had met mine as I danced with Casmiel. In that moment, doing something that was one of my strengths, I had felt much more her equal.

"Dancing may help you with riding," she said. "Balance and coordination are important for both." She stepped forward and put her hand lightly on my knee. Her touch sent a tingle up my leg that had nothing to do with magic and everything to do with nerves.

"Grip him hard with both knees," she said. "Yes, like that. See how when you do that your lower leg comes completely off his side? You have no power if you have to ask him to turn or go forward. Now quit gripping with your knees. Good. Relax completely. Use your thigh and calf muscles. That's where the strength of your seat comes from."

She stuck her hand behind my thigh, and a giggle escaped me. No one had ever touched me there.

"Sorry. I'm not trying to tickle you. This"—she touched me firmly—"is where you are going to have to build a lot of muscle. Now stand up in your stirrups. Any time you're having trouble with your position, this is a good way to remind yourself where your legs are supposed to be. When you stand up, you're forced to put your lower legs in the correct position, or you won't even be able to get yourself out of the saddle."

I sat down heavily, my thighs trembling with the effort of holding myself up for even a few seconds. This was not going to be pleasant.

She sent Louie out on a long rope, clucking at him to move forward.

"Now feel the way he walks. Pay attention to where his back muscles are pushing you and focus on following that movement. Sit up straight, but relax your hips."

I tried to do as she asked. It was strange to have someone talking about my hips. Of course, dance instructors had talked about them before, but they hadn't been quite so . . . blunt.

"Chest up, shoulders back. Keep both your lanterns on the road ahead!"

I might have blushed if I hadn't been so on edge. The language she used was better suited to the proprietor of a lowbrow tavern than a member of the royal family. Where had she even learned to talk like that?

Louie and I continued to amble around the arena, Amaranthine firing off instructions more quickly than I could assimilate them. As I struggled to maintain my position, something caught my eye out past the other arenas. The bright shirts of three men stood out against the summer fields, the necks of their mounts dark with sweat. They approached at a brisk trot, the center horse flipping her head, the whites of her eyes stark against her bay coat.

Instead of slowing as they approached the barn, the lead horse picked up a canter and skittered sideways over the dirt trail between the paddocks. As the riders drew closer, I recognized Prince Thandilimon aboard the unruly mare, a wide grin on his face. I straightened my posture and tried to remember everything Amaranthine had told me to do. It would be good for him and other nobles to see me riding.

I smiled, raising a hand to wave. Before Thandilimon could return the gesture, the dust kicked up by the horses engulfed us and Louie let out a tremendous sneeze. I tipped forward in the saddle as his head flew down, and I tumbled over his shoulder to land in the dirt. My hip smarted, and I coughed amid the settling dust. Louie had come to an abrupt halt, placid as ever, and peered back at me before turning forward with a sigh.

"Don't move," Amaranthine said, closing the distance between us in a few strides.

I tensed as she approached, waiting for the inevitable reprimand.

Instead, she crouched down and put her hand on my shoulder. Her touch comforted me with its balance of certainty and gentleness.

"Go slow. Make sure everything's working," she instructed.

"I'm sorry," I said, embarrassed. Looking stupid in pants was apparently the least of my problems.

"It wasn't your fault," she said, scowling in the direction of the barn. "That idiot brother of mine is going to get someone killed letting his horse run in from the trails. I've told him a thousand times not to do that."

"I still shouldn't have fallen off," I said. "All Louie did was sneeze."

"The important thing is that you're all right." She pulled me up onto my feet. "If I get you injured, my father, my brother, and both our kingdoms will be after my neck."

"I'm fine," I said, brushing the dirt off my breeches. My hip ached, but she didn't need to know. "Did the prince see me?" I asked hesitantly.

Amaranthine rolled her eyes. "Doubt it. Idiot was probably too busy trying to keep his seat on that ill-mannered mare of his."

I cast a glance over to the barn, but the men had disappeared inside. I cared what the prince thought, but in a way it was more upsetting to think I'd disappointed Amaranthine.

"Arms and legs still working?"

"I suppose so." I moved all my limbs experimentally, still a little shaky from the fall.

"Then you're getting back in the saddle." Amaranthine gestured impatiently at the left stirrup.

I quashed my fear, walked to Louie's side, and let her toss me onto his back again.

A sunlength later my legs felt as though they were made of pudding. I staggered around like a kitten as Amaranthine showed me how to remove Louie's saddle and bridle and put away the equipment in the tack room. She did so with ruthless efficiency that allowed no room for small talk, leaving me to dwell on my failure to improve her opinion of me.

Relief flooded me when we stepped into the barn aisle and I saw Casmiel approaching. He greeted us and kissed my hand. Even Amaranthine smiled to see him. His presence made everything feel lighter.

"We received some new border reports I thought you'd like to see, so I came to escort you to the castle," he said, and then turned to Amaranthine. "Are you coming back with us?"

She shook her head. "You know how it is down here. There's always shit to shovel."

"Keep it off your boots!" he said with a laugh, and touched her shoulder fondly.

On our way back to the castle, I mumbled a prayer to the wind god, hoping that studying Directorate business would help me forget my utter ineptitude in the saddle.

Casmiel's study was even lovelier than I expected. Bookcases lined the walls on either side of his desk, with greenery interspersed among the multicolored spines of the volumes. A small set of the wind god's chimes jingled softly in one of the windows, and the crystals hanging below the clappers cast shards of light all through the room.

"Have a seat," he said, gesturing to a circle of heavy leather chairs. He sat across from me once I had selected my own, a strategic position designed to put us on even footing for the conversation to come. In spite of his blithe nature, I could tell that Casmiel should never be underestimated.

"Thank you," I said as he handed me a tall glass of pale tea served over crushed ice with a sprig of mint sticking out of the top. It smelled herbal and vibrant, green as spring.

"How do you feel things are going so far?" he asked.

"All right. The riding lessons will be challenging." Or rather, my instructor would. "The breakfasts have been nice, but the conversations have mostly been about parties and fashion. I'd love to learn more about issues important to the crown as well."

"The other nobles may try to distract you with tea parties and frippery," Casmiel said. "You will have to earn your place here.

Show my brother, Thandi, and the Directorate that your voice is to be trusted. Queen Mirianna was more than a figurehead and an entertainer. She was the conscience of the king. His anchor. May she rest with the Six." He made a fist and placed it over his heart.

"May her rest be eternally peaceful," I murmured, mimicking his gesture and sketching the symbol of the shadow god.

We both took a moment of silent reflection, and I let my eyes wander over Casmiel's shelves. Most of the volumes in his office were not books but records of the kingdom. He had them categorized by type and year, the colored bindings allowing for quick reference. The man held the reins of the kingdom in his hands.

"I hope to be worthy of Queen Mirianna's memory," I finally said. "And also to make my own future."

"In that case, let's go over those border reports and see what you think. Apparently the bandits are getting hungry, especially in the southeast." He pushed aside the tea tray, and we spent a sunlength poring over reports and records that the Directorate had reviewed the previous morning, seeing if we could parse out any further information from them. Messengers occasionally interrupted us to bring Casmiel the latest updates on Directorate business, leaving me in awe of how adeptly he handled the competing needs of all who relied on him.

"You're a quick study, my lady," Casmiel said near the end of our session. "Most members of the Directorate don't have the eastern trade routes memorized as well as you."

"Thank you," I said, delighted. My head swam with information. I'd be up late making notes, but unlike riding, that was something I knew I could do.

Another knock sounded on the door, and a page entered. "A noble's house was defaced by the Recusants, and he's demanding retribution," the page said. "The king has requested that the Directorate convene in half a sunlength."

Casmiel dismissed the page and sighed. "Our time is up, I'm afraid," he said. Outside, the afternoon was fading into dusk. "If you have time to review those expiring trade agreements, it would be a great help to me."

"I'd be happy to," I said, thrilled that he trusted me with such an important task.

He bade me farewell with a kiss on the hand, and I left his study with renewed confidence and a sheaf of papers in my arms. I hobbled down the hallway, my legs stiff and aching from sitting still for so long after the punishment of my riding lesson. But a crash sounded before I'd stepped more than ten paces away. I stopped in my tracks, as did a page who was hurrying by. Perhaps Casmiel had knocked something off one of his shelves. He might need help cleaning it up.

"My lord?" I asked, turning back to tap on the door.

Silence was the only response. Magic prickled into my fingertips as dread made my pulse pound in my ears.

I knocked more loudly, then pushed open the door.

Scattered papers danced across the floor as a breeze gusted in through the open window. Casmiel lay on his back amidst them, one arm thrown out to the side. One of his eyes stared vacantly in my direction. A white arrow protruded from the other, the shaft glimmering with otherworldly light.

SIX

✦ *Mare*

BY THE TIME I SLIPPED BACK OUT TO TOWN ON FOOT, the afternoon had given way to twilight. Lamps winked on in windows and on the street. I was eager for nightfall, when the lights would glow like fireflies throughout the city—until the mournful call of a hunting horn sounded in the distance.

Traffic slowed to a stumbling stop. Heads bowed, and hands covered hearts.

My trembling fingers found their way to my chest as though struggling to contain the heart within. A lone rider cantered down the street through the parted crowd, her horse's shod hooves sending up dust and sparks. Her white cloak fluttered behind her, the hood pulled up to shroud her face in shadows. She raised a horn to her lips and blew another icy tone, the brass catching flickers of lamplight as blue tassels swung beneath it.

A great hole opened inside me. The White Riders meant a royal death. Who in the Six Hells could it be?

The whispering began as soon as the final horn call faded into silence.

"Surely it's not the king."

"The Havemont princess, perhaps?"

"No! The White Riders ride only for the Mynarian royal family. She's not Mynarian yet. Besides, a foreigner is a foreigner no matter how long—"

"The daughter! It could be the daughter," a voice interrupted.

"The magic users must have been behind it," someone said.

With those words, the crowd exploded into chaos.

There wasn't time for me to end up in a street brawl, or to finish my original mission. I needed to get back to the castle, preferably before anyone discovered my absence. I shoved through the crowd, fighting my way up the street. Closer to the castle wall, liegemen prowled with swords at the ready. I cursed and pushed down a surge of fear and anxiety.

I extricated myself from the crowd and ducked into a narrow space between two houses. Every shadow seemed to reach for me with dark fingers, and I shuddered as I passed the outline of a white circle on the side of a building, barely visible in the dim lamplight. I crept through backyards until I found what I'd hoped for—an ornate metal trellis that climbed all the way to the top of a house. I latched on before I could lose my nerve.

The tang of iron and the green scent of crushed cypress leaves tingled in my nose as I scaled the trellis, the metal biting into my hands. My arms ached by the time I reached the roof. I pressed myself flat against the stone tiles and crawled carefully to the peak for a better view.

A cohort of at least a hundred liegemen stood at attention in front of the main gates of the castle. Onlookers hung back closer to the city streets, wary of the steel that glinted in the liegemen's hands. Far below me, pinpoints of light sparked in the darkness as sets of vigil candles were lit. Each grouping of six candles drew a small cluster of people. Fools. Vigils provided nothing but bruised knees. Praying to the Six wouldn't bring back the dead. Having lost my mother, I knew that better than anyone.

The wide swath of open ground between the city folk and the liegemen scared me. A royal death alone wasn't reason to keep mourners at such a distance. Foul play must have been involved in whatever had befallen my family. Alone and unarmed outside the castle walls, I'd be an appealing second target. Then again, trying to sneak past that many liegemen was just as likely to end in death. All my options lay somewhere between shit and manure.

I made my way back down the trellis, relieved when my boots finally hit solid ground. A slightly discordant hymn drifted through the streets as I hurried toward a side entrance to the castle wall. Unsurprisingly, the way was blocked. Four liegemen stood guard over the lone door, torchlight filtering between the iron bars behind them. I let the shadows of the buildings swallow me as I sneaked closer to the entrance. Street traffic was so light and intermittent it couldn't be used as cover.

Perhaps I could sneak in with a delivery. Or if I could get close enough to—

"Heya!" A pair of hands grabbed me from behind, shoving me out into the light.

I whirled around and struck at my assailant, but my fist flew through empty air.

"Don't think so, m'lad," he said.

Before I could retaliate, my back hit the cobblestones of the street. A burly liegeman stood over me with the tip of his blade resting on my throat. Hells. I'd forgotten about the perimeter guard.

"If you think you're getting in, you're mistaken." A sadistic grin was evident in his voice, though I could barely make out his face with the gas lamp shining behind his head. "No one is allowed in or out, by orders of the king."

"I wasn't trying to get in," I said, racking my brain for an excuse.

"Sure you weren't. Why were you sneaking around in the shadows, boy?" He pressed his sword into my neck. The blade stung my flesh.

"Just looking for a friend, sir." My voice trembled.

"You look a mite scrawny for an assassin. Or maybe you're one of those filthy magic lovers." He spat beside my head. "Maybe I'll kill you first and ask questions later."

My heart pounded in my chest. What a stupid way to die. I was going to have to reveal my identity, and my father would never let me out of his sight again.

"Gammon, what did you turn up?" a familiar voice called from across the street.

"Nils!" I squeaked.

"You know this street rat?" Gammon kept his eyes on me as he spoke to Nils.

"I can't say I know that many street"—Nils stepped closer and looked down at me, recognition dawning on his face—"rats."

I swallowed hard, staring up at him. Standing over me in his uniform, he looked every bit the authoritative liegeman, sheathed sword buckled at his narrow waist. He held his spear at the ready, the strong muscles of his arms visible below the short sleeves of his shirt.

Silently, I pleaded with him to think of a way out of the situation—any way that didn't involve being forced to play the princess card.

"Stand down, Gammon. I know this one." Nils sighed and drew his spear back into guard position.

The blade vanished from my throat. I touched my neck and my fingers came away red with blood.

"Sometimes I don't know why I bother," Gammon muttered, sheathing his weapon.

"You did good work," Nils assured him. "No telling what's out here tonight."

Nils pulled me to my feet, frowning as he glimpsed the cut on my neck.

"What have I told you about leaving the castle grounds without permission?" He squared his stance and glared at me.

"That it's inexcusable, sir." I hung my head, falling into the act.

"That's right. I don't care if it's your night off. Stable hands only leave the grounds on praise days. Tonight you could have been killed." His brown eyes bored into me. Had I been a real stable boy, I would have quaked in my boots.

"I'm sorry, sir," I said.

He grabbed me by the back of my shirt and shoved me toward the gate. "Back on duty, soldier." He nodded to Gammon, who saluted before vanishing into the shadows with remarkable stealth for a man of his size.

Nils marched me to the castle wall. I kept my head down, slumping so he had to drag me in like a cat by the scruff of its neck. The key bearer unlatched the gate, eyeing me mistrustfully as we passed through. As soon as we were out of their line of sight, Nils dropped the act and enveloped me in a hug. I squeezed him back, inhaling the familiar clean smell of his uniform.

"You picked a hell of a night to go out on the town, little Mare," he said when I stepped out of his embrace. "The White Riders—I worried it was you."

"I'm fine," I said, trying to reassure myself as much as him.

"You're lucky I was at the gate and that I just got promoted." He glanced back in the direction of the wall.

I nodded. "What in the Sixth Hell happened? Who was it?"

"I don't know. Only personal guards were invited to the great hall for the announcement. The rest of us were immediately put on duty and told that no one comes in or out until morning."

I cursed under my breath as tears stung my eyes. "I can't believe this is happening. I need to find out what's going on."

Nils put a comforting hand on my back. "Maybe you should turn yourself in to the liegemen at one of the doors. At least you're already within the walls. How bad can it be?"

"I can't. If anyone learns I was out tonight . . ." I didn't have to finish the sentence. We both knew that my remaining freedom would be gone in a heartbeat.

"What are you going to do? I wish I could escort you in, but I've got to get back to my post before the others get suspicious."

"I'll figure something out," I said, and stepped forward for a farewell hug. His arms closed around me more gently this time. Behind him, a scattering of vigil lights glowed in the windows of the castle. One burned far away from the rest, like a single bright star alone in the night sky. Princess Dennaleia's rooms. And just like that, I knew how to get in.

SEVEN

🪶 *Dennaleia*

STILL SHAKY FROM THE EVENTS OF THE AFTERNOON, I could barely keep myself composed enough to write a letter to my mother. My pen skittered across the page, leaving legibility somewhat to be desired. I wrote reassurances of my safety while longing to tell her the truth: that Casmiel's death terrified me. If I had still been in the room with him, maybe I'd be dead too. How had it even happened? Where were the guards? And most importantly—why had he been killed?

I would have given anything to talk to Alisendi, but she was still somewhere between Havemont and Mynaria on her way for my wedding bazaar. I wished both she and my mother were here so that we could pray in the Sanctuary together as we used to back home. Maybe that would bring me some comfort. But my parents had agreed it would be better for my acclimatization to come to Mynaria on my own, and Alisendi was coming for the bazaar only because it made sense to visit before she took on responsibilities that would make it harder to travel. My father almost never left Havemont, thanks to his duties. And after my wedding, winter would come more swiftly in the north, meaning that my mother was unlikely to visit any sooner than next summer.

As I brought out the plum-colored wax to seal my letter, the vigil candles in my window flickered—the only warning before a person in filthy clothes clambered over the sill and thumped to the floor.

I screamed, and magic surged out of me before I could stop it. The vigil candles flared, sending a burst of sparks into the room.

"It's only me!" the intruder said, staggering up and nearly crashing into my harp.

I scurried backward, grabbing a poker from beside the fireplace and brandishing it in what I hoped was a threatening manner. As I opened my mouth to scream again, I recognized the smudged face.

"Amaranthine?" I said.

Her clothes were barely more than peasant rags and hung on her in a way that disguised her gender better than I would have imagined possible.

A firm knock sounded at the door.

"Your Highness?" the muffled voice of a liegeman called through the heavy wood.

Amaranthine ducked into my bedroom and dove under the bed as the guard cracked the door. I whipped the fire poker behind my back, hoping my skirts would conceal it.

"Is there a problem?" the liegeman asked.

"No. I'm sorry. I'm so jumpy since this afternoon, and I thought I heard a noise outside."

"All right," he said. "Let us know if you hear anything else." He scanned the area as I stood stiffly and tried to look anywhere but the bedroom. When he finally closed the door I exhaled, grateful he hadn't bothered to investigate further.

"What are you doing in here?" I said, dropping the poker and crouching to peer under my bed.

Amaranthine slid out and stood up. "Please . . . can you tell me who died?"

My stomach dropped. I thought she had been mourning with Thandilimon and the king this evening. How could she not have heard what happened?

"It was Lord Casmiel," I said softly.

Her gray eyes snapped to meet mine. "No!"

"He was shot in his study this afternoon." My voice faltered. "I had just left."

Her eyes welled, and she swiped at them with her fists. It hurt me to see her suffer. In a few steps I closed the distance between us and put my arms around her as though she were my own sister. She remained tense, and I stepped back when it became clear she wasn't going to return my embrace. All emotion had vanished from her expression.

"What happened?" she asked, her voice hollow.

I explained what I'd seen. My hands shook as I relived the moment all over again.

"A white, glimmering arrow? That's strange," she said, her eyebrows furrowing.

I nodded. "It's unusual to paint arrows. If the arrow were crafted for an individual marksman, or a tournament, it could make sense for it to be painted. But an assassin would never be foolish enough to leave any identifying markers behind with a target. On the other hand, it also doesn't make sense for the arrow to have been army made. If you're outfitting an army, it's too time-consuming and expensive to paint arrows. Besides, if you were going to go to the trouble to paint them, you'd probably use a dark color for stealth. Unless maybe you were fighting in snow." I'd been turning the problem over in my mind all evening but still couldn't draw any conclusions.

"How do you know all that?" she asked, taken aback.

"I read a lot," I said self-consciously.

"What about the glimmering?"

"I don't know," I said, my gaze jumping back to the windowsill, where the vigil candles still burned, half melted and sagging at strange angles from the burst of heat my power had caused.

"I should go," she said. "Can I use your washroom?"

"Why are you dressed like that anyway?" I asked.

"It's none of your business," she replied.

"I think it is now, seeing as you decided to sneak in my window." It felt good to snap back at her, to be in my own space instead of hers, where I could feel free to speak my mind.

"Fine. I don't always stay on castle grounds. This is a way to make sure I don't get noticed," she said.

Sneaking outside the walls must have been what Casmiel meant by "unconventional" sources of information.

I sighed. "You're going to need something else to wear." I set the fire poker back in its holder and dug through my closet. With her height and figure, it was going to be a challenge to find something that wasn't so small as to be vulgar. I pulled out a simple dress in sage green that I hadn't worn in Mynaria yet. It would do.

"Thanks," she said, the fight gone from her voice. Her fingers trembled as she touched a reddish-brown smudge on her neck before disappearing into the washroom.

Was that blood? What had she been doing out in town?

Amaranthine eventually emerged, her face clean and her expression subdued.

"Can you help me with the laces?" she asked, turning around.

"Of course," I said.

Auna always made it seem so easy, but my fingers fumbled as I pulled the dress snug. The material drew in around Amaranthine's waist, accentuating the graceful curve of her hips. All at once the room felt hotter, and my magic prickled beneath my skin to make me even clumsier. The smell of the outdoors still clung to her, mingling with the rose and lavender of the soap she had used to wash up. Even though she had touched me during my lesson, it felt different to have my hands on her. By the time I had finished tying the laces, my cheeks burned.

"Thank you," she said, turning to face me. The smudge on her neck was gone, but now I could see the source. A thin cut rested beneath her jawline. I opened my mouth to ask how she'd obtained the injury, then thought better of it. It would be kinder to give her a place to put some of her grief.

"I'm sorry for your loss," I said. "Casmiel spoke kindly of you. He said you had a good heart."

She sighed. "If I had a good heart, I'd be doing my 'duty for the kingdom,' as my father always says. Serving the crown like Thandi."

"Were things different before Thandilimon was born? Weren't you the heir?" I asked.

"I don't remember. I was only a little more than a year old when he was born. My father believes that kingdoms should pass from father to son, so it's always been all about Thandi."

"I see," I said, though I didn't understand the purpose of placing one gender above another. As eldest, my sister had always been destined to be queen of Havemont, even if I had been a boy or she took a consort.

"I wouldn't have wanted to be heir anyway," she added.

"Why not?" I asked. The power of the crown gave us the capacity to help people and to change our kingdoms for the better.

"Ha!" Her laugh was sharp and brief. "A lifetime of pretending I know what's best for an entire kingdom full of individuals? Every day of my life scheduled to the hilt? Deciding who lives and who dies for their crimes? Marrying someone I don't give two buckets of manure about because it's what's right for my kingdom?"

"Of course. Who would want that?" I said sarcastically. She described the future for which I had spent my entire life preparing.

She shrugged. "Not me."

"I do hope Thandilimon will come to love me," I said. Besides being useless, being trapped in a loveless marriage with someone who didn't respect me was my greatest fear. While an epic romance was unlikely in my situation, I still wished for it. Love would make the years easy. Loneliness would make them hard.

"Good luck," she said. "Partnerships can be built, but love can't be coaxed. Love should feel like the first time you gallop a horse flat out. It should make your blood sing. It should terrify you. And some part of you should recognize it the first time you meet the other person's eyes."

There was a challenge in her every word, and knowledge of things I had never experienced. I stared, dumbstruck, unable to argue and not certain I wanted to. Her version of love wasn't the kind circumstances had given me.

"I should get to my quarters now." Amaranthine bundled up her peasant clothes and crossed the room toward the door.

"Of course," I said. Talking to her left me as exhausted as if I'd just finished one of my history tutor's infamous three-sunlength exams. So much for making friends.

She opened the door and disappeared down the hallway, shaking off a liegeman who offered to walk with her. She was lucky my guard had changed shifts at some point after her arrival and didn't seem concerned about her presence in my rooms—a fact that unsettled me further. Liegemen should have been at peak vigilance after what happened to Casmiel. Between that and how the conversation with Amaranthine had rattled me, my nerves felt like they were on fire. I needed a prayer more than ever.

Although my mother and sister couldn't be with me, I could still pray alone. Perhaps it would settle my magic and allow me to sleep. It also wouldn't hurt that the more pious I appeared, the less likely it was that anyone would suspect me of magic.

"Excuse me," I said to one of the liegemen. "Could you take me to the Sanctuary, please?" I didn't think anyone would begrudge me a few moments there to honor Casmiel's memory.

"Of course, my lady," he said.

We walked deeper into the royal wing to a heavy wooden door, the lintel adorned with six orbs of polished glass in a circle—the symbol of the Six Gods. The hinges made no sound as I entered. Before me lay a circular area with soft lighting and six well-tended altars arranged in evenly spaced nooks. A deep calm came over me as I paced through the empty room.

I began with earth, for my soul felt heavy. The stone felt almost alive beneath my thumb, and the magical tingling in my palms eased. Rock was slow to change, but it would in time. Even the most difficult things become easier to bear. Next came water, which I had never much liked, perhaps because its primary incarnations on the mountain had been snow, ice, and frigid rain. I dipped my finger into the shallow basin of water and let a single drop fall into the offering bowl. At the altar of air, I blew on the miniature chimes, their discordant jingle sending a shiver down my spine.

At the shadow god's altar I swept my hand through the darkness beneath a richly ornamented box to acknowledge the power of the unknown and the afterlife. For the spirit god I closed my eyes and took the time to remember Casmiel: his courtesy, his reassurances, and the confident way he'd swept me across the dance floor. If I could help the crown get to the bottom of what had happened to him, it would be at least a small repayment of his kindness and mentorship during the brief time I'd known him. I would make the alliance a success in honor of his memory.

I saved fire for last because it felt like home. The wooden offering chip was smooth and small between my fingers.

I promise to do all I can.

I sketched the god's symbol and tossed the chip, but before it hit the flames, magic burst from my fingertips to swallow it. The power came easily, twisting nearly out of my control. The chip exploded in a shower of sparks, and the buzzing of my magic finally relented. I was suddenly exhausted even as my heart raced with fear—and wonder at strength I never knew I had. Something was very different about my magic in Mynaria. I would have to get to the bottom of that, too.

EIGHT

✦ *Mare*

MY FATHER AND THANDI DEMANDED I COME TO THE
Directorate meeting the morning after Cas's funeral, no doubt to
punish me for my mysterious absence the day he died.

Father shuffled the papers in front of him several times before
speaking, trying to keep his composure. "We must discuss the
circumstances of Lord Casmiel's death," he said.

Director Hilara smiled almost imperceptibly. She was lucky I
didn't pick up my chair and hurl it at her. It was one thing to dislike
Cas as she always had, and entirely another to look that smug when
his body had been buried for less than a day.

"He who would do such a thing is walking outside the path of
the Six," Director Eadric said. "He must repent and find the light.
Tread back to the walkways of the stars, the wind, the fire . . ." His
gaze wandered up the wall to the ceiling.

I barely managed not to snort in irritation. The man's flighty personality was enough to make me want to "walk outside the path of the Six" and punch him in the face.

Father ignored Eadric. "Revenge is the priority. And dismantling any threat to our kingdom."

I sighed. My father always rode with his sword out in front of him. One day he was going to fall on it.

"I agree. We must avenge him as soon as possible and show that Mynarians are not to be trifled with," Thandi said. "The arrow that killed Cas was white. Could that have some significance? It makes little sense to paint an arrow unless it was meant to be used in the snow—or to send a message."

I knew exactly where he'd gotten that idea, and it was no surprise he failed to credit her. Dennaleia was a lot smarter than she looked, I'd give her that.

"There's no snow here," Eadric said, his forehead creasing in puzzlement. "If we send some clerics to meditate on this at the High Adytum, the Six may guide us. . . ."

"The only place around here where there's snow is Havemont. Or Zumorda," Captain Ryka said, tapping her voting piece on the table as she spoke. The horseshoe nail made a dull clanking on the stone. She wore mourning whites instead of her usual riding leathers, her red-rimmed eyes betraying the freshness of her loss in spite of her calm demeanor.

"Havemont wouldn't dare jeopardize the alliance, especially with their princess here," the king said.

"Zumorda's crest is a white dragon," Ryka said. "White arrow, white crest. The connection is obvious."

"A potential Zumordan threat should not be overlooked, but

what of the local rebel group? Their symbol is also white," Lord Kriantz noted, though as an ambassador, he could not participate in votes. The man seemed to have a better head on his shoulders than the rest of them, at least.

"If we'd made the alliance with Zumorda back when the opportunity existed, perhaps this could have all been avoided," Hilara remarked.

If nothing else, the woman was persistent. Given her apparent glee over Cas's death, it was no surprise she'd rather talk about alliance opportunities than search for his killer. I stared her down, wishing my glare would burn holes through her face. Her seemingly ageless skin glittered with a shimmery powder that brought out the gold flecks in her eyes and would no doubt be the latest fashion by midwinter.

"Zumorda won't let so much as a merchant's caravan into their kingdom, much less an ambassador," said Lord Tommin, the director of trade. "We can't build alliances with people who won't allow us to export goods and who do not respect that the trade guild knows no borders. Horse traders can enter for the fair in Kartasha, but there's a significant amount of paperwork—"

"After the attack, the Elite Guard had a look around Lord Casmiel's study," Captain Ryka said, cutting him off. "We haven't even been able to figure out where the arrow was shot from. Also, some of the first to arrive at the scene noted that the arrow seemed to glimmer."

"Perhaps we should examine the arrow. Did you bring it, Captain?" Thandi asked. It was somewhat reassuring to know he had at least half a brain in that thick skull of his.

"Yes. I've kept it with me since it was recovered." Ryka pushed a narrow box to the center of the table. Her usually steady hand trembled, giving away the truth of what she felt beneath the stoic mask she wore.

Pity welled up in me, tightening my throat. It was the last thing that had touched Cas, and the only evidence we had. No wonder she carried it with her everywhere.

Everyone leaned forward, and I stood, craning my neck to see as she opened the box.

Nothing remained inside but ash.

Ryka stared at it in shock.

The table flew into an uproar, disbelief and fear traveling like wildfire through the group.

"This is heresy!"

"I'll hunt them down myself!"

"Zumorda must be behind this!"

The king raised his hand for silence.

"The first priority should be increasing castle security," Lord Tommin insisted. He had a thin, reedy voice and a bulging gut that pressed up against the stone table. "We can't have our families put in danger."

The man didn't even have any children, but it was no surprise that a gluttonous merchant would rather lie around eating exotic confections than pick up a sword.

"Captain?" the king asked. "How many more liegemen can we put on duty?"

Ryka rubbed her temples. "I have about fifty ready to take the oath. Beyond that, we'd have to pull in trainees."

"We'll need a far larger army to face Zumorda," Tommin said.

"I know that," Ryka snapped.

"We haven't yet determined that Zumorda is to blame," Hilara said.

"But why would anyone kill Casmiel? He was pure of heart. A servant of the kingdom," Eadric said dreamily.

It was unfortunate that such a reasonable question had to come from such an unreasonable source, because no one bothered to answer it.

"We need to mount a counterattack against Zumorda right away," Tommin said.

"Border defense should be our primary concern," Hilara said. "We can't retaliate without assessing our current allies and evaluating our strength."

The conversation devolved into a heated argument.

As much as I hated to be on Hilara's side, a nagging voice in the back of my mind kept asking if Zumorda had truly been behind Cas's death, or if perhaps the Recusants could be to blame. Maybe the two had worked together.

If only I'd gotten more out of that damned informant back at the Deaf Dog.

If only Nils and I had made Alen answer more questions.

"What about an investigation? Indisputable evidence that Zumorda is behind this?" I finally spoke up, but my voice was lost in the chaos of the room.

I crossed my arms and sat back in my chair, turning my eyes heavenward and begging the Six for the fortitude to survive the rest of the meeting. Grief lodged itself deep in my belly. If the idiot directors were too busy worrying about their own necks to investigate properly, then I owed it to Cas to find out what had happened. It was the least I could do for the one family member who had loved me for who I was instead of who I was supposed to be.

After the Directorate meeting, I headed to the stables for Dennaleia's daily lesson. I set her to work immediately, my mind elsewhere. I should have been out in the cresthaven searching for answers about Cas, the arrow, and Zumorda. But my father had kept me close since Cas's death, and I didn't want to give him reason to further tighten the restrictions. I took it fairly easy on Dennaleia since I was preoccupied, but she still winced when she dismounted at the end.

"The soreness will get better in time," I said. We entered the barn with Louie in tow.

"I hope so," she said, and cross tied the horse to untack him.

I had to give her some credit. In spite of her obvious discomfort, she wasn't one to complain, and she never had to be told how to do anything more than once. She wiped down and put away Louie's tack without a single piece out of place.

"Can you show me your horse?" Dennaleia asked as she pulled the cover over her saddle.

"I suppose," I said, surprised by the request. "His stall is at the other end of the barn. Walking might help with the aches."

Dennaleia stopped several lengths back when we got close to my horse's stall. I clucked softly, and Flicker stuck his head over the half door.

"This is Flicker." I wrapped my arm around his neck as he put his head over my shoulder.

"Isn't that dangerous?" Dennaleia asked.

"It could be," I said. "But I trust him. I'd never do it with another one. They all have their quirks. Flicker gives hugs." I scratched an itchy spot under his mane until he tilted his head in bliss.

"I think I'll decline hugs from anything that can crush me."

"He'd only crush you if I told him to," I said, smirking a little at the alarmed expression on her face.

"That's not comforting!"

"Don't worry. He hasn't even learned those maneuvers yet. He's still in the early part of his warhorse training. He won't be finished for another year or two." I patted him fondly.

"If he's in training like the others, why does Thandi refer to him as a cull?" she asked.

"It's that tall white stocking that goes up over the knee on his front leg. Every autumn after we bring in the broodmares during the Gathering, we wean the new foal crop and then sort the young stock and sell the ones that aren't worthy of breeding. Sometimes we'll ship out older horses too, if they didn't work out in the training program."

"But what's wrong with a white stocking?" She stepped forward and cautiously held out her hand for Flicker to sniff.

"The last thing you want going into battle is a big splash of white that attracts the eyes of the enemy, and his marking is too large to cover with a wrap or armor. That's why he's a gelding. But we aren't at war . . . so while the purity of bloodlines is important, he's not likely to see a real battlefield where his color will matter." I paused. "You shouldn't ask me about Flicker. My friend Nils says I could bore a person half to death going on about him."

"It's nice to talk with someone. So if this is the only way to get you to talk, I'll ask you about Flicker more often." She seemed oddly pleased.

"If that's what you want," I said. I didn't believe for a moment that she wanted to hear me yammer on about my horse.

"What else do you enjoy besides riding?" she asked.

"I used to sing sometimes," I said, not sure why she was pretending to be interested.

"You do have a musical voice," she observed.

Her compliment threw me off guard, and I searched for some sign in her expression that she was mocking me. When I didn't find it, heat crept into my cheeks and I turned to Flicker to hide it.

"But you don't sing now . . . ?" she asked.

"My mother was a talented musician. When I was little, she used to have me sing with her. But then she died, and everyone stopped expecting anything from me." I couldn't keep the bitterness out of my voice.

"That must have been hard," Dennaleia said. Her sympathy made me uncomfortable.

"I have to go." I headed off any further conversation. I had stalls to clean, and the day had been hard enough without dredging up memories of things I preferred to forget.

When I got back to my rooms later that evening, Nils was waiting outside my door. My heart lifted a little at the sight of him.

"I got your message a few days ago," he said. "I'm sorry I couldn't come sooner."

"I figured. Come on in." I beckoned him into my receiving room, relishing the fact that my father would fall over dead if he knew. Having men in and out of my chambers at odd times of the night was an infraction that even Cas couldn't have overlooked, and Nils and I had been making a habit of it for ages. The liegemen at the door exchanged nods with Nils, an acknowledgment of all the blackmail material they had on one another. Our secret was safe with them.

Once we were inside, Nils stepped forward and enfolded me in a tight hug. I let myself get lost in it for a minute, his familiar embrace easing the endless stab of grief.

"I'm so glad to see you," I said. Long shadows danced throughout my receiving room, cast by the vigil candles my maid had lit in the window for Cas.

"How was the Directorate?" he asked softly.

"A disaster. They couldn't even settle on a plan for the investigation." Idiots. I summarized the meeting for him, adding some profanity-laced commentary.

Nils sighed. "Why am I not surprised?"

"I still can't believe he's gone," I said. As angry as I was with the Directorate, the weight of Cas's loss was stronger.

"I'm so sorry, Mare. He was a good man," Nils said. "Any theories on who did it?"

"No. And what bothers me even more is that I can't figure out *why*." I studied his warm brown eyes as if they might hold an answer.

"Not even one? You're usually the queen of conspiracy theories."

"The only person out there who even smells like trouble is the queen of Zumorda, and she's been reigning quietly for years without showing any sign of interest in us. The ambassador from Sonnenborne seems eager to collaborate, and he has enough tribes under his banner that he might as well be king of that godsforsaken desert. With Sonnenborne and Havemont as allies, we have Zumorda surrounded on its northern, western, and southern borders. The queen would have little to gain and possibly everything to lose by starting a war with us. It doesn't add up."

"True, but she's almost too quiet. How do you keep the peace in a kingdom that large and strange? We've never heard rumors that they have any kind of military. And why do Zumordans insist on accessing Mynaria by way of Havemont instead of soliciting a treaty directly with us? It makes no sense for them to travel so far north. It's inefficient."

"I wish I knew." I lit the lamp on the table in my sitting room to push back the darkness.

"Could someone within the kingdom be responsible for Cas's death? On the Directorate, even?" Nils asked, settling on one of the leather couches. I sat down beside him with my legs tucked beneath me.

"Would any of them be foolish enough to take the risk of being punished for high treason?" I asked. "Hilara has always hated him, but she's too cautious to resort to murder to get her way. The only others who could have done it are the Recusants, but they don't seem very organized. And still—why? Cas wasn't a fundamentalist."

"Mare," he said softly. "Maybe it's time for you to talk to your brother and father. You've seen a lot on the other side of the wall—even what we learned from that Recusant the other day. That information could lead them in the right direction and help with the investigation."

"Hells no," I said. "And what investigation? Those idiots could barely come up with a plan to fortify the castle, much less actually seek out the killer. Besides, they have their own spies." I crossed my arms.

Nils sighed. "Do they listen to them?"

"Not as often as they should."

"Exactly. Maybe they need to hear a broader perspective from someone they'll take seriously."

"Right. As if they would take me seriously, especially when they find out I've been outside the wall nearly every day for the past three years," I scoffed. "The only person who might have listened was Cas, and he's dead." A fresh wave of grief rose with my words. I took a deep breath to push the feelings away. The night air smelled of clean linen and a hint of alfalfa drifting in through the open window.

"They might listen."

"No. They'll yell at me, I'll get assigned extra guards, and I'll be upbraided for endangering myself, especially in light of what happened to Cas. I may not be an important player politically, but I'm sure picking off members of Mynaria's royal family would still send a strong message. My father and the Directorate will be all too conscious of that danger. If I'm going to do any information gathering, which of course I will, they'll be the last to know about it."

"You're anything but unimportant, Mare." He brushed a loose strand of hair out of my face. I couldn't help but soften at his touch.

"I see how you seduce all the ladies, Nils. Pretty slick." Though I teased him, sometimes I missed the time before—the time when we had been more than friends.

"My heart beats only for you," he quipped, throwing his arm around me. "Even though half the liegemen think I might be interested in boys after that stunt we pulled to get you back in from the city the other night . . ."

"Right," I said, rolling my eyes and shoving him away. "I'm certain half the kingdom can vouch for your interest in women."

"I have no idea what you're talking about!" He looked at me wide-eyed. "I can't help it that women keep throwing themselves at me. I don't even want most of them."

"I think you want enough," I retorted. "Someone at dinner was talking about you and Lady Elinara getting caught behind the practice fields."

"Well, the lady does enjoy a bit of . . . jousting." He waggled his eyebrows.

"Oh, for the sake of the Six." I put my hand over my face in mock disgust, grinning behind my palm.

"In all seriousness, Mare, be careful if you decide to cross the wall again. The city isn't as safe as it used to be. I won't always be there if you get yourself in a mess, and Gammon isn't the only one who might stick a sword in your neck."

"I know." I ran my hand along the arm of the couch. The danger was irrelevant. Cas deserved justice.

"And I know you're going to do it no matter what I tell you." He smiled. "That's what I love about you."

"I need to figure out what happened to Cas. I don't trust the Directorate to do their job."

"You're going to need help," Nils said.

"That's why I have you."

"You know I'll do anything I can," he said. "But they have us on double shifts right now. Sneaking out is going to be more difficult.

And there are only so many channels of information I have access to." He couldn't risk getting in trouble—it could cost him his job.

"I need someone both political and tolerable, which is about as likely as finding a unicorn in Flicker's stall tomorrow," I said.

"It wouldn't hurt to do some research in the library too," Nils said. "Surely some information exists about what that white arrow signifies, or what kind of magic would make it burn up?"

I wrinkled my nose. "I'd rather clean stalls. With my hands."

He laughed. "That's my little Mare. Shall I go, or would you like company for a while?" He pulled me close, brushing his lips against my forehead.

I hesitated. Asking him to stay was unfair. He had other places to be, and other women willing to give him more than friendship. But I didn't have anyone else.

"I'd like it if you stayed," I said, hating myself for the tremor that crept into my voice.

And he did—his solid form the only barrier against my sorrow.

NINE

🔥 *Dennaleia*

MY WEDDING BAZAAR WENT ON AS SCHEDULED about half a moon after Casmiel's funeral, the morning after Alisendi arrived. Swaths of gauzy fabric hung from the high ceiling of the queen's bower and solarium, billowing gently in the morning breeze. The room blended seamlessly from inside to out, stone interior walls giving way to trellises covered with climbing vines and brilliant blooms. Merchants were stationed throughout the area, tables piled high with the finest wedding wares: dyed silks, rich tapestries, and exotic confections. Courtiers in the bright colors of summer sipped cold drinks as they wandered the room and garden.

I should have felt emboldened by Alisendi's presence, but I wasn't in the mood to put on my manners for a party and court my future ladies-in-waiting, even with my sister by my side. I wanted to do something useful.

"Have you chosen your wedding attendants yet, Your Highness?" a velvety voice asked.

Hilara stood beside me, tall and resplendent in a violet gown. Tight curls framed her face, the rest of her black hair up in an elaborate arrangement woven with lavender ribbons. Perhaps I should have been flattered that she chose to attend my party, but I had to repress my irritation. She had power. She could have been with the Directorate, helping find Casmiel's killer or dealing with the Recusants. Instead, she was parading around setting fashions.

I pasted on my best diplomatic smile. "Not yet, my lady," I said. "It will be a difficult decision with so many wonderful choices." Never mind that I barely knew anyone but Amaranthine, who was glowering in the shade of a nearby tree. She had managed to get away with wearing formal riding attire instead of a dress, looking both striking and wildly out of place among the other noblewomen.

"Have you any suggestions?" I asked.

"Certainly, Your Highness," she said. "Nairinn of Almendorn's place at court is secure and strong. She won't marry until she finds a person of the proper status, so you could count on having her by your side for at least a few years. Annietta of Ciralis has connections in the far north, which could be advantageous should we ever pursue further exploration there. Ellaeni of Trindor would be a unique choice, definitely more valuable than one of the provincial girls since she's the only current representative of the Mynarian fleet. But she hasn't been here long and isn't likely to stay." Hilara gestured to each girl in turn—a well-dressed brunette entertaining several other girls by a fountain, a pretty redhead looking at gemstones with my sister, and a girl with the straightest, blackest hair I'd ever seen standing by herself, looking uncertain.

Beyond Ellaeni, Amaranthine caught my eye again. She was

making a surreptitious attempt to escape the garden, but within a few steps she was blocked by a blond girl intent on showing off her jewelry to anyone who would give her half a second's worth of attention.

"And there are some with whom you shouldn't bother," Hilara said, following my gaze.

"Thank you for your thoughts, my lady." Her comment irked me even though I didn't owe any loyalty to Amaranthine, especially when soreness from my riding lessons plagued my every move. Besides, I was still upset about our conversation in front of Flicker's stall. I thought I had finally gotten her to open up, and then she'd shut me out twice as forcefully and made a point of vanishing immediately after every lesson since.

"Choose your allies wisely, Your Highness," Hilara said. "Maybe someday you'll be able to make up for losing the best one you had." She turned and moved off toward the merchants, her words leaving me chilled in spite of the hot morning sun.

"She's as friendly as a hungry mountain bear, isn't she?" my sister said, walking up as Hilara vanished into a cluster of eager admirers.

"They all are, unless they want something," I muttered.

Alisendi gave me a look straight out of my mother's repertoire of Meaningful Glances for Misbehaving Young Ladies. "You'll want things from them too one day. It's part of the game."

I shrugged.

"Come on," Alisendi said. "This is supposed to be fun! We get to pick out all the things for your wedding. I can hardly believe my little sister is going to be a married woman." Her green eyes sparkled with all the excitement mine should have held.

"Neither can I," I said. The wedding had always seemed like a far-off thing, and the alliance had always seemed so certain. Now, my future rushed toward me faster than ever, and Cas's death and the trouble in its wake had my faith in the alliance shaken.

"You're lucky. Prince Thandilimon is so handsome. And these Mynarian guards . . ." She stole an unsubtle glance at the rear end of a liegeman as he paced through the party.

"I can't believe you said that." Sometimes it seemed impossible that my sister and I were related. If it hadn't been for the fact that looking into her face was like looking into a warped mirror that showed a taller, prettier version of me, both of us with our mother's hair and our father's eyes, I would have had some serious questions about our respective parentage.

"Are you still holding out for Olin?" she teased. Ali had always given me a hard time about not fancying any of the boys back home. Her crushes changed more quickly than the wind in a blizzard, but I didn't see the point in mooning over some other boy when I had always been promised to Thandilimon. Eventually, I got so tired of her harassment that I chose one at random: Olin, the baker's son. But after a while it became clear that my supposed crush was doomed when Olin started courting Ryan, one of the handsome squires Ali fancied.

Fortunately, I was spared any further mocking as other young noblewomen surrounded us to vie for my attention. But the girls always lingered within earshot of Hilara, making it clear that they courted her as eagerly as me. With Hilara's political power she might as well have been queen, and winning my favor was likely only a ploy the girls used to impress her. My irritation increased and my hands tingled in warning as my magic stirred.

"It's a warm morning, is it not, Your Highness?" someone said. Behind a table piled high with intricate tapestries stood a short, round man with an elaborately sculpted beard that came to a sharp point beneath his chin. He smiled to reveal teeth tipped with silver. "Your ice has melted," he said, gesturing to my glass. His words carried the hint of a vaguely familiar accent.

"So it has," I said. It wouldn't have been remarkable, except that a servant had just brought me a fresh drink. The zings running through my fingers let me know exactly how it had melted so rapidly.

"I thought you had that under control," Alisendi whispered. All the humor on her face had been replaced with worry.

"I do," I said. "It's fine." My nerves felt like they were on fire. I needed to calm down. Alisendi and I hung back at the merchant's table, letting the other girls wander on to the next display.

Nearby, Amaranthine had escaped the blond girl and was talking to one of the guards stationed by an archway. She gesticulated wildly, telling some story that had the poor liegeman going red in the face. How she could be so friendly with a random liegeman and so cold with me outside of our lessons was utterly baffling—and infuriating. When they both had their laughter under control, she squeezed his arm in farewell and slipped past him out of the party.

She had never even said hello.

A surge of magic flew from my fingertips and a flame ignited on the corner of one of the textile merchant's wooden display racks.

Alisendi took in a sharp breath, and I grabbed her hand to silence whatever was about to come out of her mouth. But before either of us could speak, the bearded man on the other side of the table flicked his finger almost imperceptibly, and a burst of air extinguished the flame, carrying the smoke away on the breeze.

I stared at him in astonishment.

"Master Karov of Sigil Imports," he introduced himself. "We import the finest weavings from all of the Northern Kingdoms." He studied me with sharp eyes and a knowing smile, adjusting a tapestry to cover the damaged corner of the display rack.

I swallowed hard. "Princess Dennaleia of Havemont, at the service of the crown and the Six." Falling into manners and formality did little to calm my jangling nerves, but I did not know what else to do. My sister also introduced herself, her face still white with shock.

"I am honored to make the acquaintance of two such lovely ladies. May I interest either of you in a tapestry?" Karov said.

My gaze skittered over his wares as I clamped down on my panic. If he told anyone I had set that fire, neither Amaranthine nor Hilara would be my biggest problem. Then again, he had also used magic to put it out, so logically he couldn't implicate me without also incriminating himself. Still, the thought did nothing to settle my nerves.

To calm myself, I dredged up what I knew about tapestries and tried to examine his offerings with a more critical eye. Tapestry weaving was largely a far-north art, and my mother had a vast collection insulating the castle against the brutal winter winds in Spire City. Unsurprisingly, many of Karov's weavings were equestrian themed, portraying hunting and battle scenes. Though he showcased a variety of styles that were clearly from different parts of the Northern Kingdoms, every tapestry was tightly woven and of the highest quality.

"Were these made on a low-warp loom?" I asked, running my fingers across the edge of a small but complex tapestry depicting the mountains of my homeland. A lone mountain bluebird winged across the top of the weaving, bright against the wintry landscape.

"You have a discerning eye, my lady," Karov said. "Our imported weavings from the north are all made on low-warp looms in order to achieve the utmost levels of detail."

Looking more closely at the image, I frowned. Something wasn't right about the mountain range—at least as viewed from Havemont. From Spire City, sharp peaks surrounded Mount Verity, not the rolling hills pictured in the foreground of the tapestry. But the lopsided profile of the mountain was unmistakable, if a little misshapen.

"Where is this from?" Alisendi asked, pointing to the tapestry.

"The northeast," he said with a smile.

My sister and I exchanged a glance. There was only one side of the mountains that gave way to rolling hills, and it wasn't in Havemont.

It was in Zumorda.

And now that I knew that, his accent was unmistakable. Seeing the understanding dawning on my face, he simply tapped on the tapestry hiding the burned spot on the rack and smiled.

Another threat.

"How much do you want for it?" I asked. Maybe if I spent enough at his table, I could guarantee his silence.

"For you, Your Highness? Consider it a gift." He pulled the little tapestry off the rack and rolled it up, tying it with a thick silk ribbon. "Come see us again. We have many other wares that might interest you."

I tucked the tapestry under my arm, grabbed Alisendi, and hurried away. When we had almost caught up to the other noblewomen, I shot a nervous glance back at Karov just in time to see Hilara approach his table. Coin exchanged hands as she purchased something, but with a move so deft I barely caught it, Karov rolled a small sachet into the tapestry before passing it across the table to her. A fresh wave of dismay rolled over me. If they were colluding in some way, it could only lead to terrible things, but I didn't know what to do with the information. The possibility of my own magic being discovered was too risky.

"The Six help me," I said.

Alisendi began to sketch out the symbol of the fire god in front of her, but I caught her hand.

"The wind god," I whispered. "The wind god is seen as more powerful here."

She gave me a worried look but complied, and we reentered the group of noblewomen.

As the sun beat into my skull and I prepared to make my way toward the next cluster of party guests, a stab of envy for Amaranthine hit me. She didn't have to cope with underhanded threats from courtiers and Zumordan merchants. By now, she could be anywhere: back in her rooms, riding her horse over the hills, or even out in the city. She had the freedom to do anything she wanted, at least until the king and Thandilimon thought better of it. Although Thandilimon was nice enough, and Amaranthine was certainly difficult, it bothered me that he acted as though he knew what was right for her. Someone as proud as Amaranthine would never bow to anyone, whether it was her brother, her father, or her husband. It wasn't in her.

And with everything that had gone wrong since my arrival, I was starting to wonder if it was in me, either.

TEN   ✦ *Mare*

MY SCHEDULE FINALLY LINED UP WITH NILS'S A FEW
weeks after Cas's funeral, so we escaped the castle and headed for
the Pelham. There wasn't much time between Dennaleia's afternoon
lesson and a stupid music performance later in the evening, but it was
better than nothing.

The city had changed since my last time out. Merchants kept
their windows shuttered, and strangers on the street avoided eye
contact. Every other building seemed to be tagged with the white
circle of the Recusants. Some had black slashes through them—the
mark of the fundamentalists who opposed them.

Upon arrival at the pub, we shoved our way into a secluded
booth away from the cluttered tables near the bar, hoping to avoid
any fights. I slapped a coin down on the table that a mostly toothless
barmaid soon replaced with two battered mugs of ale.

Nils made a face after his first sip. "This stuff tastes like horse
piss, as always."

"I don't want to know how you came up with the basis for that comparison," I said. The ale didn't taste that bad—it had an uncomplicated zing to it that was perfect for a blazing-hot summer day, and the Pelham had a deep enough cellar that it was served remarkably cold.

"So what's the plan?" Nils asked.

"Watch. Wait. Drink your damn pint," I said. Hopefully some answers would come our way if we kept our ears open, but mostly I was glad to be out. Between paranoid courtiers and extra guards everywhere, I'd had enough of the incessant itch of eyes on my back.

"And what do you plan to do with the information we glean? Have you thought any more about talking to your father or brother?"

I shook my head. "Only if I discover something compelling enough."

"This is about more than Cas, Mare. It's a chance to get leverage with them that might help you later." He nudged my foot under the table.

"What do you mean?" I asked.

"I'm asking what you plan to do with your life. Have you thought about it? I'm pretty sure the king and your brother have. Why do you think your father parades you past strings of nobles every time you actually eat dinner at the royal table?"

"To keep me out of his way." I sat back in my chair, uncomfortable with his line of inquiry. "He doesn't care what I do as long as I don't meddle in anything that actually matters."

"No. It's so he can marry you off to the first person who expresses interest."

"I have some choice in the matter." What Nils said was true, but I didn't want to admit it.

"You say that, but he could make your life difficult enough that marriage would seem like a better choice than whatever else he put in front of you. It's like training a horse—make the right thing easy and the wrong thing hard."

"Who says marriage is the right thing for me? Just because everyone else is riding their horses backward off a bridge doesn't mean I ought to." Though I'd happily train Flicker to do just that if it meant avoiding marriage to some idiot of my father's choosing.

"It's an analogy. Plans for you must be on your father's mind, especially now that Princess Dennaleia is here and Thandilimon's role will change. It'll affect you as well."

I took a deep breath and exhaled slowly. "Okay. You're right. But I don't have a bastard's clue what to do. I don't see a way out."

"You're cleverer than the whole Directorate put together. You'll think of something." He reached across the table and gave my forearm a firm squeeze.

"All I can do for now is keep a sharper eye on their plans," I said. "Lord Kriantz invited me to a music performance tonight. I was going to try to find a way out of it, but maybe it will be an opportunity to find out what my brother and father have been doing."

"That's a start." He nodded.

"Doesn't help me figure out the future, though." I needed to get away from my family. There had to be a way to do it without shackling myself to someone I had no use or feelings for.

"The princess has to be trained, and that will buy you some time. Or you could always make things simple and marry down."

He winked at me suggestively.

"Nils!"

"Kidding, kidding," he said. "Although pretending to marry me might work if it weren't for my job at the palace. Pulling off a false marriage under that much scrutiny would be tough."

"If the marriage were false, I'd rather marry a woman," I said. "At least then no one would be able to question the legitimacy of it based on lack of children." No matter how vague my life plan was, spending half a year out of the saddle to have a baby definitely wasn't part of it.

Nils flipped his mug to signify the need for another drink and scanned the room for our server. She was sprawled across the laps of two men who looked like they had never seen reason to bathe, giggling as one of them dropped coins down the front of her dress.

"Looks like my refill might take all night," Nils grumbled.

"There's one way to remedy that," I said, and took off for the bar before Nils could talk sense into me. The corner we'd been sitting in was too quiet anyway.

"Six help us," he said, and hurried after. The late-afternoon crowd near the bar wasn't too wild yet, but they did seem close to the bottoms of their pitchers.

". . . magic-loving scum is going to ruin our kingdom," a bearded man ranted. "Heard the arrow that killed Lord Casmiel was augmented with magic. If those slimy Recusant bastards can enchant arrows to fly farther and strike true, they must be plotting a war right here in our streets!"

His audience at the surrounding tables muttered their agreement. We'd stumbled into a group of fundamentalists. I ordered two more mugs of ale and pretended to ignore the conversation in hopes of hearing something useful, keeping my head down like the hooded woman hunched over her drink beside me.

"It had to be magic. The spears would've caught 'em otherwise," an older man at the table said.

Nils tensed at the slang word for liegemen, and I put a steadying hand on his arm.

"Those magic-lovers ain't that hard to catch," a woman said. "They all have that same slippery look about 'em. And white paint on their hands."

"Hear, hear!" someone else said, and swung his mug of ale through the air, splattering half the others at the table.

"Caught one walking down my street just yesterday," the bearded man said. "He tried to scare me off with a handful of sparks. Made sure he'll think twice about doing that again."

The whole group chuckled in an unfriendly way that made me edge closer to Nils.

The woman next to me whirled toward the bearded man and drew a serrated knife from her belt. "I've been looking for you," she growled, and plunged the knife through his hand.

The man shrieked like an animal. Not only was his hand was pinioned to the grimy bar, but the flesh around the blade began to smoke as the knife grew white-hot. I stared, frozen in horror. Sure, I'd heard of magic, but I'd never seen it used like this before.

"Magic-loving bitch!" someone shouted. The fundamentalists overturned their table, but the woman apparently had allies throughout the room who leaped up to meet them. Fists flew. I stumbled back into Nils, fear making my stomach drop.

"You killed my husband, and I hope you burn in the Sixth Hell," the woman said to the man she'd stabbed.

She turned toward me and I caught a glimpse of bloodshot eyes and short, sandy hair before Nils yanked me from the fray and out a side door into a filthy alley. I dashed for the road, dismayed that we'd chosen not to ride. Horses like ours would have likely been stolen from the hitching rail outside the Pelham before our drinks were even served, but having them would have made for a faster escape.

"Let's go this way!" I pointed to another alley halfway up the next block as the tavern fight behind us started to pour into the street. We leaped over a rag-clad man lying unconscious in front of the entrance who reeked of urine and stale beer. Nils matched my stride and then pulled me the rest of the way through the bad part of town at a pace I could barely match, my lungs burning and my mouth dry.

"We are *not* going back there," Nils said as soon as we entered one of the side gates through the castle wall.

"Not today," I said, panting as we marched up the hill toward the castle, still shaky from our near miss. "But we did learn something valuable. What if the Elite couldn't figure out where Cas's killer shot from because magic was involved? We can go to the gardens and look for evidence."

"I should be compensated for keeping you company," he grumbled.

"You should thank me for making sure you're never bored," I replied, and cut across the groomed lawn in front of the stables toward the gardens.

We trudged through endless archways adorned with climbing vines and elegant topiaries all the way to the back of the castle. Peering up at the window of Cas's study as we entered the closest atrium of the garden, I walked headlong into someone standing in the path.

Princess Dennaleia stepped back and smoothed her skirts, clearly flustered.

"Excuse me," she said, taking in my grubby peasant garb with a wary eye.

"What are you doing here?" I asked. As far as I knew, she ought to be off doing some insipid court task by now.

"Looking for answers," she said, her expression turning grim. "Can't say I expected to meet anyone else here, though."

I smirked at her subtle jab at the Directorate, impressed that she was brave enough to investigate Cas's death on her own. And in spite of my diligent efforts to avoid getting too friendly with her, it moved me that she cared about him.

"This is Nils," I said. "He keeps me out of trouble. Or gets in it with me."

Nils bowed and gave Dennaleia his most charming smile—the one that turned most women's brains to mush.

"Nice to meet you," she said, and then turned back toward Cas's window, her gaze jumping between it and a piece of paper in her hand.

I nearly laughed outright at the confusion on Nils's face. He wasn't used to women finding other things more interesting than him.

"So how in the Sixth Hell did someone make a shot into a second-story window from down here?" I asked.

"The only places to shoot from are the top of the garden wall or the roof of that shed," Nils said.

Dennaleia shook her head. "The angle isn't right. Lord Casmiel would have had to be standing right in front of the window. He wasn't."

I remembered then that Dennaleia had been the first to see him dead. "So, what would the angle have been?"

"I calculated the trajectory at somewhere between ten and fifteen degrees," she said. "But in order for that to be the case, the shot can't have been made from this garden. None of the structures are tall enough." She showed us her paper, which had a detailed diagram of the garden and window—and enough mathematics to make my head hurt.

"Well, we know the Recusants are capable of enchanting weapons," I said, shuddering at the memory of the burning knife. "So assuming the arrow had magical assistance, what else would fall on the path you calculated?"

All three of us surveyed the area and stopped at the same time on a tall tree two gardens away.

"That's too far to shoot from," Nils said. "The archer wouldn't be able to see him through the window."

"Maybe he wouldn't have needed to see if magic was involved," I said.

We strode through the gardens to the base of the tree.

"There," Dennaleia said, pointing into the branches.

A small white circle was painted on the trunk, high enough that it was barely visible.

"I'll take word to the captain," Nils said. "I need to get ready for my shift anyway."

"Don't tell her I was here," Dennaleia and I said at the same time.

Nils laughed. "Your secrets are safe with me."

"I don't want Ryka questioning me," I said. She'd want to know how we'd made this discovery, and I couldn't have her find out how narrowly we'd escaped the brawl at the Pelham.

"Some of the noblewomen invited me to a tea and embroidery session, but I told them I didn't feel well so that I could come down here instead," Dennaleia admitted sheepishly. "And Thandilimon told me not to worry about things involving the Directorate. . . ."

Maybe I'd underestimated her.

"You won't get a hard time from me about breaking the rules." I shrugged. "But there's one more thing I don't understand. If the Recusants are being beaten in town—murdered even—why would they leave traces that would implicate them in Casmiel's death?" It didn't add up. No assassin was stupid enough to leave a mark. Why would a small rebel group like the Recusants risk persecution by the crown?

"It makes me wonder if someone else is involved," Dennaleia said.

"Or another kingdom," I said grimly. Perhaps Zumorda was rising after all.

ELEVEN　　　　　　　　　　🔥 *Dennaleia*

AMARANTHINE BARGED INTO THE DRAWING ROOM half a sunlength after dessert had been served. The string quartet had already begun to play, and the musicians paused awkwardly between pieces, waiting for a cue to continue. The Six only knew where she'd been since I saw her in the garden earlier.

"Ah, Your Highness. So lovely of you to join us," Lord Kriantz said to Amaranthine. He stood and escorted her to a chaise. Her hair was put up but in slight disarray, and her dress laced so loosely Auna would have had a fit at the mere idea. Still, she looked lovely, as if she had brought a bit of the wild summer evening inside with her. I shifted my weight in my chair, all too aware of the corset bones digging into my ribs.

"At least she's reliably late," Thandilimon grumbled, rolling his eyes.

Beyond him, the king shot Amaranthine a look that could have liquefied half the armory.

I glanced at Alisendi, who merely raised her eyebrows.

As the music picked up once more, Thandilimon took my hand, cradling it in his palm. While the gesture was thoughtful and reassuring, his fingers did not fit well between mine, and my hand ached before the minuet was even half complete. By the time the piece ended, I was grateful for the applause that allowed me to let go to show my appreciation for the music.

Amaranthine clapped as well, the baron leaning over to whisper something in her ear. Lord Kriantz tapped the inside of his ring with his thumb as they spoke. She laughed. Somehow one sentence he spoke was more engaging than anything I ever said. I wanted her to like me, but nothing I did seemed to help—not even helping to find the Recusant symbol in the garden. Frustration seethed in my stomach, and a dangerous tingle raced into my fingertips.

"Are you all right?" Alisendi asked.

"Oh, yes, of course," I replied, silently cursing her ability to read my moods.

"You've been scowling ever since my sister came in," the prince observed.

"I'm sorry, Thandilimon," I said. "I suppose seeing Princess Amaranthine reminded me of how sore I've been from my riding lessons."

"No need to apologize. And please call me Thandi as the rest of my family does. We'll be family soon." He smiled.

I managed to return his expression, grateful for the familiarity his nickname offered.

"At least Mare is keeping company with Lord Kriantz." Thandi nodded respectfully in the baron's direction. "I pity him the suffering, but perhaps he'll encourage her to do something useful for the crown. He's provided some excellent counsel to the Directorate."

I pushed aside thoughts of Amaranthine and took advantage of the opportunity to ask what I really wanted to know. "Is the Directorate still investigating what happened with Casmiel?"

A flicker of sorrow passed over his face. "Yes, Captain Ryka is looking into some evidence found in the garden today. I won't go into the details, though. I wouldn't want to bother you with such dull things."

I probably knew more about it than him.

"But I think Directorate business is quite interesting, and so important to the kingdom. If I can offer assistance in any way, I would be more than happy to," I said. Maybe he would give me an opportunity to make myself useful, and to make my years of lessons worthwhile. Since Casmiel's death, no one had asked me to do much of anything.

"I am sure that it would only cause you stress. But now that Cas is gone, we could use some help with royal correspondence. I'll speak to someone about it as soon as I have the chance if you are lacking things to do." He patted my hand and smiled, looking pleased with himself.

"Perhaps," I said, disappointed. At least Amaranthine had put my calculations to use.

My sister nodded encouragingly, and I could see that she agreed with him. Any service to the kingdom was a worthy pursuit. Although he had asked for my thoughts from time to time, Thandi had shown no inclination so far to help prepare me to sit on the Directorate or contribute to political discourse in a meaningful way. If wearing a crown gave me power, I wanted to use it to make the world a better place, not to plan garden parties and poetry readings and write letters. The idea of being stuffed into a study somewhere to handle correspondence on behalf of the crown was not particularly alluring, but if necessary, I would do it.

I sighed and turned my head toward the string players, steeling myself for another dull court tune. Before I could fully exhale, something odd flickered in my peripheral vision. An unfamiliar servant passed behind us, moving more quickly than his job would ever call for. Something about it made me reach nervously for Thandi's arm, but before I could touch him, the servant drew a dagger from his boot and lunged for the king.

"Look out!" I screamed, but it was already too late.

The king's personal guard drew his sword and shielded him, nimbly avoiding the assassin's blade as it sliced through the air. Thandi pulled me out of my chair and urged me toward the door. I stumbled and lurched away from him, my knees smarting as I fell to the unforgiving stone floor. Beads popped off my dress and scattered like hailstones as I scrambled away, following my sister toward the wall.

I turned around when I hit the edge of the room, clinging to Ali. The assassin had missed his target and was cornered by the empty fireplace. He snarled in frustration as he faced off against the king's guard—the only liegeman in the room with us. This time, a swift strike from the assassin took out the guard, and the liegeman toppled to the ground with blood pulsing out of a wide gash in his neck. My whole body shook. There was nothing I could do, and no way to escape. A few of the noblemen beat on the heavy wooden doors beside us, more interested in saving their own lives than that of their king. The doors held fast, barred from the outside. Someone had turned against us. I couldn't imagine who.

Lord Kriantz was the exception to everyone else's panic. He slipped in front of the king like a shadow, and Thandi and Amaranthine came up to flank him. An acidic taste coated my tongue as the assassin struck at Lord Kriantz, who barely dodged the blow in time. I adjusted my position to shield Alisendi. If only one of us made it out alive, it had to be her. The burn of magic rose in my chest. I clamped down on it and prayed for the fire god's mercy and the strength to keep it under control.

The assassin attacked again, his blade biting into Thandi's arm. A cry escaped my lips as Thandi gritted his teeth and pulled the arm in close to his side. Amaranthine retaliated, kicking at the assassin's legs, but he dodged and lunged again for the king. Lord Kriantz used his forearm to shove the assassin's blow aside with the swift grace of a snake. Behind the king, an oil lamp exploded, showering everyone with glass and sparks. My control was slipping.

"Do something!" Alisendi whispered.

The assassin struck at Amaranthine, catching her shoulder with his blade, and her yelp of pain brought another unstoppable rush of magic. As little as she seemed to like me, the idea that a person as bold as her could be taken down in a closed room without a fair fight filled me with white-hot anger. The magic exploded out of my control.

The assassin ignited from the inside out just as a short blade shot out of Lord Kriantz's sleeve and embedded itself in the man's throat. His body swelled and bloated until gore erupted from beneath his cracked and blackened skin, viscera catching fire as soon as they hit air. As flame consumed him, the power drained out of me in a rush, leaving me weak. I huddled against Alisendi's side. White-faced and trembling, she held me close.

"What in the—" Amaranthine stumbled back from the burning body as Lord Kriantz swooped in to smother the remaining flames with a wall tapestry.

I gagged as the smell of burning flesh and carpet stung my eyes and throat. Footsteps scuffled in the hallway as the doors were finally unbarred. Liegemen burst into the room, naked steel in their hands.

"Fetch the captain of the guard immediately," the king roared. He grabbed a sword from one of the guards closest to him and waved it around as he stomped through the room. "Someone will answer for this!"

"Yes, Your Highness." The senior liegeman gestured for the others to lower their swords and begin escorting everyone to safety. The room slowly emptied of people, some hurrying away as quickly as the liegemen would take them, and others lingering to crane their necks at the smoking body on the floor.

"Your Highness, are you all right?" A liegeman reached down to help me to my feet and then pulled Alisendi to hers. Even with his assistance I could barely trust my quivering legs. The liegeman brought us out to stand beside Thandi, who gripped the cut on his arm, his jaw set against the pain. Amaranthine stood on the other side of him, not looking particularly bothered by the blood seeping through the ripped shoulder of her dress.

"What in the Sixth Hell just happened?" Thandi asked.

"You got yourself sliced up," Amaranthine answered. "Let me

see it." She reached for Thandi's arm.

"No. The healers can deal with it." He jerked his arm away.

"Or you could let me do it so you don't bleed out before they get here," she snapped. She pried his fingers from the wound, and he winced as she yanked the fabric away from the cut.

"Ouch!"

"It's not that bad." She tore a piece of trim off the sleeve of her gown and tied it tightly around his arm above the wound. As soon as she was done, Thandi pulled his arm back, cradling it protectively. Amaranthine shot him a disgusted look.

I was merely relieved that they were both in one piece. Thank the Six I hadn't lit one of them up instead. If any harm had come to them or Alisendi because of me, I might as well have gone to the Great Temple and turned myself in to the priests as a heretic and let them do with me what they saw fit.

"Lord Kriantz!" Amaranthine shouted down the hallway.

"Yes, Your Highness?" The baron strode toward us, turning away from the two liegemen to whom he'd been speaking.

"Your knife," Amaranthine said. "Is that an enchanted blade?"

"Not that I'm aware of, my lady."

I kept my arms wrapped tightly around myself and peered back into the room behind me. Seeing the blackened corpse alongside the chair, I doubled over as my stomach churned. If anyone found out that it had been me who set him ablaze, I would be ruined. Never mind that I couldn't explain how it had happened in the first place. Ever since I had arrived, my magic had become increasingly out of control. According to my mother, it should have faded with age, not grown. Yet somehow I had just killed a man.

"Not that you're aware of? Then which of the Six Hells did that fire come from?" Amaranthine asked.

Alisendi squeezed my arm, but I didn't acknowledge it.

"Your speculations are as good as mine. My blade was forged in Sonnenborne. We prefer simple steel to magic," Lord Kriantz said.

Amaranthine frowned at him. She started to say something else but shut her mouth instead, her full lips pressing into a pensive line. Her gaze flickered to me.

I quaked beneath her scrutiny, afraid she somehow saw the truth.

"Are you all right?" Amaranthine asked me.

"I don't feel well," I said. My head spun, and my body threatened to follow.

"Get her to her rooms," she told a liegeman nearby.

I sagged against the wall, grateful for Amaranthine's take-charge attitude.

"I'll come along to make sure she's all right," Alisendi said with a tremble in her voice.

The liegeman nodded to Amaranthine and guided us from the scene. Dark spots hovered at the edges of my vision as we walked away.

When the door to my rooms closed safely behind us, Alisendi sank into one of the chairs and put her head in her hands.

"This is so much worse than I thought," she said. "If anyone finds out that was you—"

"I know," I snapped. "I didn't mean to do anything. It's been different since I've been here."

Ali chewed her lip the way she always did when there was something she wasn't telling me.

"What?" I asked.

"Nothing. But things haven't been very stable in Havemont since you left."

"What do you mean? What does that have to do with what happened tonight?" I couldn't believe she'd been holding things back from me. We used to tell each other everything.

"Zumordans have started springing up like weeds these last few weeks. They're everywhere now, gathering to protest being banned from the High Adytum."

"But why? Banning them wasn't even part of the original terms of the alliance," I said. "Everyone here seems to think it was, but why didn't we know?"

"I've reviewed the original decrees. The wording is vague," Ali said. "Ten years was plenty of time for them to find loopholes. Now groups are forming who believe only in the Six, who are certain that the magic users are going to strike out against us."

"The same thing that's happening here," I said softly. I couldn't reconcile the fear in me—both for my kingdom and myself.

"If anything happens to the alliance now, we won't have the Mynarian liegemen we need to hold back the Zumordans. If it falls apart completely, Zumorda might try to annex us to prevent this happening again. And in the meantime, those who oppose them are growing more restless and violent by the second. If anyone finds out that you yourself have some kind of gift, something big enough to kill a man, what then?"

"Both sides will see me as a betrayer," I whispered. "Everyone will be out for my blood."

"You have to find a way to stop it. Get rid of it," Alisendi said.

"It's the only way you'll be safe."

I stood up and stepped over to where she sat. She moved over without a word, and I wedged myself in beside her like we used to do as children, curling up together in the same chair. She put her arms around me and let me cry on her shoulder, softly rubbing my back until the tears eased.

But even after my cheeks were dry, I still didn't know how to do what she asked of me. She might as well have asked me to cut out my heart or stop drawing breath.

TWELVE

✦ *Mare*

AMIDST THE CHAOS I SLIPPED BACK INTO THE DRAWING room and retrieved the assassin's blade from where it had fallen. The heavy dagger was adorned only with a plain white pommel nut and had the heft and edge of something well made.

"That looks Zumordan," Lord Kriantz said over my shoulder.

"Really?" I turned to him. "How do you know?"

"The style looks like one I saw in Kartasha a few years ago," he replied, wiping his own knife clean of blood and soot.

"I can take that, Your Highness." A liegeman who looked barely old enough to be in uniform stepped forward and reached for the knife in my hand.

"I don't think so." I pulled it away from him and stepped back, nearly knocking into Lord Kriantz.

The liegeman continued to hold out his hand. "It's quite sharp, Your Highness, you shouldn't—"

"Oh, piss off," I said, losing patience.

The young liegeman's eyes widened and then shifted into a glare.

"The captain will be here shortly," he said.

"I'll give it to her when she arrives," I lied. I had no intention of turning over the knife—not until they made me. The blade could lead me to Cas's killer, Zumordan or otherwise. Knowing the Directorate, they'd only argue over it for a moon and then shove it in a drawer somewhere to collect dust.

"I will help see that the blade winds up in the proper hands," Lord Kriantz cut in.

I shot him an annoyed look, but our combined words had the desired effect.

"Fine," the liegeman said. "See that you do." He turned on his heel and walked away.

I made a rude face at the liegeman's retreating backside. As soon as he was out of sight, I flipped my grip on the blade so it lay against the inside of my wrist and then pressed my arm into the folds of my skirt. With the blade sufficiently hidden, I ducked back out into the hallway. Lord Kriantz followed close on my heels.

I made my way through the lingering nobles and liegemen, moving as neutrally as I could to avoid drawing attention. Right before I got clear of the crowd, Lord Kriantz spoke.

"May I walk you to your chambers?" he asked.

I hesitated for a moment, but company sounded like a good idea under the circumstances, and the sooner I got away, the less likely it was that Captain Ryka would catch up to me. Maybe having Lord Kriantz with me would reduce the likelihood of my being followed.

"All right," I said. We strode away from the crowd until their voices faded away behind us.

"Do you mind if I take a look at your blade?" I asked as soon as we were out of earshot.

"Of course not, my lady." He pulled the small knife from his wrist sheath and handed it over as we continued toward my rooms.

"Sonnenborne workmanship," I grumbled. Knives were hardly my area of expertise, but there was nothing unusual about it as far as I could tell. It was a simple blade, unadorned, clearly made for the exact purpose for which it had been used. "Does my father know you've been toting this thing around in your sleeve?"

"No, but I doubt he'll complain, since it saved his life tonight. We Sonnenbornes don't make a habit of going anywhere unprepared. The desert is unforgiving, as are its people." He slipped the knife back into its concealed sheath, and the mechanism that had released it clicked back into place.

"So what were you doing in Zumorda a few years ago?" I asked. Few were brave enough to cross the border, especially to visit the cities closest to his holdings. Not one of them had a good reputation.

"Horse trading. It's one of the better markets for Mynarian culls, as I'm sure you know."

"Right." What he said was true, but unenlightening. Exhaustion weighed me down as the heightened energy of the fight faded away. "By the Six, I'm weary of puzzles and deaths."

"As are we all, I'm afraid," he said.

Before Cas's death I had rarely worried about my ability to take care of myself within the castle walls, but tonight it was nice to have another person with me. We walked on in silence until we reached the door to my rooms. The two liegemen moved aside to let me enter, and Lord Kriantz followed me in.

"Thanks for helping get that liegeman off my back," I said. "And fighting for my father. If you hadn't . . ." As strained as my relationship was with my father, I didn't want any harm to come to him. Lord Kriantz had made all the difference. Everyone else had only tried to save themselves—except Dennaleia, who had been too busy cowering in the corner. Half fainting away was probably covered in one of her handbooks on how to be a proper lady.

"Of course. I'm happy to help at any time. Speaking of which, it's best you let me look around in case any other dangers are hiding in the shadows." He stepped gracefully around me.

"I think it should be fine," I said. "The liegemen never leave their posts."

"Like the ones stationed outside the drawing room tonight?" he asked, pulling back my curtains.

"You're right." I rubbed my temple. "Anything is possible. I suppose it's better to check than to wind up dead."

He prowled around the room a moment more, his dark eyes raking every surface.

"I think you're all clear, my lady." He stepped forward and took my hand, brushing his thumb across my palm. "You were very brave tonight."

"Any half-wit would have done the same," I said gruffly, though his compliment pleased me.

"I disagree. A few people here seem to have trouble with . . . inaction."

"Spoken like a diplomat," I said.

"Spoken like an ambassador," he replied with a gentle smile. "This is not my kingdom. I do not presume to know how it should be run. If anything, I hoped to learn some things here that might be applied to Sonnenborne as we develop our own system of governance."

"You don't have to be polite with me. The Directorate is obviously more interested in slinging manure at one another than doing anything about investigating Cas's death."

Lord Kriantz nodded but didn't speak.

"Why did you help me, anyway?" I asked.

"Alliances are not only built from the top down, my lady," he said. "And I am as interested in the source of these attacks as you are. A threat to Mynaria could be a threat to Sonnenborne. I'm eager to ensure that both our kingdoms remain safe."

"Well, if the Directorate won't find out where this thing came from, then I will," I said, scowling at the blade in my hand. Brushing the blood grooves with anxious fingers, I flipped the knife over. It shone brightly even in dim light.

"I have no doubt you will," Lord Kriantz said. "I should be off. Let me know if there is anything else I can do for you."

"Thank you, Lord Kriantz," I said.

"Good night, Mare. Stay safe." He bowed and exited the room.

I appreciated someone who knew not to overstay his welcome. I set the knife down on my vanity and paced over to my couch. The cut on my shoulder stung when I probed it with my fingers. The torn fabric of my dress had stuck to it. I grimaced as I pulled the ripped material away, but the wound was shallow.

I rang for my maid, Sara. It wasn't the first time I'd come home cut up from something or other, and it was better not to waste the healers' time with something she could handle. Summoning Nils held more appeal, but he was on duty.

A knock sounded on my door. "Come in, Sara," I called from the bedroom.

But instead of my maid, Captain Ryka appeared in the doorway with four of her Elite liegemen.

"I trust you know what happened to the assassin's weapon," she said, her gaze steely.

"I was going to bring it to you tomorrow," I lied, cursing the liegeman who had ratted on me.

She shook her head. "I know you too well to believe that, but this isn't the time to play around. Cas was my husband. Don't stand in the way of my investigation—or my revenge." She didn't scare me as much as she had when I was a child, but her words still made me quake a little.

"There's no evidence that this was even connected to the other attack," I argued.

"That's my problem, not yours. We'll be taking the blade now," she said.

"No!" I leaped to my feet, but she snatched the dagger from my vanity before I made it halfway across the room.

"If you aren't going to show up to the Directorate, don't meddle in our business," she said, and marched back out, letting the door slam behind her.

"Maybe if you got anything done, I wouldn't have to," I said, and threw a shoe at the closed door. Perhaps I should have followed her, but I didn't have any more fight in me, not after tonight.

Without the blade to take to town to research, my only resource left was the library. The thought of locking myself in there to pore over books made me sob with boredom. I needed another ally, preferably someone well-read. Someone who might be able to parse out details about the blade and arrow that would identify the true enemy. Then it struck me that I already knew the best-schooled person in the palace: Princess Dennaleia. And fainting aside, she clearly had her wits about her based on her speculations about the white arrow and the calculations she'd done to figure out from where the archer had made the shot.

I had no other choice—I'd have to get her on my side as soon as possible.

THIRTEEN   🔥 *Dennaleia*

THE MORNING FOLLOWING THE ASSASSINATION
attempt found me in the royal library. Noblewomen clustered around
me, their bright dresses whispering over the soft carpets. Thandi had
suggested I socialize with the other highborn girls at court before
my sister left. In light of recent events, she had elected to return to
Havemont as soon as enough liegemen could be spared to escort
her. In the meantime, I had to suffer the frustration and boredom of
listening to the other girls carry on about nonsense when there were
many deeper concerns at hand.

Underscoring the importance of developing closer relationships
at court, a letter from my mother had arrived early that morning.
After a few words of sympathy over Casmiel's demise, the rest of
her message was devoted to the importance of the alliance and
my duty to see that our two kingdoms rose to meet this new and
uncertain enemy as one. It closed with a reminder to spend my

praise days wisely and to devote my time equally among the Six. I knew what that truly meant—that I needed to keep my hands out of the fire, so to speak.

I thought I'd kept my gift from her all those years after she'd caught me in the hearth. If she knew something I did not, she should have told me before formal letters had become our only way to communicate. She should have told me how to stop it before I killed a man. But for now I still had to do as she wished and be the leader and ambassador my people required.

Trapped amidst the other girls as they vied for position by my side, I struggled to catch a glimpse of the books we passed while still keeping an ear on the conversation.

"Did you hear that the Count of Nax is going to marry that provincial woman from the east?" the blond girl on my left asked.

"No!" Annietta of Ciralis covered her mouth in shock. "But she's so strange. Practically Zumordan. What if living so close to the border has tainted her with magic?"

"My father says she's doing it to throw suspicion off their family. He thinks they're supporters of the Recusants," a voice added from the back of the group.

How they could gossip about weddings in light of Casmiel's death and the assassination attempt made little sense. I chose not to comment, instead turning my head to admire the king's book collection. Dim light filtered through tiny windows near the top of the vaulted ceiling, casting a cool glow over the tall bookcases. The depth and breadth of the Mynarian library were consistent with its place at the center of the Northern Kingdoms. Shelves towered over us on either side, sections marked with intricate wooden signs painstakingly carved by master craftsmen. Inhaling deeply, I reveled in the familiar smell of ink and parchment.

The cluster of girls stopped in the poetry section, eager to choose poems for the reading in a few nights' time. They giggled as they pulled books from the shelves, skimming for suggestive lines they hoped would win the attention of the men or women courting them. At least my sister managed to hold back. I was fairly certain she knew all the dirtiest poems by heart, but she wisely comported herself with dignity.

"What do you think of this one, Your Highness?" The pushy blonde shoved a book under my nose.

I smiled politely and took it from her.

"Callue is always a classic choice," I said, returning the book to her. A burst of shoving ensued as every other girl tried to get her hands on another volume of Callue.

My sister rolled her eyes and mouthed "Horomir," and I covered my smile with a hand. Vili Horomir penned the naughtiest poems in the Northern Kingdoms, generally filled with terrifying euphemisms for parts of the male physique. If the girls wanted suggestive poems, they ought to have consulted my sister instead of me.

I quietly stepped out of the way, wondering if it would ever seem less strange to have everyone leap to imitate what I did— everything from my dresses to my choice in poetry. Only one other girl hung back from the crowd, smiling timidly at me. I remembered her from my wedding bazaar as Hilara's third recommendation. The shy one from the sea.

"Hello," I said. "I don't believe we've formally met."

The girl blushed. "Ellaeni of Trindor, Your Highness." She curtsied.

"Not interested in Callue?" I asked, keeping my tone light.

"Oh, Callue is nice. I . . . I'm not sure what to choose. Getting up in front of people makes me nervous. And the only person I would have wanted to read for is back home." She bowed her head, a curtain of shining black hair falling across her cheeks.

"Well, I've found that making people laugh tends to be a good antidote for all those things. If you like, I can show you some of my favorites by a different poet," I said, excited to make a suggestion of something I truly loved.

"That would be wonderful, my lady." She brightened.

I escorted Ellaeni around the other girls to a later part of the alphabet and pulled a thin, plain volume from the shelf, thumbing the book open. "This is one of my favorites. Razkiva mostly writes humorous rhymes about animals."

She smiled as she read the poem.

"This is perfect, Your Highness," she said.

Unfortunately, I couldn't linger too long with Ellaeni for fear of showing favoritism, but I made a mental note to connect with the girl later, away from the others. With her diffidence, she seemed as though she needed a friend. I turned to face the group and begin my rounds when a voice far too loud for the indoors burst out behind me.

"There you are!" Amaranthine said.

Everyone stopped what they were doing and stared. Amaranthine's riding clothes already adorned her familiar form, her braid only moderately tidier than it usually was in the afternoon.

"Hello, Lady Amaranthine." I curtsied, both to remind her of her manners and because every other girl had dropped her book to watch what was unfolding. My sister glanced between me and

Amaranthine with a questioning expression.

"I need to talk to you," Amaranthine said.

I smiled in an attempt to reduce my irritation as magic prickled through the palms of my hands. "Perhaps we could speak after my riding lesson today?"

"No, I need to talk to you right now," she insisted, not even sparing a glance for the other noblewomen.

I gritted my teeth, hoping no one could see. "As you wish," I said. "Why don't we step outside?"

"No," she said. "Back here is fine. It'll only take a moment."

She darted behind a bookshelf, leaving me to politely excuse myself from everyone else to follow her. My sister, thank the Six, took command of the situation and started urging the noblewomen to practice reading for one another. The librarian's eyes followed me as I went after Amaranthine, accompanied by his furious scowl of disapproval.

"Amaranthine, I'm sorry, but this isn't the best time—" I began.

"What do you know about Zumorda?" she interrupted me.

Tingles shot through my palms and I clamped my hands down on the shelf behind me in an attempt to hold in the magic. A surge of disappointment followed the rush of power. My gift had been quieter since I'd killed the assassin. I'd foolishly hoped that it had been permanently drained away. If I could kill without meaning to, there was no telling what might happen next now that it was rising up again. The thought made me sick to my stomach.

"Listen—Lord Kriantz said the blade used in the assassination attempt the other night is probably Zumordan. I don't know how to verify that, and I was hoping you could help."

"Why don't you ask the smith? Or the weaponsmaster? Or even the captain of the guard?" I asked. The Zumordan merchant from my bazaar also crossed my mind, but Amaranthine wouldn't have known to ask me about him. I couldn't imagine what sort of demented reasoning would lead her to me for information about a weapon.

"They won't know." She shook her head. "Havemont is the only kingdom with a major city close to Zumorda, and I know you've spent a lot more time at your studies than me. I want to know how a blade of their design could have ended up here. It could point to them as the source of the attack, and perhaps also as Cas's murderers. There could be spies in our midst. Or maybe they're working through the Recusants."

"This is none of my business," I said. While a part of me leaped at the idea that I could finally be of help, I needed to get away from her before something went up in flames. Also, getting tangled up in anything to do with Zumorda was a dangerous proposition. "Thandi and the Directorate haven't asked me—"

"This isn't Directorate business. This is my business." Amaranthine stepped aggressively toward me, so close I could smell the cinnamon of her soap.

"I don't know anything!" I shrank back against the shelf.

"I know that," Amaranthine said. "What I want you to do is find out. See if there's a way we can verify that the blade is Zumordan. And perhaps see if there's any information on the kind of magic that killed that assassin. Or Cas. A connection between the two."

"I wouldn't know where to begin." A lie. Figuring out where to find obscure information in the library was a game I used to play with my tutors—one at which I had been quite skilled. Probably the section on weapons crafting would be my best chance for information on the blade, but it would make sense to start with geography and political history in order to narrow down the specific region from which the weapon came. It couldn't hurt to take a look at some architecture books, and perhaps even census records if any were available. The numbness in my hands and face subsided, soothed by the familiar mental exercise of research planning. At least the magic quieted more quickly than it had leading up to the assassin's death. It seemed to have less fuel, somehow.

"Perhaps you could look here in the library." Amaranthine stared at me, her gray eyes bright.

"You're already here," I pointed out. "You can look yourself."

"I'm not a scholar," she said. "You are."

"Well, you're the first person here to acknowledge that," I muttered. Gratitude welled up—stupid, foolish gratitude that she recognized something so important. It felt good to be seen.

"Can you do this? Please? I know you don't owe me anything, but this might help catch the bastards who killed Cas and tried to kill my father."

I couldn't decide what to do. I wanted to help because it was my duty to Mynaria, and because she was asking me to use the skills I'd been so frustrated that Thandi and the Directorate had not yet taken advantage of. She was also handing me the perfect excuse to research my own magic. But it was a risky thing she asked of me. Too risky.

"I care about my family," she continued. "They may be dim-witted sometimes, but they're still my family. And this is my kingdom. And I won't have some bitch queen tormenting us from afar and playing with us like pawns."

"Well, what do you know about the blade?" I asked, curious in spite of my fear.

"Before Captain Ryka took it from me, I noticed there wasn't any crest on it. The metal was very bright, maybe even silver. It had a white pommel nut—does that seem Zumordan to you?"

"I don't know. Their pennants are white, but that isn't enough evidence to accuse them of attempted assassination," I said.

"Captain Ryka mentioned their crest but didn't say anything about the pennants. See, you already know things that might help," Amaranthine said.

"Don't you think researching magic could be problematic?" I asked. "There isn't likely to be much information here, and given that magic use is treason—"

"It's a little risky, yes," she admitted. "But if it helps us figure out who is behind this, I don't care. Some things I've seen in town make me unsure whether magic itself is the problem. It's whoever is using it against my family."

I still hesitated, but a spark of hope came alive in my chest. She didn't hate magic users unquestioningly. Maybe she wouldn't despise me if she knew the truth. And helping her would allow me to look into my own abilities.

I couldn't say no.

"All right, fine. I'll see what I can find out," I conceded.

"Dennaleia," Amaranthine said. "Look at me."

The intensity of her gaze made my stomach jump into my throat.

"Thank you," she said, vanishing as quickly as she'd come.

I leaned against the wall for a moment, wondering what in the Six Hells I had gotten myself into. Everything about Amaranthine was so extreme—the way she spoke, the way she moved, the way she looked at me.

I pressed one hand against the wall, hoping the cool stone might quell the buzzing in my palms. Instead, the stone gave beneath my touch. I jerked my fingers away as though it had burned me. An indentation in the shape of a finger remained in the wall.

"Your Highness?" a tentative voice said behind me.

Fear shot through me as I turned around. Ellaeni peered around the end of the row of shelves.

"The others were wondering if you could help them pick some poems too, my lady," Ellaeni said. Her face was neutral. Friendly, even. She hadn't seen anything. I exhaled shakily.

"Of course!" I said. I grasped my skirts to steady my trembling fingers and followed her back to the group.

The tittering and whispering stopped as soon as the girls saw me. Only my sister looked at me with a what-in-the-Sixth-Hell expression that meant I'd have to come up with an explanation later.

"Please excuse the interruption," I addressed the group. "I would love to see the poems you all have selected."

They smiled back falsely, smug with their knowledge of the latest gossip. It would be all over court by nightfall that Amaranthine and I had caused a scene in the library. I shouldn't have offered to help her. She had taken me down a notch in front of people with whom I should be building up sway. My resolution to obey my mother's wishes was not going as planned.

I commented and nodded over each girl's poetry selection, trying to pay everyone equal attention, but Amaranthine's request hung over me. When the time came for lunch, I let the girls get halfway to the great hall before I excused myself, insisting that I'd forgotten something in the library. My sister gave me a dubious look, but I waved her off with an innocent smile.

I stalked back through the library aisles like a thief. None of the volumes were about Zumorda; the Mynarians had done a good job of purging every book on magic. History and architecture yielded no results, and as I'd feared, no census information was available. Even the geography section held nothing except the most simplistic of maps. The detail stopped at the Mynarian border on the west side of Zumorda, and the Havemont border in the north. After what felt like sunlengths wandering through the library, the only remotely promising thing I managed to pick up was an enormous tome on swordsmithing techniques that gave me a headache just looking at it.

As I passed through the religion section on my way out, a strange chirp came from one of the shelves. I stopped short. A bright blue bird with a belly that faded to white perched on top of a thin green book sticking out from the other volumes on the shelf. Impossible. Mountain bluebirds didn't live on the plains—only north, in the mountains where I had grown up. When I stepped closer, the bird fluttered out one of the high windows.

I took the book down from the shelf. Crisp pages yellowed with age parted to reveal an illustration of a man with his hands raised in the air. A storm swirled around him, not of rain and thunder, but of stars trailing streaks of fiery light. It looked like one of those celestial events when the gods sent stars shooting across the sky, but the man had somehow brought them to earth.

It wasn't a book on religion. It was a book on magic. Curiosity and fear slithered over each other inside me.

Somehow the book had been misshelved or preserved—perhaps due to the design on the cover. At first glance the six colored dots looked like the same ones used to denote the gods, but they were in the wrong order. I thumbed through the book, growing more and more apprehensive. It seemed to be a record of the most powerful mages and their work. The introduction outlined the six Affinities: wind, water, earth, fire, shadow, and spirit. Each Affinity corresponded to one of the Six Gods.

Alongside the profiles of the great mages, complicated diagrams showed the relationships between the Affinities, remarking that strength in multiple Affinities was rare—and dangerous. I had always thought my Affinity was fire. But there had been the time the door slammed, and earlier today when the stone had softened beneath my touch. Dread raced down my spine.

Surely my gift couldn't be more than fire. But then again, I had also thought it small—until I killed that assassin. There was only one way to find out. In an empty corner of the library I sat down in a chair and closed my eyes. Carefully, I let my magic rise into my fingertips, the familiar numbness spreading up my arms. Instead of fire I daydreamed of a soft breeze, summoning it in through the window high above me.

A gust blasted through the library, flipping the pages of the open books on a nearby table. My heart raced as I wrestled the magic back in. When I opened my eyes, my head spun and I gripped the arms of the chair to steady myself.

"There you are!" Alisendi appeared at the end of the aisle and hurried toward me, distressed. "Where did that wind come from? What are you doing back here?"

"Nothing," I said. I shoved the green book under the swordsmithing tome.

"You missed lunch," Ali said. "Thandilimon wanted to know where you were."

"What did you tell him?" I made a weak attempt to tidy the books my magic had disturbed, unable to meet Ali's eyes.

"That you'd forgotten a book in the library and you have a tendency to lose track of time when reading," she said, exasperated. "But you're not at home now—you can't just disappear like that. People find it peculiar."

I started to make up an excuse, but Ali deserved to know at least part of the truth. Once she left, she'd take the secret of my Affinity with her and I'd be alone with it again.

"I was trying to research your suggestion," I whispered. "Maybe there is a way to make the fire god's gift disappear." I traced a circle on the swordsmithing book, thinking of the colored dots on the one beneath it.

"Let's hope to the Six there is," she said. "But I'm leaving in less than a week."

The subtext was clear—without her, there would be no one to provide excuses for me.

"I'll be all right," I said, ignoring how much the words felt like a lie and how desperately I knew I'd miss her.

"Will you?" she asked, taking my hand, her expression grave.

"I must," I said, picking up the books and clutching them to my chest. "Let's go. I'm going to be late for my riding lesson."

Thank the Six she didn't know that apparently fire wasn't the only thing I needed to suppress.

FOURTEEN ✦ *Mare*

PRINCESS ALISENDI'S FAREWELL TOOK HALF A
morning, wasting yet more valuable time. Captain Ryka wouldn't
let any members of the royal family ride with the escort for fear of
our safety, so we waved good-bye from the front courtyard as her
carriage and armed escort disappeared into the city.

Dennaleia stood straight, but I could see the sorrow etched in
her face as she watched her sister leave. Her expression didn't change
as we headed to the stables for her lesson.

"Have you found anything at the library?" I asked.

"Not yet," she said with a sigh, clearly tired of hearing the same
question day after day.

"I can't stand being trapped in here," I said. "Let's go for a trail
ride."

"Is that allowed?" she asked.

"It's safe as long as we stay on the acreage within the castle walls.

Besides, who's going to stop us?" I said, casting a hostile glance at Captain Ryka, who had come down to the barn with us to drill the latest recruits. Even after she'd taken the knife, the Directorate hadn't bothered to question me as a witness to the assassination attempt—more proof that Cas had been the only one of them with full use of his wits.

I tacked up Flicker in his war saddle and strapped on my horn, bow, and quiver to give us practice carrying the cumbersome trappings of the hunt. We climbed onto our horses at the mounting block, which Dennaleia now did with ease. She had gotten past the soreness caused by riding nearly every day, no longer leaving her lessons shuffling stiffly.

As I led her away from the guarded paddock, two liegemen rode up.

"You have to be joking," I said.

"For your safety," one said. "Captain Ryka's orders."

I rolled my eyes. If the captain wanted me to stay out of her business, the least she could do was stay out of mine. "Fine, but stay out of earshot or I'll spend the whole ride coming up with new ways to insult your mothers." I motioned Dennaleia forward.

The city spread out in our view as the horses picked their way up the trail. Beyond the rooftops, the wind rippled through the golden summer grass like waves on the sea. Trees arched over us, providing welcome shade from the afternoon sun as we made our way into the low foothills bordering the back gardens of the palace.

"Watch for branches," I said, ducking beneath a low limb and reaching out to snap off another.

Dennaleia didn't respond, but she didn't fall off her horse, either, so she must have heard.

The foliage thickened as we rode deeper into the woods, winding down a hill and through a small stream. When the trail finally opened up after the creek, I slowed Flicker until Dennaleia and I rode abreast. I patted Flicker on the neck, trying to figure out how to get the princess to talk, hoping to coax another smile out of her.

"So how are things going?" I asked.

"You mean the research . . . ?"

"That and everything else."

"I haven't found any answers yet, which is frustrating. Everything else is . . . well, it's hard sometimes."

"What do you mean?" Besides riding, I couldn't imagine what she was talking about. I hated court life, but with her grace and diplomacy, Dennaleia seemed born for it.

"I miss Ali. And I miss Havemont, too. There's no one I can talk to. Thandi is busy much of the time. And you're only training me because Casmiel ordered you."

"Who told you that?"

"Thandi," she replied.

"He would, that useless road apple," I said. "It's not that simple. Yes, I was ordered to give you lessons. But you've also proven to be more intelligent than any of those mush-minded jackasses on the Directorate." I needed her on my side. And honestly, she wasn't bad company, particularly when she let her wit out to play.

"It matters what you want too," she said.

"What I want is to see the determination you had when you first showed up here. The girl who knows half a dozen random facts about arrows for no apparent reason and can calculate a shot trajectory. The girl who gets on a horse even when it's the last thing she wants to do." Those were the things I respected most about her—the things that made me like her in spite of my intentions to the contrary.

"I've come to like riding . . . but I don't feel like that girl right now," Dennaleia said, so softly I barely heard her.

"You're still that girl," I said. I wanted her to be her best self, not only because it would help me, but because I knew that strength was in her. The events since she'd arrived were enough to break anyone's spirit. Maybe she just needed to find her way back to something she loved—something that made her feel as alive as she'd looked when she danced.

"What do you do well?" I asked.

"I play the harp. Useful, I know," she said.

"So invite me over to listen sometime. I'd like to hear you play." An unexpected burst of nerves followed my request. Music had once had a bigger place in my heart, and picking at old wounds was uncomfortable.

"All right." Her tone was noncommittal, but a blush rose into her cheeks.

"Good," I said. "Let's trot."

We picked up the pace. I hoped as we trotted through the trees that she could feel the indefinable thing I felt on Flicker's back—the way cares could fall away and leave only the wind in my hair and the sun on my cheeks.

The guards got too close and I shooed them away as the trail opened up into a meadow with a breathtaking view of the city.

Movement in the streets was barely discernible as anything but motion itself. But when we reached the peak of the vista, our horses shied sideways as someone burst out of the woods lining the meadow.

"For the Recusants!" the figure shouted. An arrow whizzed past Dennaleia's shoulder.

"Go!" I shouted, and swung Flicker around to shield Dennaleia and Louie. Both horses took off at a canter, angling away from our attacker. The liegemen urged their horses toward us, but they couldn't outrun the archer's next shot. Guiding Flicker with my legs, I unhooked my bow from the saddle and nocked an arrow.

"Keep him steady!" I shouted to Dennaleia, hoping that she could keep Louie at an even pace. Without my hands on the reins I had no way to rate Flicker's speed. I sat up straight and sank my heels deeper into the stirrups, knowing I couldn't take any chances. I didn't have three shots and targets like in drills. I had one shot to take down someone who wanted us dead.

Another arrow shot from our attacker's bow and struck the dirt behind us. I pulled my bowstring back, then stood in the stirrups and turned to let my own arrow fly, all in the space of a heartbeat. My arrow released at the peak of Flicker's stride and struck the archer in the shoulder. The person crumpled to the ground, lost in the golden grass.

"Whoa!" I said, and we pulled up our horses. They shifted underneath us, still uneasy, ears pricked toward the fallen enemy. I blew five sharp calls on my horn in the pattern to indicate an emergency, hoping that a patrol was close by to supplement our guards.

"Get down," I said. "We don't know if there are more of them."

Dennaleia slid out of the saddle and crouched beside me.

"If anyone else shoots, let go of the reins," I whispered.

She nodded and slipped her free hand into mine, sending a shiver of surprise through me. I met her frightened gaze and squeezed back gently. The seconds passed like a held breath until hoofbeats drew close and I let go. The guards slowed as they approached so as not to spook our horses, four additional liegemen behind them.

"What's the call?" the head liegeman asked as she drew close.

"An archer came out of those trees and shot at us," I said. "I took her down over there."

"Stay here," the head liegeman directed our two original guards. She gestured to a third. "You, perimeter check." She dismounted and drew her weapon, indicating that the final two liegemen should follow. I pulled a knife from my boot and trailed after them with one last nervous glance at Dennaleia. Even though she was safe with the liegemen, it made me uneasy to leave her.

The four of us picked our way cautiously across the meadow toward the spot where the archer had fallen. My stomach churned. The silence in the meadow could mean that I had killed her. I had never shot a person before.

We heard the archer wheezing with pain before we saw her. She lay on her side with my arrow sticking out of her right shoulder. Her short, sandy hair matched the sun-bleached meadow grass. She wore the expression of a cornered stray—and a face I recognized.

It was the Recusant woman I'd seen stab that fundamentalist at the Pelham. Dread drew its slow claws down my spine.

A bow lay beside her, a crude and simple instrument that looked a little warped from ill care. No wonder her aim had been so poor.

We had been lucky. She lunged toward the bow with her good arm, but the liegemen seized her on both sides and I stepped on the end of the weapon before she could get a grip.

"Why did you do this?" I asked.

She hissed with pain and spat toward the feet of the liegemen.

"The alliance must be stopped at any cost," she choked out. "But I wasn't after you."

The words offered no comfort—only a rising tide of fear. Of course Dennaleia had been the archer's target. Her death would guarantee the disintegration of the alliance.

FIFTEEN

🪶 *Dennaleia*

THE DIRECTORATE QUESTIONED THE ARCHER IN THE
Great Temple, no doubt for the symbolism it provided: the leadership
in Mynaria would not tolerate heretics. When I walked in alongside
Thandi, I half expected to go up in flames. My gift had continued to
regain strength since the death of the assassin, and the air around me
once again felt like it could combust at any moment.

The dome above the transept let in light and air, chimes hanging
from thin cords tinkling in the breeze. The lower tones of the larger
chimes in the temple garden were dimly audible even from inside,
soft and dissonant under the whispered conversations all around as
the Directorate settled down for business.

"Where's Amaranthine? Shouldn't she be here?" I whispered to
Thandi. I hadn't seen her in days. With the castle on lockdown since
the capture of the archer, there had been no riding lessons.

"Ryka wanted her to come, but she refused. She said that she had nothing to add to her statement, that you would be witness enough, and that she had 'better things to do.'"

It hurt that she hadn't shown up. She'd made herself scarce since the attack, and the king's paranoia about my safety meant all my days had been scheduled to the hilt. But in spite of the liegemen trailing me everywhere, I had felt safer crouched in that meadow with her hand in mine. I missed her. Evidently she didn't feel the same.

The Directorate faced the rows of empty temple seats from the middle of the transept, their chairs arranged in a semicircle. Thandi and I took our places on the dais behind them. Once the king settled into his seat between us, silence descended on the room.

"Bring in the heretic," the king said.

Ryka signaled to her liegemen, and a group of four dragged the archer down the aisle and forced her to her knees in front of us. She held her head high in defiance, her shoulder swathed in bandages and her right arm bound to her chest.

Director Eadric rang his bell and got up without waiting to be formally invited to speak. He teetered forward until he was within a few paces of the archer and then squinted down at her, looking as if he smelled a particularly pungent onion.

"Have you pondered traveling the infinite paths of purification and repentance? To find your way back to the truth of life, to the Six Gods who watch over us all, benevolent, beauteous, leading our souls into the realms of virtue . . . ?"

She responded by spitting at his feet.

Eadric tilted his head at her and then turned to the rest of the Directorate. "We should perform a cleansing ritual," he said, and then paced around the transept waving his miniature chimes and chanting toward the patch of sky visible through the high glass dome.

I couldn't fathom what would make anyone think that a cleansing ritual was a good use of time during what should have been an expeditious interrogation.

Before Director Eadric had even finished easing his creaky rear end back into his seat, Thandi rang his bell.

"Motion for Princess Dennaleia to speak," Thandi said.

Everyone but Hilara raised their voting pieces in my favor. Clearly the woman would have been as happy to see me shot. I swallowed hard and stood up.

"Three days past, Princess Amaranthine and I were trail riding when this woman came out of the trees and shot at us," I said. "Before she fired, she shouted, 'For the Recusants.' Amaranthine shot her in the shoulder and then summoned additional guards."

I took my seat.

"Did you shoot at Princesses Amaranthine and Dennaleia?" the king said. He tapped impatiently on the arm of his chair.

"Yes, and I'd do it again." The archer looked straight at me as though she'd burn holes through me if she could.

"Why did you commit the treasonous act of striking out against members of the royal family?" The king looked about ready to run the archer through. It was fortunate for her that weapons were not permitted in the temple.

"To stop the alliance. All should be allowed access to the High Adytum, no matter their beliefs," she ranted. "You fools don't understand the forces at work, and if you did, you'd fear the trap you've set up for yourselves by blocking access to those who keep the world in balance. And if I'd still had my husband by my side, I would have taken her in one shot, like I did the steward who brokered this fool's alliance." She spat again, and the liegemen surrounding her stepped in.

Several members of the Directorate gasped and the king surged to his feet, reaching for the empty place where his sword was usually belted. I sat frozen in place, numb with shock. She'd only been trying to kill me. If stopping the alliance was the main objective of the Recusants, in a way Casmiel's death was on my hands too. My arrival had been their cue to attack. Thandi leaped up, ringing his bell for order until everyone quieted.

"Captain, what evidence was found at the scene?" Thandi asked, returning to his seat. Though his voice was steady, his grip on the arm of his chair left his knuckles white.

Captain Ryka stood. "An unremarkable bow and a quiver of white arrows. Two of them had been fired, and we recovered those from the field. But let's go back to the beginning." She faced the archer. "How did you murder Casmiel? That was a difficult shot with no clear line of sight, and assuming you used the same weapon we found at the scene three days past, you'd have better luck shooting flies in a windstorm."

"The arrow was enchanted to seek him," she said, looking almost pleased.

"And to go up in ash?" Captain Ryka prompted. "How?"

"My husband's fire Affinity."

It shocked me that she let the information go so easily.

"Where is your husband now?" the king demanded.

"Dead." The rage and grief was plain on her face. "Dead because of your stupid alliance and the antimagic zealots who have taken it upon themselves to 'cleanse' the city. People found out about his fire Affinity, and he started getting attacked on the street every night on the way home from work. Joining the Recusants was the only way to fight back. Stopping the alliance is the only way to make Mynaria a safe place for people like him to live."

My pulse pounded in my ears. No wonder she didn't bother lying. She had nothing left to lose. And her husband had been killed for his Affinity—one that might have been just like mine. Except he'd clearly had half a clue how to use his.

Hilara rang.

"Who was responsible for the assassination attempt on the king, and where did you obtain the Zumordan blade used in that attempt?" she asked. "Did your husband enchant that weapon?"

She wanted an explanation for the assassin going up in flames, and the archer's husband might have been one. Only Alisendi and I knew that it had been me. I took deep breaths and focused on keeping my face expressionless.

"My husband did whatever would serve our cause," she replied. "Not that it matters now."

"Tell us who else was involved in plotting the attempt on the king," Hilara asked.

"I have nothing left to say," the archer said.

"She's playing the fool. These Recusants are clearly working with the Zumordans to take down the alliance and the crown. We should torture her until she confesses. Motion to torture the prisoner!" the director of agriculture said.

"Denied," Thandi said, overruling the possibility of a vote. At least he saved the Directorate the embarrassment of that.

"Make no mistake—you will pay for my brother's death," the king said. "We will hunt down everyone dear to you until you reveal the names of anyone else who had a hand in it."

"I have no family. My husband is dead. There is nothing left you can take from me." The archer's eyes were cold.

The king sat down and slammed his fist on his chair. I flinched.

"Motion to hold this prisoner for further questioning about her associates," Hilara said.

The directors raised their voting pieces unanimously.

"Motion to begin detaining, questioning, and punishing all those connected to the Recusants or anyone suspected of having an Affinity," the Captain Ryka said.

All twelve directors raised their voting pieces again.

A scribe recorded the votes as my heart plummeted.

"At least we know who is behind these attacks now," Ryka said. "We'll catch the scum."

I couldn't feel my hands, and I could hardly hear over the frantic beating of my heart as they dragged the archer away. They thought they knew who was responsible for all the attacks, but the archer hadn't revealed anything about the Zumordan blade. She'd said herself that she had nothing left to lose, so why not confess?

"It's all right," Thandi said, misreading my distress. He took my hand. Numbly, I let him. "She can't hurt you now."

"Of course." I nodded.

But it wasn't the archer I feared. It was the Directorate hunting down magic users—and catching me first.

✿ ✿ ✿

Back in my rooms I frantically thumbed through the green book from the library in search of answers about how to hide my Affinity—or better yet, get rid of it. The author of the book had a scholar's interest in the subject but wasn't a magic user himself. Long, dry passages described how those with Affinities could use the power in themselves or the environment, but didn't explain how it was done. He recommended that exercises be done to condition and develop a gift, with no explanation of what those exercises might be. He warned that repression of power could lead to sudden outbursts, and that large expenditures of magic could drain the user for a time. The only somewhat useful note was a mention of the High Adytum, and how working with one's power in spaces designed for it allowed more focus and control.

I couldn't start sleeping in the castle Sanctuary to keep my Affinity in balance, and I couldn't walk around firing off sparks at random to keep the power from slowly building within me. In a book on great mages, there was no section on princesses who started fires. It was filled with men who could sink fleets of ships with one spell and women who could change history by writing in their own blood. That kind of magic was legend, not reality; theirs were gifts that belonged to gods, not mortals.

I slammed the book shut and shoved it under my bed in frustration.

I passed the rest of the afternoon writing and discarding half-drafted letters to my sister, trying to distract myself from my fear. I wanted to ask Ali how to do what she said and get rid of my Affinity, but she wouldn't have answers, and I would be a fool to incriminate myself in writing. The only answer was to find those responsible for the knife attack so that the Directorate would put their investigation to rest, which meant I needed Amaranthine—even though it upset me that she hadn't shown up for the questioning. Maybe her request to hear me play the harp wasn't the overture of friendship I'd hoped. Maybe the way we'd held hands after we were attacked hadn't meant anything. She didn't care about the crown. She had no reason to care about me.

By the time Auna came to ready me for dinner, setting the entire city on fire and riding back to Havemont on a stolen horse had started to seem like the only viable solution to my problems. Auna stood behind me at my vanity, my hair half twisted up into layer upon layer of knots. The thought of one more pin stuck in it made me want to scream.

"This is the latest fashion in Mynaria," Auna said, "but I'm adding a few special braids and charms like we use in Havemont. We'll start a new trend!"

Auna's excitement was not contagious.

All I could think about was the Directorate meeting, and it twisted my stomach into knots even more complex than the ones in my hair.

"Are you sure you need to put all of it up, Auna? I don't want to be late for dinner," I said.

"But of course, my lady! We can't have you looking like a child. You must look like a queen. Remind them who you are. Make sure that the proper people approach you. Things are different here than in Spire City," Auna said.

I scowled into the mirror, wishing she would tell me something I didn't already know.

"I miss Havemont," I said. "People were less complicated there. The only person who doesn't behave like a sycophant is Amaranthine, and that's only because I have nothing to offer her." That wasn't entirely true, of course, but Auna didn't need to know about my research.

"Don't waste a moment's thought on her, my lady. I'm sure it won't be much longer before she's married off and you won't have to see her again."

My stomach clenched at the thought. Mare, married? I couldn't see it, and the suggestion irritated me. Sometimes it seemed like she was the only person in Mynaria with any sense, even though she managed to find her way in and out of trouble as often and nimbly as a mountain goat.

"Try not to let Lady Amaranthine vex you. Soon you will have a husband and children, and they will keep you far too busy to think of home or of the princess," Auna said.

Her knowing smile unnerved me, as did the thought of children. While I wanted them, they had always seemed so far off. But now it was entirely possible I could be a mother by this time next year.

"Of course, Auna. You are right." I tried to smooth the brooding expression from my face. Auna's ability to channel my mother terrified me sometimes.

"In the meantime you should focus on your relationships with the other nobles as your mother suggested," Auna said more gently.

"Everyone wants something from me. I don't think I have that much to give." I chose my words carefully, knowing that through Auna they could one day find their way to my mother's ears. While my face remained impassive, anxiety still gnawed at me. Thandi had been a wonderful resource in deciphering the true intentions of the lesser nobles, rising steadily in my estimation as it became clear how well he knew the intricacies of his court. But of the noblewomen I'd met so far, only Ellaeni had impressed me with her lack of obsequiousness and her neutrality about court happenings.

Perhaps that was why Amaranthine was so threatening—she seemed full of secrets, but also transparent in a way no one else was. There wasn't a thing in the world she could possibly want from me other than a pair of eyes to pore through library books. If she were to be my friend, it would be on her terms and by her choice. Whether or not I liked her hardly mattered, even if I did extend an invitation to her for something other than horseback riding.

Research on the knife should have taken precedence. I wanted to be able to give her some useful information, if only to prevent any further harm to the members of the royal family. Rising to the task might prove to her that I was something more than a dull-witted courtier. I needed her as an ally. I wanted her as a friend.

When she told me on the trail ride to invite her over, she had given me an opportunity. No queen would turn down an opportunity, and vacillating about it wouldn't solve any problems. The moment Auna left the room, I smoothed my skirts and called for a page to deliver an invitation.

SIXTEEN ✦ *Mare*

GETTING OUT OF THE CASTLE WAS THE HARD PART. Getting directions and meeting times at the Deaf Dog was the expensive part. But getting into the Recusants' gathering place looked like it might be easier than I had expected.

Around the time the Directorate was probably beginning their pointless questioning of the archer who had tried to kill Dennalcia, Nils and I stood outside the abandoned Sanctuary where the Recusants were purported to meet. The neighborhood smelled like a stall overdue for cleaning, and the few people we saw scurried away from us into the shadows like bugs. A dilapidated set of wooden chimes hanging near the door creaked against one another in something too weak to be called a breeze.

It was easy to see why the Recusants had chosen the building as their meeting place. A wide swath of weed-choked ground separated it from the other nearby buildings. All that space between the buildings meant that in broad daylight there was nowhere to hide and spy. The front entrance appeared to be boarded shut.

"Well, we'll have to break in," I said.

"Subtlety has always been your strength." Nils chuckled.

I shrugged and started off toward the building, but Nils grabbed my arm. "What if there are people in there?"

"We'll tell them we're looking for a place to get married and are charmed by the old-fashioned majesty of this fine building."

"You're deranged."

"Let's try the back," I said.

We stomped over the spindly weeds through what must have once been the temple garden and made our way along the side of the structure. The high windows were boarded up with planks streaked with bird chalk, abandoned nests wedged between them. Across the street the clang of a blacksmith's hammer rang out, the only sound breaking the silence of the early afternoon.

Around the back we found a second entrance, also boarded up. A white circle the size of my palm marked the topmost board near the top of the frame. I tugged the handle, not entirely certain that the whole thing wouldn't fall apart when I yanked on it, but the door swung open on silent hinges. The boarded-up exterior was a ruse.

The Recusants had left much of the interior intact—restored it even. While the apses looked as though they had never been painted with aspects of the gods, the floor had a brightly painted star, each point corresponding to one of the gods' colors. But they were in the wrong order. I frowned, perplexed.

"There's nowhere to hide in here," Nils said, surveying the heart of the Sanctuary.

"Sure there is," I said, and pointed to the cross-work of beams on the ceiling. The Sanctuary was designed in an old style, with notched beams made for climbing that would allow the clerics to open the high windows during summer. The windows, of course, were gone, but the beams remained.

Nils looked a little sick. "You're suggesting that we hang from the rafters like a couple of bats?"

"If it gets the job done," I said.

"You first," he said.

"Fine by me," I answered, and pointed to the closest beam. He boosted me up and I climbed into the deepest chapel—the one for the wind god—and concealed myself in the wide well of the window between the boards that had been haphazardly nailed to both the inside and outside of the frame.

"Can you see me?" I asked.

"Not at all," Nils said.

Dust motes danced through the light slanting in through the slats of the boards across the window. Nils looked like a mirage, like some artist's idea of the perfect man.

"The light suits you," I said.

Instead of responding, he stepped a few paces away, toward the front door. I was inching forward to crawl back out when an unfamiliar voice asked, "Can I help you?"

I froze.

"Hello," Nils said, and cleared his throat.

I slid backward as quietly as I could, tucking myself into my hiding space.

"Are you new?" the voice asked. "The service doesn't begin

for another half a sunlength."

"Service?" Nils asked.

"You must be lost." The voice sounded disappointed, and female.

"Well, I could be convinced to stay," Nils said. I could almost hear the wink and smile accompanying the phrase. The owner of the voice must be pretty. Over Nils's shoulder I could see only the barest hint of a head crowned with dark curls.

"It's risky," she said. "Not everyone likes the kind of service we do here."

"Well, I'm nothing if not a man of service. Tell me more," Nils said.

The girl giggled and I rolled my eyes. How did he get away with it? But I knew. It was that chiseled jawline, those warm brown eyes, and the way he looked at people like they mattered regardless of their station. And even though by now he had to know that he always got what he wanted when it came to women, there was always still a hesitation, a question, in the way he stepped close—always asking for permission before he touched. She must have seen it too.

"You can stand in back with me," she said. "And if you decide not to stay, slip out the door. Not everyone wants to join the cause."

"Who could resist an invitation from a girl with your eyes?" Nils said. "Show me the way."

She laughed, and they walked off toward the front door of the temple, out of earshot. I breathed a sigh of relief. I was committed to my hiding place now, though. Eventually other people trickled in, settling on blankets on the floor until the Sanctuary filled with a low hum of conversation. To anyone who barged in, it would have looked like an oddly timed service for the Six. They could have passed it off as a prayer group, the very thing they supposedly stood against.

The conversations in the room died down to a hush as a man with a gray beard came to the front of the temple and stepped up onto the dais. He wore the simple clothes of a craftsman—perhaps a cobbler. He opened a leather satchel and unwrapped a silver bowl that he set on the table.

"Anyone who wishes to be tested may come forward," Graybeard said.

Three young men stood and came hesitantly up to the dais. Each one held a hand over Graybeard's silver bowl, and each time Graybeard shook his head. Then, as they took their seats, he put his own hand over the bowl, which lit up with a soft, silvery light.

"May the Six protect us and our Affinities," he said.

That he asked the Six for protection startled me. I thought the Recusants believed only in the power of magic, not the Six, but that didn't seem to be the case.

Graybeard led them through something that almost took the form of a praise day service, the difference being that instead of merely acknowledging each of the Six Gods, he also acknowledged the Affinities tied to them. By the end of the service, I was truly puzzled. There hadn't been any secret information, or plans to destroy the royal family, or even any mention of the alliance. At the end, everyone trickled out of the Sanctuary except for four people who clustered up near the dais until all the others had departed. I hoped Nils had found somewhere to lurk nearby.

"Yashti is lost to us," Graybeard said. "They're questioning her today. No doubt her treason will be discovered and she'll be punished. We'll soon have to relocate."

Thank the Six I'd found them before that happened. I held my breath and shifted my weight, trying to ease the cramps from crouching for so long.

"It was only a matter of time," a thin woman with sharp, shrewlike features said. "They were always extremists, and she hasn't been right since Alen died. It's no surprise she'd run off on her own, delusional enough to think she could single-handedly assassinate a member of the royal family. Of course the spears got her."

I leaned closer to catch the softer voice of the next person who spoke.

"She and Alen would both still be here if they hadn't taken the shadow man's money," said a younger man with hunched shoulders. Though he was the youngest of their group, he had a weariness about him that suggested he'd lived through more than most his age.

"Yashti made her choice, and we cannot save her now," Graybeard said. "If we spend time hunting anyone, it should be the source of that other eruption of magic. All I've been able to determine is that the signature was like Alen's—but he had already been dead for two days. There's someone out there with a fire Affinity. Someone exceptionally strong."

It sounded as though they were talking about whoever was responsible for my father's would-be assassin going up in flames. If they didn't know who had done it, they couldn't be the ones responsible—so who could?

"If we find that person, they may kill us," the shrew replied. "We don't know whose side they're on, and there aren't enough of us to take on someone that powerful."

"We should work on the magic itself," the young man said. "Just because we've been labeled Recusants doesn't mean we should lose track of our original purpose. We don't have time to hunt down rogue members of the Circle or waste time trying to find a mage who surely would have already found us if he wanted to. If we work together, there's still a chance we can create some kind of siphon to reduce the ambient magic here and make it safer to use and develop our powers. That burst we felt released quite a bit, but it's building up again. If we could set up a loop that would keep going in perpetuity without necessitating our presence, we could—"

"Is no use." The last member of their group finally spoke, a small woman with dark gray-streaked hair whose features almost reminded me of Dennaleia's. Her voice carried a thick accent, the consonants sharp. Zumordan. "Even after burst, is like playing with fire with hands soaked in kerosene. Magic here is so thick you can cut."

The Recusants were working with Zumordans—that much, at least, was true. But what did it mean? I kneaded worriedly at my foot to ease the pins and needles.

"We shouldn't try to do this without Alen," said the shrew. "We should focus on continuing to use our smaller spells as we always have."

"I agree. We don't have Alen anymore. We're the only ones left," Graybeard said.

"It won't be long before they come for us too," the youngest man said. "We need to try to set up something that will help mitigate the danger even if they do."

"Building a siphon is futile," Graybeard said. "And those without any sensitivity to magic won't notice the difference either way. To do that we need people stronger than us. People with more knowledge."

"But with those in Zumorda . . ." The youngest man's voice grew even softer.

I pressed my ear to a crack between the boards to try to make out his words. It immediately gave way and crashed to the temple floor. Panic raced through me. All four of the mages turned to me at the same time, shock registering on their faces. Then anger.

"Stop her!" Graybeard shouted.

I kicked the boards on the outside of the window and they gave way with a crack, tumbling to the ground. It was a long drop.

I jumped anyway.

My ankles smarted with the impact even as I tried to roll to catch my fall—right through a patch of weeds and rocky ground that left me stained with smears of golden dandelion and bruised from the sharp pebbles. I leaped to my feet and stopped only long enough for a whip-poor-will call, a signal that Nils and I had sometimes used in the past. Then I ran.

The four Recusants came boiling out of the temple behind me. I wished I could have somehow communicated to them that I didn't necessarily have a problem with what they were doing. I didn't care if they had access to the High Adytum or not, or fiddled with magic or not. I only wanted to know that my family would be safe, but first, I had to make sure I was.

A whistle pierced the air and I veered toward it, intercepting Nils at the next cross street. We raced through alleys until my lungs burned and my feet smarted from pounding against the stones. We reentered the castle, breathless.

"They probably followed us, you know," Nils said. "I don't know how far back we lost them. It might not have been far enough."

I nodded. "Without doubt."

We took a side entrance up to my rooms.

"Where'd you get off to, anyway?" I asked, still trying to catch my breath.

"Jilli was quite accommodating of my need to stay close to the Sanctuary after the service ended."

"Of course she was."

He grinned but said no more.

I filled him in on what I'd learned in the temple before it all went wrong.

"So they're working with Zumordans and using magic . . . but they still believe in the Six?" he asked.

A chime sounded in the hall, and Nils cursed.

"My shift is in less than a sunlength," he said. "I have to go."

I nodded. "We'll come up with another plan to get out soon. There's so much more we need to look into."

We hugged, and as he left, a page arrived at my door.

"Message from Princess Dennaleia, Your Highness." The page bowed. "She invites you to stop by her chambers after the evening meal. Would you like to send a response?"

Now that I knew the archer had been acting alone rather than with the Recusants, and had been paid by a third party, I had a side to the story she probably wouldn't have heard. Though our lessons would start up again the next afternoon, it couldn't hurt to see her before then.

"Yes, please. Tell her I'll be there. Thanks," I said.

The page ducked out.

But in addition to wanting to compare notes on the Recusants, I found myself glad she hadn't forgotten me in the three days since I'd seen her last.

SEVENTEEN   🔥 *Dennaleia*

WHEN I RECEIVED AMARANTHINE'S REPLY AFTER
dinner, several things struck me at once: my furniture was arranged
all wrong, my hair was styled much too formally, and I had no
idea how I was going to entertain her. Anxiety overcame me at the
thought of her in my rooms. This was my first chance to make a more
personal connection with her, and she was my only hope to stop
the Directorate before my secret could be discovered. Moreover, I
wanted to impress her—to show her that there was more to me than
my clumsy attempts to improve at riding.

I sat down at my vanity and began pulling pins from my hair.
Calling Auna to do a casual twist seemed silly, and I didn't want
her to see how agitated I was over a visit from Amaranthine. With
each pin deposited on the table, looping curls fell around my face,
sticking out in all directions. I groaned in dismay. It still smelled
lovely from the perfumes Auna had used in it that afternoon, but

the visual impact was rather like angry mountain squirrels had been nesting in it for weeks. Gritting my teeth, I fought it back up, a few messy curls escaping. It would have to do.

I ordered in some tea, mostly so I'd have something in my hands to fuss with in the event of awkward silences, and set to work tugging furniture into an arrangement more appropriate for entertaining. It felt wrong to ask anyone to do it for me, since it wouldn't be an important visit in the eyes of anyone else. A casual dress completed my preparations. Looking in the mirror, I worried that I looked more peasant than princess, but as I contemplated another change in wardrobe, a knock sounded from my receiving room.

"Princess Amaranthine, Your Highness." The liegeman outside my door announced her as she strode in. While it had been many sunlengths since she might have been on horseback, she still wore breeches, though they were far too clean to have spent any time in the barn today.

"Good evening, Your Highness," she said with a tinge of her usual sarcasm.

"Good evening, Princess Amaranthine," I replied in an equally mocking tone.

"Ugh! I wish you would stop calling me that," she said.

"Well then, don't call me Your Highness or Princess," I retorted. "I've heard nothing else from anyone all day long and I'm sick to death of it."

"Fair enough," she replied, this time with a genuine smile. Her gray eyes burned right through me. Without the focus of my riding lesson, there was no structure for our interaction. I didn't know what to say. I pressed a finger into my palm to quiet the tingling there.

"Would you like some tea?" I poured a cup before waiting for an answer, eager to give my hands something to do.

"Thank you." She took the cup I poured. "It's nice that the nights are starting to get cooler. We're almost to the time when you start to value a cup of tea. Or better yet, hot chocolate."

"Autumn was always one of my favorite seasons at home, too. It's different there, though. The changes were more dramatic. Flowers in spring, the best food in the summer. Leaves changing color in the fall, and snow in the winter." I shifted nervously. Why was I babbling on about the weather when there were so many more important things at hand?

"Snow?" Amaranthine asked. She strode over to a chair and sat down, crossing her legs at the knee. Her teacup sat cradled in her hands, tiny ripples catching the light as she blew on the hot liquid.

"Oh yes. More snow than you can imagine if you haven't been to the mountains," I said, remembering the great banks of white built up against the castle walls in winter. It wouldn't be long before the first snow came to my home, the storm riding in with that strange metallic smell it always had. This was the first year I wouldn't be there to run outside to let the flakes melt on my tongue for good luck.

"So what did you do all those years trapped inside for the winter?"

I thought back to my time at home, searching my memories for something meaningful to tell her. "I spent most of my days in lessons of some sort. Far too many manners and meals were involved. And a lot of books, though I didn't mind those." Amaranthine didn't need to know about all the cold winter nights I had spent figuring out what I could do with fire.

"Not to be offensive, but I think I would've found all that quite dull."

"Sometimes it was. But my marriage decree was signed when I was six, so my whole life went into preparing to become queen of Mynaria. Except the overlooked detail of learning to ride a horse."

"Maybe it was fate's way of bringing us together." Her mouth turned up on one side.

"I doubt that," I said. "You certainly weren't part of my parents' plan for me to be the perfect princess." But she should have been. No one else in Mynaria had seen what I was capable of and given me the opportunity to help the crown.

"Well, fate and your parents might have completely different ideas about what your life is going to be like. So keep that in mind, too."

"Fate and my parents both seem to have things pretty well plotted out for me," I said. "It's not as though I can run off and change my mind about what I want to do." And honestly, it had never occurred to me. The certainty of a plan had always brought me comfort. But now, having traveled across two kingdoms to get to Mynaria, the world seemed a much larger place, and I wondered sometimes what another life would be like.

"Maybe it's best that you don't know what else is out there that you might have done in another life." She spoke without sarcasm. "You'd end up with a lot of regrets. Or wishing for things to be different."

"But that's already how I feel," I blurted out. "I've spent so much time being groomed for this that I have no idea what I want. And no one but you lets me do anything useful anyway. But learning to ride—doing something so new and different—makes me feel more alive than I've felt in a long time. Maybe forever." And so did sitting with her, a fact that made me more nervous by the moment. It frightened me how important it had become to me to win her over.

Amaranthine looked at me appraisingly. "And do you like riding?"

"I like it for what it is teaching me. And I'm getting to like the horses better now that they don't seem to have as much of an appetite for my fingers." I smiled.

Amaranthine laughed. "I think it's more that you've learned how not to feed your fingers to them."

"So . . . why didn't you come to the questioning today?" I finally asked.

"Having all those idiots in one room was the perfect chance to escape, of course," she said.

"You were outside the walls?" I couldn't believe the audacity of it. If I wasn't safe on the trails within the castle walls, how could she expect to be safe wandering the city streets?

"Yes," she said. "If you tell me about the questioning, I'll tell you what I saw."

I told her about the archer's admission of responsibility for Casmiel, and about her husband who had died. "But I don't think she was responsible for the attempt on the king. She didn't have any information on the weapon or know anything about the magic used that day."

"Well, I'm not so sure the Recusants are exactly what we've been told," she said. "Yes, they're opposed to the alliance, but I overheard them talking about the archer. Apparently she was an extremist, acting alone when she came after you. She and her husband had taken money from someone they referred to only as 'the shadow man.' The rest of them seem to have some other agenda, talking about a bunch of magic nonsense I didn't understand. Something about building a siphon because the ambient magic in Mynaria is too volatile."

I almost dropped my teacup. No wonder my gift had been constantly out of control. That was the missing piece. Something about Mynaria itself was fueling the volatility in my power. More important, there were people out there who knew about magic— people who could actually control it. Maybe they could tell me how to shut mine off, or protect myself. If they could siphon magic from a kingdom, surely they could remove it from a person. If I could get out of the castle, I could ask.

"I'll keep looking for answers about the knife," I said. It felt like so little in the face of what she'd done.

"So are you going to show me this silly instrument or what?" She gestured to my harp, which stood ready in the corner, the inlaid spruce warm and inviting in the evening light. Its presence offered the comfort of home, the strings so familiar that I couldn't remember not knowing how to play.

"I suppose I could," I said, feeling a rush of nerves. All the music I knew from memory seemed too trite and courtly for Amaranthine. I opened the trunk at the foot of my bed and rummaged through my music until my hands fell on an unusual piece I hadn't played in several years.

"I think we'll start with this," I said, and handed the music to her so I could put the rest away. Our fingers brushed, sending my thoughts scattering like a flock of birds. Magic hummed in my fingertips, and I feared she could feel the heat of it when I touched her.

I sat at my harp, took a deep breath, then fell to playing and quickly forgot Amaranthine's presence. The piece began with unusual rhythms, paced deliberately, and then blossomed into increasing complexities. My fingers rose and fell with the changing tempos, weaving melody and countermelody into notes that hung in the air like stars. The music washed away my nervousness, filling me with tranquillity and purpose. Eventually the melodies departed as they had come, intricately finding their way out from the rhythms and back into a simple and haunting tune that came to a dark conclusion.

I let the final notes ring in the air and looked up at Amaranthine. She stared back at me with a soft expression I had never seen on her before. My face warmed. Her appreciation for my playing sent a heady rush of pleasure through me—one I had never received from any other audience.

"I don't think you needed the music," she said. "Your eyes were closed for at least the last twenty bars of that. It was stunning."

"Oh, it's nothing," I said, though the compliment set off sparks inside me.

"I'd love to hear something else." She leaned forward.

"What do you want to hear?" I asked.

"Anything," she replied.

My mind rushed through the options before settling on something I was certain she would know: "The Soldier's Cup." It was a Mynarian tune that had originated as a drinking song but became so popular that even the smallest child could sing the refrain. I smiled at Amaranthine and began to play. She laughed as she recognized the melody, and as I progressed through the simple song, she hummed along. I hoped for her to sing, but she never went beyond humming the chorus.

I leaped into another song without pausing to ask for a request. She didn't even hum that one, so I skipped the bridge and cut to another. It wasn't until I played a slow, sweet ballad that she finally sang along. The words were so soft at first that I could barely make them out, but as her confidence grew, her voice strengthened into a rich alto that rose and fell with the melody, smooth and dark as Havemont velvet. I picked up a descant above her, letting her carry the melody as I added another dimension to the music. The song had several verses, and with each one we sounded better. She startled me by picking up a low harmony when I dropped back to the melody, finding her way to the notes like a trained musician.

"I haven't sung in forever," she said when we finished, her cheeks flushed.

"You should never stop," I said without thinking.

She didn't respond, but blushed and turned her head to the side. This Amaranthine was not the prickly girl I knew from my riding lessons or the troublemaker always outside the castle walls. She was something else, something more—a person who could fall into the music with me and leave us both breathless.

I started another song that would suit her voice, and she picked up again. We played for many sunlengths beyond the time for a polite visit, and finally stopped when my fingers cramped and the remains of the tea had long ago grown cold. Deep in the night, with tired fingers and a weary voice, I felt like myself for the first time since arriving in Mynaria.

When it came time for her to go, I walked her to the door, both of us dragging our feet as if it would slow time itself.

"I wish you didn't have to go." The words fell out of my mouth, and I blushed.

"Well, I can't exactly sleep on the floor in front of your hearth like a pet," she replied with a smile.

"I know you can't, but I had so much fun tonight. This is the best time I've had with anyone since I got here."

"Don't tell my brother. He's bound to be jealous." Her eyes glowed in the low light of the room, her gray irises darkening into pools that threatened to swallow me whole. "I had a wonderful time too. Thank you." She reached out.

Something welled up in me, a desire for her to touch me. My whole world narrowed to the two of us and her outstretched arm, followed by a rush of disappointment when she dropped it back to her side.

"I'll see you tomorrow," she finally said. "Good night, Denna." The nickname warmed me like an embrace.

"Good night, Mare," I said, but she was already out the door and down the hall. I craned my head around the liegeman outside my door until she disappeared around the corner, and then I reentered my rooms with a sigh. Her absence left my chambers colder.

I took the swordsmithing book to bed with me and read by the light of the oil lamp, filled with humming magic that wouldn't let me sleep. Just when my eyes grew almost too heavy to stay open, I stumbled over something interesting in the chapter on regional differences in forging techniques. The book stated that steel forged by easterners had an unusual rippled appearance thanks to the extra folding of the steel. If I remembered correctly, the dagger used in the assassination attempt had been bright and shiny.

If that was true, there was no way the blade could be Zumordan.

EIGHTEEN

✦ *Mare*

I SADDLED FLICKER BARELY A SUNLENGTH PAST DAWN and joined Captain Ryka and the liegemen trainees for a session of mounted archery. It felt more necessary than ever after Denna's close call out on the trails. A sweet melody still played through my mind from my evening with her, filling me with excess energy. It took more effort than usual to get Flicker into our familiar rhythm, the beat of his canter easing the tension in us both until we rode balanced and steady, the snorts of his breath as regular as a metronome. When we queued up to shoot, I boldly lined up right behind the captain, a spot no one ever wanted because she was impossible to outdo. Her leather jerkin fitted her like a calfskin riding glove, simple and scarred as those worn by her liegemen. Behind me, the trainees muttered challenges to one another out of Captain Ryka's earshot.

"A pitcher of ale for the best score," one man suggested.

"And a round for his or her friends, too!"

"Forget ale. I want the first shot when we go out to round up more Recusants," another said. "Filthy heretics."

"An even better prize!" another trainee agreed.

Trainees tended to be overzealous due to inexperience, but it bothered me how pervasive the hatred of the Recusants had become. It crept into every conversation like poison.

Ryka moved like an extension of her chestnut mare as she nudged the horse up into a canter from the line. She nocked and shot with precision and efficiency, her arrows flying swift and true at the exact peak of her horse's canter strides. There was no ego or showmanship in it—only the practiced motions of someone who had spent years doing little else.

I pulled together my energy and tried to imitate Ryka's stony calm. By the time it was my turn to shoot, Flicker and I moved as one. My three shots departed with the elegance of a math equation, each arrow striking the heart of the target. The trainees gaped after my second round of bull's-eyes alongside the captain's, asking what I'd had for breakfast and where they could get some.

Though the archery had been taxing on both my mind and my body, I stayed lively as I curried Flicker afterward. Knowing more about the Recusants gave me a sense of purpose, as did knowing I had Denna on my side.

"Mare!"

I looked up to see Denna herself hurrying toward me.

"Mare, I found something," she said breathlessly, her flushed cheeks the same shade of rose pink as the dress she wore.

"What is it?"

She came closer and whispered urgently. "The knife. I think I found out something that might help us with the knife." Her green eyes shone as she gave Flicker a pat on the shoulder in greeting.

"You did?" Hope surged in me.

She nodded emphatically, running her hand down Flicker's burnished neck.

"Let me put Flicker out. We can talk outside," I said. The barn bustled with activity, and I didn't want anyone to overhear. After one last brush of Flicker's coat, I led him to the pasture, Denna following behind. With the wind at our backs, the scent of her rose perfume wafted over me, making me wish she were closer. My preoccupation with her since last night was starting to scare me a little. Singing with her had unlocked something between us, and now I couldn't turn back.

Flicker took off into his paddock with the usual fanfare. I stepped upwind of Denna and pushed my silly thoughts away as I hung Flicker's halter on the fence.

"What did you find out?" I asked.

"I think the knife is a fake," she said. "It's forged in the style of a Zumordan blade, but the metal is wrong. I remember it being very shiny, which could mean that the steel wasn't forged correctly."

"How in the Sixth Hell can you tell that?" I peered at her.

"I found a section in this book on swordsmithing that I've been reading. If the blade were Zumordan, there would be a grain-like pattern in the steel. I should have found the information sooner, but the book is at least eight hundred pages and I'm only halfway through."

"You're amazing," I said. She had found the key we needed. If the blade was fake, it could point to an enemy other than Zumorda.

Then we could figure out where the forgery had come from.

"Oh no, not at all. You could have found it yourself if you'd been the one doing the reading." She favored me with a demure smile, filling me with warmth that had nothing to do with the sun. I liked it when she smiled at me like that, which made me uncomfortable. I shouldn't allow myself to be so captivated by someone betrothed to my brother.

Her eyes sparked with excitement. "Perhaps someone else in the cresthaven might know more. That time you came through my window, you said you'd been in the city. Is there a contact you might be able to use to find out where a replica of a weapon could be acquired? I have one idea, but it's not anyone I know well enough to be a trustworthy source."

"Contacts in the city I can help with. So can Nils. But how are we going to verify the blade when Captain Ryka has it?"

"We'll simply have to steal it." She stood straighter, taking on a stubborn air.

"Taking something from the captain's ready room is an invitation for multiple stab wounds. I could never do it alone," I said. Even as I spoke the words, a plan formed in my mind. The patrols rotated regularly, and I could get the schedule from Nils, and it wouldn't take much practice to remind my fingers how to pick a lock with a bent hairpin. . . .

"I'll help you," Denna said.

My thought process ground to a halt. "Not a chance. If you get injured or caught sneaking around in the middle of the night . . . I don't even want to think about the repercussions." While trouble was no stranger to me, Denna couldn't risk getting involved.

"You're the one who got me tangled up in this." She set her jaw stubbornly, determination flashing in her eyes. "You can't ask for my help and then expect me to bow out as soon as it gets hard. Besides, I could be a distraction. I don't have to actually do anything that would result in stab wounds."

I didn't like the direction the conversation was going.

"Make me a deal," she said. "I'll help you get the knife back. If our suspicions are correct, you handle telling the king, and I'll stay out of that. In return, you take me outside the walls when you go searching for more information."

"You're joking." If having her help me get the knife back was a bad idea, taking her into the city where she could be injured, kidnapped, or killed was a thousand times worse. Getting drunk and swimming naked in the horse pasture pond in broad daylight had less potential for disaster.

"Not in the slightest."

"But why?"

"If I'm to be queen someday, I should see the city from the perspective of its people. I should try to understand them so that I may rule more wisely."

Her reasoning sounded questionable to me. But damn it all, I needed to find out who had tried to kill my father.

"It's not safe. What if someone recognizes you?"

"How could they?" she countered. "I haven't left the palace grounds since Casmiel's death. We didn't do a cresthaven tour or even a formal introduction due to the safety concerns. There's no way the king would let me out of here."

"Which also makes it even more difficult to sneak you out."

"We'll come up with a disguise of some sort. Please? I'll do anything you want," she begged.

"Let me think about it," I said.

"There's no time to think about it," she said. "This is the first lead we have. It should be pursued right away."

She was right. But sneaking her into town was a terrible idea. Still, I was a tiny bit intrigued by the challenge of getting her outside the walls.

"All right. We can talk through the details after your riding lesson this afternoon. I have to get back to my rooms for a fitting." I made a face.

"Yes!" She clasped her hands together and bounced on her toes with a brilliant smile.

No one else's happiness had ever been so contagious to me. Like the night before, I wanted to reach out and touch her, to somehow acknowledge the energy that crackled between us like lightning. But I didn't dare. Instead I stood there smiling back, wondering what I'd gotten myself into.

NINETEEN   🔥 *Dennaleia*

AFTER MY DISCOVERY IN THE SWORDSMITHING BOOK,
I thought nothing could bring down my high spirits. But as Ellaeni
and I enjoyed lunch in the queen's bower where my bazaar had
been held, thunder growled and rain began to splatter on the stone
pathways of the garden outside. The wind turned cool, gusting into
the room as lightning danced across the sky. Servants rushed to pull
wooden shutters into place to close off the indoor portion of the
bower from the garden, and raindrops knocked on the wood slats
until they pounded down in a rush, a song of taps and drips.

"Late-summer storms are always the strongest," Ellaeni remarked.

"So much for my riding lesson," I said, disappointed, jabbing
my fork into a thick slice of yellow-and-purple tomato in my salad.
Since my talk with Mare about the knife in the morning, the next
step in our plans had been constantly on my mind.

"Are you enjoying riding?" Ellaeni asked with a smile.

"Amaranthine seems to have a strong personality."

"That's one way to put it. But there is more to her than people realize." Like the way she could sing.

"I would like to know her better," Ellaeni said. "She reminds me of someone back home. Someone I miss dearly." Ellaeni glanced out a rain-blurred window, her expression wistful.

"I miss home, too," I said. Though Ellaeni and I came from different places, we had that in common.

"In Trindor I had my own ship," she said. "A crew that answered to me."

"Really?" I asked, intrigued. It seemed entirely out of character for someone as shy as Ellaeni, who could barely read poetry without stuttering.

"Yes. Much like horsemanship here, mastering the sea is a rite of passage for the Trindori. Coming here, being landlocked . . . I'm grateful to see rain. The water god has not forgotten me after all," she said, sketching his symbol in front of her. "All these dry days, these clothes I can't move in . . . I've almost forgotten who I am." There was a sharpness to her then as the rain washed away her diffidence, a flash of the girl who knew herself.

"Why are you here?" I asked. "Could you not better serve your people as a captain?"

"I still plan to," she said. "But my mother is old friends with Hilara, and the two of them decided I ought to spend at least one season inland." She impaled a tomato wedge with unnecessary force.

I did my best to keep my face neutral, but some quirk of my lips must have betrayed me.

"I see Hilara is no friend of yours, either," Ellaeni observed.

"It's no secret that Havemont was not her first choice for an alliance," I said, not sure how much Ellaeni knew.

"What's no secret is her obsession with Zumordans and their magic," Ellaeni said. "She probably thinks they have some spell that will give her eternal youth and beauty. Perhaps they do."

"Is there any magic used among your people?" I tried to ask the question casually but felt the hum of my own magic rise with my curiosity.

Ellaeni shook her head. "No, but some Trindori have a bond with the water god that allows them to sense things like storms and red tides—the sea sense. It's a passive gift. Some people don't even believe it's real, but those with the sea sense do seem to have uncommon luck. They survive. I don't have it myself, but one of my crew members does. I've seen it enough to believe."

I sat back in my chair. At what point was a line drawn between an Affinity and a bond with a god? The gods were revered throughout Mynaria, but those with gifts condemned. Religion and magic had to be connected in some way, but if that was true, the chasm in people's perceptions of the two did not make sense.

A knock sounded at the door of the bower, and a page entered the room.

"Message from Princess Amaranthine, Your Highness," he said. "No lesson today due to the weather. Instead she has invited you for a visit to her receiving room as soon as you'd like to stop by."

"Thank you," I said. "Please send my acceptance."

The page bowed and hurried away with my message.

"She must like you if you've garnered that sort of invitation," Ellaeni noted.

Heat of a decidedly nonmagical variety rose in my cheeks. The idea that Mare liked me was both thrilling and scary—thrilling because it seemed like I'd won over one of the most difficult people in the castle, and scary because my focus on my duties was veering off course. I needed to concentrate on the success of the alliance and on Thandi.

Ellaeni simply smiled. "Feel free to go," she said. "I can see you have places to be. Thank you so much for the invitation to lunch."

"The pleasure was mine," I said, and squeezed her hand in farewell.

Mare's chambers were only a short walk from the bower, and there was no point in returning to my rooms. Auna would badger me into setting up some entertainment for the nobles or encourage me to respond to my mother's letter. I wasn't in the mood to lie to my mother today. I picked up my skirts and hurried toward Mare's rooms, but as I rounded the last corner, I collided with someone.

"Oh, excuse me!" I stumbled to the side and dropped my skirts to catch my balance.

"Princess Dennaleia," Thandilimon greeted me. A smile came easily to his face.

"I'm so sorry." I flushed with embarrassment and stepped away from the wall.

"I apologize," he said. "I wasn't watching where I was going. You're exactly the person I was hoping to find. I thought your riding lesson might be canceled due to the storm."

"Yes, it was," I said. His apology made me feel even more self-conscious. It certainly wasn't his fault that I had nearly knocked him over. I bit my lip and looked down the hallway past his shoulder toward Mare's room and took a few small steps in that direction, hoping he would take that as a hint that I still had somewhere to be.

"Wonderful! In that case, would you like to accompany me for a walk? I was hoping to show you a few areas of the castle that you might not have discovered on your own." He offered me his arm.

"Actually, I was on my way to see Amaranthine," I said.

"I'm sure you could use some relief from her by now," Thandi said.

I hesitated. It should have been easy to overthrow my plans with Mare for my future husband. The prince came first, and my duty was to him.

"All right," I conceded, hoping my frustration wasn't visible on my face. I took his arm and we started off back the way I had come.

"I apologize that I've been absent lately. The Directorate has been terribly busy questioning the Recusants we've dragged in. Father expects me to attend every session." He looked down at me as we walked, his blue eyes searching my face.

"That must be quite tiring, my lord. Have they discovered any leads on the knife attack yet?" If I was going to be stuck spending time with him, I might as well get some information to take to Mare.

"No, nothing yet. We're trying to find out who their Zumordan supporters are, but Hilara keeps slowing the process. She's still pressing for some kind of treaty or alliance with them."

"That's puzzling. One would think everyone would be of a mind to find the people responsible as quickly as possible, no matter who they are," I said.

"Agreed. Either way, I'm sorry we haven't had more time to spend together lately. It's been so difficult with the castle locked down, and before that with all your riding lessons." His earnest expression made me feel even guiltier for not caring.

"Yes, the riding lessons take up quite a bit of time," I said.

"I hope my sister is minding what few manners she has."

"We may be quite different, but I don't think she's a bad influence," I said. It was the most diplomatic response I could manage.

"Of course not. I'm sure a lady of your taste would not be swayed by any of her wilder ideas."

If only he knew why I'd been in such a hurry, or that I had every intention of having her help me get outside the castle walls.

"I don't think she's different in a bad way," I said. "The expectations placed on her aren't the same as those on you or me. She is who she is partly because of that, as we are who we are because of the expectations placed on us."

"It's generous to think about it that way," he replied.

Our conversation cut off as he released my arm so we could walk single file down a narrow staircase near the back of the royal wing. I stepped carefully, half certain that I'd tumble to the bottom of the stairs in a heap of gray silk and further ruined dignity.

At the bottom of the stairs we stopped in front of a door. The wood was heavy and thick, riddled with scars of age. Thandilimon lifted a lamp off a nearby hook and escorted me inside, his hand on the small of my back. Lamplight pooled at our feet as we entered an empty hall, our steps echoing against the stone floor. Wall sconces were fewer and farther between than in the castle upstairs, the areas between them dim and laced with shadows.

Thandilimon surprised me by taking my hand instead of

offering his arm again. My heart beat faster. I breathed in deeply to try to calm myself.

"This is the way to the armory," Thandilimon said.

"Pardon me, my lord, but is there something you wanted to show me down here?" Being alone with him in the dark made me nervous, and the longer we wandered around, the less time I would have to spend with Mare.

"To be honest, I just needed to get away from everyone for a little while. Having so many Directorate meetings to discuss Zumorda and the Recusants is exhausting. I doubt there's anyone down here except the liegemen who patrol now and again. I know you probably aren't interested in weaponry, but this is where we house the unique treasures the crown has accumulated over the years. You might be curious to know about the passages, too."

"Passages?" I said.

"Yes. There are underground passages that lead to different areas within the castle, and also outside to the barn. They provide us escape routes in the case of a siege. That's the entrance to the armory." Thandilimon pointed out a heavy door to our left. "If you keep following this passageway, you'll end up near the great hall. The library is on the left about halfway there."

"There is a back way into the library?" I perked up. It would have been useful to know that when doing my research on Zumorda.

"Indeed. And if you follow the southern path from the staircase we came down, you'll find a tunnel out to the barn. It comes out in the feed room. I don't recommend going down there, though. It's not lit, and if you take the one next to it by mistake, you'll end up in the back of the dungeon."

"I can't imagine why I would need to go down any of them," I said, already wondering if there were any that could help Mare and me get into town.

"Mare and I often use the barn tunnel when we were trying to skip out on our history lessons. I'm not sure they ever did figure out how we were getting down there." He smiled at what must have been a fond memory.

Something in his grin brought Mare to mind, and the resemblance made me smile back. He dropped my hand and put his arm around me, gently brushing his fingertips along the top of my shoulder. My heart pounded in my ears so loudly he must have been able to hear it. We stopped in front of a closed door, and he set down the lantern. But instead of opening the door, he took both my hands.

"Dennaleia." He looked into my eyes, that sincere tone back in his voice again. "I know things haven't gone as expected, but do you think you can be happy here in Mynaria someday? With me?"

My mind raced, searching for the right answer. Happiness would feel more realistic once the alliance was finalized and the unrest in the kingdom had been addressed. But it seemed important that he believe in me, and in *us*. Otherwise I'd never be the trusted adviser to him that Casmiel had hoped I would become.

"Yes, of course," I said.

"I'm glad you feel that way," he said, his voice warm.

Then he leaned down and kissed me.

I waited for emotions to well up the way Alisendi had described when recounting her trysts, but I only felt panic that I didn't know what to do. His mouth was wetter than I expected, his upper lip damp with sweat. I tried to kiss him back. He stepped closer and attempted to deepen the kiss, but I pulled back and broke away.

"Was that all right?" he asked.

"Um, I suppose so." I didn't know what else to say. Admitting that the thought of kissing him again made me want to run to my rooms wasn't an option. I swallowed hard. Soon we would be married. Surely it would get better with time.

"I won't do anything you don't want me to do."

"Of course."

He kissed me again on the hand and then the cheek. I stood perfectly still, as though I were afraid to scare him off, when in fact it was I who wanted to flee.

"Let's go, then," he said, smiling at me. "I can show you the other passageways."

I nodded silently and followed him onward, sending mental apologies to Mare with all my heart. A page would have to be sent with an excuse for why I had not appeared as promised. I hoped she would forgive me.

TWENTY

✦ *Mare*

LONG AFTER DENNA SHOULD HAVE ARRIVED TO VISIT, a page delivered a vague apology from her. I was annoyed, but the plan I'd crafted required two people, and it wasn't something Nils could be caught doing—I needed help. I sent a message asking Denna to meet me before the change of the midnight guard shift. Something that had been tight all day loosened in my chest when she edged down the directors' hall like a shadow, but there was no time to examine the feeling. We had to stay focused on obtaining the dagger.

"I'm so sorry about this afternoon," she said, the apology pouring out in a rush. "I ran into Thandi on the way to see you and I couldn't get away. He took me down into the tunnels, and—"

"It's fine." I cut her off. "I'm just glad you're here now." I tried not to think about whatever my brother had been up to with her in the catacombs. When he was younger, he used to like to try to talk pretty girls into going down there to kiss him, and the thought of him kissing Denna when she should have been scheming with me was irritating.

I explained my plan to recover the knife, showing Denna the hairpin I planned to use to pick the lock of Ryka's ready room. With the details sorted, we stalked our way along the rough stone wall of the hallway, taking advantage of the long shadows cast by the few sconces that still burned in the middle of the night.

"Do you see him?" Denna whispered.

"Shh." I put my finger to my lips, waiting for the guard to pass the hallway where we stood concealed.

Denna teetered a little bit as she leaned forward to peer around me, and I caught her barely in time to keep her from lurching into the suit of armor we were hiding behind. Why Captain Ryka insisted on keeping such half-rusted wastes of space on display was a mystery. I glared at Denna, even though I knew she couldn't see me in the dark. The girl clearly hadn't done enough sneaking as a child. Even getting this far had been like trying to lead a warhorse over eggshells.

Chain mail jingled as the liegeman walked past. It was time. The whole plan hinged on us making it to the door of the captain's ready room and managing to break in during the brief period when the guard was around the corner. I stepped out from behind the armor.

"Heya!" the liegeman shouted, turning with his halberd at the ready.

Shit.

The liegeman chuckled as I emerged into the dim lamplight— one of the least friendly sounds I'd ever heard. "What are you doing here, *Your Highness*?" he asked, dropping his guard. "Slumming for some fresh liegeman meat?" He waved his halberd suggestively.

It figured that I'd run into Jox—the only liegeman cocky and stupid enough to talk down to a member of the royal family. One day I'd get him dismissed in a way that ensured he wouldn't bother anyone else.

"Yes, Jox. Obviously. That's why I'm here. Because I can't stop thinking about you." I paced past him, trying to lure him farther away from Denna. I hoped she had the common sense to take advantage of the opportunity and run. We could regroup and get the knife another time.

"Maybe you're smarter than the rumors say," Jox said, completely missing my sarcasm. "Though those trousers make you look like one of us. You should try skirts sometime. They're easier for a man to get into."

"Sartorial advice from a liegeman," I said. "Now I've heard it all."

"Let me show you what a real man is," Jox said. "I'll be off my shift in a quarter of a sunlength, but I could leave a few minutes early." His predatory gaze made me wish I had a better weapon than the bent hairpin clutched between my fingers.

Gods, I hoped Denna had escaped. I risked a glance over Jox's shoulder and barely held back an entire rainbow of curses. Behind him, Denna inched her way along the wall, heading for the door of the captain's ready room. If she made the slightest noise, he'd turn and catch her. I did the only thing I could think of—leaned back into the nearest suit of rusted armor and knocked the whole thing to the floor. Metal screeched across the stone as pieces scattered.

"Oops." I batted my eyelashes. "I'm *so* sorry, Jox."

He spat a curse and began picking up the pieces. I bent down to help him, making sure to drop as many as possible. By the time he shooed me away, happy to see me go, the hallway stood silent and empty again. I deliberately exited past the door to the ready room, hoping to figure out where Denna had gone.

The door stood as firmly shut as when we'd first entered, but I could hear papers rustling on the other side. Against all odds, she had made it in. The trouble was that now I had no idea how she was going to find the weapon, or more importantly, how she would get out. The only other means of escape was the second-story external window. And if Denna could climb down a wall—in the rain, no less—I'd eat my damned saddle. The ornamental one. Crusty gold filigree and all.

I trotted downstairs to the nearest exit, grabbed a lantern from a hook near the door, and stepped out into the rain. Fat droplets soaked through my shirt. Thunder rumbled overhead, and a streak of lightning zipped across the sky as I peered up at the dark window of the captain's room. Of course there was nothing to see.

I sighed and trudged out onto the path that most closely hugged the castle wall. Not more than twenty paces past the window stood a small stone building sheltered by tall trees and covered with a tangle of vines. The door creaked open at my touch, releasing the smell of stale air and wet earth. Inside was hardly better than out; no matter where I stood, drips found their way through the roof and onto my head.

I held up the lantern, surveying the contents of the shed. Most of the tools were piled haphazardly in the corners. In the far back what I needed hung crookedly on the wall: a half-rotted ladder held together with rusty nails. It would have to do.

I pulled it down and carried it to the window, setting it against the wall. Climbing it seemed like the worst idea I'd ever had. But leaving Denna to fend for herself in Captain Ryka's ready room wasn't an option.

I put my foot on the bottom rung of the ladder, which creaked ominously as my hands slipped on the rain-slick wood. I preceded each step up the ladder with a cautious test of the next rung. Rain stung my cheeks and stuck my hair to my neck in dripping strands. At the top I grasped the sill, stretching up onto my toes to look in through the window. Through the blurry glass all I could see was the tiniest spark of light, just enough to hint at Denna's silhouette.

I knocked softly on the glass, afraid to tap too loudly in case sentries kept watch on the roof. The last thing I needed was to be shot full of arrows at the top of a wobbly ladder. The light in the room winked out, but nothing else happened. I tried again, this time tapping a snippet of rhythm from the first piece of music Denna had played for me. Moments later, the window creaked open.

"Mare?" she whispered.

"I can't believe you sneaked in there! If you had any idea how close we came to—"

She cut me off by holding up the knife, the blade gleaming as lightning flashed. "I got it."

"By the Six," I said, feeling a thrill of delight in spite of being soaked to the skin. She passed me the knife and I slipped it through my belt. "Come on, let's get out of here."

"Wait . . . you want me to climb out the window?" she asked.

"How else are you going to get out? The guard has already

changed and won't switch again until dawn. Captain Ryka will be up by then."

Denna shook her head. "I can't."

"It's not that high up. No higher than your window." I put my hand up and caught her chin as she tried to look to the earth below. "Don't look down."

"But—"

"You can do this. I'm going to climb down a few rungs. All you have to do is swing your legs down, and I'll make sure you hit the ladder before you let go. It's like dismounting from a horse."

"I can't." Denna retreated back into the window until only her hand remained on the sill.

"You have to." I put my hand over hers. "Please. Trust me."

Her hand trembled beneath mine and I squeezed to steady it.

"It's not hard with a ladder."

"I don't know, Mare . . . it doesn't look particularly sturdy."

I had my doubts about the ladder, too, but this wasn't the time to admit it. "It's not going anywhere," I said. "And once you're on, I'll go down first and hold it steady for you."

"I can't." She withdrew her hand. "I'm going to have to— Oh, no." Her eyes widened. "Someone is outside the door!"

"Get out here. Now." I pulled the window the rest of the way open, rain spattering the inside of the glass and running down in rivulets. "Take my hand. Trust me."

She shook like a leaf in the storm as she swung a leg over the windowsill. I reached up and grabbed her calf, hoping that it might give her some sense of security.

"The same as getting off a horse," I said. "Swing over onto your stomach and drop down to the ladder. Slowly."

She took a deep breath. Even I could hear the voices now—voices that were going to discover us if she didn't hurry. I cursed under my breath. Denna laid her chest on the sill, her leg still dangling out the window.

"That's right. Like dismounting. I'll guide you." I spoke as softly and soothingly as I could, trying to keep the urgency out of my voice. Keeping my hand on her leg, I carefully stepped down a rung, making room for her on the ladder.

"The door is opening!" she whispered. The window swung wide as she scrambled to hang on.

"Drop now!" I said.

She dropped her other leg down toward the ladder, her chest still resting on the window frame. She was enough shorter than me that her toes could barely touch the first safe rung to stand on. Light filled the room and weakly drifted out to where we hung. I pulled.

Denna slid down onto the ladder, her feet catching on a rung. My shoulder muscles strained as I supported her, throwing my chest forward to keep us both from pitching off the ladder. The rickety wood sagged with our combined weight, creaks sounding along its length. Resting my head against her back, I pressed us into the wall as voices carried out through the window.

"What happened to the door?" a voice said.

"I don't know," Jox answered. "I didn't see anyone near here except Her Royal Horseness over in the other hall."

"Look—the window's open. That must be what you heard," the first liegeman said, his voice conversationally close.

I held Denna so tightly, I was sure my arms would go numb. The rain pounded down on us both until her shirt grew as soaked as mine, but everywhere we touched felt hot and alive, charged with the fear of being caught. Finally, the window banged shut, and a shaky breath fought free of my lungs. I waited until I was sure the liegemen were gone, and then eased my hold on Denna.

"Let's go," I said. "One rung at a time. Go slow. Don't look down. I'll be right here."

She nodded her understanding, shuddering as I pulled my body away from hers and the rain hit her back. I climbed to the bottom first, more grateful than I'd ever been to feel the wet earth soaking through the soles of my boots. Denna followed, her movements slow and deliberate. I offered her a hand as she reached the ground, and she stepped off the ladder into my arms. She sagged into me, and for a moment I was afraid she might cry. But when she looked at me, she had a small smile on her face.

"We did it," she said. "I can't believe we did it."

"It was all you," I said. She was so clever and brave, filled with small miracles that had made everything possible. Unexpected tenderness welled up in me, and my fingers were drawn to a clump of wet hair stuck to her cheek. I tucked it behind her ear. She caught my hand with hers, pressing it to her cheek.

"I knew you'd distract that guard. And I knew you'd get me out of that room somehow," she said. "Because I trust you."

In the deep dark of the garden I could barely make out her features, but I felt her when she turned her face into the palm of my hand. As her soft lips brushed the inside of my wrist, my blood sang. Any common sense I had completely vanished as impulse took over and I leaned forward. Her breath hitched as my focus narrowed to the curve of her mouth.

A thunderclap shook the sky, and we stepped back from each other, suddenly shy.

"We need to get inside," I said, shaking off the strangeness of the moment, afraid of the direction things had almost gone. "I wish I had something to wrap the knife in."

"I have a handkerchief," Denna offered, producing a sodden square of silk from one of her pockets.

I raised an eyebrow.

"It's clean."

"Right. It'll do for now." I took the handkerchief and wrapped the wet fabric around the blade before shoving the whole thing into my boot. We took the ladder back to the shed, Denna supporting the other end as we made our way through the rain-slick paths of the garden, and put it away.

Denna stayed attached to me like a burr in a broodmare's tail as we ducked down into the tunnels beneath the castle, coming out in a broom closet close to my rooms. We sneaked past the hall guards and slipped into my chambers unnoticed. As soon as the door closed behind us, I exhaled what felt like the first full breath I'd managed all night.

Denna's eyes met mine and she gave me a crooked grin. And then she giggled. It started out small but bloomed into peals of laughter loud enough to wake the whole castle.

"Shhh!" I said, trying to control my own laughter. It was futile. We both collapsed onto the rug in front of the fire, laughing until tears ran down our already wet faces into our damp clothes.

"You're insane!" I said.

"I know. I can't believe any of that worked! Some god of trickery must have been watching over us." Denna brushed back the damp strands of hair that clung to her neck, her milky skin glowing in the low light of the fire.

"Let's hope that little god stays with us, then. We have another adventure to plan," I said. I took out the knife and held it out to her. "Can you tell if it's fake based on what you read?"

She took the blade from me and held it close to the light of the fire. "There's no grain in this metal," she said. "If what I read is true, this is definitely a forgery, but we need better evidence to confirm it. We could see about finding a true piece of Zumordan weaponry in the city. Or perhaps inquire about where one might obtain a high-end forgery." She handed over the blade and I set it on the floor.

"See? I'll never need to go to the library again as long as I have you," I teased.

"But you should," she replied, her eyes glittering. "So when should we go to the city?"

"As soon as we can. Tomorrow afternoon?"

"What about riding?"

"With the way this rain is coming down, it's going to be far too muddy to ride tomorrow. It might be muddy in town too, but clearly you don't mind getting dirty. . . ." I gestured to her soaked clothes, which sent us into another fit of giggling.

"I don't! I can do it."

"All right. Come by my rooms around the time you would usually be going to your lesson. Tell anyone who asks that we're going to be cleaning tack or something. And just to be safe, you'd best have an alibi in case we don't make it back before dinner. Whatever you have to say to get out of any other obligations."

"My friend Ellaeni should be able to help cover my tracks. I can't wait!" She leaned forward and threw her arms around me. "Thank you for today," she said.

"You're welcome," I replied, clumsily returning her hug. Our wet clothes clung to us, but beneath them the heat of her body burned against me. We both shivered, then parted, the awkwardness returning.

"I'll see you tomorrow," she said, eagerness shining in her eyes. She waved a quick good-bye and disappeared into the hallway. I shook my head, hoping the night patrol wouldn't catch her, but knowing she'd probably manage a good excuse if they did.

Sunlengths after she left, after I was dry, after I had changed into nightclothes and slipped into the warm cocoon of my bed, I still felt the phantom press of her arms around me.

TWENTY-ONE ✤ *Dennaleia*

THE NEXT AFTERNOON, THE RAIN GAVE WAY TO
brilliant sunshine and a cool breeze that made the trees shiver and
sway. Autumn would be here soon. I met Mare outside the barn,
eager for our adventure.

"Ready?" she asked. She wore old riding clothes far too shabby
for a princess, her russet hair twisted up in a knot she could easily
stuff into a hat.

"Yes," I said. Excitement rushed through me. Since the previous
night I hadn't been able to stop thinking about the moment we'd had
at the bottom of the ladder, wondering what it meant and what her
intentions were. She had looked at me as though I was everything—
and it scared me how much I longed for it to happen again. Thandi
should have been the one on my mind, but I couldn't banish thoughts
of Mare.

"Are you sure we won't get caught?" I asked.

"No. But we managed all right last night, didn't we?" Mare gave me a sideways smile as we ducked into the barn, leaving the wind outside behind us. She ushered me into the granary and closed the door. The room smelled like rolled oats and dried corn, molasses, and the rich green aroma of pressed alfalfa cubes.

"What now?" I asked.

"I'll hold the door. There's a change of clothes for you in the empty grain bin farthest from the hay."

"I can't wear my riding outfit?"

"Your riding habit cost more coin than some of the townspeople see in a season, and there are thieves who would be more than happy to strip you for it. The city isn't as safe as it used to be." Mare folded her arms. "Hurry and change—we don't want to get caught."

I reached into the bin and pulled out some rumpled clothes made of rough fabric. I wrinkled my nose.

"I didn't say this would be glamorous," Mare said.

"I don't care." I squared my shoulders. Surely if I could crawl out of a second-story window in the pouring rain, it wouldn't kill me to wear peasant clothes for a few sunlengths.

"Good." She smiled at me again, a sweet reward.

Mare turned to face the door, listening to make sure no one approached. I pulled off my riding jacket and reached to unlace the corset beneath it. My fingers immediately snarled the strings into a knot. I cursed under my breath, though not as colorfully as Mare would have.

"Problem?" Mare asked.

"My laces are stuck. Can you help?" I hoped my voice sounded calm. The thought of her touching me filled me with anxiety. I hadn't even been able to hug her the previous night without shivering with an unfamiliar emotion. She gestured for me to turn my back to her and began deftly loosening the tangle I'd created. Her fingers brushed me gently as she worked the knots free.

The corset finally gave way, freeing me to take a deep breath. I raised my arms and she pulled it over my head, rolling it up and stuffing it into the bin where my change of clothes had been. Any chill that might have lingered from the wind outside was gone.

"Mare . . ." I turned around to meet her eyes, not sure if I was going to thank her or try to say something more.

"I'll let you do the rest yourself," she said before I could find words. "I have to watch the door. Hurry." She turned and walked to the door, once more facing the exit while I pulled on the breeches and belted the tunic.

"I look like a stable hand," I said.

"That's exactly the point." She winked at me, and my cheeks warmed.

We stowed the rest of my clothes in the bin and darted out the door past rain-soaked hedges and flower beds to the garden that backed up against the wall surrounding the castle.

"Where's the door?" I asked, breathing hard from running.

"No door." She grinned. "We climb."

"You're joking," I groaned, my arms throbbing at the thought. "I'm still recovering from that blasted ladder!"

"I'm afraid it's no joke, my lady. Leg up?" She boosted me into the tree the same way she helped me onto horseback, her hands cupped beneath the ball of my foot. I scraped my palms on the rough bark, sending a shower of leaves and water droplets down onto her head. She came up on an adjacent branch, so graceful that the leaves barely rustled.

"What now?"

"Over the wall." She stepped from branch to branch until she was able to swing a leg over the stone wall. "Come on."

I gritted my teeth and began the climb. It wasn't far, but each branch felt as though it were farther than I could ever hope to reach.

"You're going to rile every gardener on the grounds if you keep shaking the branches like that." Mare laughed at me, her gray eyes shining.

"It's not every day," I panted, and grabbed another branch, "that a princess finds herself climbing trees."

"Maybe not for you," she pointed out, holding out her hand to help me onto the wall. I clung to the rough stone, thankful to be out of the tree.

"How do we get down from here?"

"We jump," she said. "I'll go first and help you down." And with that she slid down from the wall, tucking into a roll as she met the ground below. She came up smiling. "Your turn."

"This is insane," I muttered. I flipped onto my stomach, feeling nothing but air under my feet. Trusting her came so easily now.

"Bend your knees with the impact." Her voice floated up over my back. "Go."

I hesitated only a moment before closing my eyes and letting go. We tumbled into a heap at the base of the wall.

"You all right?" She hopped up and brushed off mud and leaves.

"Yes," I gasped as she pulled me to my feet.

"Let's go!" Mare beckoned. Though she didn't offer it, I took her hand as we trotted along the wall toward the cresthaven. I half expected her to pull away, but instead she laced her fingers through my own without looking back. Our hands fitted together like the interlocking pieces of a puzzle.

The roofs of houses appeared on the hill below as we approached the front of the castle grounds. They stabbed up into the sky in various shades of brown, the edges of the clay tiles still damp with rain. Mare pulled me away from the castle wall and through a narrow trail between two fenced yards. The sounds of the city buzzed in my ears long before we reached the street. Shod hooves rang against cobblestones, the wind punctuated by the occasional shout.

"Are you ready?" Mare paused and turned to me, dropping my hand.

"Yes." Despite my nervousness, I was.

"Follow me." She strode out from the alley as though she belonged there. I stayed at her heels, a nervous shadow. Though the street was relatively empty, I feared that all eyes were on me. It was different from the experience of being watched as Princess Dennaleia. Recognition was something to fear instead of something to expect. I longed to take Mare's hand again for security and comfort.

This close to the castle, opulent residences towered several stories high over the cobbled street. Ornate wrought-iron fences separated us from the manicured gardens behind them. Sculpted in shining metal, horses danced across the garden gates, their manes and tails flying as though the wind was trapped in the iron with them.

"Where are we going?" I whispered.

"You don't need to whisper." She laughed. "Nils is going to

meet us at the Deaf Dog pub."

"I feel like people are looking at me," I said. My magic simmered along with my tension, and I dug my fingernails into both palms to suppress it. Burning off a little by melting the lock on Ryka's door hadn't done enough to keep it at bay.

"That's because you aren't looking at them, silly. Look around. People are busy, and out of the corners of their eyes they only see what they're expecting."

As usual, she was right. No one returned my furtive looks, and I soon relaxed. Street traffic increased as we made our way farther from the castle. The fancy houses gave way to buildings that housed many families, laundry lines strung between windows, and children charging through the street so close to carts that it made me gasp. The scent of trash drifted out from alleys to mingle with the wet ground and the hundreds of bodies around us. Mare kept me close, her eyes constantly skimming the crowd, giving a wide berth to anyone with shifty eyes or an unsavory appearance.

"Quit wrinkling your nose." Mare smiled when she turned to look at me. I tried to straighten my face, but apparently my attempt failed. She laughed outright and pulled me to the side of the street to enter one of the many stone buildings. A wooden sign above the entrance depicted a sleeping dog next to a mug of ale.

"I've never been to an alehouse before," I said as we entered. The city noise faded as the door closed behind us, a welcome reprieve from the chaos of the street. Worn tables sported rings left behind by long-forgotten drinks. Nils nodded at us from a table in the corner and stood up to greet us as we approached. He wrapped Mare up in a hug and lifted her right off her feet as I stood awkwardly behind them. A little stab of jealousy needled me at his ease with her.

"Nils, I'm sure you remember . . . Lia," Mare said as she gestured to me.

"Of course," Nils said. "Nice to see you, Lia." He winked and took my hand to stop me from curtsying out of habit. "No need for that here," he said, leaning forward to speak softly in my ear. I smiled. It was hard to be jealous of him when he was so kind.

We settled ourselves at the table. Thankfully, Mare ordered for me without being asked. I wouldn't even know what to ask for—food and drink had always been brought to me as a matter of course. The woman who brought our ale was full-figured and cheerful, smiling as she deposited a foaming glass in front of me.

"Drink up!" Nils said. Mare and Nils raised their glasses. I rushed to do the same, foaming beer spilling over the sides of the glass and all over my hand.

"To freedom," Mare said.

"To freedom," we echoed, the clink of our glasses reverberating through my fingers. I followed their example and took a hefty swig of the drink, the foam burning up into my nose. It smelled sweet, like apricot, but left a bitter taste in my mouth. I cringed, and Mare and Nils burst into raucous laughter.

"You should see the expression on your face!" Mare said.

"I've never had beer before." I turned away from her laughing eyes to glare at the cloudy drink. It only made them laugh harder, so I took another sip for spite. I held the foam in my mouth and let it burn for a moment before swallowing it with a second grimace, earning another round of laughs.

"So, information first?" Nils asked once he'd regained his composure.

"Yes," Mare said.

Nils put a coin on the table, crown side down, which quickly vanished into a server's hand. A complicated dance of flatware and glasses followed. Not much later, a nondescript man sat down at our table next to Nils. I knew it was all part of the plan, but the man still made me nervous. Maybe people on the street wouldn't recognize me, but surely a spy might. I gulped more of my drink, hoping to calm my nerves.

"What type of weaponry do you seek?" the informant asked.

"Blades," Mare said. "Zumordan. Or custom, if you can't manage that."

He placed his fingers on the edge of the table, and Mare and Nils exchanged a glance.

"The food is good," Nils said.

"For custom blades, try Morland at the Cataphract Square Market. He's the best in the business—even the captain of the Mynarian Guard goes to him." The informant hesitated, almost as if he was reluctant to part with the rest of his information. "Go to the Aerie at the Blitz for things related to the dragon. You'll find the entrance marked with a bluebird, and the pass code is 'etheria.' It will only work once, and only today. Don't test those limits."

We nodded our understanding, and the informant departed. Pass codes and dragons and the Blitz—the Mynarian black market. What had I gotten myself into? I put back the rest of my beer to quell my fears.

"So Captain Ryka makes a habit of ordering custom blades,"

I noted. "Clearly she had nothing to do with what happened to Casmiel . . . but could she somehow be involved with the attempt on the king?"

Mare considered the idea. "She was one of the quickest to blame Zumorda for the attacks in that first Directorate meeting."

Nils frowned. "Captain Ryka has served our kingdom reliably for years. What would she gain by framing Zumorda and weakening the crown?"

"I don't know, but you have to admit security has been awfully easy to get around, even with the reserves pulled in," I said.

Nils snorted. "That's because half those idiots can hardly hold a sword."

"What about Hilara?" I asked. "She seems . . . friendly with the Zumordans. Could they be conspiring?"

Nils and Mare both frowned.

"I can see why she might have been involved in Cas's death, but why would she try to take out my father? If anything, that would destabilize the kingdom too much for her to gain any advantage," Mare said.

I shifted uneasily, remembering my wedding bazaar, when Hilara had accepted that sachet from the Zumordan merchant. There had to be more to it than that, but Mare's point was valid.

A spirited discussion began between Mare and Nils about who might be to blame and the best way to proceed. I pulled my second beer closer with sticky hands and nursed it through their conversation, noticing that my magic had dulled to a steady hum in my bones. Our food came, and I picked up a roll and bit into it, flaky pastry giving way to a spicy filling that sent hot butter running down my chin.

"Well, someone certainly has an appetite for peasant food," Mare said.

Her beauty suddenly struck me with the force of a spring avalanche on the mountain. Those mischievous gray eyes. Her teasing voice. The freckles that were becoming as familiar to me as the stars in the night sky.

"Thank you," I said, feeling a little giddy. "You've done so much for me. Bringing me here. Teaching me lessons. I'm so glad we're friends."

She touched my arm gently, and goose bumps rose from there all the way up my neck. A strange new feeling washed through me, warm and dark. All at once I understood what Alisendi had meant when she talked about the thrill of her flirtations.

I wanted Mare.

I was promised to her brother.

I was in deep trouble.

TWENTY-TWO

✦ *Mare*

DENNA SEEMED A LITTLE TIPSY FROM HER ALE, bobbing along cheerfully between Nils and me as we made our way through the city toward Cataphract Square. The buildings around us became smaller and simpler, the roofs covered in thatch instead of tile or stone. The symbol of the Recusants decorated many more buildings than the last time I'd been in town, often with the black slash of the fundamentalist zealots through it.

As we neared the heart of the city, we saw more and more blades strapped to belts, and had to dodge a number of brawls. Nils and I exchanged concerned looks over Denna's head. The Recusants and the fundamentalists must have been responsible. I'd never seen the city so violent. I hoped the bladesmith at Cataphract Square would have answers for us, because returning to the safety of the castle was starting to seem like a good idea. And the Blitz was not somewhere I wanted to take Denna.

Bodies pressed all around us as traffic flowed in both directions, growing increasingly heavy as we walked down a hill. The market unfolded before us, with vendors situated around the edges of the square and a grand fountain in the middle.

The weapons vendors were easy to spot even from across the square—an array of shining blades hung high above their market stalls to catch the sun, out of reach of thieves. A gap stood in the middle of the row like a missing tooth. As we drew closer, my worst fears were confirmed.

"He's gone," Nils said.

All three of us exchanged a look.

"Heya." I approached one of the vendors adjacent to the empty space.

He looked up from the blade he was sharpening and set down his whetstone.

"Where's Morland?" I asked. "We had an order to pick up."

"Dodged town a coupla days ago," the vendor said.

"But open market lasts two more moons," I said, puzzled. No vendor would want to miss the harvest festival, much less Denna's wedding. The influx of people could result in their best sales of the year.

He shrugged. "More business for the rest of us."

"Thank you," I said, and we walked away, swerving to avoid a man on a rickety homemade platform who was yelling about redemption and the Six and cleansing the Recusants from the city.

"We have to go to the Blitz before dark. It's our only other lead," Nils said.

Denna's eyes wandered over the crowd. I wished there was a

way to magically transport her to the castle.

"We have to keep her safe," I said.

"I've got my sword," Nils said. "No one will bother us."

"I'm fine," Denna added. "We have to see this through."

"All right," I reluctantly agreed.

We left the thickest crowds behind, working our way out into the adjacent neighborhood. The condition of the streets quickly deteriorated north of Cataphract Square. Walls and buildings were even more frequently tagged with white-outlined circles, and fewer marked with the black slash. Apparently support for magic users was more prevalent in the poorest part of town. People without homes slumped against buildings, hats pulled low over their faces as they napped in the afternoon sun. The smell of filth hung in the air, barely eased by the breeze at our backs.

"You!" A man leaped out from behind a building, pointing a knobby finger at Denna.

She yelped and stepped backward into me. I wrapped my arm around her waist to steady her. Nils put his hand on the hilt of his sword.

"You're one of them," he said, his finger trembling. "Touched by the Six! The Six. The Six, the Six, the Six," he muttered to himself, running his other hand through his stained and scraggly beard.

Just what we needed—some nutter drawing half the city's attention to Denna with his crazy pseudoreligious nonsense. Denna hid behind me and Nils, clutching my arm, fear written all over her face. I tensed as well, ready to bolt.

"Back off," Nils said, his voice low and dangerous.

We edged away from the man.

"Sparks!" the man shouted, spittle flying out of his mouth. "Her heart. Her heart! The Six . . . she has a heart of sparks."

"Run," I shouted.

"Sparks!" he yelled as we sprinted away.

We ducked down a dirty alleyway, dodging puddles of garbage and animal shit. At the end, an unmarked door stood before us. I shoved it open and stepped through, pulling Denna along behind me. The dark swallowed us, and it took a minute for my eyes to adjust to the lighting. A cavernous, windowless warehouse opened up before us, filled with rickety, dimly lit stalls built from scavenged materials. The paths between them were shrouded in near darkness, patrons of the Blitz moving through them like shadows.

"Is he going to come after us?" Denna asked me, her face taut with worry. In the odd half-light of the Blitz, she looked otherworldly, as though there truly was a spark of something bright and miraculous beneath her surface. I had to keep her safe.

"He was a crazy old man," Nils said. "You shouldn't worry about him. Let's get this over with."

I nodded my agreement, but Denna still seemed on edge.

The three of us stayed close together as we navigated the paths of the Blitz, stopping only to ask one of the market masters for directions to the Aerie. Bugs scuttled past our feet as we made our way to the darkest corner of the warehouse. As the spy had indicated, a peculiar lantern in the shape of a bluebird hung from the entrance, cobwebs trailing from its bloated glass belly. We entered the shop through heavy fabrics that muffled the sounds of the Blitz when they closed behind us. Inside the Aerie, dim light showcased a variety of wares that ranged from scrolls to herbs, powders, and small ceramic containers.

Behind the counter stood the familiar bearded form of the textile merchant from Denna's bridal bazaar.

Denna took in a sharp breath.

"Master Karov, at your service," the man said in accented tones. "May I help you?"

"We're looking for something specific," I said, unsure how to proceed.

"And what is the word for what you are looking for?" he asked.

"Etheria," I replied.

Karov smiled, showing teeth tipped with silver. "How interesting. It is a rare night that I have such youthful men and women visiting me."

My face must have betrayed my surprise at how easily he saw through our disguises.

"Worry not. We Zumordans care not for gender. Only power." He looked at Denna, who eyed him mistrustfully. "Very interesting indeed."

He reached beneath the counter and released a latch, causing the entire countertop to flip over and reveal another set of wares.

Denna's eyes immediately darted to a tiny lady's dagger, the leaf-shaped blade bright against the dark-red velvet lining of the box holding it.

"See something you like?" Karov asked.

"Is that a Zumordan blade?" Denna asked, stepping forward.

"Yes," he replied, plucking the dagger out of the case and holding it up for us to see. Its surface rippled in the low light as though a pattern had been burned into the steel.

"Look at the steel," she said, marveling. "This blade is true."

I pulled the dagger out of my boot and showed it to Karov. "Would a Zumordan blade ever look like this?"

"No," he scoffed, placing the lady's dagger back into its case and taking the assassin's weapon from me. "An expensive forgery, yes, but not Zumordan steel." He held his other hand over the hilt and waved. "The handle is false as well."

"How do you know?" I asked.

He pulled out the lady's dagger again and made the same hand motion. An iridescent dragon shimmered over the surface of the handle for a second and then vanished.

I stepped back. Denna's research hadn't revealed that Zumordan weapons held magic. She leaned closer to the blade, fascinated.

"Is this weapon magical?" I asked Karov, pointing to the assassin's dagger.

"No," he replied. "There is no life in that blade."

"How can you tell?" Denna asked.

"I can feel it, of course," he replied. "All those with an Affinity can feel the life in a Zumordan weapon. Touch it."

Denna reached out, hesitantly, until her fingers brushed the handle of the lady's dagger. She withdrew as if it had burned her.

"Did it hurt you?" I asked Denna.

"No, no. I'm fine," she said, though her expression was unsettled. I wondered if she had felt anything when she touched it—and what it meant if she had. Had Karov and that crazy man on the street seen something in her that I had not?

"How much for the blade?" I asked.

"Six hundred."

I shook my head. The price was too steep. Even if I came back later with the money, spending that much in the Blitz seemed like a sure way to blow my disguise or end up with someone's knife in my back.

"What do you know about the Recusants?" Denna asked.

I gave her a sharp look.

"Troublemakers," Karov said. "Too noisy for the likes of me. They've made messes they can't clean up."

He must have meant Cas's death, but nothing about Karov made me inclined to trust him. We had to leave before our line of questioning gave us away.

"Thank you for your insight," I said, and passed him a handful of coins. "For your trouble."

"Come and see me again," he said, nodding to each of us until his eyes stopped on Denna. "There are other things I could show you."

Denna stared back at him warily but held her ground, and there was a hunger in Karov's gaze that made me shudder.

"Should you need to call on me again, drop this to the ground and speak my name," Karov said, producing a bright-blue feather from a pocket inside his coat and handing it to Denna.

"Let's go. Now," Denna said, already pushing out through the curtains.

I followed, surprised by such abruptness in contrast with her usually perfect manners.

The three of us hurried away from Karov's stall, but I felt like his eyes stayed on my back even when we burst back out into the sunlight. We walked swiftly out of the slums until the streets were once again filled with regular people going about their daily business, but the uneasiness never left me.

TWENTY-THREE　　　🔥 *Dennaleia*

OUR SPECULATIONS ON THE WALK TO THE CASTLE
yielded no insight. Mare tried to make a case that Captain Ryka or
Director Hilara should be the primary suspect, Ryka because she
hated magic users and would want to frame them, and Hilara because
I mentioned seeing her consorting with Karov at my bazaar. Nils
refused to hear any suggestion that besmirched the captain's name,
and every time I pointed out that Hilara supported Zumorda and it
would make no sense for her to frame a kingdom she supported, the
argument started all over from the beginning.

Eventually I stopped trying to contribute and dwelled instead
on the way the Zumordan dagger had felt soft and alive in my hand,
less like a weapon than an extension of myself. My magic had risen
to meet it, and power still seethed uncomfortably beneath my skin.

By the time we got back, all three of us were short-tempered,
and Mare turned silent and pensive after Nils left us to report for his

shift. Thus it was no surprise that Mare and I ended up arguing over the best way back into the castle. We stood alongside the wall near where we had tumbled down earlier in the afternoon, with the sun now low over the hills. The wall took on a faint orange tone in the late-afternoon light, and Mare's hair glowed bright as flame where it peeked out from beneath her cap.

"I can go in through the gate. You can't. We can't take the chance of you being recognized," Mare said.

"I'm not climbing any more trees." I was already tired, and the thought of going over the wall again held no appeal.

"Then come up with a better idea!" She threw up her hands.

"You're the one who knows your way around. I thought you had a plan!" Panic rose in me. Ellaeni could pretend I was in her rooms for a private dinner for only so long. If we couldn't get back in, and our disguises were discovered, the consequences would be dire. My magic surged and some dry grass nearby began to smoke. I clenched my fists and said a mental prayer to the earth god for patience and calm.

"I did have a plan—a plan about how to get you out."

"Don't you think getting back in is a pretty crucial part of that?" My temper grew shorter by the moment. Some part of me recognized that it was silly to be so agitated, but I could not quell the frustration—or the magic that had been begging for an escape since I'd touched Karov's blade.

"Let me boost you up," Mare said.

"For the last time, no!" I pushed off from the wall with one hand, intending to head toward one of the gates. But before my hand left the stone, magic raced from my fingertips. The rocks seemed to come to life beneath my touch, growing hot as the mortar between them crumbled into dust. A portion fell in with a thunderous crack, leaving only a heap of smoldering rubble. All the rage I'd felt only moments prior completely vanished as though it had poured out of me into the stone.

"What in the Sixth Hell was that? Are you all right?" Mare asked, concerned.

I stared at the rubble, too afraid to answer her. If Mare discovered my gift and told Thandi or the king, my life would crumble like the wall. Even more disturbing was that I had no idea how I'd made the rocks give way. The incident in the library had seemed like a fluke—I thought perhaps it was my fire gift that had melted my fingerprint into the wall. My power had never been of the earth. Something was much more wrong with me than the unstable ambient magic in Mynaria could explain.

"Did that creep at the Blitz put an enchantment on you?" She touched my shoulder.

"Maybe it was that dagger," I said, latching onto the excuse. "It was Zumordan."

"It must have had an enchantment on it, like the arrow that killed Cas. I don't trust Karov, especially knowing that he's somehow connected to Hilara. This has to be his fault somehow. Come on and help me fix this." She crawled through and beckoned for me to follow, her expression drawn and preoccupied.

We crouched down on the other side and stacked the rocks as best we could to close the hole, the stones still warm with magic in my hands. I took slow breaths, trying to calm myself and ignore Mare's sidelong glances. Between the assassin, the homeless man yelling at us in the street, Karov's dagger, and the collapse of the wall, it couldn't take much longer for her to figure out that I was the common denominator.

By the time we finished patching up the wall, the filth on our clothes made a more perfect disguise than we'd started with earlier in the afternoon. Mare didn't even bother brushing the dirt from her breeches after she stood. She gestured for me to walk beside her as we made our way to the barn.

Crickets hummed in the grass, serenading the setting sun.

"I'm sorry I argued with you about getting back in," I said.

"It's all right. I should have thought it through a little better," Mare conceded.

"Well, I still shouldn't have been so belligerent about it." A yawn punctuated my words as we entered the granary.

"It's all right. Let's get you changed." Mare watched the door as I pulled off the peasant clothes. As reluctant as I'd been to don them, my riding habit now felt dreadfully stiff in comparison, even without the corset.

"Don't you have something else to wear?" I asked her.

"Nah, people are used to seeing me look like this or worse. It's nothing new."

"That's so unfair." I shot her a rueful look. As skeptical as I had been about wearing peasant clothes, I had to admit it was liberating. I didn't have to perform my role as princess, and I understood now why Mare valued her freedom and anonymity in town.

"You still look like a bit of a wreck yourself. We'd better keep to the shadows." She smiled. "I'll walk you."

I smiled back. It struck me then that it was the first time she had accompanied me back from the barn. For once she didn't disappear into her horse's stall or take off like there was somewhere else she'd rather be. We set off together, walking companionably side by side without needing any words.

Dusk hung heavy in the sky as we approached the castle. Birds winged to their nests for the night as we made our way through the gardens, gravel crunching beneath our feet. The heady perfume of late-summer blossoms greeted us through each arched gateway, every garden a miniature universe of sensory delights. I closed my eyes and breathed deeply. Mynaria had its charms.

"Oof." My eyes flew open as I bumped into Mare, who had stopped.

"Look there," she said. A spark drifted between the trees, winking out into the dark.

"What was that?" I said, curious.

"Shhh," she said. "Keep watching."

"I don't see anything."

"Wait. There!" She put a hand on my shoulder and pointed across the garden, where another tiny light drifted. Another followed, and soon more and more of them moved among the trees, leaving soft yellow trails through the dusk.

"What are those?" I whispered, full of wonder.

"Fireflies," Mare replied. "We're lucky to see them so late in summer."

She took my hand without further words. I squeezed back and stepped closer to her. We stood there as night crept over the gardens, making the fireflies glow ever brighter in the dimming light.

When Mare finally released my hand and headed toward home,

I trailed behind her, letting her lead. I could have stayed forever in that garden with her and the fireflies, empty of magic, filled with hope, wanting nothing more than to share that space with her. Had the garden felt as magical and surreal to her?

"I had fun today," I finally said when we stopped in the stairwell leading up to my rooms. "More than fun. It was the best day I've had since I got here."

"Be careful—my troublemaking ways are corrupting you," she joked.

"I mean it. Everything. The pub, the market, the fireflies . . ." I wished I could take her hand again and capture the perfection of the day there between us.

"It was nothing. I'm glad you enjoyed yourself. Next time we'll plan better. And stay out of the Blitz." She tucked a wayward lock of hair behind her ear.

My fingers twitched reflexively, as though itching to have done it for her.

"See you tomorrow," she said, and departed with a quick wave.

"See you," I echoed. As she walked away, something tugged on the thread that held me together. If she pulled too hard, my life was bound to unravel. Somehow my desire for her friendship had turned into something more pressing—something more like need.

TWENTY-FOUR   ✦ *Mare*

THE MORNING AFTER OUR ADVENTURE IN TOWN, I DUG
the blade out from the back of my vanity drawer, still wrapped in
Denna's silk handkerchief. Delicate pine trees decorated the edge of
the cloth, embroidered in an asymmetrical pattern that shone with
silver and green threads. I paused with my hand on the edge of the
weapon, hesitated, and then slipped the silk handkerchief off and
tucked it back into the drawer before leaving my rooms. I liked
having something of hers.

The hallways to my father's study had never seemed so long, and
I wanted to run instead of walk. However, I doubted that arriving
out of breath was likely to help my case. He needed to take me
seriously, as did the Directorate. What Denna and I had discovered
could change everything.

"I need to speak to the king immediately," I told the liegemen
outside the door.

The liegeman on the left cleared his throat. "I'm afraid King Aturnicus is not here at the moment, Your Highness."

"Do you know where he is?"

"Directorate business, I believe."

I growled in frustration. "I need to see him. I'll wait for him in here."

"Well . . . I suppose that might be all right." He peered out from the visor of his helmet, squinting as though my face made no sense to him.

"Of course it's all right." I straightened and looked him in the eye. He hesitated only a moment longer before opening the door. I couldn't believe a new recruit had been assigned to guard any room of the king's—more proof that Captain Ryka wasn't doing her job. It raised my suspicions all over again in spite of Nils's defense of her. Captain Ryka had loved Cas dearly and would never have hurt him, but concocting a war with Zumorda would certainly be a good way for her to find herself in a grave alongside him. Maybe that was what she wanted.

My footfalls made little sound on the plush rug as I entered the room. Stacks of vellum and parchment were scattered haphazardly across the desk, and more piled on the floor. How could my father ever manage to find anything in the chaos? I had never paid close attention to castle business, but the stacks had grown since Cas's death. The mess made me wonder who had been taking care of trade agreements and guild petitions since then.

The door to the study swung open as I reached out to examine a few loose pages hanging off the edge of the desk. Lord Kriantz and Captain Ryka entered the room alongside my father. Lord Kriantz smiled slightly and acknowledged me with a nod. The captain said nothing.

"Amaranthine, I just spent two sunlengths arbitrating a disagreement over the Trindori trade channel. I don't have time for nonsense right now." My father sighed, taking off his circlet and setting it down on a pile of papers.

"This is important," I said. "I have reason to believe the knife used in the assassination attempt on you is not Zumordan." Given my suspicions about the captain, I probably shouldn't have said anything in front of her, but at least Lord Kriantz was there as a witness. The more people who heard the truth about the weapon, the more likely the Directorate would be to listen. They had to.

"That can't be." He waved me away from the desk and settled himself in his chair. "The captain has assured me that the blade is almost certainly of Zumordan origin."

"There is no one else who would attack us," Captain Ryka said. "Zumorda is the only kingdom with something to gain. I spoke to one of Casmiel's most trusted informants about it yesterday. She's going to look into the matter with some of her contacts."

"Yes, but this blade is forged incorrectly." I pulled the knife out of my boot. "Look at it. There isn't any grain in this metal. Zumordan weaponry is forged from steel folded many more times than that of our blades. The result is a blade with a distinct grain in it. Morland, one of the only bladesmiths capable of this kind of custom work, has disappeared, and—"

The captain stepped forward. "I don't suppose you have an explanation for how the lock on the door of my ready room got melted, Your Highness," she said, her voice icy.

"I don't know what you're talking about," I said. Captain Ryka didn't scare me. In spite of her uniform and the years she had on me, as a member of the royal family by blood, I still outranked her.

"Amaranthine, your help is not necessary. The Directorate has already proceeded with measures to determine if anyone else on the grounds might have been involved. A knife is not going to tell us the identity of the killer," my father said. He didn't seem to have listened to me at all.

"Don't you realize it changes everything if I'm right?" I said. "Don't you think the origin of the attack is as important as the specific person who did it? Out in the city I—"

"We're at peace with our neighbors. The only unknown is Zumorda. No one else would threaten the peace between our kingdoms," my father said. "We've already caught most of the Recusants. It's only a matter of time before we follow the trail of poison to its source." My father's patience was wearing thin. So was mine.

"And I'm quite certain that the blade is Zumordan," the captain added. "There's more than one way to forge a blade, even in Zumorda. Everything adds up."

"Repeating yourself doesn't make you more correct!" I changed my hold on the knife and pointed it at the captain, my knuckles whitening with the force of my grip.

"Give me that weapon." My father stepped forward with an open hand. "Now."

"Why should I if you don't think it's important?" I retorted.

"Amaranthine, I'm done with your games. Give me the knife," he said.

"This isn't a game! You're the one ignoring important evidence in favor of sitting on your ass, mumbling unsubstantiated explanations with the rest of those morons on the Directorate!"

"Amaranthine!" My father's voice boomed through the room like a thunderclap. He grabbed my wrist and the knife fell to the floor. "We have a plan, and we will adhere to it. You will not interfere with matters that concern the Directorate."

"You're going to get us all killed." I jerked my arm free.

"Amaranthine, listen to me—"

"No, *you* listen. I'm tired of not being taken seriously. None of you have ever given me a chance! How am I supposed to do anything useful around here when you won't even let me?" My voice rose.

"If you wanted to be useful, you'd get married and learn to run an estate like a proper royal daughter! I ought to ship you straight to the middle of the Sonnenborne desert and see how you like your freedom then!" he shouted.

"Fine." Tears pricked the corners of my eyes.

"Amaranthine is always welcome to visit Sonnenborne." Lord Kriantz edged between my father and me. "Let's discuss this later and let the princess get back to her duties. I'll escort her out."

"Thank you, Endalan. We can finish our discussion about your bandit concerns over lunch. Captain, please send a page for Director Hilara—I need an update on the tax assessment project she took over from Casmiel," my father said before directing his steely gaze to me. "We are done here, Amaranthine." He pulled out one of his desk drawers and shoved the knife into it, sending a shower of papers off the desk to slide across the floor.

"Yes, Your Majesty." I stormed out alongside Lord Kriantz and kicked the door shut behind me, uttering a lengthy stream of profanity that carried us all the way to the end of the hall. Lord Kriantz, prudently, said nothing.

"How stupid do they have to be to not see the evidence right in front of them?" I finally managed a coherent sentence.

"It does seem unwise," he said.

"Thank you," I said. Some of the fight drained out of me at his words. It felt good to be listened to.

"Perhaps we could share a meal sometime and discuss the matter at more length," he suggested. "With all that is happening near my borders already, I don't think any kind of potential conflict with Zumorda should be taken lightly."

"All right," I agreed. At least one person was willing to listen, and both my brother and father seemed to favor him. Maybe he'd be able to talk some sense into the rest of the Directorate. Things couldn't possibly get any worse.

Even in my black mood, I had to go on with Denna's lesson as planned. I packed us a picnic lunch to take out on the trails, as I was in no hurry to return to the castle anytime soon. Denna came down dressed in a shade of green that matched her eyes and smiled when she saw me. All I managed in response was an expression that probably made me look like I'd taken a hoof to the teeth.

"Are you okay?" she asked, regarding me with worry.

"Other than wanting to slap half the Directorate with a hitching rail, I'm fine," I said.

"Do you want to talk about it?"

"No." I scowled at the door to the barn. "Where are those thrice-damned grooms?"

They finally appeared, leading Flicker and a dark horse behind him.

"Isn't that the horse that bit me?" Denna asked, shrinking back a little.

"Yes, that's Shadow." The time had finally come to put her on the horse she'd be riding for her wedding. She was more than ready.

Shadow was dark where Flicker was light, and delicate rather than built for battle. Her sleek coat shone in the afternoon sun, her mane and tail jet black and her coat the rich brown of dark chocolate. Her head was fine boned, and she had a long forelock the grooms had swept to the side out of her expressive eyes.

"Is she going to bite me again?" Denna sidled closer to me.

"No. She probably thought you had a treat that first day," I said. I pulled a worn black cachet from the tangle around my wrist and showed it to Denna. "Shadow was my first training project. You have nothing to worry about. She'll take care of you."

"All right." She put her hand on my arm, sending a jolt up to my shoulder. "I trust you."

I softened with her touch, hating myself for it. Denna had become a source of comfort—someone I relied on. That was never a good thing. Reliance on people created weaknesses for others to exploit.

The grooms got Denna mounted up, and I climbed aboard Flicker. We probably shouldn't have been riding out on our own, but if anyone inquired, it would be much easier to ask for forgiveness than permission. Besides, the last people I wanted to talk to for any reason were my father or Captain Ryka.

"You don't have to ride Shadow any differently than you'd ride Louie," I told her. "Keep the same position and use the same leg cues. The only difference you might notice is that Shadow is more sensitive. She's going to respond more promptly." Instructing Denna at least gave me something else to think about. Flicker had already picked up on my mood, tossing his head and sidestepping a little as we rode away from the barn.

Denna nodded her understanding and tried it out without having to be told. Soon she had Shadow walking, trotting, cantering, and halting with the barest touch of her seat and hands.

"This is different," she said breathlessly. "It's like going from a slow dance partner to one who is light and lithe. Or switching from a pavando to a galliand."

"I wouldn't know a galliand if it bit my horse on the nose, but I'm sure that's a good analogy," I said.

Denna grinned and nudged Shadow into a walk. We made our way into the woods, and I tried to forget the disastrous morning.

"I suppose you didn't have any luck getting your father to hear our evidence," Denna said.

My impulse was to respond with a biting reference to where he and the Directorate could shove parts of each other's anatomy, but I stopped the comment on the tip of my tongue. Denna was only trying to help.

"It was a disaster. My father won't listen, and neither will Captain Ryka. Lord Kriantz was the only one who seemed to think there might be merit to what we found," I said. "And it ended with my father's usual speech about how I ought to be getting married so that I'm out of his sight." The anger rose in me again, and with it, hurt. I broke a thin branch hanging low over the trail, wincing as it snapped in my palm.

"I'm sorry," Denna said. "You deserve better. They should have listened to you."

"I don't know," I said. The world didn't owe me, or anyone else, half a piece of horse shit. Flicker was the only one I could count on to carry me.

"No. You do. You deserve to be heard." Denna shook her head. "At least you tried. We did something. That's more than the rest of them can say."

"It's not over," I said. "We have to stop them, or at least make sure they're making the right choice. I want to stand behind my kingdom, not against it. And what if someone is still out there who could attack again?"

"We'll keep watching and listening. Maybe it's time to see if there's anything to be learned at court," Denna said. "We can do this."

"You're right," I said. Her support eased my fears.

We continued in companionable silence until the trail widened and opened into a field.

"I know what else might help," Denna said. She shot me a mischievous smile. "Race?" She nudged Shadow into a canter without waiting for my answer.

I squeezed Flicker's sides and we tore out across the meadow, the horses running with the wind at our backs. The cool air and the speed of the horses brought tears to my eyes, and I let out a whoop of excitement as Denna urged Shadow into a gallop, Flicker and I at her left flank. I glanced over to see a smile on her face and not the slightest bit of fear. Her green eyes sparkled in contrast with her rosy cheeks, joy so clearly written on her face that it swallowed me too. Watching her made me light-headed, my anger and sadness forgotten. I half expected to take flight from the saddle and soar into the sky.

We finally pulled the horses up on the far side of the field and they huffed with exertion, sweat beginning to slick the hair on their necks.

"It's like flying," Denna said, wiping the wind tears from her face.

"There isn't anything else like it in the world, is there?" The gallop had cleared my head, and the world felt new again.

"No, I've never done anything like that," Denna replied. "I feel like I have half an idea of what it's like to be free."

I smiled at her, but it was bittersweet. Neither of us would ever truly be free. She would be married by the time winter came, and if my father had anything to say about it, my marriage would follow not long after. The thought crushed me. Freedom was so fleeting for us, as swift to come and go as a breath.

We walked the horses around the perimeter of the field and up a trail leading to a small copse of trees. Low, thick branches provided a good place to tie the horses and a sheltered place for our picnic. Laughing, we struggled to pin down the blanket and the food to keep the wind from picking everything up and whisking it away. The horses flicked their ears toward our conversation, letting their lids grow heavy until they napped, each with a hind leg cocked. For a while, the lives Denna and I led down at the castle disappeared.

When we finished our food, I stretched out on the blanket, closing my eyes and letting the sun warm my face. The clean, cool wind carried the smell of grass and earth. As I lay there, Denna rested her head on my stomach, then turned her face to the sky, her eyes shut.

Her closeness made me afraid to move, as if I could destroy the moment with a single twitch. There was such innocence in her gesture, and yet it made me long for something decidedly not innocent. If only she didn't belong to my brother. For a moment I indulged the thought of pulling her up alongside me until I could feel her long lashes brush against my cheek, until her lips were only a whisper away—

"Are you holding your breath?" she asked.

I exhaled in a rush. "Oops," I said, grateful she couldn't see my face as heat rose to my cheeks.

She laughed a little. "It's all right, I'm not going to use this opportunity to stab you or tie you up or something."

"You'd never be able to take me!" I said.

"I know I wouldn't. You're strong."

"Not all the time," I said, but my cheeks warmed even more with the flattery. Was she flirting with me? What a dangerous game that would be, especially given the uncomfortable feelings the idea stirred. I could not have her. It was nonnegotiable.

"Will you come to the chamber music before dinner tonight?" she asked.

"I wasn't invited," I replied.

"Consider this your formal invitation." She reached for my cachets, skimming her fingers over the bands and sending a burst of goose bumps up my arm. If she had any idea how that made me feel, she'd stop. But I didn't want her to.

"How many cachets do you have?" she asked.

"Thirty-four cachets for forty-three horses," I answered. "The thick one is a ten-horse bracelet. I need to get some of the others redone that way."

"So many," Denna murmured. Her fingers continued to play across my wrist, turning and twisting the cachets until she finally set my arm down across her belly. I closed my eyes, remembering the first day we'd met, her luminous green eyes shining up at me as I rested my hand in that same place and reminded her how to breathe.

We lay there quietly, the seconds turning to sunlengths, until the inevitable time came when we had to go home. We packed up reluctantly and mounted, the horses eagerly pricking their ears toward the barn and their evening meal. We took it easy on the ride back, talking and laughing about nothing, and in those moments I knew what Denna meant when she told me only riding had ever made her feel so alive.

TWENTY-FIVE   🔥 *Dennaleia*

THE SUNNY AFTERNOON GAVE WAY TO A COOL EVENING
that settled in the stones of the castle and left everyone craving warmth
as we gathered in the drawing room for an evening of music. Heat
radiated from the earthenware cup I held close, warming my hands
and sending the spicy aroma of cinnamon curling up to my nose. The
smell created a bridge between my old life and new, mulled wine
reminding me of winter holidays with my family, but something in
the scent also bringing Mare to mind. I shivered and smiled into my
cup, recalling how it felt to lie with my head pillowed on her that
afternoon. She was so strong, yet so soft. Beneath the smell of horses,
earth, and the still-damp grass was a fragrance uniquely hers, spicy
sweet like my wine.

High on the pleasures of the afternoon, I had finally written
to my family. Though I omitted my adventure in the city, I did
tell them the most important thing—that I now had allies I could

trust and rely on. Between Ellaeni and Mare, I had the beginnings of friendships I knew would give me strength and support through the years to come in Mynaria. This news would give my parents confidence that, in spite of everything, things were unfolding as they should for my ascension.

Riding Shadow and composing letters had left me weary but content, but the peace of the evening didn't last long. Escorted by two liegemen, a messenger stumbled into the drawing room, barely able to stay on his feet, his clothes filthy from days of hard travel. He stopped before Captain Ryka and the king, executing a bow made sloppy by fatigue.

Ryka stepped out of the crowd. "Your report, soldier?"

"Zumordan bandits," he said. "They raided a town on our side of the border, in the southeast. The last town on the road to Kartasha."

The room filled with murmurs as everyone digested the news.

"The Directorate will have to reconvene tonight," said the king.

"Ugh," Thandi said under his breath beside me.

I squeezed his arm reassuringly. It had been a long day of meetings for him already.

"We'll do it immediately after dinner," the king declared. "Captain, please question the messenger for further details and see to the preparations."

Captain Ryka saluted and disappeared to attend to the tasks the king had requested of her. I didn't understand how this had happened. While the focus had been on rounding up Recusants within Lyrra, the borders should have already been fortified. That had been an issue even before Cas's death, and Captain Ryka was the one responsible for overseeing the defense of the kingdom. Perhaps Mare's suspicions about her weren't so out of line after all.

From that moment on, conversations among the nobles revolved around Zumorda and what countermeasures needed to be taken. Glasses were drained more quickly than usual, a third round already being served while the musicians were still setting up their instruments.

In spite of the larger problems, my primary concern was whether or not Mare would remember to attend. She would undoubtedly want to hear the news about the border right away. I hovered behind Thandi on the periphery of several conversations, smiling when required but having difficulty focusing. Lord Kriantz never strayed far from either Thandi or King Aturnicus as we worked our way around the room. Hopefully he was doing what he could to get them to consider Mare's evidence.

"We'll be the first to pledge our riders as border support," Lord Kriantz told a group of anxious courtiers.

"We are lucky to have you on our side, Endalan," Thandi said.

"As we discussed, it may be wise for you to return to your holdings soon," the king said. "We'll need your people strong and united to take on Zumorda if that's what it comes to. We can't have the enemy eroding our defenses before a war has even begun."

Lord Kriantz nodded. "I'll get my affairs in order as soon as the countermeasures are agreed upon and send for a new ambassador to take my place. My people will need me as a leader more than as a diplomat in the coming moons."

Hilara stood to the right of the king, her face stony. She said nothing, but her stillness was more terrifying than any of her cutting words. Without saying anything, she turned and walked away from the conversation, which continued on without her.

I anxiously rearranged chairs as everyone settled in for the performance, saving a place for Mare by my side. I pulled the chair so close that the wooden arms nearly touched, and then nudged it back in the other direction, but only a finger's length.

Mare had to come.

As the musicians took their places and waited for the cue to begin, she appeared at the door. My heart raced at the sight of her, in complete contrast to what I had been telling myself all night—that I would feel calmer once she arrived. Though she was late as always, this time the reason was written on her body. Each step she took sent shimmers over the iridescent material of her skirt, the blue fabric cascading to her feet like a waterfall. For once her dress was properly laced, showing off her narrow waist and every curve that departed from it.

My mouth went dry. Thoughts of the messenger, Ryka, and conspiracies against the crown fell away, leaving only a sharp pang of longing and the swirl of my magic tingling to the surface. Even her hair was perfectly in place, all of it up in a series of waves and twists so complex, I couldn't decipher the architecture of it all. She smiled at me, her eyes sparkling in the low light of the room.

I tore my eyes away, aware too late that I'd been staring. Judging by the peculiar silence that heralded her arrival, the rest of the room had experienced a similar reaction.

"Good evening, Your Highness," her familiar alto voice spoke in front of me.

"Hello," I squeaked.

"You'd think no one in this room had ever seen a princess before," she said nonchalantly.

She didn't look like a princess tonight. She looked like a queen.

"Close your mouth or you'll swallow a bug." She grinned, her eyes dancing with amusement as she seated herself beside me.

"I . . . I . . . wasn't expecting—"

"Nice to see you dressed appropriately for a change." Thandi's voice shot over my shoulder toward Mare as he sat down beside me.

"Bite my backside," Mare replied, her expression placid.

The musicians began to play, but they were impossible to focus on. Even the lilting flute melody of a tune I loved could not distract me from her. No matter where I looked in the room, it was as if she burned beside me.

My wine was gone in moments, but the fuzziness in my head did little to distract me. Mare's hand lay over the arm of her chair, her fingers tapping along with the music. She had gotten her cachets rewoven, the four wide ones and three narrow drawing attention to her strong, graceful wrist scattered with light freckles. I shifted to rest my arm on the side of my own chair until my hand lay so close that I could almost touch her.

My eyes charted their way across her face. The powder she wore could not fully hide the delicate freckles scattered like stars across her cheekbones. I wanted to trace the constellations in them, to memorize each and every pattern I could find on her skin and warm it with my touch. I kept still and tried to keep my breathing even, extending one finger tentatively across the gap between our chairs.

The room burst into applause, and her hand lifted from the chair to join in. Thandi nudged my other side, and I applauded numbly.

I tried to clear my head, but I'd hardly heard a note of the music. Nothing else, not even Thandi, could command my attention with Mare beside me looking as she did.

When the music began again, she folded her hands in her lap, straightening to listen. I did the same and accepted another cup of wine from a servant in hopes that it would still my trembling hands. Once the last piece of music ended and the applause died away, I finally had an opportunity to talk to Mare.

I reached toward her. "Mare, I need to talk to—"

"Dennaleia, have you met Lord Balenghren?" Thandi asked, gesturing to a paunchy man across the room with Ellaeni on his arm.

Ellaeni's annoyed expression told me everything I needed to know about Lord Balenghren.

"Actually, I wanted to talk to Mare for a minute," I said.

"You've been spending so much time with her lately." He frowned. "Surely it can wait until tomorrow."

I stared back at Mare over my shoulder as he led me away. She shrugged, and from the corner of my eye I saw Lord Kriantz already working his way through the room to her.

Lord Kriantz took her arm, whispering something in her ear. She laughed, her head thrown back and her elegant throat silhouetted in the light behind her. They drifted toward the refreshment table as Thandi tugged me in the opposite direction. I kept my head always slightly turned in her direction, waiting for her to let go of his arm, trying to catch her eye, but she followed him out the door without her eyes ever leaving his face. As she left the room, the light inside me was snuffed.

TWENTY-SIX

✦ *Mare*

OUT IN THE HALLWAY, SCONCES BURNED STEADILY with warm light in contrast to the slight chill in the air. I might have even enjoyed the soft and unfamiliar rustle of my skirts around my legs if disappointment hadn't swallowed me when Thandi dragged Denna away after the music.

I sighed. Dressing myself properly to surprise her had certainly had the impact I'd hoped for, and I'd liked the way she looked at me—maybe more than I should have. Yet I had still ended up on Lord Kriantz's arm at the end of the performance instead of in her receiving room talking like I'd hoped.

"What troubles you, my lady?" he asked.

"Nothing," I said. No one needed to know about my confused feelings for Denna.

"I hardly believe that. Your expression changed the moment we left the room." He looked at me appraisingly, concern in his dark eyes.

"I'm a bit tired, my lord," I lied.

"Well now, knowing that, I'm even more grateful that you made it to the music tonight. It's always lovely to see you. And, since I have your ear, there was something I wanted to discuss."

"Oh?" I quickened my pace. Maybe he had news about the knife.

"Yes. Perhaps you'd like to take dinner with me in a private room?"

"Of course," I agreed.

I let him lead me to one of the many private alcoves off the great hall where courtiers sometimes entertained smaller groups. Lord Kriantz must have known I would accept his invitation, for when he pulled back the curtain to the dining alcove and invited me to sit, a feast was already spread on the table. Though fall had nearly arrived, he had chosen a summer meal—grapes, soft cheese, rolls stuffed with peppered meat and slathered with spicy fruit sauce, and even a small bottle of sweet white wine infused with brandy.

"Is there any chance you might return to the Directorate?" Lord Kriantz asked once the pages had left.

"Why bother? They won't listen to me even if I come," I replied. "Did anything interesting happen this afternoon?"

"That depends on what qualifies as interesting to you," he said.

He was such a politician. No wonder my father and Thandi liked him so much.

"Don't know." I shrugged. "Have any of the captured Recusants provided any useful information?" I popped a grape into my mouth, not expecting him to tell me anything helpful.

"So far, the investigation hasn't led to much," Lord Kriantz said. "The questioning hasn't been very organized, and no one knows how to test whether or not specific people are magic users. The worse news is that we're receiving more and more reports that the Recusants are popping up in cities all over Mynaria. It's far more widespread than we thought."

"Really?" I asked. I hadn't imagined that dissent over the alliance would be so pervasive.

"Yes. And the discussion early this morning was rather fraught. Apparently the Trindori brokered a trade agreement with some Zumordans without consulting the crown. One of the Recusant factions was helping transport goods up the canal. When the fundamentalists got wind of it, the riot brought traffic on the canal to a standstill, and from the sound of it, they haven't sorted it out yet."

"That's quite a bag of snakes to untangle. What is the Directorate doing about the Recusants in other cities?"

"Detaining everyone they catch," he said. "Though local authorities also don't have consistent procedures or equal amounts of resources, depending on the territory. They're trying to get some of that addressed now. As for the knife, no further investigation has been conducted, but I put word in with a few people this afternoon."

"Typical," I said. Their idiocy was astounding. "Let me guess—they've been focusing on some kind of pointless local project instead."

"Security, mostly. Every time a noble can't find one of their family members for a sunlength or two, chaos ensues, more liegemen are requested. . . . I'm sure you can imagine the rest."

"Witlessness at its finest," I said. I couldn't bear to talk about it anymore or I'd start throwing dishes. "Any luck getting my father to turn over one of his prize horses to you yet?"

"Perhaps." Lord Kriantz smiled. "It will involve some negotiating. Hopefully he'll come around before I return to Sonnenborne, which may be sooner than expected thanks to the banditry. We're still rather new to this business of being civilized. I can't leave my people without leadership."

"It's a pity you're leaving so soon," I said, and meant it. He'd only arrived earlier that summer, and it wasn't uncommon for visiting diplomats to stay for a full year. It would have been nice to have more time to see if his influence could benefit both the Directorate and me.

"The tribes under my banner still need a guiding hand," he said. "A firm one. We Sonnenbornes are a powerful people united, but life is hard in the desert. There is always a temptation to return to a state where each person lives only for themselves."

I nodded, though it was hard to imagine the kind of society he described. The conversation turned to horses, and we chatted amicably over the meal until only crumbs remained. When the bell rang to call the Directorate to their meeting, we stood up and paused at the end of the table in front of the long curtains that separated the alcove from the rest of the great hall.

"Thank you for the invitation," I said.

"We must do it again," he said. He kissed my hand in farewell but then took the opportunity to pull me a little closer. "Perhaps we could go for a ride sometime?"

"Perhaps," I said, putting some space between us. I'd enjoyed his company but didn't want him getting the idea I was available to be courted. Still, he was a useful ally, and alienating him would be a mistake.

"Good evening, my lady. May we meet again soon," Lord Kriantz said, and favored me with an amused smile before slipping through the curtains and away to the meeting.

TWENTY-SEVEN   🪶 *Dennaleia*

MY PLANS TO TALK TO MARE ABOUT THE BORDER
attack were dashed first thing in the morning when I was ushered
straight out of bed into fittings for my wedding gown. Servants
bustled around me with a rush of pins, ribbon, lace, and fabric, all
of which my small form was expected to support. Morning light
cast a pale glow in my receiving room, supplemented by many
lamps hung at different heights on the wall to give the seamstresses
good visibility. But the gossip proved far worse than the poking and
prodding.

"I hear an offer might be made for the hand of Princess Amaranthine," a seamstress said with a mouthful of pins.

"Who?" another asked.

"No one knows. Mina said it was some lord from the north, but
Lynette claimed it was a southerner with a string of horses for her to
train." They both laughed.

I twitched, causing one of them to yelp as she stuck herself with a hemming pin.

"Are we done yet?" I asked, impatient to escape and get some answers of my own.

"Almost, Your Highness," the first seamstress said. "But we haven't been able to find your attendant, Lady Ellaeni? She should have been here for her dress fitting a sunlength ago. Her dress won't be ready in time if we can't get her fitted this morning."

I muttered a prayer for patience to the god of earth. My talk with Mare would have to wait until my riding lesson. "I trust you sent someone to look for her?" I asked.

"Yes, my lady. She doesn't have a personal maid, so we weren't sure who to ask," the seamstress said.

Both of them stared at me, expecting a solution to the problem. I hadn't talked to Ellaeni the previous night. I'd been preoccupied with Mare's departure with Lord Kriantz, and Thandi kept us moving around the room with little opportunity to speak at length with anyone. Ellaeni had spent most of the evening on Lord Balenghren's arm. I had caught her eye only once, as she stood alone by a table of discarded glasses, tracing the symbol of the water god over and over where someone's water had spilled, her expression troubled.

"I will find her," I said. I had a feeling I knew where she might be. But if I was correct, sending another person to fetch her felt wrong.

Once the seamstresses had put away my gown and Auna had dressed me, I went in search of Ellaeni. The halls bustled with morning activity, pages darting amidst the other foot traffic and liegemen standing sentry at every junction. Though more than a moon remained until the harvest ball and my wedding, decorating had already begun. Servants guided twisted garlands of silk leaves in orange and red from sconce to sconce in each corridor. I hurried past them, trying subtly to shake my hands free of tingles that wouldn't ease. If Ellaeni was where I suspected, I feared what I might find. It wasn't like her to disappear without so much as sending a message. Taking a deep breath, I pushed my way through the heavy door of the Sanctuary.

The door swung closed behind me, dimming the commotion of the castle to a distant hum. My magic quieted as well, eased by the peace of the Sanctuary. Beneath the altar of the water god, Ellaeni sat with her skirts around her and her face in her hands, sobs racking her lithe frame. I crouched and touched her shoulder.

"Ellaeni," I said softly.

"Oh no," she said, trying to wipe the tears from her cheeks. "Dennaleia—I mean, Your Highness—I'm sorry, I—" She put her head back in her hands and rocked forward, choking on another sob.

"I am only Denna right now. What happened?" I wrapped my arm around her like I would my sister and held her until she found her voice.

"The letters stopped," she said. "There's been a riot over the canals. They've started rounding up the Recusants in Trindor, and I'm afraid they've taken Claera."

"Claera?" I asked tentatively. Ellaeni had never spoken that name before.

"The chief cook on my ship. She was everything to me," Ellaeni said. "She took such care with my crew and with me most of all. I'd visit her in the galley at night, and she'd have saved me something special. We'd have eaten dreadful salted meat and black radishes for dinner because it was all we had left at the end of a long haul, and I'd go down there to find she'd carved one of those ugly black radishes into a beautiful flower to have something pretty to give me." Another tear trailed down Ellaeni's cheek.

"I'm so sorry, Ellaeni. I understand. Mare is like that for me. She's my best friend. I would be lost without her," I said.

"No. Claera is not only my friend . . . she's my heart. My parents forbade me to speak of her while here at court. They don't approve of someone of my rank associating with a cook." Ellaeni searched my face with hope and fear.

Understanding dawned on me. They had been lovers. I blushed over my mistake at comparing their relationship to mine with Mare.

"Why do you think they've taken her?" I asked.

"She has the sea sense," Ellaeni said. "And now that the Recusants are being persecuted and anyone suspected of magic hunted . . . I worried a little when her letter didn't come last week. But the mail should have arrived again today, and there was nothing. Between that and the riots . . ." Her voice caught.

"Oh, Ellaeni . . ." My heart broke for her.

"I would give anything to make sure she is safe. My rank. My ship. Whatever it takes," Ellaeni said. "Every night, she's the last thing I think of when I fall asleep. Every morning, I feel her loss when I wake."

No wonder Ellaeni had been so unhappy about being sent to Lyrra. She hadn't just left behind the only life she knew. She had left the person she loved most.

I took Ellaeni's hand and squeezed it. "I'm sure she thinks of you every day, too," I said.

"You think so?" Ellaeni asked.

"I'm sure of it," I said. "If you come with me, maybe we can see about getting you into an attendant's dress. And I'll see if there's anything I can do to help you find out where she is." I was not truly sure I could help her, but only a terrible friend wouldn't try.

Ellaeni turned and wrapped her arms around me. "Thank you, Denna. It's good to be able to talk about Claera. To have someone who knows."

I returned her embrace and pulled her to her feet.

She grimaced at the tearstained state of her dress.

"Maybe if we say a prayer, something can be done about those spots," I said.

She nodded, and we stepped to the altar of the wind god.

"Let's close our eyes," I said. My magic came softly in the Sanctuary, subdued and easy in my hands. I sketched the symbol of the wind god and invited the tingles out. A gentle breeze dried the spots on Ellaeni's dress, and then I released the power. The chimes at the air altar jingled as the magic dissipated in a final gust.

Ellaeni opened her eyes and stared at her dress in wonder. "The wind god truly is powerful here," she said.

"Indeed," I said, dizzy from the outpouring of power, and more than a little surprised that it had worked. My magic really was easier to handle within the confines of the Sanctuary.

She took my hand and squeezed it. "Thank you."

We both circled the room and offered prayers to each of the gods in turn. My emotions churned in me as I tossed the offering chip to the fire god. Ellaeni couldn't possibly remain at court more than a year—she needed to return to Claera, and I would support her in that. But if I lost Ellaeni, I hoped Mare might stay. I needed at least one person by my side I could trust, and I couldn't see myself eventually ascending to queen without Mare's friendship and counsel.

All the boring meals, poetry readings, and dress fittings I had to sit through would be bearable knowing I could seek out her company at will. She gave me the perspective I needed, shedding light on the world in a way I would not have considered. Then again, if marriage was what she wanted, I couldn't stand in her way.

I had to find out the plans for her future.

I couldn't go to Thandi—he wouldn't understand. He already had trusted advisers and confidants he'd known since childhood. Unfortunately, King Aturnicus was the only other person with the authority to give me answers. As soon as I had escorted Ellaeni to my receiving room for her fitting, I sent a page to arrange an audience with the king before I could second-guess myself.

However, nervousness hit once I was confronted with the king staring expectantly at me from across the massive desk in his study. I took a deep breath to steady myself, as I had done in my early riding lessons.

"What brings you here, Princess?" King Aturnicus asked me.

"I heard a rumor, Your Majesty," I said, twisting my skirts in my hands. "I heard that Amaranthine is possibly going to be married later this year, but she hasn't said anything to me about it, which makes me think maybe she doesn't know, but if she doesn't know, then someone has to be planning it, but I can't imagine anyone would be planning it without—"

"Stop." The king put up his hand, and my rambling ceased

immediately. "Who told you that?"

"Some servants were talking about it. They didn't know to whom, though," I added, realizing that I might be implicating someone by mentioning the rumor. He let out a heavy sigh.

"It is unfortunate that the rumor began, and it's not entirely accurate. A proposal has been made for Amaranthine, but no binding agreement has been confirmed. Her suitor was kind enough to allow her the time to consider his offer and let you and Thandilimon remain at the forefront for now."

My eyes widened at the words "binding agreement." That binding agreement would take away the one person I trusted implicitly. Was that what she wanted?

"Please remind me why you have an interest in this, Princess Dennaleia," the king said. He frowned and leaned back in his chair, which creaked as he shifted his weight.

"I don't want to interfere with anything that will benefit the kingdom," I said, "but I've found Mare to be a valuable source of advice and company in my time here in Mynaria. I would never keep her here against her will, but I feel that she might be important if I one day ascend the throne. I value someone who gives such good, honest counsel."

"Are we speaking of the same individual? The one who showed up properly dressed yesterday for the first time in her adult life?" the king said, his tone sardonic.

"I believe so," I said, allowing my mouth to quirk into a partial smile. She had looked outstanding. But I couldn't tell him the other reasons I wanted her to stay—how she had taken me to see the city, how we'd broken into Ryka's ready room, and how when she looked at me I felt like I could fly.

"Amaranthine still has things to learn. She must accept that her kingdom comes first. She is eighteen and already past the age when she should have been betrothed. I had hoped you would be an example to her rather than the other way around," he said.

"Oh, I've tried, Your Majesty." The lie came easily, but I hated myself for it. I didn't want her to be like me. I wanted her to be herself.

"I'm sure you have, my dear. Perhaps you should begin spending more time with the other nobles and spouses of those on the Directorate. That would be a great asset to Thandi."

"Yes, Your Majesty. I apologize for intruding into family business. I only wanted to offer some thoughts on ways that Amaranthine might contribute to the crown in the future."

"Speaking of my wayward daughter, I'm sending Thandi down to observe your riding lesson today. He needs a respite from Directorate business, and I'm sure he will be interested to see what you've learned."

"Of course, Your Majesty." As if the business of Mare's marriage weren't bad enough, I wouldn't even be able to talk to her openly with Thandi there.

I should have cared about the chance to ride with Thandi and impress him with what I had learned.

I didn't.

"It was nice of you to stop by, Princess." The king waved me out of the room.

I strode out into the hallway with confidence, but my facade crumbled within minutes of walking away. The king had already made his decision. I could only wait to see what Mare's would be.

TWENTY-EIGHT

Mare

THANDI TROTTED ZIN UP AS I LED FLICKER AND Shadow out for Denna's lesson.

"What are you doing here?" I asked. I'd hoped to finally get some time with Denna to share with her what Lord Kriantz had told me about the Recusants and the rioting in Trindor.

"Making sure you've taught my future wife something useful." He gave his horse a few hearty pats on the neck. "Besides, Zin and I could use the exercise."

"We're riding out. You probably don't have time."

"Oh, but I do. Father has given me the afternoon off from the Directorate. They're wrapping up their discussion of how much border support is needed to prevent further raids. My vote has already been cast."

"Fine." I made a lengthy show of checking the girths and stirrup leathers on both horses while we waited for Denna.

His horse fidgeted, swinging her head around to nibble at his boots.

"You shouldn't let her get away with that," I said.

"And you shouldn't be riding a cull. Or a horse with war breeding," he retorted.

"Forgive me if I fail to take advice from someone with only four cachets to his name."

Thandi scowled at me. "Some of us don't have time to spend all day down in the barn, Mare. Some of us take our responsibilities seriously and care about the crown."

I snorted. "If you run this kingdom like you trained that horse—"

"Don't even pretend you know anything about what I do," he snapped. "Let's both stick to what we know."

Denna cleared her throat, alerting us to her presence. I scowled in Thandi's direction one last time before turning to Denna and handing her Shadow's reins. She smiled as she took them, and the tension bled out of me.

"Lovely to see you, my lady," Thandi greeted Denna.

"Always a pleasure, my lord," she replied, swinging up into the saddle with ease. "I'm sorry for being a few minutes late."

"It's no problem. I had the chance to chat with my charming brother," I said with the warmth of a winter gale.

"We're taking the hill paths, I presume?" Thandi started his horse in the direction of the trail without waiting for an answer.

"I suppose so," I muttered under my breath.

Denna gave me an apologetic look.

"Walk with me, my lady." Thandi gestured to Denna to ride up alongside him. She squeezed Shadow into a jog to catch up, leaving me to follow behind them barely within earshot.

"We may have had a breakthrough with the Recusants," Thandi said.

"Oh?" Denna asked.

"Another of their leaders here in Lyrra has been captured along with something far more valuable. He has some sort of artifact—a silver bowl—that seems to identify those with Affinities. He's been tight-lipped about how it works, but it's only a matter of time before we break him down. Then we can begin testing anyone suspected of magic."

They must have caught Graybeard. I wasn't sure if that was good or bad.

"But what about the Zumordan blade?" Denna asked. Shadow danced sideways a little, betraying Denna's tension.

"Figuring out the secret of the bowl takes precedence. We know that the Recusants are responsible for Casmiel. And discovering who the magic users are should lead us straight to the Zumordans behind it."

His logic didn't make a whole lot of sense, especially from what I'd seen of Graybeard and the meeting he held at the abandoned Sanctuary. But before I could point out the rampant idiocy in the Directorate for the umpteenth time, Thandi urged his horse into a trot.

I willed my eyes to burn holes through his red jacket as it bobbed through the trees. He didn't deserve Denna; she would never reach her full potential with him. He'd have her writing letters and doing cresthaven tours and embroidering thrice-damned baby blankets her whole life when she could be researching for the Directorate and learning to be a true monarch instead of just a pretty face.

Flicker increased his pace and tossed his head, reacting to the tension throughout my body. I had to think about something else or I'd end up unhorsed before we made it halfway into the hills. I fumed my way up the trail until we got to a meadow, the spread of golden grass a welcome escape. Flicker and I cantered away, making a loop around the edge of the field. I focused on his strides, hoping to find peace in the familiar three-beat rhythm of his hooves on the grass. My body took over from my mind, and I relaxed into the quiet place where nothing existed but me, Flicker, and our forward motion.

I asked Flicker for a flying lead change as we turned toward the others, Thandi's bright-red jacket and Denna's deep-blue one beacons against the golden meadow. Flicker switched leads effortlessly, his chestnut ears pricked toward the other horses. I slowed him to a trot, then a walk, in no hurry to get close enough for conversation. Denna put Shadow through her paces in the distance. They looked like a pair now, a beautiful and delicate contrast to Thandi and Zin. I could barely remember Denna as the awkward beginner who fell off her horse because of a sneeze.

"You've done your job, sister," Thandi said as I rode within earshot. For once he seemed pleased with me, and it brought an unexpected swell of emotion. I couldn't recall the last time he'd looked at me with gratitude or approval.

"She truly has," Denna said. "I might have been able to learn without her, but I don't think I would have found so much joy in it." Her face was radiant as she spoke.

"In fact, she rides so well I don't think you need to teach her any longer," Thandi continued. "You can have your afternoons back to yourself. I'll let Father know."

My brief moment of camaraderie with him shattered.

"But I don't feel ready!" Denna exclaimed, shooting me a panicked look.

"You are." I hated to agree with Thandi, but she was. For the purposes of what she needed to know, she had already surpassed the level of competence she required. To keep her in lessons would be selfishness on my part.

"But—"

"You can still ride Shadow anytime," Thandi reassured her. "Perhaps we should plan to ride together regularly. I would like that."

A weight settled on my chest. Afternoons without her would be empty. He would take my place in her life as friend and confidant. As Thandi and Denna discussed their plans, I stayed silent, staring down at the dying grass beneath Flicker's hooves. I did my best to maintain the facade that had once been second nature—complete impassiveness no matter what. But it simply wasn't possible with Denna. Over the past moon she'd broken through all my walls, and now I lay defenseless.

"Should we head back now?" Denna asked.

Nausea dug its claws into my stomach, a sharp physical response to the thought of my future without her close.

"Mare?" Denna finally looked over from Shadow's back, concern in her glass-green eyes.

"I don't feel well," I said, breaking away from her gaze to stare at Flicker's ears.

"Probably from riding the ghastly gaits on that cull," Thandi joked.

Denna nudged Shadow closer. "Truly, are you all right?"

"Something from lunch must be disagreeing with me. Go on ahead. I'll catch up."

Thandi snorted in annoyance and spurred Zin toward the trail at a brisk trot.

"Go," I repeated, refusing to meet her eyes.

"If you're sure," she said, slowly turning Shadow and sparing me one last glance before cantering off toward Thandi.

As they disappeared into the trees, I dismounted and numbly sat down. Flicker lowered his head to nuzzle at the grass for something to eat. I waited to throw up, praying for some sort of release from my feelings, but the sickness never came.

Half a moon passed in which I didn't see or hear from Denna, and both my life and the weather grew colder. Autumn had finally arrived. My few invitations to her were met with regretful declines that cut closer to the bone each time. There was always something else on her schedule—she had been swept fully into court life with room for little else. I missed her with a kind of smarting ache that stirred to life with the smallest reminders: when the shimmering sound of a harp drifted from one of the drawing rooms as I paced through the castle late one night, when I rode through the field where we'd nearly been shot, and when a server at the Deaf Dog brought me the wrong drink and I found myself with a mouthful of apricot beer.

The evening after the apricot beer and a failed attempt to track down someone who might know Morland's whereabouts, I returned to my chambers to find a sealed note from Denna on my vanity. Initially, I didn't even want to look at it. I lingered in my bath, hiding from the chilly weather and easing away the faint aches left in me by a hard ride and my trip into town. I didn't know what to expect. Probably a polite thank-you note for the lessons, or maybe an invitation to another social event where I'd get all of five minutes of Denna's time before my brother dragged her away. It crossed my mind to simply burn the note unopened.

But by the time the bathwater grew cold, I had resigned myself to reading it. I sat down at my vanity swathed in a robe, pulling the thick fabric around me as though it might protect me from the contents of Denna's note. The wax seal, which was deep purple and embossed with a lone pine tree and a star, separated easily from the paper and left a plum-colored stain on the parchment.

> Dearest M,
>   I need to talk to you. Please meet me in the back garden three sunlengths after dark.
>   Yours, D

I folded the note and then immediately unfolded it and read it again, my heartbeat echoing in my ears. She wanted to see me alone. I told myself not to get excited over something so small, but I couldn't slow the beating of my heart.

Drying myself in a hurry, I pulled out my black breeches, then second-guessed myself and pulled out all the darkest dresses I had, tossing everything onto the bed. By the time my hair was almost dry, the room had devolved into total chaos. I sent Sara away when she tried to assist me—I didn't want her knowing my plans. When Nils showed up to get me for dinner, he found me in the midst of the disaster, still wearing nothing but underclothes.

"Whoa. Should I even try to come in here?" He picked his way over the discarded garments on the floor until he got close enough to envelop me in a hug.

"Shut up," I mumbled into his shoulder.

"Is someone coming courting tonight?" He pulled back and winked.

"Hardly!" I turned away with flushed cheeks.

"So what are you wearing? We're going to get lousy spots at the table if you don't have something picked out. And I'm guessing that underdress wasn't what you had in mind."

I rolled my eyes. "I need a dress, but it has to be dark."

"I think you should wear this one," he said, picking up a deep-blue dress off the bed.

"Why? I already rejected that one on the basis of breasts. As in too much of them showing."

He grinned. "But that's exactly the basis on which it's a good idea. Especially if you're trying to impress someone."

"You're disgusting." Denna was a friend, and a tight dress would probably have limited impact on her. Though I had to admit her reaction to my attire at the last music event had been quite rewarding.

"I know you too well, Mare. Something is going on with you. But I won't question it. A lady should always have her secrets."

"As long as her secret doesn't involve what she caught from the last liegeman she bedded. Right, Nils?" I waggled my eyebrows.

"Now you're the disgusting one," he laughed. "Truly, wear this dress. It looks smashing on you."

"All right." I finally gave in, pulling the dress over my head. "Can you lace me up? Surely you know how after the number of girls you've had in and out of their dresses."

"Well, sometimes I don't take them all the way out of their dresses for that reason," he said.

"Lace it already, bonehead. You don't even have to do it tight. I like being able to breathe."

"As you wish, my lady," he said, pulling the laces snug.

After a merry dinner with Nils and his friends, I excused myself to sneak out to the garden. I slipped into the closest servants' stairwell outside the great hall to avoid the patrolling liegemen, walking to the back gardens using a convoluted route and listening carefully for anyone else who might be outside.

Despite my paranoia, the night was still and cold, even the animals safe in their nests and dens. As I got closer to my destination, it occurred to me that Denna might be putting me on, or that Thandi could have sent the note. I tried to quell the ragged beating of my heart by sheer force of will, my breath fogging in front of me in the crisp autumn air.

When I finally arrived in the back garden, it stood empty. I settled myself on a stone bench on the north side of the square yard, shuffling my feet against the flagstone path. I shivered in the dark, tucking my hands deep into the folds of my cloak and holding my arms close against my body. I wished I knew the exact time. Was I early or late?

As I stood up to pace to keep warm, Denna appeared, like a shadow separating itself from the darkness. She stepped through the other side of the garden to smile at me, her eyes shining from beneath the hood of her cloak.

"I'm so glad you came!" She rushed up to me.

"Of course." I smiled.

"It's freezing out here." She wrapped her arms tightly around herself and bounced in place.

"Your suggestion, not mine. You could always have me scaling your walls again to climb in your window," I joked.

"Next time you're welcome to do that. In fact, maybe I should have you teach me how to climb too."

I laughed at the serious expression on her face. "I doubt Thandi would approve of his wife scaling stone walls in the middle of the night."

"Probably not, but it's not for him to say."

"Isn't it? What's going on, Denna?" I asked.

"It's all my fault," she said woefully, sitting down on the bench from which I'd stood up a few moments before.

"What do you mean?"

"It's all my fault," she repeated, hanging her head as her smile faded.

"Explain." I sat down beside her. She turned to me, her face pale in the moonlight.

"I spoke to the king a few weeks ago." She took a breath. "I heard that someone was going to make an offer for your hand."

"What?" It was the first I'd heard of any such thing.

"I'm fine with that if you want to get married, truly I am. But

I hadn't heard anything about it from you, which made me think that maybe you didn't know. Then I got worried. And a little selfish. I don't want the king to send you off unless it's what you want, so I tried to explain to him how important you are to me. Instead, they've ended my lessons and scheduled every day until the wedding up to the hilt. Games in the parlor. Poetry readings in the garden. A fashion show and discussion with the lady courtiers."

I groaned. It all made sense now. Any interest in me on Denna's part undoubtedly made my father and brother eager to separate us so that I wouldn't be a bad influence. If they had been planning a marriage for me, removing Denna from my daily life might make marriage seem like a more reasonable option.

"Oh, please don't be angry." She clutched my arm. "I . . . I can't lose you. You're the only thing that matters to me here, the only one who has made me feel at home . . . well, not at home exactly, but alive. Happy. I feel so many things I didn't know I could feel, and it's all because of you. I value your opinions and your thoughts, and you're so perceptive, and I can't be here and do this without you, I can't."

"Oh, Denna," I said softly. I wasn't upset with her. Every word she spoke I could have said about her in return. But I didn't dare confess that. "I'm not angry," I said. "But you're right—it could be because of your talk with my father that Thandi's been putting together all these events. My father probably thought you were getting too close to me and didn't want you to be corrupted by my influence."

"I know, but my intention was exactly the opposite. I wanted him to see how good you are, how wonderful you are. All he's missed out on by not keeping up with you and paying attention to what you have to say. Now I've made a mess of everything, and it is all my fault, and I'll miss you so much—" She bit her lip.

"Shhh, it's all right," I said, wrapping my arm around her shoulders. Her teeth chattered, and I held her close to ward off the chill. My pulse raced as she nestled into my arm. She felt perfect there, the sweet rosy smell of her hair warming me as though summer had never left.

"I'll always be your friend," I said. And though the words were true, they didn't quite feel like enough. But what more could I offer?

"You're the best friend I've ever had," Denna said, and startled me by throwing her arms around my neck.

She held me a moment, and then a moment more, and I cautiously returned her embrace. She melted into my arms, tucking her head up against my neck.

"I'm sorry it's so cold out," she whispered, her voice muffled by the folds of my cloak. "This is no way to meet. I have to see you again—I don't care what Thandi plans."

"I want to see you again too." The intensity between us frightened me. It felt like it could go in a dangerous direction, but there was no way I could turn away from it.

"We're going to have to work something out," she said firmly, pulling back from my embrace. "We still need to figure out who was behind the forgery of that knife."

Grudgingly I let her go, the cold rushing in to surround me again.

"Do you have anything in mind?" I asked. "Because this garden is only going to get colder when winter comes, and there will be even more eyes on you now. If we start visiting each other, they'll only rearrange your schedule to make it impossible all over again."

"Ugh!" She swatted a bush with her hand. "We'll have to be creative. How hard was it for you to climb that wall when you broke into my rooms that first time?"

"Oh, Hells," I said. "I was sore for two days afterward."

"I have an idea," she said excitedly. "Ropes! Ropes from the barn. Can we get some rope, or some extra halters? We'll make something that makes it easier for you to climb."

"We always have lots of old halters lying around. I'll see about it tomorrow," I said. Her cleverness delighted me.

"Good. Then we'll meet tomorrow night, my rooms, after whatever nonsense they've planned for me. Four sunlengths after dinner should be late enough. A great deal has happened at court."

"I haven't had much luck in town, but we should still compare notes. I'm in."

"Really? I know this is crazy. You don't have to do it if you don't want to."

"I'd visit you even if you were on the fifth floor and I had to figure out a way to fly," I said.

"Mare!" she exclaimed, and hugged me again. "I'm so glad." She pulled back slowly, her breath misting into the dark. She stared into my eyes, searching there for something. I had no idea what she was looking for, though her eyes were filled with hope and fear, and something else I couldn't identify. I knew what I wanted her to see—that I would always be there for her in any way I could.

"I'll see you tomorrow," she finally said, briefly cupping my cheek with her cold hand before hurrying out of the garden.

I sat on the bench, shivering with the chill caused by her absence, and not completely sure what to make of our exchange except that she wanted to see me. She wanted me to come to her window tomorrow. It was enough.

TWENTY-NINE

Dennaleia

COOL NIGHT AIR BLEW THROUGH MY BEDROOM,
making the flames in my hearth flicker and spark behind the fire
screen. Shivering, I moved closer to the warmth, holding my hands
toward the rearing horses that decorated the metal. The horses had
wind-tossed manes like the ones on the fences and gates that Mare
and I had walked past out in Lyrra. Even now, I could almost taste
the bittersweet beer and feel the comfort and freedom of being close
by Mare's side. She would arrive soon if everything went according
to plan.

Behind me, a knotted series of halters and ropes trailed from
the thick wooden leg of my bed out the open window. Procuring
them had been as easy as Mare promised—she had smuggled them
in through the barn tunnel, packed them up in a gift box covered in
bright ribbons, and had her maid deliver them to my chambers.

Sitting through a hideously dull poetry reading with a pleasant expression on my face earlier in the evening had been easy. Knowing I would soon see Mare made everything bearable. Thandi had remarked on how happy I looked, and I responded that the poetry was especially lovely. It wasn't true, but that didn't matter. The dim light of the parlor had made his blue eyes look the exact same shade of gray as Mare's. Seeing pieces of Mare in him brought an easy smile to my face. If getting to see Mare made my time with Thandi more enjoyable, it was one more way that she made my life better—one more reason that I could not ever lose her.

I put on my cloak and pulled a chair up to the window where the rope dangled. The chill didn't stop me from peering out my window every few minutes until Mare stood in the garden below, her face barely visible between the arborvitae that lined the castle wall. I waved, resisting the urge to call out a hello as she gave the rope several experimental tugs. Climbing didn't look easy, but she managed to pull herself up, the old horse halters and ropes holding firmly.

When she clambered through the window, my hands and feet lost all sense of what they ought to be doing. She pulled up the rope and closed my shutters, and then we stared at each other for a moment that stretched out until I knew my cheeks burned as scarlet as the red silk covers on my bed.

"So, um, how was your day?" I finally asked.

"Oh, you know, the usual. Got drunk on cheap ale down in Lyrra. Growled at a few children. Kicked a few puppies." She pulled off her hat, letting her braid tumble down her back.

"You did not!" I giggled.

"Well, it's about a quarter true," she said, her eyes sparkling with merriment. "I did spend the day down in the cresthaven, and Nils and I did go to one of the more unsavory pubs we frequent, since we haven't had much luck at the Deaf Dog. Though I'm not sure how much longer we can keep going to the Pelham. The streets feel dangerous now."

"Tell me what the Pelham is like," I said. It honestly didn't matter, but the sound of her musical voice was so welcome to my ears that I could have listened to her read the treasury inventory of all four Northern Kingdoms. Happily.

We sat side by side on my chaise.

"It's dark," she said. "The kind of place where you don't want to eat anything you drop on the table. And pretty much everyone in there looks like they'd take the food right off your plate if you don't keep an eye on 'em. The ale is cheap but goes down easy. Most of the serving girls are missing a few teeth and don't look like they've ever found use for a hairbrush."

"Mmm," I said. I plucked a sprig of arborvitae from the sleeve of her black shirt and twirled it between my fingers. As I tossed it into the fire, my magic rose unbidden to incinerate it right before it hit the flames. I sat back quickly, but Mare didn't seem to notice.

"What's troubling is that information is harder to come by now. In spite of so many Recusants having been rounded up, they seem to keep appearing, and the violence against them keeps increasing. They've left what used to be their meeting place, and no one has any leads. They're too wise now to reveal their locations," she said.

"I've heard from a friend that they're springing up all over the kingdom," I told her, thinking of Ellaeni and Claera. "They're being persecuted everywhere as well. I fear for some of my friends."

"Yes, Kriantz mentioned that too. But you have friends among the Recusants?" Mare asked. "If you do, that could be very helpful! We could ask them—"

"No, no." I shook my head. "One of my friends is courting someone who has a gift. That's how I found out. But she hasn't received a message for a long time and fears something has happened. I've been trying to look into it for her."

"Does the person have a fire gift, by any chance?" Mare asked.

Fear flickered in me, a mirror of the flames in my hearth. "No," I said. "Water."

"Pity. The Recusants mentioned someone with a fire gift, someone powerful. But they didn't know who it was, only that they had sensed a burst of magic the night of the assassination attempt on my father. I was hoping maybe your friend's love might be the explanation for that."

"No, I don't think it was her." My mouth got drier by the minute.

"Maybe once they start testing people more comprehensively, they'll track the person down. It might provide some of the answers we're looking for."

I swallowed hard. It couldn't be much longer before paranoia made the Directorate start testing courtiers.

"Mare? I have to tell you something." I trembled with fear, but the words were unspooling and I couldn't go back. "That night the assassin tried to kill the king . . . I was so afraid. And when he struck out at Thandi, and then you . . . I was scared you would be hurt. That you might die."

"That makes two of us," she said. "But it doesn't matter. He's dead." She touched my arm reassuringly.

"I know. But there's something else I need to tell you about that night," I said.

"What do you mean?" she asked.

My throat closed on the words. I couldn't speak them.

Instead I gazed into the heart of the fire and released the barest bit of my magic into the world. Sparks lifted out of the fire, drifting into the room, burning more brightly as they rose. My control wavered as they grew close to the ceiling, and I clamped back down on the magic. The sparks popped all at once, showering us with cinders.

Mare stared at me, dumbfounded.

My cheeks burned with shame and fear. When she'd said she would always be my friend, she hadn't known my secret. But I wanted her word to hold true—and that meant I needed to tell her.

"Please forgive me," I said. "My mother told me to hide it, to take the secret to my grave. And it was always such a small gift, a parlor trick. Not real magic. But ever since I came here, it's been out of control. It's stronger than me, Mare, and stronger every day. I'm afraid. I don't know what to do."

"It was you," she whispered. "Not Lord Kriantz, not the knife. You burned that assassin."

I nodded, tears stinging the corners of my eyes. "I never meant to do it. I was so scared. When he struck at you and Thandi, I couldn't hold it back."

Mare's expression was indecipherable.

"Please don't hate me," I said, my voice small. My lip quivered, and I tried to keep my chin up even as my gaze fell from Mare's face.

The floor swam in my vision as tears pooled.

She put a tentative hand on my arm.

"Nothing could make me hate you," she said.

"But it's forbidden. It's dangerous," I said, daring her to contradict me.

"Yes," she said. A heavy pause hung between us. "But it means a lot that you trust me with the truth."

I swiped away the tears with a shaky smile. The weight of carrying my secret alone in Mynaria had finally been lifted.

"What are you going to do?" she asked gently.

"I don't know," I said. My problems were far from solved. "If they start testing everyone, it's only a matter of time before someone finds out. The alliance will collapse. I keep thinking that maybe after I'm married, I can do something about the Recusants. They have to be held responsible for what happened to Cas, but maybe there is more they could do for us. Some way they could work for the kingdom instead of against it. If there is a way to remove or hide my Affinity, maybe they know a way. . . ."

I shivered. Releasing the magic had somehow left me colder than before, and the air in the room was still cool from when I'd had the shutters open for Mare. I rubbed my hands together and tucked them under my arms, neither doing much to make them feel better.

"Give those to me," Mare said. She scooted closer and reached out, beckoning with her fingers when I didn't immediately comply.

"My hands?" I squeaked.

"Yes, silly." She took my hands, the warmth of her touch sending a shock through me. "Denna . . . I don't know that much about magic. But I don't think the Recusants were entirely responsible for Cas. We have to figure out who forged that knife and why they wanted to frame Zumorda. Perhaps that person or power is behind what happened to Cas. But most important, I'm not going to let anyone hurt you."

"Thank you," I said. I wanted to cry again with the relief her words brought me. She knew, and yet she wasn't running away. She knew, and she still held my hands as though they were the most precious things in the world. She cradled them tenderly, massaging the warmth back into my fingers. Magic hummed through my entire body. I didn't dare move or speak lest it make her stop or result in me accidentally lighting something on fire. Even with the riding calluses, her hands were silken in comparison with Thandi's. The care she took with me, with every touch, was exquisite—as if she knew my body without having to be told anything about it.

"Can I ask you a question?" she asked.

I nodded.

"What does it feel like? Using the magic?"

Of all the things for her to ask, I hadn't expected that.

"It makes my hands tingle when it surges up," I said. "Using it makes me feel like I'm giving away pieces of myself, but there's a thrill in it too. Sometimes it feels dangerous and out of control and like I have no idea what I'm doing."

"Sounds kind of like the moment right before you kiss someone," she said. She smiled a little and dropped her gaze.

Her comment lingered with me the rest of the night, as did the way she'd accepted my Affinity with such unexpected gentleness and grace. Every time she looked at me, I felt like the only person in all the kingdoms. She lit me from within.

Long after she left, the fire in the hearth still burned brightly, a fitting accompaniment to my emotions. The first night I had felt this way was when Mare and I were in the garden among the fireflies. Something about the way they drifted through the garden had made me feel so alive, and yet standing next to her had grounded me. Staring into the fire, I imagined that little pieces of flame separated from it, rising up to drift through the room as the fireflies had that night.

A spark landed in my half-empty teacup and hissed out in the lukewarm liquid.

And for the first time it didn't scare me that my magic came with such explosive ease in Mynaria—I simply watched the pinpoints of light drifting lazily through my bedroom, fantasizing about that night I'd stood in the garden with Mare. And just as I had pulled the sparks out of the fire, I put them back one by one, each spark spiraling back to the heart of the flame until it dimmed to nothing but embers.

I came out of the trance as if waking from a dream—a dream that left me barely able to hold myself upright or keep my eyes open. But in that moment I was sure of something for the first time: my magic was no parlor trick, or the result of too many prayers to the fire god.

I had an Affinity. A powerful one.

I would never be able to hide it.

And it wasn't Thandi who had shown me the size of my gift, accepted me, and grown the spark into a fire.

It was Mare.

With that knowledge came the realization that I was absolutely, without any shred of doubt, profoundly in love with her.

If only I had been anyone else in the world, maybe I could have told her. But my future was set in stone.

THIRTY

✦ *Mare*

SNEAKING INTO DENNA'S ROOMS BECAME A DAILY HABIT. Her Affinity should have frightened me but instead made me feel closer to her and honored that she trusted me with that terrifying part of herself. I tried to convince myself that our stolen sunlengths together were enough, until one night when I stayed over so late that I fell asleep beside her and woke up the next morning with her small form curled up next to me, the warmth of her back pressing into my chest. I loved the soft skin of her shoulder and the gentle curve of her waist and the sound of her sleeping breaths. And though in that moment we were almost as close as two people could be, it still didn't feel close enough.

When it came time to meet her the evening after I spent the night in her bedroom, I could no longer shake my uneasiness about what the future might hold. As soon as we sat down, she launched into an exasperated speech about plans for the wedding. I could hardly stand to listen. I wanted her to belong to me, not my brother.

"Denna," I interrupted her when she finally paused in her rant. "I'm wondering if there is something else you haven't thought of." It was now or never.

"What? Oh Hells, did I forget something for the wedding?" She sat upright, a look of total panic on her face.

"Possibly," I said drily. "Did you forget that in less than a moon you're marrying my brother?"

Denna stared at me. "Of course not. That's the whole point."

"But you do realize what that means," I said. I hoped she would take the hint, because spelling it out in detail hurt with every word.

"I don't understand."

"You. Thandi. Married. Prince. Princess. King. Queen."

"Yes, yes, yes. What does that have to do with anything I don't already know?"

"Denna, I'm not going to be climbing up any ropes into a room you're sharing with my brother." All our moments together were stolen, and once she moved in with my brother, there would be none.

"I know." Her voice faltered.

"And you aren't going to be able to sneak out. When you get married, spending time with me is not suddenly going to be all right. It'll be quite the opposite. They'll have you busy with twice the things you're doing now. You'll be expected to host every event that ever gets planned in these walls. You'll have to do cresthaven tours. Hopefully they'll wise up and put you on the Directorate right away. There's no way you're going to fit me in, sneaking or not."

A series of emotions crossed Denna's face that I couldn't quite decipher.

"Why do you care so much, anyway?" she asked. She stood up and faced me.

"What?" Her challenging tone took me aback.

"No, Mare, truly. Why does it matter?" she pressed.

"Because . . . because I care about you," I finished lamely.

"You can care about me just as much when I'm married. You can show that you're my friend by helping me get through all this, by making it more bearable. By staying here and offering me your counsel and friendship." She leaned closer.

"Yes, but—"

"But what, Mare? What do you want from me?"

My chest tightened and my throat closed against the words that needed to be spoken. She didn't understand that friendship wasn't enough anymore, and I didn't know how to tell her. It would destroy everything.

"Mare, you have to tell me why this matters to you," she said.

"Because . . . because I don't want to be without you," I said.

"But you aren't going to be without me! Not unless you marry someone else and leave." She stepped back and threw up her arms.

"Yes, I will," I said, finally snapping. I stood up. "Denna, you don't understand what it will be like. You're not going to have a life of your own. I may play a small role in it if I stay here, but it isn't going to be like it is now. And I don't want things to change, unless change means I get to spend more time with you, not less."

Plus she'd be married to my brother and sharing his bed. My future would be that of a spinster, growing old alone, withering away as I watched them build their life together. I had to speak now, before it was too late.

"Denna, the truth is that I wish it were me, and not Thandi, who you were slated to marry. I'd suffer the crown if it meant a life with you." Every word hurt. I had pulled out my still-beating heart and laid it on the floor before her. There was only one more thing to say. "I love you." Tears rose to choke me.

She stared at me as if I'd struck her, so still that I couldn't begin to imagine what was going on in her mind. Telling her my feelings had been a terrible mistake.

I turned away, my chest caving in. At least I could marry someone else or make a life on my own, never having to wonder if things could have been different.

"I have to go." I sniffled, stupid tears already running down my cheeks. I hated that Denna was seeing me so weak and broken. I went for the window, grabbed the rope with shaking hands, and swung my leg over the edge. Then suddenly she was beside me, gripping my arm, her eyes gleaming with tears of their own.

She pushed me back against the wide frame of the window, and my breath hitched in my throat. In spite of knowing that I had to flee, my body stayed frozen in place, unwilling to let go of my final moment close to her. An unanswered question formed in the charged air between us. She brushed a tear from my cheek with gentle fingers, and every inch of my traitorous body responded with longing so fierce it burned.

"I can't lose you," she whispered.

Something like hope flickered in my chest.

She leaned forward and kissed me.

THIRTY-ONE

Dennaleia

MARE'S BODY WENT RIGID AT MY TOUCH. I KISSED her slowly, deeply, every feeling I had for her pooling into my lips as I tasted the sweetness of her. An icy wind cut through the open window, making no difference in the heat between us. She had awakened me to the world, and now it was my turn to bring her to life by showing her how much she meant to me. The rope slapped against the windowsill as it fell from her limp fingers, and I knew I had won.

"I love you, too," I whispered.

All at once her hands were everywhere, fumbling to get a grip. She pulled me in so close that I was almost in her lap, her inner thigh pressing into my hip as she kissed me again. A jolt of heat burst in the pit of my stomach as she softly bit my lip, teasing me more deeply into her embrace. When we finally broke apart, breathless, I couldn't even feel the cold.

"Mare," I said softly, holding her face in my trembling hands. Tears still lingered on her face, and I used my thumbs to brush them away.

"I should go. . . ."

"No, stay." I kissed her cheek. "Please." I tugged her down from the windowsill and back over to the couch. She followed me on unsteady legs. I held her hand as she sat down, afraid that if I let go, she'd try to flee.

"I didn't expect that," she finally said, squeezing my hand.

"Me either. I've never felt this way about anyone before." I looked into her eyes, hoping she would understand.

"I haven't either." She exhaled shakily.

"I didn't know. If I had thought you felt the same way about me that I felt about you . . ."

Her eyes snapped up to meet mine. "You mean you've had feelings for a while?"

"Yes." I blushed. "But I didn't know if you did."

"Well, now you know the answer."

She pulled me close. I inhaled the perfect smell of her, the spice and the sweetness heady and intoxicating. She tipped my chin up and brushed her lips over mine again, stirring a hunger deep inside me. I put my arms around her neck to draw her even closer. I needed her to teach me how this was done. My head swam with the sound of her voice and the feel of her lips.

She kissed me until I was breathless, until I could hardly see straight or stand upright. And even though I was exhausted and she insisted she had to go, I could hardly bear to stop touching her. Her face looked different than I'd ever seen it before, flushed with exhilaration that I had wrought. The tears were gone from her cheeks, replaced with a ruddy glow that came from more than the fire.

We walked hand in hand to the window, each pace as slow as I could make it. When I shivered from the cold air blowing in, she engulfed me in her arms again. A sigh escaped my lips as I pressed my head into her shoulder. She rested her chin on top of my head, putting her neck in a convenient place for kissing.

"If you don't stop that, I'm not going to be able to leave," she said.

"That's exactly my plan," I mumbled between kisses, enjoying the way her pulse fluttered against my lips. I never wanted to stop.

"You aren't making this easy."

"Can you come back later?" I looked up at her hopefully.

"I can't," she groaned. "I'm already late, and I promised Nils and his friends a round of cards. He's already been complaining that he hasn't seen me in days."

"Well, I'll let you go on one condition . . . you have to come back tomorrow. And stay." My own boldness shocked me, but I wanted her so badly I didn't care.

"I think I can manage that." Her smile curled against my cheek.

When she disappeared out the window, I watched until my teeth chattered with the cold, finally closing the shutters when I was certain she wasn't coming back. I didn't know what had come over me. I couldn't bear to see Mare hurting so much. I had tried to bury my love for her, knowing my marriage prevented a future for us. But this—her feeling the same—I was unprepared for. Guilt ate at me as I thought of Thandi, but all I wanted was to revel in knowing she loved me.

THIRTY-TWO

✦ *Mare*

I JOGGED AROUND THE CASTLE TO A BACK ENTRANCE that I sometimes used coming back from the barn. The liegemen at the door didn't spare me more than a cursory glance. Perhaps the cold air was excuse enough for the red in my cheeks. The low hum of conversation greeted me as I crossed the wide room and made my way among well-worn tables that mostly stood empty. A few groups clustered over games of cards, sipping from heavy mugs of strong black tea to keep themselves awake for the night shift. I swept my hands through my hair in a weak attempt to tidy myself as I approached the table where Nils sat. I'd never hear the end of it from the men if they thought I'd been with someone, and there sure as all Six Hells wasn't any way I'd tell them the truth.

"Heya, Mare!" Rowlan, one of Nils's friends, waved at me. Nils turned around to face me, a welcoming grin on his face. The familiar warmth of his brown eyes brought me back down to earth a little. I strode over to his table and slid in beside him. Unfortunately, there was one person at the table I hadn't been counting on.

"Late as usual. What a surprise," Thandi said by way of greeting.

"Didn't expect to see you slumming it down here," I said. Seeing him brought me back to reality with the force of a winter storm. Denna still belonged to him. Even if she loved me, she hadn't made me any promises.

"They're my friends, too. Besides, I like a game of quat as much as you do." He was full of manure as usual. The only one he could call much of a friend was Rowlan, and that was only because they were regular sparring partners in arms class. I doubted any of the liegemen would step above their station by claiming to be friends with the future king.

"Funny that you like the game even though I always manage to beat you," I replied.

The other guys at the table chuckled at the challenge, jostling one another as they always did.

"You can take my place, Mare. I'm on duty in less than a sunlength—lots to do before the Gathering tomorrow." Brin, another of Nils's friends, tossed his hand down onto the table and stood up.

"Thanks." I switched to Nils's other side and slid into Brin's place. It put me at a diagonal from Thandi, which was better than facing him straight on. Looking at him across the table, I was torn between guilt and pride. She loved me. She had kissed me.

"So where were you?" Nils asked between turns.

"I lost track of time. Sorry." I stared at the table, my fingers twitching on my cards.

He sat back, an amused smile on his face. "Really?"

"Probably with Lord Kriantz getting aroused over horseflesh." Thandi rolled his eyes.

If only he knew how wrong he was. Still, my cheeks burned. The men laughed, all looking at me now.

"I wasn't with him, not that it's any of your business," I finally managed to stammer.

A flash of understanding crossed Nils's face, and he sat back upright. "I heard you've been having trouble with Lessi, Rowlan. She still got you by the short hairs?"

Rowlan groaned and put his head in his hands, earning another round of laughter from the table and blessedly putting attention elsewhere.

"She wants me to dress as a cat for the harvest masque in town. Can you believe it? A blasted cat!"

"She'll probably put a bow with a little bell around your neck." I snickered.

Rowlan's expression morphed from dismay to raw horror. "I'm never going to live this down. Never."

"You've got that much right," Nils said, wiping tears of laughter from his eyes.

"What about you, Thandi? How's the pretty princess from Havemont?" Rowlan asked, clearly desperate to change the topic of conversation.

Thandi shrugged. "She's clever, and we get along well. It's about the best one can hope for from an arranged marriage. She'll make a fine queen."

I feigned interest in my hand, shuffling the cards back and forth in no particular order. If any of them deduced my opinion on the topic, I was doomed. Part of me was relieved that he didn't seem overly keen on Denna, but his lack of appreciation for her also made me want to kick him. She deserved more.

"So have you gotten anywhere with her yet?" Rowlan waggled his eyebrows.

Thandi played his card and smiled slyly. "What do you think?"

If I could have gotten away with smacking the smirk off his face, I would have. And the worst part was that I didn't know if he was bluffing. Ice coursed through my veins at the thought of him touching her. She couldn't have kissed him, could she?

"That's a definite yes, then," Rowlan said. "Dammit, I'm out of trump cards. You always block me, Thandi."

"Romancing her a little can't hurt. We're stuck together either way," Thandi said.

He had definitely kissed her. I dug my fingernails into my thigh as everyone else laughed. It was true—they were stuck together, moving toward the same unchangeable goal. It would leave me wanting. I played a trump and took all but two of Thandi's counters off the table. Beating him didn't hold the sweetness it might have before I knew he'd kissed her.

"Damn. You always have the card you need at the end." Nils shook his head.

"'Pennies come to the patient,'" I quoted.

"Dammit, Mare," Thandi cursed, taking back the counters he'd managed to keep on the board.

"Nothing you don't deserve," I said.

The longer I sat at the table, the heavier my limbs felt. The lightness of being with Denna dissipated, replaced with the reality that she was destined for my brother. I had to choose a future. And though it would break my heart to leave her, it would destroy my soul to stay.

"Are you all right?" Nils turned to me with concern in his eyes.

"Kind of tired. I'd better go," I said.

"I'll walk you part of the way."

I didn't have the heart to object, so I waved good-bye to the other players and my brother, though I didn't meet his eyes. I knew what I would see there. Confidence. Arrogance. A future of certainty before him, married to the girl I loved.

"What is wrong with you?" Nils asked, putting his arm around me. "You came in there high as a kite and now you look like you want to vomit or punch something. Maybe both."

"I do," I growled, and shrugged his arm off.

"So . . . do you want to elaborate on that?"

"My brother is such an arrogant ass. Doesn't appreciate a damn thing he has."

"I assume you're not talking about all this." Nils gestured to our surroundings.

"I'm talking about Denna. It's like she's an object, another thing he gets to have because he's going to be king someday."

Nils cocked his head to the side but didn't speak.

"She's worth so much more than that, but he doesn't see it. There's so much she can do for this kingdom, and no one is giving her any opportunity." My vehemence grew the longer I went on.

"I'm not sure that's exactly what he was saying," Nils said. "I mean, it *is* an arranged marriage. A political alliance. You're lucky if you so much as get along with a person you're stuck marrying, from what I understand. And he seems to appreciate her intelligence and think she'll make a good queen."

"I have to get out of here," I said. "Maybe I should ask my father for some of the unclaimed territory up north. Go start a horse-training business."

"In the middle of nowhere? That should go well."

"I don't want to watch the life of one of my closest friends be slowly ruined." The explanation was less than half-assed. Her kisses still burned on my skin.

"Why are you so upset about this? I know you've been spending a lot of time with her lately, but—"

"I don't know what to do." I didn't know how to admit what had happened between Denna and me. How it had changed everything.

"It's all right, little Mare. Choosing a direction for your future is a big decision. Think about the people here who love you . . . and the people you love." His voice was gentle as he squeezed my shoulder.

His words cut deep. My decisions were bigger than me, and Denna wasn't the only one I loved. He mattered too. I took his arm until we reached the bottom of the stairs and then pulled him into a hug.

"Thank you for being my safe place. And my best friend," I said.

"Of course," he replied. "I always will be."

I gave him a farewell kiss on the cheek and climbed the four sets of stairs to my portion of the royal wing, but when I reached my hall, I found an unexpected guest. Lord Kriantz stood outside the door to my rooms.

"What brings you to this drafty part of the castle?" I asked, trying to conceal the mess of emotions still warring within me.

"There's a small matter I wanted to discuss with you," he said.

I hoped to the Six he finally had some useful information about the Zumordan blade or the Recusants. Anything, really. I beckoned him into my receiving room and shut the door.

"What was it you wanted to discuss?" I collapsed into one of the chairs without much dignity, already exhausted from the evening.

"Marriage," he said.

My body went hot and then ice-cold in the space of a breath. I sat up in my chair, wide awake again.

"You look like a spooked colt," he said, smiling through his dark beard.

"I apologize, my lord. It wasn't what I expected you to say." I couldn't imagine what in the Sixth Hell he was thinking. I'd rather have horseshoe nails hammered into my skull than get married. Besides, I hardly even knew him.

"You don't need to decide right now," he continued. "I did want to let you know that I've discussed it with King Aturnicus, and he is pleased by the idea of a match between us. However, obtaining your consent is equally important. I think it could be good for both of our kingdoms, and good for us as well."

"But why?" I asked. What deranged logic had led him to think marrying me was a good idea?

"Your knowledge of horses would serve me well in the breeding program I'm developing." He leaned forward. "I hope to create a new breed with the endurance of the desert horses and the strength of your Mynarian war steeds. I want a partner, not a piece of property, who can help me build Sonnenborne into a powerful kingdom, and I know that you would never settle for less. Since I'm the elected ruler of the tribes under my banner, which comprise the largest settlement in Sonnenborne, our marriage would also create an alliance between our two kingdoms. If Zumorda is truly behind the attacks on Mynaria, we must present a united front. Havemont, Mynaria, and Sonnenborne must stand as one. I don't know how else we could expect to take on their forces." He spoke with the passion of someone who believed in his mission.

"I don't know what to say," I said. At least that was one thing it was easy to be honest about. I liked him well enough, but leaving Mynaria hadn't ever been part of my plan—if the random bits of thought I had about my future could even be labeled a plan. But Lord Kriantz's suggestion of a partnership was more than I would get from most suitors. And I was curious about his plans for the Sonnenborne horse-breeding program.

"That's why I don't expect your decision at present. Please, take your time to consider my offer. The Gathering, harvest ball, and Thandilimon's marriage are at the forefront right now anyway. The border raid has pushed up my timeline to return home, but I still want you to have some time to decide."

"Of course." I was still too stunned to say anything else.

"I'll leave you to think, my lady. I am sure your day has been quite long enough." He stood and walked past me to the door.

"I'll consider your offer," I said, my mouth dry. As if I hadn't already been confused enough.

"I am glad to hear it. Good night, Mare." He bowed slightly at the door, and favored me with another smile. "If there is anything else I can do for you in the meantime, please let me know."

"Good night, Endalan."

As the door closed behind him, images of my future flashed before my eyes, and I did not recognize myself in any of them. Was I ready to become a wife? A Lady of Sonnenborne? Gods forbid, a mother? I supposed he was handsome enough, though I had never spent more than a moment or two considering it. I stared into the fire long after he left, trying to get a grip on what to do. I couldn't decide if I should stay or go, or if it was worth it to fight for Denna or better to walk away while we might still remember each other fondly. I didn't know if I should try to go forward alone or take the easy way out that Lord Kriantz had offered. At least one thing about his proposal held appeal—my future would be on the back of a horse, and that was the one place I knew for certain I wanted to be.

THIRTY-THREE 🔥 *Dennaleia*

EARLY-MORNING LIGHT FROM AN OVERCAST SKY GAVE everything a washed-out look, the restless hooves of the horses carving half-moon divots in the grass as we waited to depart for the Gathering. Somewhere out in the hills, the king's broodmares and foals awaited us. My bones crawled with the hum of magic, and every time I thought of kissing Mare, it rose dangerously close to the surface. My reservations about riding out intensified as Shadow and I joined the other gatherers at the base of the hills. If I set something on fire, the most important members of the Mynarian court would be the first to see it.

"Ready for the ride?" Ellaeni asked as I approached the group, running her hand down the dappled neck of her gray horse.

"As ready as I will ever be," I said, easing Shadow to a stop beside her. "Any news from Claera?"

Ellaeni shook her head, her face somber. "My mother sent

word that the canal riots have ceased and most of the local Recusant factions have been dismantled. But many people went missing over the past moon. Claera would never reach out to my parents anyway, even in desperation. Not after how they've treated her."

"I'm so sorry," I said.

We fell into a grim silence.

A brisk wind stirred the horses, making them fidget and champ at their bits. More than twenty nobles and liegemen waited near us on horseback, while another dozen or so circled the outdoor arena to warm up. I scanned the crowd for Mare and Flicker, craning my neck in hopes of catching a glimpse of her bright hair or Flicker's telltale white sock. Maybe having her nearby would put me more at ease. I needed to see her face and know that the previous night hadn't been a dream. Shadow sidestepped, agitated by my tension, and Ellaeni's gelding pinned his ears. I patted Shadow absently and tried to take steady breaths.

With no hope of rest after Mare's departure last night, I had frantically thumbed through the pages of the green book from the library. I thought about using Karov's feather, but my skin crawled every time I thought of his weapon and how keen his interest in me was. I couldn't trust him. Even if my magic couldn't be entirely hidden, there had to be ways to stop it from surging at random. But according to the book, control was even more elusive for those with multiple gifts, as the rules that applied to one Affinity might not apply to another.

When I couldn't make sense of any more words, I came back to the picture that had caught my eye in the library. Even in the midst of the storm of fire and stars, the mage looked calm and in control.

That wasn't me.

"It's almost time," Thandi said as he rode up, his mare doing her usual impatient jig.

"I'm ready," I said, forcing a smile. I could hardly stand to look at him with my mind so full of his sister.

I glanced back at Ellaeni, but she seemed preoccupied.

Thandi nudged Zin forward, and I urged Shadow to follow.

"This is always my favorite part of the fall," he said. "Nothing stirs the blood quite like a gallop through the hills. Did you do any jumping in your lessons?"

I shook my head. "No, I'm afraid not."

"Well, beware the ditches. And the logs. Follow the pennant bearers if the terrain gets too rough—they usually take the safer paths, as it's hard to jump carrying a flag." He gestured to several riders clad in blue with bright white trim, each one carrying a flag stuck into a holder strapped to his or her stirrup. The pennants rippled in the breeze, long orange triangles of fabric snaking out behind the hindquarters of their horses.

His helpfulness only intensified my guilt, and my magic continued to seethe with nowhere to go. We trotted into the hills, snippets of laughter and rumor drifting through the crowd. Upwind of me, voices spoke of war. Of the Recusants who had been captured. Of the ride against Zumorda. The Gathering wasn't the only thing stirring people's blood.

"Are you nervous, my lady?" Thandi asked.

"A little bit," I admitted.

"Don't worry," he said. "This isn't Shadow's first Gathering. She'll take care of you, and so will I."

I shrank into the saddle, embarrassed. After this long in Mynaria, I shouldn't have needed anyone to take care of me.

"Where's Amaranthine?" I asked. Even her name on my lips brought heat to my cheeks.

"Who knows?" Thandi shrugged. "Probably back at the stables. She said something about helping with the mares and foals when they come in."

We broke into a trot, ending the conversation. As I posted with the rhythm of Shadow's hoofbeats, the bright, brassy notes of a trumpet call echoed through the trees, urging us onward. Trees lined the wide trail, which skirted the base of the hills rather than twisting up into them like the ones I'd taken with Mare. Thandi and I kept a brisk pace, passing others as we made our way to the front of the group. Ellaeni stayed close too, her presence providing a little comfort. The king's blue-clad form bobbed ahead of us, the back of his riding jacket emblazoned with the crossed wheat sheaves and arrows of the Mynarian crest in gold thread.

"Let's ride up with Endalan," Thandi said, pointing ahead.

At the king's flank, Lord Kriantz rode a horse unlike any of the others. She stood only a little taller than Shadow, dwarfed by the warhorses all around, and had a peculiar coat that gleamed like polished gold. Lord Kriantz rode with the confident seat and steady reins of a master horseman, the mare's thin neck arching proudly before him. If his seat hadn't been so good, and he hadn't been so lean himself, he might have looked comical astride the beast with her spindly legs, narrow barrel, and strange convex face. Even the horse's tail was thin, the sparse white strands ending right below her hocks.

"Heya!" Thandi called out to Lord Kriantz. "I was wondering if you'd ever bring out your horse."

Lord Kriantz grinned. "I've enjoyed your warhorses, but riding Pegala will always be like coming home. She'll still be fresh when your mounts are puffing their way back to the barn." He patted the horse's golden neck, earning a flick of the mare's large ears.

"Maybe so, but you'll want one of our horses if we ride against Zumorda," Thandi replied.

"You can count on my sword alongside your own," Lord Kriantz said.

Thandi nodded, his gaze growing steely.

Their conversation shifted back and forth between horses and war, leaving me no desire to comment. Instead my mind swirled with thoughts I could barely handle—my Affinity, Mare's tears and kisses, and how increasingly probable it seemed that all this would end in fire and chaos.

We found the broodmare band as the trail opened up into a meadow deep in the heart of the hills. A mare snorted warily as we approached, though we were not the only humans present. Several herd guardians already stood in the midst of the horses, their brown uniforms smudged with the dirt and grass stains of several days' travel. The guardians mounted as we drew closer, using their horses to gently guide stray mares back into the center of the herd. Colts and fillies pranced alongside their mothers, the most curious ones stepping toward us, ears pricked and short tails flicking from side to side.

Our group split in the middle and cut wide around the edges of the meadow, Thandi indicating for me to follow him, though his mare flattened her ears at Shadow. We stopped on the other side, the other riders following a set of hand signals with which I wasn't familiar. Though I didn't know what came next, my heart beat faster in anticipation.

"Get ready," Thandi said, his face alight with intensity.

We rode forward until the herd of horses broke into a trot. Then the horn sounded. The herd bolted, and we flew with them. The touch of my heels wasn't needed to urge Shadow forward. I stood in my stirrups as Mare had taught me, using my lower legs to absorb the impact of Shadow's gallop. In mere seconds we entered the trees, which flashed by far too quickly to count. Shadow's hooves beat over the earth with the others, barely in control.

I struggled to keep close to Thandi without coming within kicking or biting range of Zin. Ellaeni rode at my flank, her gray horse wild-eyed with the excitement of the gallop. Lord Kriantz had separated from us, his mare's long legs spiriting her down the trail, a golden ghost amidst the trees. All we could do was follow. My thighs burned, already weak from half a day of riding, and as we crested a hill and began the perilous descent, I grabbed a handful of mane and whispered a prayer to the Six.

The herd funneled into the valley trail, and I breathed a sigh of gratitude as the pace slowed to an easy canter. Shadow still breathed hard, her neck damp and strides labored as she worked to keep up with the warhorses. As Lord Kriantz had promised, his horse barely even sweated, her golden coat still shimmering in the afternoon light. The low, gnarled trees and heavy underbrush kept the herd on the open trail, channeling them safely toward the castle. The hard part was over.

Thandi rode up alongside the king's black horse, sharing a grin with his father. In that moment, I finally felt Mynarian. There was a future for me with them, and it comforted me. I urged Shadow to extend her strides to catch up to them, to ride where I belonged. I needed to claim my place, to ride where I ought, even though every limb in my body still ached at the thought of Mare.

As I drew within a few horse lengths of the king, a sense of wrongness hit me in the space of a heartbeat just before a burst of violet flame engulfed him.

I screamed.

The king's horse reared, and Shadow skidded to a halt, nearly catapulting me out of the saddle. I clutched her mane and struggled to right myself as she shied away from the center of the trail. I got control of my reins in time to see the king topple from his horse, purple fire licking at his livery, the golden crest of Mynaria burning across his back as though it had been stitched specifically for that purpose. Liegemen converged on him, yanking off their jackets to snuff the flames. But when they pulled back, the king remained still.

Lord Kriantz and a few liegemen rode into the trees, checking the perimeter for any signs of the attacker. Shadow shifted uneasily beneath me as I gagged on the smell of burned flesh.

Captain Ryka crouched beside the king, putting her cheek to his face. "He's still breathing!"

Thandi leaped from the saddle, handed Zin's reins to a nearby rider, and rushed to his father's side.

"He lives," Thandi whispered the words like a prayer.

I dismounted from Shadow and clutched my stomach. This

couldn't be my fault. It couldn't. I would never hurt the king. I would never hurt anyone. I tried to think back to moments ago, whether anything had been smoldering. I felt sick, but not that strange emptiness and exhaustion that often came from using my power. It couldn't have been me.

Lord Kriantz trotted his mare over. "I couldn't find anyone," he said.

Thandi clenched and unclenched his jaw, staring off into the trees for a moment before turning to the liegemen surrounding him. "Croden and Lianna, survey the area again. You with the bay gelding, ride for a medic and a litter, as swiftly as your horse will carry you. The rest of you, ride on. We still have to get the broodmares in."

Everyone reacted quickly to his confident orders, the horses moving swiftly into the trees and down the trail. For the first time, I saw the man who would be king one day. A strange silence came over the forest as the riders' hoofbeats faded in the distance. Between the quiet of the forest and the stillness of the king's body, it was hard to believe that he might survive.

"Is there anything I can do, Your Highness?" Lord Kriantz asked.

Thandi looked up at him blearily. "Stay close. I may need your counsel, friend."

"As you wish, Your Highness."

"How could this happen?" Thandi croaked. "He doesn't bear the mark of any weapon."

Lord Kriantz spoke with gravity. "This was no ordinary attack, Your Highness. There must be magic behind it. How else could the flames burn violet?"

Thandi's expression darkened. "If a magic user is responsible, we will find him." He hung his head over his father's body. "We will find him, and we will quarter him."

I trembled. There was no mercy in his voice. There would be no room to explain that the existence of my Affinity did not make me responsible.

"Perhaps it is time to begin testing all those present today with the Recusant artifact," Captain Ryka suggested. "The perpetrator could be hiding among us."

Numbness spread through me.

"Yes." Thandi nodded his agreement. "At once."

THIRTY-FOUR

✦ *Mare*

THE CHARRED MASS ON THE LITTER BARELY resembled a human, much less my father. I hit my fist against the stone wall of the stables over and over as the medics converged on the litter and whisked him away, Captain Ryka following swiftly behind. As angry as I was with my father for so many things, the thought of him so close to death undid me. After all, he was the only parent I had left.

I should have been on that ride, and I would have been if I could have handled being around Denna without my heart lighting up like a bonfire. If any harm had come to her, I would never forgive myself. I didn't follow the medics—there was nothing I could do. Instead I waited at the door of the stables, ready to lend a hand with the horses. At least that was one thing I knew how to manage. I brushed the grit from my hand and stepped out into the dusk.

Lord Kriantz rode in first, the neck of his golden horse still arched and lively. I held her as he dismounted, and then I passed her reins to his private groom.

I looked him in the eyes, willing him to know what I asked without having to speak the words.

"He may still live, my lady," he said gravely.

I nodded absently, my eyes darting to the other riders coming in. They all wore the same expressions. Exhaustion. Fear. Sorrow.

Lord Kriantz clasped my arm gently. "I am so sorry, Mare. If there is anything I can do for you or your family—"

"What happened?" I interrupted.

He leaned closer.

"The attack was magical," he said, his voice pitched so that only I could hear.

I stiffened, and he stepped back. That didn't make sense. It seemed as though most of the local Recusants had been captured. Denna would never hurt anyone. Who else could there be on the loose with an Affinity?

"Did things go well with the mares and foals?" he asked more loudly.

"Yes. Fine. They'll be ready for the culling . . . if it goes on next week as scheduled," I said.

The high-pitched whinny of a weanling calling for its mother echoed from the holding pen. The sound cut through my heart. Though they'd be fine in a few days' time, today the loss of their mothers was still raw. Everything that mattered to them was gone.

"Good. Please let me know how I can help." Lord Kriantz put a comforting hand on my shoulder.

Thandi walked in, already off his horse. Zin's head hung low, her sides streaked with dry sweat. She heaved a sigh as a groom took her reins.

"How bad is it?" I asked him.

Thandi shook his head, his blue eyes inscrutable.

"Tell me how bad it is," I said, grabbing him by the shoulders like I used to when we were young.

"It's bad, Mare, all right?" He waved me off. "I can't talk now. I have . . . I have things I need to take care of."

I took his forearm to stop him for a moment. "I'm here if you need me," I said.

He squeezed my arm in return and nodded.

Lord Kriantz gestured to Thandi. "Let's get to the castle. The Directorate will need you. Mare can walk in with Princess Dennaleia."

My disloyal heart quickened.

Thandi nodded mechanically and followed Lord Kriantz up the hill, four liegemen falling into place around them. Thandi's shoulders didn't look wide enough to carry the burden of being king yet, even for a day. How strange to think of my brother as a man. A little over a year younger than me, and already a man. A king, if the Six claimed my father.

I sat down on a hay bale and leaned back against a stall, watching the parade of hooves go by as the last of the Gatherers rode in. I didn't stand until Denna and Shadow approached the barn, and then I flew to my feet to help her from the saddle. Her drawn face barely brightened when she saw me, but that flicker was enough.

She tumbled from Shadow's back into my arms, all salt and sweat and bedraggled curls that still smelled sweet as summer roses.

A groom led her horse away, and I pulled her close, holding her as if she were my only anchor.

"It was so awful, Mare," Denna murmured in my ear. "He was right in front of me."

I pulled back and took a ragged breath. If only I had been there for my father—and for her.

"But he'll live. He has to," she said. She relayed the story of the afternoon in a trembling voice.

"But where did the fire come from?" I asked.

"I wish I knew, but it wasn't me. I swear! I would never hurt anyone." Her eyes welled. "But Lord Kriantz . . . he looked at me afterward as though he was looking through me. I think he might know about my Affinity." Her face was pinched with fear.

"He couldn't possibly know," I said. "His people don't use magic. Most Sonnenborne tribes don't even worship the Six."

"But what if he tells people it was me?" she whispered.

"Why would he do that? He's been trying to help us."

"I don't know. I'm afraid," she admitted. "Thandi said if they found the mage, they'd kill him. Captain Ryka suggested testing everyone on the ride today. Thandi agreed. Who else will there be to blame?"

"No one is going to kill you," I said.

"I missed you today," she said. "Until . . . until the accident, I could hardly think of anything else." She looked like a scared little girl, as lost as one of the weanlings calling for its mother. But the only person she called for was me, and that call could be answered.

"I missed you too," I said, my voice raw.

We left the stables in silence and held hands through the garden where no one could see us. I followed Denna to her rooms like a lost dog. I sat at her vanity and sent a page for a change of clothes while Auna bathed her in the adjacent room, feeling like I might lose all sense of myself if I didn't stay close.

After Denna dismissed Auna for the night, she finally whispered my name.

"Mare."

The way she said it sounded warm. Like home. Like the fire in the hearth and the flush in my cheeks when she drew near.

"Denna," I answered.

She crossed the room and took one of my hands, stood up on her toes, and brushed her cheek against mine. The contact sent a shiver through my body. No matter how many times we touched, I would never get used to the perfect way she felt against my skin.

I wanted to tell her how dishonorable it was to the crown that I stood before her, dishonorable to allow my heart to beat the way it did for her. I'd let down so many people before, but this was a new level, even for me. But she needed me. And I needed her. And damn her head—it fitted on my shoulder like the only place it was meant to be.

She pulled me to the hearth and we sat down together. I took her hand into my lap and traced the lines on her palm.

"Lord Kriantz asked me to marry him, you know," I said.

She drew back her hand and closed her fingers.

"What did you tell him?" she whispered.

The weight of the question sat between us. I wasn't sure whether to laugh or scream or weep.

"Nothing yet. I'm still considering it." I shrugged. All it would take for me to turn him down was the promise of Denna's love—the promise of a future for us together. But she had to offer it without being pressured. She had everything to lose.

"You have to be joking," she said. "We still have work to do. There's still someone out there we have to stop." A spark popped out of the fire and sizzled out on the stone floor.

I eyed it warily, and she took a deep breath.

"I can still help that cause if I'm married to Lord Kriantz. Maybe there is more he could tell us." I finally met her eyes, wishing they didn't make my stomach feel so strange. Wishing they didn't make me want to kiss her.

"But if we can't figure out what's going on, the kingdoms will fall to war with Zumorda. And you'll be down there too close to the front lines. . . ." Her voice shook.

"What makes you think I care? What does it even matter? I can't stay here, Denna. I can't watch you marry my brother." My voice almost broke with the words.

"But Lord Kriantz doesn't love you!" she sputtered.

"And you love my brother? How is that any different?"

"It's you I love. I'll think of something before the wedding. Give me more time, please. I need this," she pleaded. "I need you."

She stood up and then knelt in front of me.

"Please," she said, taking my hands in her own. "Please stay with me tonight."

A war raged in my heart.

She kissed the backs of my hands.

I shouldn't stay.

She put her hand on my knee and ran it slowly up my thigh

until I took a sharp breath.

I needed to leave.

She crawled forward, pulling herself up into my lap, and then touched my cheek, soft as a feather, sending goose bumps clear up into my hairline.

I licked my lips.

She put her mouth to my neck, placing a soft kiss where my pulse throbbed beneath my skin.

I stopped being able to think.

"We shouldn't do this," I whispered.

"I know."

She led me to her bed and laid me down beside her. I let her hands wander over me, losing myself in the patterns she traced over my skin. When she brought her lips to mine, we kissed until we could barely breathe, until I couldn't resist sliding my hand up her thigh, hiking the nightdress over her hips, her smooth skin like warm silk beneath my fingers.

Denna grew bold with my touch, finding her way beneath my shirt until she slipped the fabric over my head. Her mouth moved over my exposed skin, awkwardness quickly blooming into desire. When she put her hand between my legs, the last of my shyness vanished. The confidence in her touch left no question that she craved every inch of me, and I couldn't get enough.

"I've wanted you so long," she whispered.

I could have wept with the force of what those words made me feel. This—*this*—was what I had waited for. She was what I had always needed. I pulled the nightgown over her head so that our bare skin could meet, entranced by the way her gentle, insistent fingers were building an unstoppable feeling inside me.

Denna kissed my neck and trailed her lips over my shoulder as my body flooded with pleasure so total that I felt nothing else. She held me close until the intensity subsided and I finally caught my breath. As soon as my limbs worked again, I reached for her, eager to reciprocate. She pressed against me hungrily, slick against my fingers. She exhaled in my ear, a soft unself-conscious sound, and my own body filled with desire all over again as she cried out and clenched her thighs around my hand.

After we found our clothes and she finally fell asleep, I lay awake, pressed against her, trying to memorize the way she fitted so perfectly against me. I needed her more than I'd ever needed anyone. She softened my harsh edges. She made me better—she made me less who I was and more the person I wanted to become. The only trouble was that she had never been meant to be mine. Her breath rose and fell steadily, the only accompaniment to the occasional spark popping from the embers of the dying fire in her hearth.

I closed my eyes, but sleep would not come. The image of my father's burned body haunted me, and with every minute that passed I became more certain that the calls of the White Riders' horns were only a breath away.

But it wasn't the White Riders that woke us.

THIRTY-FIVE

Dennaleia

THE DOOR OF MY BEDROOM BURST OPEN BEFORE DAWN, filling the room with lamplight. I sat up and rubbed the sleep from my eyes, ready to dismiss Auna—until a face appeared.

Thandi.

He didn't say anything, and somehow his silence was worse than any words.

Behind me, Mare stirred, cold air replacing the warmth of her body as she sat up and unwrapped her arm from my waist. Without looking, I could feel the icy stare she leveled at her brother. But all of us knew who would win. His jaw clenched and unclenched over and over. I shrank into the covers, pulling them around me as though they could shield me.

His eyes skated over me and landed on his sister, his gaze sharp as a drawn sword.

"I can't . . . I can't believe you," Thandi finally said to Mare. "I came looking for you to talk about Father, and this is what I find?"

"She's my friend, Thandi," Mare said, crossing her arms.

Though I had called her the same, hearing it from her lips stung. Friends kept each other company, always quick with a supportive word or an embrace. But friends did not kiss in a way that lit one's whole body on fire. Friends didn't undo one's ability to think with a single touch, and they didn't do what we'd done last night.

But my future belonged to Thandi—if he would still have me.

I would lose her no matter what.

"We aren't children anymore. You can't keep doing what you want with no regard for the kingdom," Thandi said. The lamplight darkened the circles under his eyes.

"Did you ever stop to think that Denna isn't a piece of property, Thandi? That she has her own desires and cares? Because if you did, you might have noticed that she's twice as smart as either of us. You've hobbled her before even trying out her paces."

Thandi strode across the room toward her, the lantern in his hand swaying, light and shadow dancing across the room. Terror for her rose in my throat. I wanted to shove the words back into her mouth, to get her to leave while he still allowed her some dignity.

"And have you been trying out the paces of my future wife?" he asked, venom in every word.

"Unlike you, I listen to her," Mare replied, her voice as cold as his.

"She didn't do anything wrong," I said. I was the guilty one.

"We can talk about this later," he said to me.

"I'm sorry," I said. Except that I wasn't. And that only made me feel worse.

"As for you, Mare, any choice you had about marrying Lord

Kriantz is gone. I hope you enjoy your future in the middle of the desert," he said.

I wanted to pull the covers over my head and go back to sleep, and wake up to a world where this was not happening. My emotions boiled over until the coals in the hearth glowed orange, and I clamped down on my feelings. If Thandi saw magic, he would have more than one reason to kill me.

"You can't make me do anything." Mare stared at him, defiant.

"Enough," he said. "Guards!"

Liegemen entered the room, faces impassive.

"Please escort my sister to her rooms and see that she stays there. I want liegemen posted at all exits . . . including the windows," Thandi instructed.

Panic flickered across Mare's face. The liegemen flanked her, driving her out of the room. She would be caged like an animal, and there would be no way for me to get to her. The door swung closed behind them, leaving me alone with Thandi. My heart smashed holes in my chest with every beat.

Thandi approached my bedside. He bowed his head, undoubtedly searching for words of accusation. The worst part was that they would be true. He must hate me for my betrayal. Even if it hadn't been spoken aloud, the way I looked at her had to be evidence enough. I clenched the covers to keep my hands from trembling. Many minutes passed before he finally spoke.

"You know you promised, right? Promised yourself to me?" he asked, his voice breaking at the end of the question.

"I know," I whispered.

"Did I do something wrong?" He looked up at me, his eyes

searching my face, begging me to tell him something of which he could make sense.

I didn't know how to explain to him that my feelings for Mare had nothing to do with him. He didn't hobble me—the rules of my life did. And it wasn't his fault she lit me up like a midwinter parade, every color of the Six bright in my heart when I looked at her. It wasn't his fault that she had done that almost since the first time we'd met, since the first time she'd touched me.

"We have to do our duty," he said. The resignation on his face made him look so much older.

"I know," I whispered again.

"Mare has to do her duty too. War is coming."

I nodded, my eyes not focusing on anything at all. Without her, my future stretched before me like a yawning darkness. After this, it was inevitable that she would be taken from me.

"I know you don't have to love me, but I thought maybe you could. Someday," Thandi said.

Guilt poured over me in inescapable waves. I had wronged him, and in doing so had betrayed my kingdom.

Worse, I knew that given the chance to do everything over again, I would willingly make the same mistakes twenty times over.

There could not possibly be forgiveness in his heart. Maybe there shouldn't be.

"I'm sorry," I said. I didn't know what else to say.

The silence between us was broken by the discordant wail of hunting horns, the same mournful calls I'd heard when Casmiel passed.

The new king hung his head and wept into my sheets.

THIRTY-SIX   ✦ *Mare*

THE DISSONANT CALLS OF THE HORNS CRACKED ME IN
two, and I fell to the floor as the hoofbeats of the White Riders
took the city. My father was gone, and I'd never even had the
chance to say good-bye. There would never be a chance to salvage
our relationship, or for me to prove that I was anything other than
useless. Thandi was king. Denna's future held no place for me, and
my brother would send me to Sonnenborne as promised. I could fight
all I wanted, but under the king's command I would be powerless.

I lay on the stone floor until I shivered, past the breaking of
dawn. When Sara found me there, she peeled me off the floor and
guided me into bed.

I woke only when someone sat down beside me and placed a
familiar hand on my shoulder.

"Heya," Nils said.

I opened my eyes halfway and squinted at him blearily, searching through my muddled brain for words.

"Nils!" I choked out, and sat up.

He folded me into his arms as he always had, rocking me as I fought tears. I clung to the familiar feel of him under my hands, his solid form and tidy livery the only things I could still count on.

"How did you get in here?" I asked.

Nils shrugged. "They said you can't come out. Didn't say anything about me coming in."

"Figures. Thandi's always been shortsighted that way. You have to get me out of here." I tugged at his shirtsleeve.

"I can't," he said, shaking his head. "You know why. I answer to him now. What in the Six Hells did you do to get locked in your rooms, anyway?"

"Thandi found me in Denna's bedroom this morning." The words tumbled out in a rush. Nils had told me a hundred tales of waking up in the wrong bed; I hoped he would understand without me spelling it out.

Comprehension dawned in his eyes. "I see."

"I told her I loved her," I admitted, my voice barely above a whisper. I studied the patterns on my duvet, tracing an embroidered swirl with my finger, afraid to meet his eyes.

"Well, that's progress," he said.

The simple words filled me with gratitude. I fumbled to grasp his hand. Whichever of the Six Gods had gifted him to me could never be thanked enough.

"I don't know what I did to deserve you," I said softly.

"We've been through a lot together. You've always been with me through the scandals and heartaches, and now it's my turn."

I brought his warm hand to my cheek and turned to lightly kiss the familiar contours.

"So does he know?" Nils asked.

"He must."

"Did he catch you in a compromising position?" He smirked.

My cheeks burned. "It doesn't matter. She'll marry him anyway. Duty clearly matters to her more than whatever this is between us. The crown comes first."

"Denna didn't say anything in return when you said you loved her?"

"Well . . . ," I began hesitantly. "She kissed me. And then she said it back." I almost didn't want to tell him, because that was one thing I wanted to hold close—the way she'd taken me so by surprise and made me believe even for a moment that things could work out.

Nils raised his eyebrows. "And last night?"

"I couldn't stand to leave her after the Gathering." I pinched my arm to keep the tremor out of my voice. "I told her I'm considering marrying Lord Kriantz. But she won't hear of it."

"Neither will I," he snorted.

"But his holdings are close to Zumorda. Maybe by going with him I could find out what's truly going on. Or, once we got close to the border, I could make a run for it. Ride alone into Zumorda to warn the queen that her kingdom is being framed."

"You're deflecting. This has nothing to do with that and you know it. Don't run away from your feelings. And I'm not sure I like the idea of you riding alone into Zumorda any better than you going with Lord Kriantz."

"What other choices do I have? Even if it weren't for Lord

Kriantz, I'm not going to be sneaking through Denna's window when she's sharing a room with my brother. This was all a horrible mistake."

"But maybe if you hadn't been caught, you would have had more time to make your case."

"What case?" I wailed. "I have no case. I have nothing to offer her. I barely know what I'm going to do with myself, which means I have nothing to give her, especially nothing on a par with being queen."

"Is being queen what she wants?"

"It's her duty. And her duty is the most important thing to her." I turned my head back into the pillow. "Gods, I am stupid. Incredibly stupid. How did I get so stupid? You should have beaten the stupid out of me when you had the chance."

"You aren't stupid," he said, touching my head tenderly. "You're in love."

I hated and loved him for being so right.

"And now . . . now with my father . . . our time is gone," I said, barely able to get the words out as I held back tears. "I can't talk about this anymore. Can you stay and keep me company for a while?"

"Why, so we can start a whole new set of rumors around here?" he teased.

"I don't want to be alone." I could feel the grief waiting to swallow me again.

"All right." He stretched out on the bed and propped his head up on his elbow.

I snuggled up beside him, though it didn't close the wound

where my heart had once been.

"Tell me stupid liegeman stories," I said. "Or better yet, stupid liegeman jokes. They know the best dirty jokes."

He laughed, and obliged, and eventually I fell into a fitful sleep.

THIRTY-SEVEN

🔥 *Dennaleia*

I SAT ON THE DIRECTORATE FOR THE SECOND TIME two days after the death of the king. The windowless room at the heart of the castle where the Directors met was stifling even with a chilly wind blowing outside. Under any other circumstances, I might have held my head high to be at the table with the Directors, but I wasn't at the meeting based on my own merits. Thandi had not let me out of his sight since the White Riders had called out the death of his father. Although I walked the palace with him, and had stood freely beside him as he knelt before his horse to accept the crown from the clerics of the Six, he had me as trapped as Mare. It was still too soon, but I longed for word from my family—some note of reassurance or advice about how to untangle the mess my life had become.

From the moment of the king's death, our faces, together, took the place of his. Each day, Auna dressed and bejeweled me in the most lavish finery I owned. But while the outside of me shone with perfection, inside I was shattered and lost. Everything depended on me keeping control, on holding myself together until I could find a way to get to Mare. I had less than a moon until the wedding to figure out a way to keep us together, to stop Lord Kriantz from taking her away, and to somehow find and get rid of the Recusant artifact before my Affinity could be discovered. The artifact had already unearthed one magic user at court, and though he had never done anything but serve the crown, they still sent him to the dungeon screaming.

The faces around the table were weary after two days of ceremonies and the accompanying administrative tasks. No time had been provided for anyone to grieve—none existed when an assault on Zumorda had become the top priority. Thandi's coronation the day before had felt more like an addendum to the king's funeral than an occasion in its own right. It was all obligation and little celebration. Even the wine we drank afterward was sour on our tongues.

Now, we planned for war.

"The Zumordan border will be most vulnerable near Sonnenborne," Lord Kriantz explained, gesturing to the map spread out over the table. "Their cresthaven lies in the northern mountains, and my people can attack from our border in the south."

Thandi nodded, a crease between his eyebrows as he placed several glass counters on the map. "I think we can send in reinforcements, but we'll need to keep the bulk of our cavalry at our own border in the east. Perhaps build upon the existing cavalry we sent after the bandit attacks," he said.

"That should be fine, provided we time things correctly. Kartasha is Zumorda's largest fortified city in the south. If you can take it once we've secured this area here, we'll be positioned well," Lord Kriantz said. "The queen will be hard-pressed to take back the land."

Thandi nodded again.

Did he even know what he was agreeing to? Not all of his riders would return. They would sacrifice their lives for revenge—revenge that might not even be owed to them. But I saw what was behind it. Sadness could not hide the smoldering in Thandi's eyes when he spoke of his father. I twisted my skirt anxiously under the table at the thought. If he found out about my Affinity and thought me to blame, his rage would burn brighter than any flame I could call.

"And as we discussed, the lands south of Kartasha between the city and my borders will be added to Sonnenborne," Lord Kriantz said, tacking a red string on the map to denote the new border.

"Wait." Captain Ryka spoke, crossing her arms. "I'm still not comfortable with attacking the southern part of the country when the seat of power is in the north. It doesn't make sense to me."

"We don't need to take the whole kingdom. It would be foolish to try, at least during the initial assault. We need to send them a message that neither Mynaria nor Sonnenborne is to be trifled with," Thandi explained.

"With winter coming, the northern Zumordans will soon be confined to their cities. The snows make the northern roads nearly impassable for several moons," Lord Kriantz added. "I'm sure Princess Dennaleia can attest to that, as her cresthaven suffers from similar seasonal limitations."

I nodded a reluctant affirmative.

"This is all according to the plans we'd been working on before my father passed," Thandi said. "It will also bar the Trindori from making any more agreements with the Zumordans under the table. They'd have to cross through Lord Kriantz's holdings to reach their contacts in Kartasha."

"I still call for solid evidence that Zumorda is behind the attacks," Hilara said.

"What more evidence do we need?" Thandi said. "The attack that killed my father was blatantly magical. We've captured nearly all the Recusant leaders, and we've been feeding the prisoners peaceroot to quell their gifts. Who could have done it besides the Zumordans?"

Zumorda was not the only place a magic user could come from. My Affinity was the proof, even if I wasn't to blame.

I said nothing.

The captain sat back, twirling one of her voting nails between her fingers. She wore thick cachets woven from many colors, like Mare. My heart throbbed at the thought of Mare's delicate wrists, the freckles on her arms—

"You have your votes if you choose to disagree," another director reminded Captain Ryka and Director Hilara with an oily smile.

"I'll send my horses back before the culling and follow after the harvest ball," Lord Kriantz said. "Pegala and the other desert-breds are too distinctive to form a caravan, and I wouldn't want to risk Princess Amaranthine that way. She and I can travel separately from them for safety in case of Zumordan spies."

He spoke as though their marriage were already sealed. With the king's assassination fresh in my mind, all I could picture was Mare, lying on the side of the road with a white arrow embedded in her chest. There wasn't a single thing I liked about Lord Kriantz's plan.

"And the initial attack?" Captain Ryka asked.

"I already sent a messenger—my people await my command. They won't act without me present," Lord Kriantz said. "As soon as I arrive, I'll rally them for the attack and send a message by courier to you for supporting cavalry. The timeline should be no more than a moon, as winter falls in the north."

The plan was well designed. Northern winters were incapacitating. It would be spring before the queen would be able to send more forces to handle whatever bloodbath we unleashed on their borders.

"Excellent plan," Thandi said. "We can rally here in the meantime and begin training our forces. Captain, we can go over those plans before praise day."

Captain Ryka nodded, still wary. "What of the investigation, Your Majesty? Shouldn't we see it through to its conclusion and make sure to deal with any spies here in Lyrra?"

"There's no time for that now," Thandi said. "My father is already gone. We must ride against Zumorda while we still have the element of surprise. We can ferret out the betrayers once the forces depart."

"I would prefer not to send my cavalry against an enemy who may not be at fault," Captain Ryka said. "We never found Morland after he left the market, which leads me to believe he knew something about the dagger from the first assassination attempt. He's an expert forger, and it's possible the weapon is a fake. I still have two members of the Elite searching for him."

The captain cared about the men and women who rode for her, and apparently she had actually listened when Mare told her about Morland's disappearance and possible involvement. If only Mare or I had known sooner, we could have had an ally on the Directorate. Perhaps two, with Hilara also opposed to riding against Zumorda.

"Those in favor?" Thandi asked.

The metallic clink of horseshoe nails sounded as the Directorate tossed favorable votes to the center of the table. Only Captain Ryka and Director Hilara held back. I wanted to grab the nails and fling them back into the directors' faces. Instead, I sat perfectly still, cultivating an expression as blank as the polished tiles beneath our feet.

"Assigned," Thandi said, nodding to the scribe, who dutifully recorded the vote.

"Now, on to the wedding," Thandi said. "In light of the war, I would like to propose that we move up the ceremony. It makes sense for us to ride out as king and queen as we begin to gather the troops. All the resources for the feast and ceremony are already in place."

My facade crumbled and panic closed my throat. I'd counted on having until the harvest festival to find a way to Mare and to get her help solving our quandary.

"When do you propose to hold the ceremony, Your Majesty?" someone asked.

"The feast can be held on praise day following the culling, and the wedding the morning after," Thandi said. "Since all the wedding attendees will already be in town for the culling by then, it shouldn't be a problem."

My heart throbbed in my chest and magic raced through my veins. That meant the wedding would be in less than half a moon. It was all happening too fast. There wouldn't be any time to talk to Mare, to try to figure out some way to salvage any part of what we felt for each other.

"All in favor?"

The table rang with cast nails for a unanimous vote. As an outsider, I did not even get any say in the date of my own marriage.

"Assigned," Thandi said to the scribe. "And that concludes our business for the day."

Chairs scraped across the tile as the directors rose to exit the room.

I stood and braced myself momentarily on the back of the chair, reaching deep for the strength to go on, reeling from the sudden change in plan. My magic threatened to spill out and immolate everything. After all the years of preparation, I had never felt less ready to be married or more afraid of what I might be capable of doing with my Affinity. I needed answers.

There was only one person I could think of who might have them.

As soon as I was shunted to my chambers and certain of my solitude, I opened the shutters and let the wind cut through me like a sword. Shivering even in my heavy dress, I was glad to feel something besides panic over losing Mare. Auna had not yet lit the fire in my receiving room, but it came to life and crackled behind me as my power, barely contained, found an easy outlet in the fresh kindling.

Spurred by the erratic bursts of flame in the hearth, I pawed through my wardrobe until I found what I sought in the pocket of one of my cloaks—the blue feather Karov had given me at the Blitz.

"Karov," I whispered, dropping the bright blue feather before I could question the wisdom of it.

The wind swept the feather to the floor and it crackled with sparks upon impact, turning to ash whisked away by the breeze. I collapsed onto a chaise, not sure what to do. The inevitability of war loomed, making every shadow in my rooms seem sinister. To steady myself, I whispered prayers to each of the Six in turn, hoping that one of them might take pity. But before I made it to the final prayer, a bird swooped through the window, startling me to my feet. It perched on the arm of the chair at my vanity, its wings the same brilliant blue as Karov's feather.

Then the bird shimmered before my eyes, metamorphosing into a grotesque and ever-expanding shape until Karov himself stood before me.

I stared, my mouth agape.

"How interesting to see you again, Your Highness," he said, his expression smug.

"It was you in the library," I said, remembering the strange circumstances under which I'd found the green book.

Karov favored me with a silver-tipped grin. He settled himself in a chair without being offered one, and with a gesture of his hand the shutters swung closed. The fire still flickered and swelled with my uncertainty, but Karov did not seem bothered.

"What can I do for you, Your Highness?" he asked.

"Help me," I begged him in a trembling voice. "Tell me what's wrong with me and why I can't control it."

"It is simple," he said. "You have a gift. Each time you use your gift, it drains you, because you have no training. You won't be able to control who you harm, and there is a good chance you'll do damage to your closest friends and family simply because they are the ones who are around you most."

My stomach sank.

"Unless, of course, you get some proper training. That would allow you to use your gift without hurting yourself or putting others at risk." He sat back and waited for me to respond.

"So you can train me," I said. "Teach me how not to hurt people. How to hide this."

"If only I could, Your Highness." A flicker of regret crossed his features. "Perhaps I could show you some basics, but your gift is not so simple. Me, I am a creature of wind. And Zumordan, as you may have surmised. You glow too brightly in my Sight for fire to be your only gift. I imagine you've experienced other manifestations of your Affinity that aren't limited to flame?"

I recalled Ellaeni's dress, the castle wall, the gust in the library, and the slammed door. Somehow, without having seen those things happen, he knew.

"How did you know?" I asked.

"With practice, most magic users with gifts of moderate strength can develop their Sight. I can see the magic in everything. Even you."

"But I'm not Zumordan," I said. "I shouldn't have an Affinity." There had to be some mistake, some explanation.

"Mages were not always mostly Zumordan," he said. "As

we grew fewer in number, suspicion of magic increased until the religious uprising. No one knows why we started to die off and fewer were born to replace us. Many with Affinities fled to Zumorda for sanctuary. Meanwhile, the people of the other Northern Kingdoms decided that magic was not for mortals, assigning each Affinity to one of the gods of whom your people are so fond," he said. "It's all part of the same system, distorted over time."

It made sense. The godlike symbols on the green library book. How much calmer my gift was when used in the Sanctuary. There had always been a connection between the Six and the Affinities.

"So the High Adytum—that's why it's so important to magic users? That's why they've been trying to stop the alliance?" I asked.

"The High Adytum was built by magic users and the worshippers of the Six together, back when the religious and magical beliefs in Havemont and Zumorda were less divergent," Karov said. "It is the best place to work magic in all of the Northern Kingdoms. Legendary enchantments have been made there. You may find your power easier to manage in other temples and sanctuaries, too. To this day, they're still built with specifications that help control and amplify Affinities."

I nodded in numb agreement. What he said lined up with my experience.

Karov sat back and studied me intently.

"You are a rare creature indeed, Princess. And a dangerous one," he finally said. "The only advice I can give you is to trust your intuition, but be careful how far you reach with your gift. I'm sure the book you found in the library showed you how dangerous it can be when one calls on more than one power at once. And it does not help that the crown has rounded up the Recusants."

"What do they have to do with anything?"

"They called themselves the Syncretic Circle before being relabeled by the fundamentalists. Most of them have only the smallest of gifts, but they help keep balance in the kingdom. With so few magic users here, the ambient magic that exists in the kingdom is never being used. The small enchantments the Recusants perform help drain some of that away and prevent anything catastrophic from happening. Now that they are locked up, those of us with stronger gifts run the risk of catastrophic consequences for using ours. It takes a great deal of training and control to avoid setting off disastrous reactions."

No wonder I felt like I was about to explode out of my skin. No wonder it seemed to worsen every day.

"But where did my Affinity come from?"

"That I cannot answer," he said. "But Affinities are usually gifts of blood, not chance."

No blood of mine could explain my Affinity. A shudder ran through me as I questioned my entire life. While it was true I didn't strongly resemble my father, I looked very much like my mother. We were of the same mold, with dark hair, fair skin, and pale eyes, though hers were blue, not green. My parents loved each other far too much for me to be of some other man's blood.

"Why did you give me the feather?" I demanded.

"Zumorda will always shelter those with Affinities," he said. "The queen has assigned a few of us to see that those with the need will find their way to Zumorda, where they can learn to harness their abilities. And perhaps those we assist might advocate for our interests from time to time when the need arises."

His explanation seemed too simple, and the Zumorda he described was hardly the enemy it had been painted to be. But perhaps this had been his long game—to find more ways for Zumorda to deepen its grip on Mynaria through me.

"I am not joining any causes or making promises," I said. "I cannot speak for Mynaria or Havemont. I could be reduced to nothing before all this is through. They've begun using a Recusant—I mean Syncretic Circle—artifact to test everyone. If anyone here finds out about my Affinity—"

"And that's why you're a particular challenge," Karov said. "We can't offer you anything, because your disappearance or even a clear alignment with Zumorda could spark a war, particularly in light of the current political situation. But Zumorda is a place where little matters but power. So perhaps one day you will find your way out of this tangle and come to us on your own terms. When you do, we'll be there to receive you."

"I don't want training. I want to know how to make it disappear," I said. "What about peaceroot, the herb they're giving the prisoners?"

Karov chuckled. "I doubt you want to contend with the side effects. The headaches are monstrous, and it can cause necrosis in your fingers and toes, turning the flesh purple. Immunity builds up in time, and the more you take, the farther the damage spreads."

I tightened my hands into fists. It wasn't a viable option.

"Your Highness, I suggest you accept the inevitable," he said. "An Affinity, much like a heart, cannot be changed."

With those words he folded in on himself until he was once

more a mountain bluebird—apparently one of his gifts as an air mage. A gust of magic opened the shutters for him to wing out into the blustery day.

"Wait!" I cried, chasing him to the window, but it was too late. He fluttered into the overcast sky and was gone.

In spite of what I had learned, I felt no better than before he had arrived. I hated him for his words but could not deny the truth in them. Without control of my gift, I would destroy everything around me. Even the kingdom I was supposed to rule. Even the girl I loved.

THIRTY-EIGHT ✦ *Mare*

A FEW DAYS BEFORE THE CULLING, THE WIND DIED down, leaving the castle grounds bright with autumn sunshine. Gardeners raked up the red and golden leaves that the wind had torn from the trees, and in the distance horses kicked up their heels in their paddocks. I sat in my window, one leg in and one leg out, like I had when Denna had stopped me from leaving her rooms. Twisting the knife of memory filled up the emptiness. Feeling pain was better than feeling nothing.

My barely touched breakfast of shortbread and sliced apples with sharp cheese made excellent ammunition to lob at the liegemen below, which gave me some modicum of satisfaction. They couldn't keep too keen an eye on me without taking food to the face. Birds clustered at their feet, reminding me of Thandi's courtiers as they lunged and pecked at one another to get to the crumbs.

"My lady?" Sara approached me. "Someone has been sent to

escort you to the stables."

I dropped the last slice of apple back on my plate in surprise. Until now, I'd heard nothing about any plans to let me out of my rooms for so much as a sunlength. The messages I'd sent to Thandi had gone unanswered, and I didn't dare reach out to Denna. Those days were over, and her own silence made her decision perfectly clear.

"He's in the receiving room, my lady," Sara said.

I brushed the crumbs from my breeches, swung my leg back through the window, and went out to greet the man waiting for me.

He wore a snug leather jerkin depicting the silhouette of a hawk in flight, its hooked profile sharp across his belly and its right wing angling up over his shoulder. One of Lord Kriantz's men. He bowed upon my approach.

"With the king's permission, Lord Kriantz has asked that I take you to the stables, Your Highness," the man said. His accent was thicker than his master's, the vowels made soft and round by his pronunciation.

Dread hung in the pit of my stomach. There was no chance of my turning down a sunlength of freedom, and Lord Kriantz probably knew that as surely as I knew why he wanted to see me.

"Of course," I said, and gestured for Sara to hand me a cloak.

Lord Kriantz's man escorted me out of my rooms, moving like a cat ready to pounce if I tried to make a run for it. I wasn't that stupid. There was nowhere to hide and no point in dragging my feet when, if nothing else, I couldn't wait to stand under the open sky.

Traffic increased as we left the royal wing. When we descended the final staircase into the outer hall, I stopped short. Measured footfalls kept steady rhythm as an entourage made its way toward the heart of the castle. Four liegemen escorted two noblewomen and their maids, the nobles wearing a riot of color that lit up in shades of blue and green as they passed through the squares of sunlight cast in through the open windows.

One of the women was Denna.

She came into view behind the the first two liegemen, more than a head shorter than either of them. A tiara glittered in her dark hair, studded with pale-blue gems that matched the ones sewn onto the bodice of her gown. Her step faltered when she saw me, her lips parting in surprise.

With Denna in front of me for the first time in days, all I could remember was the feel of her bare skin, the press of her body on mine, and the way her kisses burned down my neck and across my collarbones. I was on fire with the memory of us together and frozen with the knowledge that she could never be mine. The only thing tempering the pain was anger that she'd chosen him instead of me, and that I had been foolish enough to let my heart go in spite of it.

Denna turned her head and kept walking, leaving me to stare after her, gripping the balustrade with white knuckles. Her friend cast a questioning glance in my direction as though she could see the shame and desire that racked my body as I stood there looking the fool.

Lord Kriantz's man urged me onward, and I shuffled the rest of the way down the stairs and out into the gardens, numb. The sunlight I'd looked forward to now seemed harsh and unfriendly. I barely saw the gardens or the people we passed with my head so full of the image of Denna decked out like a queen. Leaving Mynaria was starting to feel like the only way to survive. It was surely the only way I could ever hope to forget her.

At the stables, Lord Kriantz stood near the outdoor arena, holding the reins of his golden horse and my red one, both already saddled. Another of his men waited nearby with a bay desert horse that had the same odd conformation and metallic sheen that distinguished Lord Kriantz's mare.

"Good afternoon, Your Highness," he said, handing me Flicker's reins.

"Thank you, my lord." I quickly acknowledged him and then threw my arms around Flicker's neck, not caring if it seemed childish. Flicker craned his head around and lipped at my shirt, the familiar gesture making my eyes sting with tears. I swallowed them down and stroked his neck a moment more. My horse, at least, would never leave me or betray me. Our relationship was simple, and familiar, and more solid than anything else left in my life.

"I thought you might be ready for a ride after so many days in the castle," Lord Kriantz said.

"Yes," I said. It was unclear how much Thandi might have told Lord Kriantz about the nature of my captivity at his hands, and I didn't want to tell him anything he didn't already know.

"Let's ride in the hills where we can talk," Lord Kriantz said.

My stomach lurched with nerves, but I nodded my agreement, checked Flicker's girth, and used the fence to swing up into the saddle. We urged our horses along the path to the hills, Lord Kriantz's guard following a respectful distance behind.

"The Directorate met a few days ago to discuss the war," Lord Kriantz said as soon as we were out of earshot of the stables.

"Oh?" My sense of foreboding increased.

"The magical attack at the Gathering has made it clear that Zumorda is responsible. Plans require that I ride for Sonnenborne right after the king's wedding, which has been moved up."

Another arrow lodged itself in my heart.

"When?" I managed to ask.

"The feast will be on praise day, and the wedding the morning after," he said. "As for us, I hope you've had time to consider my proposal."

He'd given me more than enough time.

I took a deep breath of the crisp air and searched Lord Kriantz's face, his horse, his bearing, for some sign of what the right decision might be. He seemed as steady as ever, his gaze keen, his demeanor calm. If worse came to worst, I could always try to strike out on my own once we were far from Lyrra.

Emotions warred in me. No path held any joy or promise.

"Yes," I said at last. "I will ride with you." As if there was truly any other choice.

His face lit up with a broad smile.

"I am happy to hear it." He extended his arm across the distance between our mounts.

I reached for him and we clasped each other hand to forearm, more like comrades in arms than future husband and wife.

It was done.

At least I would escape. And if time was kind, I'd find something to live for besides the memory of her.

THIRTY-NINE

Dennaleia

THE DAY OF THE CULLING, I WALKED TO THE STABLES alongside Thandi like an animated corpse, feeling nothing and everything at the same time. The image of Mare standing on the staircase haunted me, and I had spent the days since desperate to close the chasm between us. A servant pressed a steaming mug of hot apple cider into my hands as soon as we arrived beneath the large tent set up alongside the arena. I clutched the cup and held it to my nose, but the cinnamon smell sent a stab through my heart. Though the warmth felt good on my hands, I discarded the mug on the nearest table, untouched, as soon as Thandi looked away.

Outside the tent, courtiers laughed and talked, most of them dressed in their best riding habits instead of the usual indoor finery. Several nobles stood around the holding pen where the weanlings anxiously milled about, taking bets on which horses would stay with the crown and which would be culled and sent out on the trading strings. I hung close to Thandi, knowing that any attempt to drift off would only be greeted with liegemen blocking my way. Still, I analyzed every opening, ready to bolt should the opportunity present itself.

Until the unthinkable happened.

The row of heralds outside the arena snapped to attention and played a sharp call on their bugles. Conversations faded into murmurs of confusion as everyone turned to face the castle. All those attending the culling should already have been at the arena, and anyone who required a heraldic declaration was already with us. Thandi offered me his arm, and I took it reflexively as the source of the disturbance came into view. Guards wearing plum livery and carrying long swords flanked someone I could not have been more shocked to see.

My mother.

Tingles raced up my arms.

She wore a crimson gown embroidered with hundreds of gleaming flowers, and the crown on her head shone with bejeweled spires that jutted into the sky like the towers of our castle back home. Faced with a true queen, I felt even less ready to become one myself. I took slow breaths, trying to quiet my Affinity.

My mother smiled at us as she drew to a halt and curtsied in greeting. Thandi bowed and kissed my mother's hand. I curtsied in return, hating the formality that meant I could neither flee nor throw myself into my mother's arms.

"Welcome to Lyrra, Your Majesty," Thandi said. "Please join us for the afternoon meal."

"Thank you, Your Majesty," my mother answered.

I glanced at her, trying to convey my questions with a wide-eyed look, but all she gave me in return was a fond and dignified smile. There was no way I could find out what was going on in front of all these people. My mother would never break protocol. Thandi led the two of us to the banquet area and seated my mother at a table that the servants had hastily set up to mimic the royal one, but before I could speak to her, he led me to our seats several tables away.

Courtiers gossiped about their shuffled seating arrangements over the luncheon of decadent harvest food: rabbit braised with wine, herbs, and caramelized shallots, crusty bread spread with honeyed cheese tempered with the last of the mares' milk, and apple pastries topped with crumbled brown sugar and toasted oats. I consumed only enough to be polite, a little of each dish as tradition dictated, glancing at my mother whenever possible. I could not begin to fathom how she had arrived so quickly or why she had not sent a messenger ahead.

After the food was cleared, it was time for the culling.

"Did you know she was coming?" I whispered to Thandi as we walked to the arena.

"I'm as surprised as you are," he said. "But this is a good thing. One of us should have a parent here for the wedding." Sadness flickered across his face.

Before I could say more, Lord Kriantz fell into step beside Thandi, and the tingling in my palms resurged. Though they only made amicable conversation about the horses, all I could see looking at Lord Kriantz was the man who was taking Mare from me. The thought of him touching her made me want to immolate him on sight.

At the arena, Thandi clasped Theeds's forearm in greeting. "Everything in order?"

"Yes, Your Majesty," Theeds said. "The weanlings are ready to run through first, and the grooms will be prepared to run through the older sets in order."

"Good," Thandi said.

"We could use Mare's eye today," Theeds said offhandedly, scuffing his boot through the dirt.

Lord Kriantz and Thandi exchanged a look.

"She's not feeling well," Thandi said.

My blood burned at his lie.

Theeds regarded him with a suspicious eye but nodded and turned to the arena to finish the preparations.

"You don't have to stay on your feet," Thandi said to me. "Endalan, would you please accompany Princess Dennaleia to her seat?"

I would have rather lain down in the middle of the ring and let the horses prance over my bones than spend any time in his company, but I had no choice.

"Of course, Your Majesty." Lord Kriantz took my arm, only a hint of displeasure on his face that he wasn't to participate with the horses. While his close relationship with Thandi had already bought him a new level of credence, only the royal family and their horse masters had any say over the culling. Lord Kriantz seated me beside my mother in a row of wooden chairs on a stone platform alongside the arena, a canopy stretched above our heads to block out the sun. He settled me in the most ornate chair, encircled me with the embroidered woolen blanket from the back, and took his seat on my other side.

I immediately turned to my mother, filled with a thousand questions.

"I am grateful to see you, Mother, but why are you here?" I asked, speaking as softly as I could.

"When Alisendi returned from her visit, she told me about the assassination attempt on the king," she replied. "I was concerned, and your father and I thought it wise not to announce my visit in order to avoid becoming a target myself."

The subtext was clear as day. Ali had told her my gift was out of control.

"What about the letter?" That was the most positive correspondence I had sent her, and the first time I had expressed confidence in my future in Mynaria—all because of Mare and Ellaeni. Things had seemed more solid than ever at that point, unlike now, when nearly everything had fallen to ruins.

My mother lowered her voice even farther. "Casmiel's death was concerning. Your struggles to adjust, perhaps to be expected. But developing relationships with Princess Amaranthine, who does not participate with the Directorate, and a coastal girl with little political power, and the intensity of your concern over Amaranthine's opinion of you—"

I bristled. She judged them without even knowing them. But guilt welled up in me at the thought of Mare.

"I have bigger problems than that, Mother," I said, barely able to keep my voice level. "The gods have become more familiar."

Her blue eyes pierced me in warning.

"This is not the time, Dennaleia," she said. "We shall talk about those things after the wedding, once the alliance is secure."

"But I need to know—"

She cut me off by placing her hand on my arm and gazing out over the arena, expecting me to follow suit. The streaks of silver in her dark hair made her look even more regal, a striking contrast to the red of the dress she wore. Confidence and majesty radiated from her as though both had been part of her since birth. I had no idea how she could be so calm under the circumstances.

Below us, servants finished the preparations, stirring a large basin of paint that sparkled with flecks of silver. They carried it to a table on the quarter line of the arena, carefully surrounding it with greenery for decoration. Within the arena, whitewashed poles laid on the ground showed the course each horse would be led through for inspection, a wide circle around the center of the arena with an entrance and exit on each side. Closer to where I sat, slender branches laden with bright magenta blossoms wove through the arena fence, secured with braided rope.

A tall black weanling was the first horse to dance into the ring. The groom dodged flying hooves as he did his best to walk and trot the barely halter-broken colt along the circle around Thandi, Theeds, and the two other members of the culling committee. The half-wild eyes of the colt broke my heart. His life had changed in an instant the moment that halter had been slipped over his head. I looked up to the castle, searching the distant windows as if I might catch a glimpse of Mare. I wished she would come to free me— gallop through on Flicker and sweep me out of my chair and over the hills clear to the ocean, where we could board one of Ellaeni's ships and never be seen again.

Below, the fussy black colt sidestepped across the center of the arena. The committee nodded approval, and Thandi dipped his hand into the silver paint.

"For wind, strength, speed, and heart, the Six shall ride with this colt as sealed by the hand of the king." Thandi stamped the horse's shoulder, the silver handprint standing out brightly against the colt's dark coat. The handler trotted the horse out of the arena to applause from the spectators.

By the fifth sunlength of the culling I barely paid attention, staring out over the arena and letting my mind wander. I shouldn't have had to sit there all day, but Thandi must have known that I would fly straight to Mare, that I would find a way into her rooms even if I had to fight the liegemen at her doors myself. Instead, I watched horse after horse being led in front of the cullers until the only things keeping me awake were the bones of my corset stabbing into my hips and fear of disappointing my mother.

Then the grooms led in a horse I recognized.

"No," I said, shooting a panicked glance at Lord Kriantz.

He shrugged.

He couldn't. No one with a soul would allow that horse to be sold. Down in the arena, the stable master's mouth drew into a hard line, and he crossed his arms. He must have known this was coming, but he didn't look happy about it. A murmur drifted through the crowd, and I shifted forward to the edge of my seat.

The handler took the horse through his paces, running as fast as he could to keep up with the long, sweeping strides. When they came to a halt in the center of the ring, the tall chestnut gelding lipped playfully at his handler, calm and easy after the half-wild weanlings and yearlings that had gone through earlier in the afternoon.

Thandi pointed to the right, sending Flicker to the cull pen. He'd go out with the rest of the sale string after our wedding.

Lord Kriantz shook his head. "Waste of a nice horse," he said.

Flicker was the one thing that mattered to Mare. If he cared for her, how could he let Thandi use the horse as petty revenge?

"How can you let him do this?" I hissed. "Flicker is everything to her."

He shrugged. "She won't need that horse in the desert. She'll have her choice of any of mine. That one's not fit for desert life."

His logic did nothing to cool my temper. Nothing in his explanation offered any care for her, or thought of her, or consideration for what she loved. Wild thoughts poured into me, thoughts of burning. I bit the inside of my numbing cheek, hoping it would stop me from blasting Lord Kriantz's head clear off his shoulders. I redirected my gaze to the ground below the raised chairs on which we sat, focusing on a few damp leaves in the dirt. Smoke wisped up as they dissolved into ash.

My mother grasped my hand in warning.

"Your temper is showing, Your Highness," Lord Kriantz said under his breath with a smile.

My body went ice cold, but it did nothing to put out the raging fire in my heart.

FORTY

✦ *Mare*

ON PRAISE DAY, THREE DAYS AFTER THE CULLING, I SAT down alongside Lord Kriantz for Denna and Thandi's prewedding feast in the great hall—the first meal outside my chambers since Thandi had locked me up. It might as well have been my last. The velvet folds of my dress hung around me like a funeral shroud, darker than the evening sky outside. Decorations glittered on the walls, streamers hung from every chandelier, and the table burst with as many arrangements of autumn leaves and blossoms as could be wedged among the place settings and serving platters.

I wished for Denna's Affinity so that I could set it all on fire.

Once everyone had taken their seats, the double doors of the great hall swept open to reveal Denna in her finery. Her dress glimmered in the colors of autumn, layers of coppery fabric fluttering over a rich burgundy satin. The bottom hem of the gown hung with enough beads and wire scrollwork to decorate every war saddle in the stables, and her dark hair was twisted up and accentuated with streaks of chestnut and white horsehair braided into the lustrous strands.

While part of me wished for nothing more than to stand up and take her hand, that time had passed. I twisted my cachets until they cut off the circulation in my wrist, tearing my eyes away from her to stare at my empty plate.

As Denna passed me to take her seat, she brushed her fingertips over my bare shoulder blade with the lightness of a feather. Goose bumps rose in the wake of her touch, and I hated her for it. My stomach churned as she sat down with Thandi at the head of the table, her mother like a mirror image on her other side. Lord Kriantz put his hand on my arm and brought me back to earth. I studied his face, his easy smile, his dark eyes and angular jawline, wishing that something there could call up even half of what Denna made me feel. At least he would take me far away from her and the chaos she wreaked in my heart.

It wasn't until the dishes were cleared, several rounds of dancing had taken place, and Thandi was distracted talking to Lord Kriantz that Denna slipped into the chair beside me. Other nobles milled around us, sipping their wine and engaging in conversation, but she might as well have been the only other person in the room.

"You came," Denna said.

"Like I had a choice," I replied. "Thandi can't leave me locked up forever." I kept my voice steady. I had to put up a wall she couldn't crack.

"I've missed you so much." Denna's hands trembled, and she clutched her skirts to steady them. "These past days have been terrible.

I wanted to come to you, but Thandi hasn't allowed me to leave his side."

"This is all my fault," I said. "I never should have said anything about how I felt. I should never have stayed with you that night." It hurt to say the words, but no other choice remained.

"But I'm glad. I wouldn't trade the past few moons for anything." She touched my forearm.

I pulled away. "Yes, you would. Your duty." I pointed to the ornate tiara atop her head.

Her face fell. "Serving the kingdom as a monarch is the only thing I know how to do. It's the only way I have power to help stop the war," she said. "But I want to find a way to make things work for us. I want to make you happy. And I can't bear the idea of going on without you. Tell me what I have to do to change your mind."

"There's nothing you can do," I said. "I can't stay. Thandi and the Directorate have forced me onto this path, and I've accepted Endalan's proposal. Isn't it what you would do? Do your duty and go along with what everyone else has planned?"

"That's different," she said. "You know as well as I do that the Recusants hold only part of the responsibility for what happened. Going to war against another kingdom when we have no proof is foolish. There's no strength in an alliance between Sonnenborne and Mynaria based on that. We don't even know if Kriantz can hold enough tribes together to declare himself king, as he seems to be planning to do."

She was right, but I didn't want to admit it. I couldn't agree with her because I couldn't stay.

"Well, my brother's being an idiot, but maybe I can change

Endalan's mind. He isn't stupid. He might listen to someone he's forming a partnership with," I said.

"There's no guarantee of that," she insisted. "This war benefits him. He gains land. I don't know if he can be trusted."

"If he won't listen, maybe I'll take Flicker and go to Zumorda on my own. Try to warn them. Either way, it's better than staying here and watching you marry my brother," I said.

"But Thandi culled Flicker," she blurted. "He'll go out on the sale string tomorrow. I've been trying to figure out how to stop—"

"What?" I said. My warring emotions coalesced into a much simpler one: fury.

"Lord Kriantz was right there with me. He said Flicker wasn't fit for desert life. If he cared about you, he should have stopped Thandi," she said.

"They won't get away with this." I set my jaw and scowled across the room at my brother. Someone would pay. My punishment had been taken one step too far. No one was going to take my horse.

"But Mare—"

I shook my head and stood. At least Flicker's culling presented a problem I could solve, unlike the disaster with Denna. I stormed across the room to Lord Kriantz and pulled him aside.

"You sold my horse," I said flatly.

"Pardon?"

"Dennaleia told me that Flicker got culled yesterday."

"I didn't have any say in the culling, my lady. I don't know what you heard, but I assure you I would not have encouraged His Majesty to sell your horse. He's a nice gelding. I offered to take him, but His Majesty pointed out that I should keep my string limited to what I can use for my breeding program."

Lies. Denna frustrated me, and disappointed me, but she had never lied.

"So things aren't useful unless you can breed them? Is that how it is?" I raised my voice.

"My lady, please don't cause a scene. I know you're upset about the horse, but we can sort it out tomorrow. And you'll have your choice of horses in Sonnenborne after we wed," Lord Kriantz said.

"I don't want a desert horse. I want my horse," I said.

"This will soothe your nerves, my lady," he said, and pressed a glass of wine into my hand and stepped over to take my other arm. "Let's talk about this later."

"There isn't going to be a later," I said. "I've changed my mind. I won't marry you. Call it off." I shook free of him and stalked toward my brother, who was deep in conversation with the Count of Nax.

Thandi saw me coming and turned his back. If he wanted to play it that way, I could join his game. I pitched the full glass of wine at him. Wine and glass shards exploded over his feet, bringing the conversation to a sudden halt.

"What in the Six Hells!" Thandi jumped back, glass crunching beneath the soles of his boots.

The crowd hushed around us, faces aghast.

I smiled.

"Your Majesty," I began. "In case you forgot, I'm your sister, not some broodmare you can send off on a trading string. If selling my horse is your idea of a punishment, you can shove your plans up your royal ass. This is over. I'm done with war, I'm done with Lord

Kriantz, and I am especially done with you." I stared him down, every muscle in my body taut.

"If you'd done what was asked of you from the beginning, we wouldn't be here now, Amaranthine," he said, his voice level.

"Is that so? I happen to believe that everyone is a player in this game. I'm not taking responsibility for your failures. So if you want to wage war on a kingdom that you have no evidence actually did anything, enjoy that. I'm leaving. You can dig your grave by yourself." I turned on my heel and shoved through the crowd. They quickly parted before me—all but one.

Denna stepped out in front of the exit of the great hall, blocking my way.

"That's unwise, my lady," I said. I needed to ride my anger straight out of the room, and she was the one person I did not want to hurt. Still, I faltered as I faced her, feeling the inexplicable pull that always begged me to close the distance between us.

"Don't go," she pleaded.

"I'm leaving," I said. "But here's something to remember me by."

I gathered her into my arms and kissed her with the intensity she'd kissed me with that first time, hoping if I kissed her hard enough everything I felt for her could be left behind when I walked out of the room. She tasted sweet, a hint of spiced apple from dessert still on her lips. And in spite of my anger that she had chosen him instead of me, and even though I was about to walk away from her forever, the feel of her against me reminded me that what happened between us had been inevitable. I loved her. She made my heart race and my legs feel like they might give way. Every second she spent in my arms was sweeter than a song, lighter than air.

I didn't stop to judge her reaction, just marched out of the room with my head held high. When the solid door of the great hall closed behind me, I laughed, a strange broken sound that echoed through the hallway. At least I was free—if I ran before Thandi sent his grunts after me. I would get my culled horse and ride straight out of town and never look back. If I rode far enough, maybe clear to Zumorda, I could start over as myself instead of the princess I was supposed to be.

"Mare?" Nils approached with a puzzled expression.

"You have the timing of the Six themselves," I said. "Walk with me and keep the other liegemen off my back. I've got to get moving before they come after me."

He sighed. "What did you do now?"

"Can't explain. I have to go. Come on." I tugged him down the hallway, casting a nervous look over my shoulder. Even through the doors I could hear the resurgence of chatter, a tidal wave that would surely follow me in some form. The liegemen outside the door shifted their weight uneasily, as if they knew Thandi would send someone after me. But they wouldn't act on their own with Nils by my side. We hurried down the hallway toward my rooms. I'd take only what I could carry and be out in less than a sunlength.

"Mare, what in the Six Hells is going on?" Nils asked. "I'm on patrol."

"I know. Just patrol in this direction for a minute," I said.

"What happened?"

"I'm leaving, Nils. I'm not marrying anyone. I'm making a run for it on my own. To Zumorda, I think."

He frowned but nodded. "If that's what you think is best, I support you. The Six know you've had enough thrown at you lately. Get out while you can. I'll always have your back." He squeezed my arm, and I smiled up at him. At least there was one person I could rely on. We rounded the corner into what should have been an empty hallway.

"Not so fast, Mare." Lord Kriantz stood blocking our way, two of his men behind him, swords glinting in their hands.

Nils and I stopped short.

"I meant it, Endalan. I'm done. I'm not going anywhere with you. Don't make this difficult." I stood my ground, glancing around for the quickest route of escape.

"If she says she doesn't want to go, you aren't taking her anywhere," Nils said, stepping up behind me.

"I'm afraid you're wrong," Lord Kriantz said. He smiled, and the expression didn't quite reach his eyes. His eyes took in the scene with the smug look of someone who knows he has already won. My anger gave way to fear.

He raised his hand, and his men surged toward us.

The soldier after me was strong but slow, and I twisted and ducked out of his grasp. I landed a few blows as it quickly became apparent that Lord Kriantz had told his men not to injure me. Nils drew his sword and sparred with the other guard, metal screeching against metal and boots scuffing across the hallway as they fought.

"Enough of this." Lord Kriantz swooped in. In one fluid motion he trapped me from behind and brought a thin blade up to my neck. The cold metal pressed into my skin enough to sting.

I froze.

"Stand down," Lord Kriantz said to Nils. "You know I won't kill her, but I'd be happy to free her of an unnecessary appendage or two."

Nils dropped his sword and stepped back, raising his hands in surrender, his chest heaving from the exertion of the fight.

"That's better," Lord Kriantz said.

I struggled in his grip, landing a solid kick on his shin, but he didn't even flinch.

"End him," Lord Kriantz said to his men.

"No!" I screamed, thrashing with all my strength.

Lord Kriantz's soldier stepped forward and plunged a short knife through Nils's neck.

My broken heart shattered.

FORTY-ONE

🔥 *Dennaleia*

WHEN MARE'S LIPS LEFT MINE, SHE PULLED AWAY everything that mattered, laying me bare before the crowd. Nothing of my true self was expressed in the ornate dress, the charcoal accentuating my eyes, or the wine-red stain on my lips. The dark circles under my eyes had been smoothed away with mineral compound, as if the loss of the only person who mattered could be erased with a smudge of makeup—as if my Affinity could be locked away beneath the right clothing. The points of my tiara dug into my skull like the jaws of a beast closing over my head to seal my fate. Mare's kiss was the only piece of truth anyone had seen tonight.

My mother stared at me from across the room as though seeing me for the first time, her face white with shock. Thandi simply turned and walked away, servants scurrying after him to attend to the wine on his trousers.

The ache in my heart grew too large to be contained by the room.

Someone took my hand. Ellaeni. Pain radiated from her eyes, and I recognized myself in her. But she had been wise enough to choose Claera at any cost, in spite of the objections of her family. One day they would find each other again.

My bones buzzed with magic, and a flower arrangement on a nearby table began to smolder. I let go of Ellaeni and shoved out the door of the great hall, afraid I might burn down the room around me. I followed the momentum of my feet, heading toward the royal wing, not sure what I would say, but knowing that I couldn't let Mare leave like that. The party—and Thandi—could wait a few minutes for me. It wouldn't be hard to make excuses. No one would be surprised that I needed a minute to regain my composure after the scene Mare had caused.

My steps echoed in the empty corridor, the absence of liegemen filling me with creeping tendrils of unease. On a feast night there should have been two guards in every walkway. A thump sounded in a nearby hallway.

I peered around the corner and froze. Nils lay on the floor, blood pooled beneath him. Mare was sobbing in anguish. A lump rose in my throat and I choked it down, afraid to reveal myself. At Lord Kriantz's nod, one of his men silenced her with a fist to the head and she slumped against the soldier, unconscious. My nerves screamed, but my feet wouldn't move.

"Burn him. Another body will help our cause," Lord Kriantz said.

His soldiers nodded. One pulled a length of golden string from his pocket and wrapped it around Nils's neck, trailing the ends over the chest of his uniform. Lord Kriantz handed Mare over to his men and stood over Nils, turning the ring on his left hand a calculated half turn. Brilliant violet flames sprang from the golden thread and engulfed Nils.

It hadn't been a mage who had killed King Aturnicus. It had been Lord Kriantz. He must have been the shadow man who paid the Recusants to kill Casmiel, too—all in the interest of starting a war to win Zumordan land. My stomach heaved and the flames in the wall sconces exploded one by one, plunging the hallway into darkness lit only by Nils's burning body.

"What the hell was that?" one of the soldiers said.

"Pick her up and let's go. Now," Lord Kriantz said.

I heard scuffling as one of Kriantz's men heaved Mare over his shoulder, but by the time my eyes adjusted to the darkness, they were gone, no doubt through the exit nearby. I cursed under my breath, colorfully enough to impress even Mare, and sidled after them. Outside, the sharp clatter of shod hooves split the crisp night air. Lord Kriantz and his men wrestled Mare's limp form into a coach drawn by two nondescript gray horses. As soon as the doors clicked shut, they trotted out the gate.

I couldn't let it happen, but there was no way I could risk using my magic to stop them, not if it meant I might hurt Mare by mistake.

I bolted to the great hall. I had to get Thandi to send liegemen to reclaim her. The party had resumed some semblance of normalcy, other than the curious eyes that followed me and the liegemen who converged as I entered the room.

"We've been asked to escort you to His Majesty," a liegeman said.

"Of course," I replied, grateful that I wouldn't have to barrel my way through the crowd to find him. It was almost too easy. The liegemen would lead me straight to Thandi, and then we could turn around and go after Mare before Lord Kriantz cleared the city gates.

The liegemen led me around the edge of the room to the antechamber behind the royal table and escorted me in. Thandi sat at the center of the small room, a servant scrubbing at the wine stains on his trousers.

"Ah, they found you," he said. He waved everyone else out until I stood alone in front of him. His eyes dodged mine, as though he couldn't quite look at me after the scene with Mare.

"Something terrible has happened." I struggled to catch my breath, my heart and lungs warring with one another beneath the constricting bodice of my dress. "Lord Kriantz took Mare. I just saw him kill Nils with fabricated fire that looks like magic. Purple flames, like the ones that killed King Aturnicus. He has a gold ring that—"

Thandi's gaze sharpened and he finally met my eyes at the mention of magic.

"That can't be," he said. "I saw Nils on patrol before I came here tonight—and people can't fabricate magic. We have to focus on finding and eliminating the real source of these magical attacks and destroying them. Zumorda."

"Are you serious? This isn't even about magic. This is about the fact that Mare was forcibly dragged from the castle by the man who killed your father!" Panic made me light-headed. All he would have to do was go into the hallway and see Nils's body to know I told the truth.

"I'm sure you're mistaken," he said. "But if you're that concerned, I'll send a guard to check in with Nils and a page to Mare's rooms to verify her presence."

I could not fathom how he could be so calm.

"By then it will be too late!" Sparks intruded on the edges of my vision. "This isn't about me and Mare. This is about our kingdom going to war for no reason. It's about sacrificing the lives of our people so that Lord Kriantz can expand his holdings and crown himself king. Do you think I don't know what I saw? That I don't deserve to be taken seriously?"

"I trust Lord Kriantz," Thandi said, his voice colder than the night air. "And surely you can understand my hesitation to trust you."

"My eyes work as well as anyone else's." My hands grew warm until my palms tingled.

"Do you smell something burning?" Thandi looked around the room in alarm.

I let go of the chair I'd been clenching. Smoke rose where my fingers had been, and fright consumed me. I hadn't meant to do it.

"By the Six." Thandi stood, his expression thunderstruck. "It's you."

"No," I said, terrified. If he held me responsible for his father's death, I would be killed. Worse, persecuting me would distract him from going after Mare.

"You . . . you're making this all up to hide that it was you. No wonder everything started after you got here. And you knew so much about the arrow . . . you must have been working with the Recusants. I can't believe I was so stupid." He backed away from me.

"None of that was me," I said. "All I ever wanted was to be the best queen for Mynaria. I didn't know anything about the Recusants until I got here. Please listen to me! We have to do something about Mare and Lord Kriantz! Don't you see? He's leading you into a war that benefits only him!"

"We must marry for the alliance to ride forward into war, but believe me, you will be tried and held responsible for any death you caused," Thandi said. He edged toward the door.

For my entire life, duty had come first. Today, it was time to stand by my heart and my kingdom. I stood up straight and faced him head on.

"No," I said. "I cannot marry someone who won't save his own sister. And I will die before I marry a person willing to sacrifice his cavalry for a war clearly plotted by Kriantz for his own gain. If you want an alliance with Havemont, bring Mare back. I'll marry her instead. Gladly." My conviction burned more brightly than my fear. My days of being afraid were over.

"Never," he said.

"Then let me go," I said, and flicked my hand in the direction of the smoldering chair. It burst into flames, and the release felt good. Like galloping Shadow. Like kissing Mare. Like freedom. More power rose to take the place of what I'd lost. I could barely hold it in, as though speaking the truth of what I wanted had finally freed my magic as well as my heart.

"Liegemen!" he called.

The door opened and several liegemen stepped in. Their salutes faltered as their eyes flew back and forth between Thandi and the burning chair.

"Please escort Princess Dennaleia to her rooms," Thandi instructed. "And post four guards at her door tonight. I'd like extra security through the wedding in case the enemy"—he looked at me—"decides to make another attack."

They swept me away from the room like trash. Temptation to burn them all sat near the surface of my skin, but I had to save my power for the one who deserved to die: Lord Kriantz. If I could stop him, all their plans would fall apart. I didn't care how dangerous using my gift had become.

After the door closed behind the liegemen, I retreated to my bedchamber so that Auna could help me undress. Once I was free of the cumbersome dress, I'd actually be able to do something. But Auna had done no more than started to take down my hair when the door to my receiving room burst open and my mother walked in.

"Dennaleia," she began.

"No. Not tonight," I said. The last thing I needed was a lecture from my mother. The hearth surged with flame, making the room uncomfortably warm. If my mother agitated me any further, the whole castle would probably burn.

"I am not here to say what you think," she said, sitting down on my bed.

I didn't believe her until she put her hand over her face and closed her eyes like she couldn't find the strength to go on. Swathed in the layers of her dress with her face in her hands, she seemed very small.

"Auna, you are dismissed for the night," she finally said.

Auna curtsied and hurried out of the room.

Mother stood up and took over where Auna had left off, removing the seemingly infinite layers of my skirts and loosening my corset with gentle hands. I could not remember the last time she had touched me at all.

"Thandilimon showed me the chair," she said as she helped slip a night shift over my head.

"I tried to tell you," I said. "I tried to ask you why this was happening. You never have time to talk to me. Everything is about decorum. Protocol. Making the right impressions on others. Smoothing things over and never talking about what is truly going on." As I spoke, sparks burst out of the hearth.

"I thought I could protect you," she said. "When you were young, your gift was so small. With the blood diluted, I thought it would stay that way. I'm sorry, Dennaleia. I was wrong."

She sat me down at my vanity, and in the mirror her eyes were shadowy with unshed tears.

"What diluted blood?" I whispered.

My mother took a deep breath. "You know that I am from one of the outer provinces of Havemont. South, in the Kavai Mountains near the Zumordan border."

I had heard the story a thousand times. How my father met her on his coronation tour. How instantly smitten he was with her regardless of the fact that she was a lesser noble. How he surprised the people of his kingdom by taking such an improbable woman as his wife, and how that choice had united the kingdom more than anyone expected.

"My mother is not truly my mother. My birth mother was Zumordan. My mother's handmaiden." The confession seemed to cost her with every word, her hands trembling.

My mother, the most regal person I knew, was of impure blood.

"My parents tried for many years to conceive a child, but it never happened. My mother and her handmaiden came to an agreement with my father, and I was born. In a way, I had three parents." She pulled herself together, speaking as flatly as though she was reciting the information from a history book. "No one knew the truth. They told me when I came of age, once it became clear that I might become a queen."

"How could you not tell me?" I struggled to speak through the tightness in my chest as my eyes stung with tears. All along, the explanation for my gift had been right there, and she had deliberately hidden it from me. My arms went numb with increasing power. The oil lamp on my bedside table exploded in a burst of flame, showering the area with broken glass. A gust of wind blew open one of my shutters so violently that the top hinge snapped.

My mother jumped, and her hands shook even harder as she finished unwinding my hair.

"No one could know," she said. "Your father and I agreed when we married. If the truth about my blood came out, it could endanger the Havemont crown. The kingdom always comes first."

"I can't hide my truth, Mother," I said. "It is stronger than I am." That was the only thing of which I was sure.

"I know," she said softly. "I'm so sorry, Dennaleia. I thought I had done the right thing. I never had any hint of magic, nor did my birth mother. We didn't know this could happen."

I told her then about the knife, the Gathering, and Karov's words of warning. I told her what Kriantz had done, and about Thandi's refusal to listen to me. I had nothing left to lose. The attack on

Zumorda had become inevitable. And with Nils dead, the Recusants locked up, and me as the only suspect for magic use, nothing that came next could be good.

"Thandi may still marry me for the alliance, to perpetuate this foolish war," I finished. "But after that, I'm as good as dead."

My mother rested her hands on my shoulders and met my eyes in the mirror.

"You are my daughter and I will always love you. And in this matter, I must admit that I do not know any better than you. But if you can forgive me for not telling you about your grandmother . . . then I will forgive you for making your own decision about this and doing what you must."

I reached over my shoulder and covered her hand with my own, wondering if I had ever seen my mother as she truly was. Yes, she was a queen, but she was also simply a person doing the best she could with what she'd been given. Not so different from me. We had both made mistakes, and we would both have to pay for them.

She kissed my cheek and departed with no further words, leaving me with the chaos of my thoughts and the insistent surging of my magic. I paced over to my bedside and removed the green book from among the singed glass shards of the lamp, stroking the cover absently. If only I had control like the mage in the book, I could burn my way out of the castle, or send a fireball after Lord Kriantz to destroy him.

Beneath my feet, the fraying edge of a horse halter peeked out from under the bed frame.

At the sight of it, memories of Mare overcame me.

My heart fell into pieces as numerous as the stars. Our moments together burned inside me more brightly than any fire: her clever words, her hand in mine, her arms around me, her fierce kisses.

Her love.

In that instant, everything snapped into place. I knew what I had to do. If sacrificing myself for the kingdom was necessary, I would risk myself to stop the war and save Mare, not die slowly being persecuted by Thandi for crimes I had not committed.

I stripped out of my night shift and pulled on my riding pants, boots, and as many layers as I could. I topped the haphazard ensemble with my simplest cloak and opened my other shutter to the night. Only the cold wind greeted me—the garden below stood empty and dark. Thandi hadn't counted on the memory of Mare helping me out the window of Ryka's ready room to give me courage.

Looking down made my stomach seize with nausea, but there wasn't time to indulge the sensation. I tossed the rope over the wall and swung a leg over the windowsill, the distant lamps of the stables beckoning me from across the gardens. I clambered down our makeshift ladder to the ground and ducked in through a door, taking the same route Thandi had shown me when we walked beneath the castle.

Once underground, I raced through the tunnels and shoved my way into the armory. Swords, axes, and maces hung on the walls, but armor and other random objects lay about in various states of filth and disrepair. I didn't know where to look for the Recusant artifact the Directorate had been using to test people for Affinities. But I was a magic user. Some part of my gift had to help me.

I took a deep breath and closed my eyes, drawing as cautiously as I could on my gift. Beside a pile of battered shields, something glowed—the edge of a silver bowl mostly concealed by a smudged rag. The glimmering intensified if I didn't look at it head on. That had to be it. I snatched it and ran. It felt alive in my hand, like Karov's dagger.

I paused at the entrance of the barn tunnel. Though there wasn't much time to spare, I could still do something more for my kingdom, and for others like myself. I hesitated only a second before taking the dungeon tunnel instead. It ended in a metal gate at the heart of the dungeon, and I could see the prisoners' cells beyond it. But a guard also stood blocking the way, and two more paced near the main entrance of the dungeon on the other side of the room.

I closed my eyes and reached with my gift for the oil lamps in the hall outside the main entrance, far enough away that they were out of sight. Once I had them in my grip, all it took was the barest nudge, and every one of them exploded. The liegemen ran out of the dungeon and into the hallway, leaving my path clear. Prisoners pressed forward in their cells, trying to see what had happened, and reached for me when I came out into the light. The cells of the dungeon were not even keyed—just heavily barred with latches that would open only from the outside.

They cried out in a mass of voices I couldn't untangle.

I held up the silver bowl, which glowed blindingly in my hands as I let my gift rise into my fingertips. Most of the prisoners shrank back as quickly as they had come forward, the voices settling into screams of fear as they pressed themselves against the back walls of their cells. But a few remained at the fronts of their cells, faces still pressed to the bars.

"It was you," a man with a gray beard said, but his words held none of the judgment or fear of Thandi when he had said the same. His voice held only wonder.

I unlatched the door of his cell and handed him the bowl. It dimmed in his hands.

"Free your people," I told him, pointing to the way out. The Syncretic Circle could return to doing their part to help other magic users in Mynaria and make the kingdom safe.

As for me, it was time to go for a ride.

FORTY-TWO

✦ *Mare*

I CAME TO WITH THE RHYTHM OF HOOFBEATS pounding into my head. Gritty floorboards pressed against my cheek, boots barely visible in front of me in the near dark. I tried to reach for the bench above me with numb hands, only to find my wrists snugly bound. All I could do was roll onto my back. Above me, Lord Kriantz looked on with an implacable expression.

"Ah, you're awake," he said. "The journey to Sonnenborne will be more comfortable that way."

"You bastard," I whispered. He'd killed Nils. I tried to channel my pain into anger, into something that I could use. I kicked out with my bound feet, hoping to burst open the carriage door, but one of his two men put his blade to my shins. My body trembled with the force of my rage and sorrow, my head throbbing. Denna had seen everything so much more clearly than me. I should have trusted her. I should have stayed by her side even if it broke my heart.

"I hoped it wouldn't come to this," he said. He spoke with no malice, only the eerie calm of someone with an objective and no regard for anything standing in his way.

"What do you even want from me?" I fought my bindings in frustration, wishing I could sit up and have the conversation with him eye to eye. We were supposed to be equals. We had been, until I'd compromised his plan.

The soldier sitting alongside him raised an eyebrow and a blade, but Lord Kriantz waved him off. I posed no threat in my state.

"Well, it's not exactly you that I want, though I would have been happy for us to have a partnership. Thandi underestimates you, I think. Perhaps in time you will agree with me that an alliance between our kingdoms is for the best in spite of the means."

"I doubt that," I said. He could drag me halfway across the world if he wanted. Eventually I would find a way to escape, and he wouldn't see me again until I found a way to destroy him for what he'd done to my friend and was about to do to my kingdom.

"Think about it from my perspective," he said. "The tribes of Sonnenborne have nothing but desert. What do you think we want?"

"Other than goats to hump, I won't begin to try and guess," I replied, straining against the ropes again. One of the soldiers jabbed me in the ribs with the toe of his boot to stop me.

"Zumorda," he said, ignoring my insult. "The resources of Sonnenborne are finite. For hundreds of years we've continued to move farther north as resources dwindle and the earth grows more arid. Without new land my people will die. We can't survive more than a few winters where we are now. You don't know what it's like to watch your own people starve in the streets, withering away in the sun. I am the closest thing to a ruler that Sonnenborne has, and I didn't work to bring so many tribes under my banner simply to watch my people suffer and waste away."

"That doesn't have anything to do with Mynaria."

"It has everything to do with Mynaria. Sonnenborne needs allies in order to take land from a kingdom as powerful as Zumorda. Yours is the only kingdom with enough strength to support us."

"So you take me? I'm worth nothing. Don't you realize that I'm a joke even among my own people? All you've done is sabotage us. The death of both Cas and my father has left us weak, and we'll be weakened further when you send our cavalry to fight a pointless war. What do you plan to do once Thandi realizes the Zumordans weren't to blame?" Words were the only weapons I had left.

"Once a war begins, the source of instigation won't matter. Thandi won't hear a word against the trusted friend who stayed by his side through the worst days of his life, though it's a pity I had to end King Aturnicus to ensure my place. But a green king is far easier to work with than a seasoned one, especially when he believes I put my life at risk to save his father. At least a generous donation to the most hotheaded Recusants made it easy to get rid of Casmiel, who was the only one who had the potential to decipher my intentions." His voice held no emotion. He had never cared for any of us.

"I will kill you with my bare hands." I lunged at him but succeeded only in slamming my skull into his knee as I fell to the floor of the carriage.

"That won't be necessary." He laughed. "You will come to appreciate me in time. This marriage is a business arrangement. I won't ask anything more of you."

I spat at his feet. I would sooner die than give him anything he wanted. Without my freedom, Denna, Nils, or even my horse, there wasn't anything left in the world that I cared for.

He laughed again. "You'll be a fun project, Princess. You certainly have the fighting spirit my people need."

I rolled onto my side away from him and fought the ropes that bound me until my wrists grew slick with blood. When I was no longer able to struggle, I lay still until the rattling of the carriage wheels numbed me. No one had seen me taken, and amidst the festivities my absence wouldn't be noticed until it was too late.

FORTY-THREE 🔥 *Dennaleia*

OVER AND OVER I WHISPERED PRAYERS TO THE SIX AS I rushed around the dark stables. The members of the Syncretic Circle hovered in the shadows outside, waiting. I didn't know how we would all get out, but if I charged the gates, perhaps they could follow. I worked in the dimness; lighting a lamp would draw attention I couldn't risk. Fumbling with Flicker's saddle, I struggled to make sense of the unfamiliar tack. I had considered taking Shadow, but Flicker was bigger—big enough to carry both me and Mare. I would bring her back or die trying.

Flicker shifted from side to side as I fought with the leather and buckles, craning his head around curiously. He was so tall I had trouble getting leverage to tighten the girth. Bridling him was a fresh nightmare, my hands shaking as I stood on a rickety stool to reach high enough to slip the snaffle into his mouth and the crownpiece behind his ears.

"May the Six keep us," I said, leading Flicker into the dark practice yard.

From the moment my leg swung over the saddle, I knew that he was nothing like Louie or Shadow. Each of his strides was big enough to unseat me, and the energy in him burned as surely as the fire beneath my skin. And though staying on was the most important thing, and I should have been more concerned about the Recusants behind me, all I could think of was Mare. With a white-knuckled grip on the reins, I pulled up the hood of my cloak and guided Flicker into the night.

"Halt!" the gatesmen called out as I approached the castle wall.

"Is that you, Princess . . . ?" One of them squinted up at me, and I pulled the hood of my cloak even more closely around my face.

"Yes," I said. "There was an unmarked carriage drawn by two gray horses that left a sunlength ago. Which way did it go?"

"Your Highness, you shouldn't be leaving."

"Tell me which way the carriage went." I hoped they couldn't hear the tremble in my voice.

"I believe it went south, as that's the only city gate open this late at night. But you can't leave. Orders of the king."

"The king's orders can go straight to the Sixth Hell," I muttered.

"Pardon?"

"I said, what's that burning smell?" I pointed to a tree next to the gate and glared at it as hard as I could, urging my magic to rise. A prayer to the fire god rose to my lips, and I murmured it into the night. A breeze stirred, but nothing else happened.

"I don't smell anything," one said.

"Are you well, Your Highness?" The other stepped forward to reach for Flicker's reins.

"Damn it!" I yelled at the tree, and tugged hard on my magic, fueling it with rage.

Half the leaves caught fire.

Flicker shied away from the burst of flame, and I dug my heels into his sides. Behind me the members of the Syncretic Circle swarmed into the courtyard, taking the liegemen by surprise. Flicker rocketed out of the gate, hooves sending up showers of sparks against the cobblestones as chaos unfolded behind us.

Flicker's snorts echoed through the chill night air as he reveled in the freedom of the darkness and the road before him. He trotted through the city as though he knew our destination, barely contained between my hands and legs. I clutched a handful of his mane, determined to stay on. My legs shook with fear and fatigue by the time we reached the city gate, and I slowed him to as sedate a walk as I could manage. I couldn't have the guards thinking I was galloping out of town on a stolen horse—especially when that was exactly my intention.

"Heya!" A guard stepped out in front of me. My hands trembled on the reins as I fumbled for something to say that would give me my freedom.

"It's my sister," I finally burst out. "I have to find her. She came this way in an unmarked carriage." I said another silent prayer to the Six, hoping that they wouldn't recognize me.

The guard looked at me skeptically as Flicker sidestepped.

"Please, sir, you have to let me go after her."

"That's an awfully nice horse you're up on, missy," he said.

"Yes sir, my father breeds horses. This one is mine because of the ugly white sock, you see. No one would buy him." Thank the Six for all the small horse-related things Mare had taught me in our days together.

"All right," he said, stepping aside. He didn't look completely convinced, but I wasn't going to wait around for him to change his mind.

"They went southeast," a second guard said quietly.

"Mack!" the first guard barked.

"Oh shut it, Brail. She looks too young to be out there, and it's the least I can do," he shot back.

I spared him a grateful look before cantering off into the darkness. Behind me, the tree I had set on fire burned at the top of the hill like a beacon. Another glance showed a line of torches descending from the castle hill—riders coming for us. We cantered faster.

The night was all shadows after the brightness of the city. I trusted Flicker to keep his footing as we made our way down the road, my eyes slowly adjusting. The moon hung close to the horizon, bright and brilliantly orange in the sky. We cantered until Flicker's neck broke out in sweat, and then slowed to a trot. Torches no longer bobbed in the dark behind us, but they would inevitably come.

Eventually a light glowed ahead of us in the distance. When I caught sight of the gray horses pulling it, magic sparked in me and I struggled to keep my hands soft on the reins. I nudged Flicker off the road into the scrubby trees and trailed the carriage until it jangled to a halt. As though Flicker understood, he stood perfectly still when we stopped, his ears pricked in the direction of the carriage. My stomach roiled, afraid that at any moment he might whinny to the other horses and give us away.

I dismounted and stole closer, Flicker whuffing warm breaths behind me.

"Make it quick," Lord Kriantz's familiar voice said. One of his men jumped out and headed for the side of the road, and the other stayed behind to help pull Mare from the carriage.

I saw her then, and fury and magic swept through me in a storm that begged for release. Lord Kriantz had had her bound hand and foot, and she fought them as they wrestled her out.

"Your struggle is pointless," Lord Kriantz said dispassionately. "This is our only stop before dawn. You'd best use it."

I willed him to drop dead, my stomach tight with rage. Mare looked even worse up close, her wrists bloodied by the ropes that bound them. Her head hung, a curtain of hair blocking her face from my sight.

"Come on!" the second guard shouted, and kicked Mare as she fell to her knees.

"There's no time to be wasted." Lord Kriantz gestured impatiently.

"She won't move," the guard said, kicking her forward onto her face. She fell easily, limp as a child's rag doll.

"Make her." Lord Kriantz's voice stabbed through me.

The guard nudged her with his toe and followed it with a kick to her side. Magic coursed through my veins, scorching the inside of my body.

I looped Flicker's reins over a tree branch and hoped Mare would forgive me for disobeying her lesson to never tie a horse by anything attached to his bit. Seconds later, the first guard's stream of urine hit the needles on the forest floor only a few paces from where I stood.

"What the—" The guard jumped back as I stepped into the dim light cast by the carriage lantern.

"I've come for her." I stared them down, letting magic pool in the palms of my hands.

There was no fear left in me. If I could have drawn the power of all Six Gods, I would have done so with no regard for the consequences, even though the air around me felt as though it could catch fire with almost no provocation.

At the sound of my voice, Mare rolled onto her side and struggled to her knees. The shape of my name formed on her lips.

The other guard drew his sword and looked to Lord Kriantz for direction.

"Well, well, Princess. Isn't this interesting." Lord Kriantz crossed his arms. "You'd best return to the city before anyone finds you missing. If you don't, perhaps Mynaria and Sonnenborne will ride against Havemont as well as Zumorda."

"And you'd best ride straight back to the hell you came from," I said.

My body burned white-hot, everything inside me rising to the surface with my anger. They would not hurt her any further.

"She's glowing!" The other guard pointed at me, his eyes wide.

"Let her go." My voice came out hollow and strangely detached. The magic had taken control of me. Power rose in unstoppable waves, waiting to be set free. I felt myself being swallowed by it, and for the first time, I didn't try to fight back at all. I reached as far as I could, taking in power from the land and the sky around me.

Nothing would remain but destruction.

"Don't listen to her—she's just a girl," Lord Kriantz spat.

"But, my lord—"

"I pay you to follow orders!" he snapped.

"Give her to me," I said, taking another step forward.

"Never," Lord Kriantz replied. "She's mine." He stepped over to where she knelt, pulled her to her feet, and put his hand around her throat. "I can squeeze the life out of her if I choose. Get on your horse and go back to Lyrra and maybe I'll let her live."

As his hand tightened around her neck, the storm within me burst free.

"Let her go!" I screamed, my words echoing through the trees.

Instead of holding back, I called on each of the gods who had ever answered me, opening myself fully to the power with no regard for the consequences. A rush of exhilaration took me as the magic flooded in. Fire came easily, sparking between my fingers until my hands blazed as brightly as the sun. Earth was reluctant but formed an anchor. I reached for the stars themselves until streaks of light painted the night sky. And finally I summoned air to guide the destruction home. A furious wind flung off my hood and whipped my hair as I brought down a storm of falling stars.

The first falling star smashed through the carriage, the explosion knocking Lord Kriantz off his feet. Mare stumbled away from him and collapsed, disappearing into the smoke rising from the smoldering ground. Time seemed to slow as pandemonium unfolded. Everything burned, ignited by the stars I pulled down.

Shouts were drowned by the thunder of rocks slamming into the dirt, shimmering trails of sparks hissing in their wake. Craters formed all around us from the impact of the white-hot stones. The two carriage horses reared up in terror, lurching and sending the whole thing over onto its side. Their legs flailed uselessly as sweaty flanks heaved in a tangled mess of limbs. As the storm raged on, they grew still, the smell of singed hair and flesh searing my lungs. Trees ignited and the road itself went up in flames as grass and bushes were charred into ash. From some distant place I mourned the horses and feared what I had become, but I could not stop the storm. It unwound from inside me in a torrent I could not even begin to control, tugging at my own life force.

Still, my focus remained on Mare, her limp form barely visible in the middle of the road. Love poured from me to shelter her, shunting the destruction away. The storm burned brighter around me even as my vision slowly dimmed and my arms lost all sensation. I stumbled backward and fell to my knees, a hollow opening in my chest. I tried to fight the darkness, but even as I reached for Mare, it took me.

FORTY-FOUR

✦ *Mare*

WHEN THE STORM CEASED I ROLLED ONTO MY BACK, wrists still bound and bleeding. Scorched earth scraped against my bare forearms, my right arm throbbing between the shoulder and elbow. Some piece of shrapnel had hit me, and the wound hurt like the Sixth Hell. When I finally dared to crack an eyelid open and sit up, bright moonlight sent a stab of pain through my temples. Trees eventually became clear in the corners of my vision, twisting into the dark, and the sharp smell of cinders hung in the cold air.

My breath caught in my throat as I took in the rest of my surroundings. I sat in the center of a lifeless blast site. The remains of Lord Kriantz's carriage were scattered everywhere, embers glowing in the wreckage. The fresh grooves the wheels had left on the road stopped abruptly just shy of where I sat, and the destruction extended deep into the trees on the far side of the road, where branches were warped into unnatural shapes.

But I was alive.

"Denna?" I croaked.

Nothing answered me. Even the animals and insects had fled, leaving the night still as death—until a familiar scraping sound came from the trees to my left.

"Flicker?" I said. My voice came out cracked and stilted as I coughed on ash. I blinked a few times, shocked. My horse stood tied to a tree a dozen paces into the woods. He nickered at the sound of my voice and resumed pawing at the dirt with his hoof.

I wormed over to the jagged remains of a wagon wheel and sawed at the ropes on my wrists and ankles until I was finally able to shrug them loose. I got up, shaky, clenching my jaw against the pain in my arm. Dirt and gravel dug into the soles of my bare feet. What remained of my dress hung on me in tatters, the edges fringed with burn marks.

I picked my way through the debris littering the road. Some pieces of the carriage were merely singed, and others charred beyond all recognition. What I at first thought was a pile of wood turned out to be the remains of a person. I looked behind me, realizing that I'd already passed another body. Two more lay closer to the larger carcasses of the carriage horses. My stomach heaved. A blackened arm extended from the nearest corpse, ending in a hand that had curled into a withered claw. On the stump of one twisted finger, a gold ring unmarred by ash glimmered in the moonlight. Lord Kriantz.

My stomach threatened to rebel, but in my heart, his death brought me nothing but satisfaction. Lord Kriantz's death meant the tribes united under his banner would likely fall into chaos. Even if

Thandi sent a messenger once his people found the remains, it would take time for word of Lord Kriantz's death to reach Sonnenborne.

Beyond Lord Kriantz, a crumpled form lay on the ground at the edge of the road, the spill of nearly black hair from the hood of her cloak unmistakable. My heart filled with love and terror. She lay so small and still. I fell to my knees beside her, my head spinning with panic and pain.

"Denna?" I said, coughing. "Denna?" I touched her shoulder gently and pushed her hair back from her face.

Her eyes fluttered open, and she blinked at me from beneath heavy lids.

"Head . . . hurts," she mumbled.

"Denna! Oh, thank the Six!" I said. Tears of relief trailed down my face as I cradled her in in my lap.

"You're hurt," she said, noting the wound on my upper arm.

"Only a scrape." It hurt a lot more than that, but she didn't need to know.

Tears welled in her eyes. "I tried to keep you safe, but I failed," she said.

"You didn't fail," I said. "You saved me." I gently pulled her up and kissed both her cheeks as though she was the most precious treasure in the Northern Kingdoms. To me, she was. And in the end, after everything, she had come for me. Chosen *me*.

I glanced up to see a row of flickering pinpoint lights bobbing in the distance.

"They're coming for us," I said, stroking her hair. "We can go home now."

Denna sat upright and her expression grew troubled.

"I can't go back," she said. "Not after this."

"But there will be no war. Lord Kriantz is dead," I said. "I'll even stay in Lyrra if that's what makes you happy, at least for a little while until things are more settled after the wedding." Watching her become queen might be the hardest thing I ever did, but if she could nearly sacrifice herself for me, it was the least I could do in return.

"That's not the problem. Thandi told me he would make me answer for my crimes even if we married. And in addition to coming after you and ruining his plans for war, I freed the Recusants," she said.

"You did what?"

"Without them doing their smaller magical workings, the ambient magic in Mynaria has grown wildly out of control. They help keep things in balance. But Thandi might also be angry that at one point I suggested I marry you instead of him. . . ."

"You crazy girl." I kissed her again, this time on the lips. The softness of her made my insides swim and dulled the pain in my arm. She sat up and returned my kiss with longing so intense I could taste it. The thought of a life without her felt impossible, and I no longer knew how I'd thought I could leave her behind.

"I think I have to go to Zumorda," she said when she finally pulled away. "Karov told me it was the only way to get training for my Affinity. If I'm remembering my geography, this is one of the main trade roads. There should be an inn not too much farther ahead. I'll go there and then onward to Zumorda. There's enough traffic on this road that I should be able to get close to the border with one of the traders headed south for winter."

I smiled a little in spite of the pain. Denna must have been the only person in the Northern Kingdoms capable of recalling details from trade maps after being half fried to death by magic.

"You can't go to Zumorda alone," I said. "If you thought Lyrra was bad, all the tales I've heard of Kartasha are worse. And we don't even have rumors of the Zumordan crown city. The streets could be paved with the bones of foreigners, for all we know."

Denna took my hand in hers. "When I got on Flicker's back and rode out of the city, I thought this would be as simple as saving you, even if I didn't know precisely how I would do it. But now I am afraid. Because this magic is so much bigger than I am. I thought it would kill me, and it's only thanks to the Six that it didn't kill you. It has to be tamed. If I stay in Mynaria, it's likely that I'll be punished for this. And even if I escape that, no one will ever feel safe around me." She gestured to the destruction around us.

I understood then that she had to go. And if I loved her as much as I said I did, I had to let her.

"All right," I said, and stood, wincing. "Flicker and I can carry you to the inn. I'll come back and deal with them." I jerked my head toward the torches in the distance. "Someone has to tell them you're dead so you aren't followed."

Though I kept my voice steady and strong for her, inside I had already started to crumble. Liegemen would come. When I spoke to them of Denna's death, my tears would not have to be feigned. One look at the liegemen's uniforms would crush me with the thought of Nils—and everything else I'd lost tonight.

Denna squeezed my hand with gratitude in her eyes. We scavenged all the silver coins from the charred remains of Lord Kriantz's men and clambered onto Flicker's saddle. I set Flicker off into a smooth canter with Denna nestled between my arms. Owls ducked from tree to tree alongside the road, hooting their mournful calls into the shadows. Part of me longed to forget the inn, turn off the main road, and find a quiet town somewhere that we could disappear to. I wanted to build a house with my own hands far away from the crown. But even though the girl in my arms would no longer be a queen, she was something greater than I could begin to fathom. Her life wasn't meant to be small.

The inn was as short a ride as Denna had promised. When she slid down from Flicker's saddle, my arms felt unbearably empty.

"So this is good-bye," I said.

"Make sure they take Lord Kriantz's ring," she told me. "I think he was somehow using it with golden thread to create fire. I saw him do it with Nils, and King Aturnicus's jacket was stitched with golden thread that could have been ignited the same way."

Nils. His name brought a stab of grief that felt like a sword driven through me. My best friend had died trying to protect me, only to have his body defiled to further Kriantz's attempts to frame Zumorda.

"Nils deserved better than that," I said, choking up.

"Yes," she agreed. "Hilara may know who to ask to decipher how it works."

"I'll make sure they take it." The ring could answer questions about Lord Kriantz's methods. Perhaps once they unraveled its mysteries, it could be buried with my father so that both he and Nils could rest in peace.

"One last thing. If you see my mother . . . please tell her I forgive her."

"I will," I said, gathering the reins to turn for home, knowing my heart would be left behind.

"Mare, wait." Denna reached up and took my hand. "I have already asked so much of you. But do you think there's a chance that you might come with me?"

A spark kindled in my chest, suffusing me with hope. It was the question I'd wanted her to ask since I found her on the side of the road.

"Give me two days," I said. "I'll see you on the sunrise of the third." My plan had already begun to form.

"And if you don't come?"

"I'll come," I said. "But if a runaway horse drags me clear to the sea and I don't make it—go on without me and know that I'll find you as soon as I can." I leaned down from the saddle.

She kissed me one last time. "I'll see you in three days," she said, and walked away.

The liegemen were understandably surprised to see me.

"Your Highness!" the first rider exclaimed as he drew his huffing mount to a stop. He was out of his saddle in seconds and tying a bandage over the crusting wound on my arm before I could object. In truth, I didn't have to feign pain or exhaustion. Sitting out in the cold waiting for them, worrying for Denna, had made every injury feel bone deep.

"Can you tell us what happened here?" the liegeman asked. "We saw it when we were barely out of the city gate. It looked like the stars were falling."

"They were," I said, summarizing events for him as the rest of his group dismounted and sifted through the wreckage. There was uncharacteristic hesitation in their motions, as if they thought the magic had left poison coating the ground. I told him how Denna had saved me and how everything had burned, explaining that she had sacrificed herself for Mynaria and for me.

"You're the only one who survived?" the liegeman asked when I finished.

"Yes," I said, and allowed myself to think of Nils. The tears came then, and I let them fall for everyone and everything I'd lost. Flicker nudged my shoulder and I leaned into his neck, grateful I had one safe place left to rest.

The stars above shone peaceful and steady, unchanged in spite of the road looking as though the sky had fallen to earth and smashed everything to pieces. One of the liegemen gave me a leg up when it was time to leave, and I squeezed Flicker forward and left the destruction behind for a second time.

When we reached the city, the gate guards let us in without question. The barest blush of dawn rose behind us as we walked the streets. No one was there to see us, but for the first time, I wore my status proudly, riding the dark streets of Lyrra barefoot in my tattered dress. We carried proof that the war was over before it could begin, and Mynaria could find a new kind of peace. Flicker's hooves rang over the cobblestones. Only the bakers were awake, the sweet smell of bread and pastries wafting out between the buildings. The sun broke over the horizon behind us as we rode through the castle gates, casting everything in a fiery glow. A tree in the courtyard had been burned into a skeleton of itself, the bare black branches reaching for the sky like Lord Kriantz's charred hand.

Liegemen swarmed us, with Captain Ryka not far behind them, the moment we halted in the entryway of the castle. A stable hand took Flicker's reins, and the captain helped ease me down from the saddle. There was barely time to change into more substantial clothes and for a healer to see to my arm before they herded me to the center of the castle for an emergency Directorate meeting. But before the Directorate, I had to face my brother.

When I entered the directors' room, he waited for me, standing, his crown on the table before him.

We regarded each other from opposite ends of the long table, each waiting for the other to speak. My chest felt crushed beneath the weight of fatigue and grief, and I wished I'd had the thought to beg a stimulating tea from the healers to get me through the last sunlengths before I could rest.

Thandi finally broke the silence, his voice weary.

"I'm sorry I doubted you," he said. His shoulders slumped.

"Be sorrier that you doubted her," I replied.

"She had an Affinity," he said. "She hid it from me. She freed the Recusants. She could have been responsible for all of it from the start."

"What she had was care for the kingdom. She set the Recusants free because they're part of what keeps our kingdom in balance. She destroyed Lord Kriantz not only to save me, but to stop the war. To save our people," I told him.

He nodded. "I don't understand the magic, but I see the truth in that now."

"Then maybe it's time to learn. To try to understand the magic users before we treat them like criminals."

Another pause hung between us.

"This is my fault," he said, leaning heavily on the table.

"You couldn't have known about the power of Denna's gift or the depth of Lord Kriantz's deception," I told him. "You would have to be a god, not a king, to see all of that."

"Yet I've still failed us both," he said. "Tell me what I can do to help things be right again. You're the only family I have left."

The time had come to make my move.

"We need to send someone to Zumorda in case Lord Kriantz's people decide to act without him," I said. "The queen deserves a warning, and it could be an opportunity to start a dialogue about an alliance. I'd like to go."

"But Mare—"

"It makes perfect sense," I said. "Sending a member of the royal family shows trust. Sending me alone shows respect for their dislike of political overtures. Director Hilara has made their customs clear to us a thousand times. I'm not asking you to let me be an ambassador. We both know I'm ill suited to that. I'll only start the conversation, and we'll build something from there. Together."

Across from me, he looked tired, uncertain, and so young.

"Please. There is nothing left for me here," I said.

"All right," he conceded.

We both rounded the table and met in the middle, face-to-face.

"Thank you," I said. "And I'm sorry for all this loss."

"As am I."

My heart swelled with sadness.

We clasped arms and stood there a moment, eyes downcast.

We took our news to the rest of the assembly—the Directorate and some of the highest-ranking ambassadors. Denna's mother stood among them, her face ashen as the captain relayed the report about the loss of Lord Kriantz and his men. News that I was to ride to Zumorda was met with shock and disbelief, but no one had any grounds to object after the revelation of Lord Kriantz's betrayal and its implications for Mynaria. Only Hilara offered an approving nod, and assurances that she knew who to ask about the mysterious power of Kriantz's ring.

When the Directorate dispersed and I finally staggered out of the room toward bed, Denna's mother stopped me in the hallway a few paces outside the door.

"Did you see her die?" she asked.

I shook my head, wishing I could tell her the whole truth, not wanting to see the grief and hope warring in her eyes. But I could at least tell her one thing.

"She wanted me to let you know that she forgives you," I said.

The queen took a ragged breath and blinked back tears. But before I could offer my false condolences, she spoke.

"Take care of her," she said.

I placed my hand over my heart. That was one thing I knew I could do.

FORTY-FIVE   🔥 *Dennaleia*

ON THE THIRD MORNING AFTER MARE'S DEPARTURE, I rose before dawn with little trouble after having spent most of the previous two days sleeping. The aftereffects of my magic use had taken a heavy toll. My forearms and hands had numb places that wouldn't warm or regain feeling no matter how long I sat in front of the fire.

Sleeping the days away had also been a useful way to avoid the curiosity seekers who descended on the inn. The blast site had become an overnight attraction, many reporting having seen it from improbable distances. Some said the star fall was an act of the Six. Others thought it was an omen of the end times. Only I knew the truth—that all that death had been an act of love. Perhaps when I tamed my gift, I would be able to make peace with the trade.

The stars had barely begun to fade by the time I stepped out of the inn, the little pack I'd purchased stuffed to the brim with my few belongings and as much food as would keep for a few days on the road. A sausage pastry hot from the oven served as my breakfast, rich with spices and melted cheese, sending up curls of steam into the morning air. From the hitching rail I had a clear view of the road to Lyrra, and I watched it as though the intensity of my desire might bring Mare to me. I hoped she hadn't changed her mind. Though I had spent the waking parts of the past two days convincing myself I could manage alone, it wasn't what I wanted.

As the sun splashed orange over the horizon and the frost that edged the fallen leaves began to melt, hoofbeats sounded in the distance. My heart soared in anticipation. Even the deadened places in my arms felt suffused with life as Flicker cantered into view around the bend in the road, his white stocking unmistakable even from a distance. Mare grinned when she saw me, and I thought my heart would burst with joy. Even my Affinity answered her, a small tingle of magic zipping through my palms for the first time since the night I had brought down the stars.

She leaped from the saddle and we fell into each other's arms. It wasn't until she pulled back that I could see the raw flesh around her wrists and the exhaustion evident in the shadows under her eyes. I touched her cheek, overcome with regret that I hadn't been able to get to her sooner, and that I hadn't saved her best friend. So many mistakes had been made, and lives had been lost.

Next time I would do better.

Next time I would follow my heart from the beginning.

"You came," I said, at a loss for better words.

"Of course I did," she replied. "You came for me first." She said it so simply, as if there had been no other choice.

She leaned forward and kissed me with a shyness I had rarely witnessed in her. A strange, wild feeling lit within me as her lips parted, warm as the morning sun. With her close, I would be all right.

"It's time to make our own life," I said.

"Yes, I think it is." Mare mounted Flicker and used her good arm to help me up.

Climbing into the saddle hurt a little, but I didn't care. She was there, and she was pressed against me, and she was everything. The future stretched out before us as rocky and uncertain as the open road, but filled with possibility.

Mare urged Flicker into a canter, and he responded eagerly, his long strides eating up the ground as we headed east.

For the first time in my life, I finally felt free—because some things are more important than a crown.

Saving a kingdom.

Knowing your heart.

Or riding into the sunrise with a girl on a red horse.

ACKNOWLEDGMENTS

Another several-hundred-page book could easily be filled with grateful words for all those who encouraged, helped, and guided me along the journey to publication. There are too many of you to name, and I'm thankful to every person who saw me as a writer long before I accepted it as part of myself.

Firstly, huge thanks are owed to my fabulous agent, Alexandra Machinist, who saw promise in this story and helped me shape it into something much greater than I could have managed on my own— then sold it in what felt like the blink of an eye. You are the kind of dedicated and passionate advocate every writer should be so lucky as to have on her side. Thanks also to outstanding assistants Laura Regan and Hillary Jacobsen, who coordinated all manner of calls and paperwork with speed and grace.

Kristin Rens, having you as the editor for my debut novel was a blessing beyond compare. Your kindness, thoughtfulness, and thoroughness carried through every part of the publication process. Thank you for loving Denna and Mare, for always asking for my opinion, and for making time to answer my questions, large and small. Many thanks to Kelsey Murphy, Michelle Taormina and Alison Donalty, Renée Cafiero, and Caroline Sun and Nellie Kurtzman and their teams, who also had a hand in bringing this book to life. From the moment I signed with Balzer + Bray, I had the support and encouragement of an incredible team. Thanks also to the brilliant and creative minds of Epic Reads—you're part of the reason I was excited to sign with a HarperCollins imprint, and I'm so happy that I did.

Long before I had any ambition or faith that I could become a published writer, my friends in the Austin Java Writing Company believed in me. Ivy Crawford, thank you for reminding me that I don't suck even when I feel like I do. You are one of the fiercest people I know, and you'll always be my one and only fix-it dyke. Enrique Gomez, you are the best big brother. Thank you for always having time to offer a word of support or encouragement. Your generosity never fails to humble me. Rebecca Leach, thank you for your excellent company at many a YA book festival, not to mention your help with copywriting and copyediting concerns of all sorts and lending me your dazzling swag design skills. Deanna Roy, your ruthless red (and green and blue) pen made sure that only the important words stayed in this book, and I will never again write lengthy passages of dialogue without remembering to "cut like the words were uttered by Sarah Palin." You are one of the strongest people and most steadfast friends a person could have, and I look forward to immolating many more napkins with you. Lane Boyd,

Emily Bristow, Matteson Claus, Delia Davila, Kurt Korfmacher, Chris McCraw, Lori Thomas, and Zabe Truesdell—thank you for your friendship and for our many nights of laughter and cheap wine. All of you touched my writing journey in some way.

My critique partners have repeatedly saved my sanity and are among the most exceptional writers I know. Ben Chiles, thank you for naming Casmiel. Thank you also for reading, cheering me on under any and all circumstances, regularly making me convulse with laughter, and most of all for teaching me the concept of friend (and robot) love.

Helen Wiley, if not for you, I'd still be flailing and melting down in a plot tangle somewhere and hoping to find the answers to my problems somewhere between tears and whiskey. Your endless patience, generous help, and incredible ability to see all the pieces of a story will always stagger me.

Paula Garner, words will always fall short of describing everything you are to me. No person could have been a better companion on my journey to publication, and I am grateful every day for your kindness, admiration, and devotion as we've walked this path together HHH in THH. Our elaborate bribery system, your castigation when I'm being a CSWH, your charming TVN, and your inimitable teakettle are things I never knew I always needed. Your honesty, trust, and love are the most incomparable and priceless gifts. Since we met, you have been my support, my voice of reason, my comfort, my ass kicker, my coauthor, and my compass. I would never have been able to navigate the past few years without your friendship. You're a keeper, Shy.

I would be remiss not to mention Malinda Lo, who went from

admired author to mentor to friend. Your enthusiasm for this book in the early days meant a great deal to me, and your feedback made it so much stronger. Thank you also to my cohort at the 2013 Lambda Literary Foundation Writers Retreat for Emerging LGBTQ Voices. That week showed me what a privilege it is to have a group of understanding readers discuss one's work (and the lasting and sensational impact of a rubber unicorn mask).

The beta readers, editors, and cheerleaders who read for me or promoted my book during the early part of this adventure made all the difference. Thank you, Dahlia Adler, Kat Bishop, Elizabeth Briggs, Jaye Robin Brown, Ginny Campen, Sylvia Cottrell, Emily Gottesfeld, Kelly Marshall, Aunt Duffy, Marieke Nijkamp, Emma Osborne, Lindsay Smith, Rachel Tobie, and Elisha Walker for your various contributions along the way.

Thanks to the Class of 2k16 and the Sweet Sixteens for being the kind of wonderful and supportive communities every debut author should be so fortunate as to have.

Thank you, Mom and Dad, for fostering my independence, supporting my writing and other creative endeavors, and letting me grow up on horseback. Horses helped me become a better person, and so did you.

And finally, a great debt of gratitude is owed to my wife, Casi Clarkson, who was there from the first draft of this book to the last. You made this book possible. Thank you for the writing den, feeding me, date nights, giving me space and time when I needed it, plot-solving dog walks, and most of all, your love.